PRAISE FOR

'*Romeo and Juliet* meets *Twilight* by way of *The Godfather*.'
The Guardian

'Stylish and exciting.'
Books for Keeps

'Kai Meyer's writing is beautiful and powerful…
he weaves a thrilling, dark and mysterious narrative
that expertly mixes fantasy and reality so well that
it is incredibly hard to put down.'
MostlyReadingYA.com

'I need to know where the story goes from here!'
Readaraptor.co.uk

'I would definitely recommend this book and am eagerly
awaiting the second installment.'
Migmag.co.uk

'An intriguing read for older teenagers.'
Welovethisbook.com

'I was absolutely gripped…
I really cannot wait to read the sequel.'
Inkscratchers.blogspot.com

ARCADIA
AWAKENS

KAI MEYER

ARCADIA
AWAKENS

templar

A TEMPLAR BOOK

First published in Germany in 2009 by Carlsen Verlag

First published in the UK in 2012 by Templar Publishing,
This softback edition published in 2012 by Templar Publishing
an imprint of The Templar Company Limited,
Deepdene Lodge, Deepdene Avenue, Dorking, Surrey, RH5 4AT, UK
www.templarco.co.uk

Copyright © by Kai Meyer

Copyright © 2009 by Carlsen Verlag GmbH, Hamburg
First published in Germany under the title *Arkadien Erwacht*
All rights reserved

English language translation copyright © 2012 by HarperCollins Publishers

Published by arrangement with HarperCollins Children's Books,
a division of HarperCollins Publishers, New York, USA

Translated by Anthea Bell

Cover design by Will Steele

Cover images copyright © by iStockphoto.com

Mixed Sources
Product group from well-managed
forests and other controlled sources
www.fsc.org Cert no. SA-COC-1565
© 1996 Forest Stewardship Council
FSC

ISBN 978-1-84877-631-9

Printed and bound by CPI Group (UK) Ltd, Croydon, CR0 4YY

For Steffi

Contents

The Last Chapter

"One day," she said, "I'll catch dreams like butterflies."

"And then what?" he asked.

"Then I'll put them between the pages of big fat books and press them until they're words."

"Suppose there's someone who never dreams of anything but you?"

"Maybe then we're both words in a book. Two names among all the others."

Rosa

Somewhere over the Atlantic the silence woke her.

She was hunched in her seat, knees drawn up, her back feeling bent and twisted after a cramped five hours on the plane. The windows were dark, and most of the passengers were asleep under grey blankets.

No voices, no sounds. It took her a moment to figure out why.

Her earphones were silent.

She glanced at her iPod display. All gone, several weeks' worth of music deleted, just like that. There was only a single genre left, a single musician, a single song. One she'd never heard before, and certainly hadn't downloaded herself. She clicked through the menu once again.

Others.

Scott Walker.

My Death.

That was it. Everything else had vanished.

She supposed the emptiness suited the beginning of her new life.

She leaned back, closed her eyes, and listened to 'My Death' on an endless loop for the next three hours, until the plane landed in Rome.

*

At Fiumicino Airport Rosa discovered that her connecting flight to Palermo had been cancelled because of a pilots' strike. The next didn't leave for another five and a half hours. She was exhausted, and 'My Death' was going around and around in her head even without earphones now.

She had to transfer to another terminal for her connecting flight. With her carry-on baggage, she stood sleepily on an endless walkway. At six in the morning, it was still dark outside, and the brightly lit interior of the corridor was reflected in the enormous glass windowpanes. Rosa saw herself on the walkway dressed entirely in black, her long, blond, witchy hair tousled as always, and the shadows around her ice-blue eyes as dark as if she'd put on too much mascara, though she wasn't wearing any make-up at all. She hadn't touched it since that night a year ago.

Her strappy dress emphasised her doll-like figure, too small and thin for seventeen years old. But then she saw a family on the walkway behind her, with fat children and carrying large bags of food, and she felt glad to be thin and have no appetite, glad that she'd come into the world *kind of different* and *oh, such a difficult child.*

There was a pregnant woman ahead of her. Rosa kept her distance without coming too close to the group behind her. Even though the plane had been almost full, she'd had her own row, and she'd built a cage around it in her mind. Her own little world by the window. But here on the ground everything was moving, there were too many people, there was too much confusion for her to draw clear boundaries.

She put the earphones back in. A strange song, it sounded like something out of a black-and-white Europe, out of old movies with subtitles. Gangsters in black suits on sun-baked beach promenades, beautiful French women in hats being throttled by jealous lovers.

The song didn't have to be called 'My Death' to make her think of these things. It was something about the heightened drama of the music, the sound of the deep, dark male voice. A death wish with an aftertaste of chilled martinis.

My death waits like
A Bible truth
At the funeral of my youth

She dreamed of drops of blood smeared over the decks of white Mediterranean yachts, of melancholy silences between lovers under the southern sun.

The walkway brought her out into the crowded departures lounge.

Other girls carried tasers or pepper spray for safety. Rosa had bought herself a stapler in a hardware store on the corner of Baltic and Clinton Streets. Her thinking was simple. An electric shock is nasty but leaves no marks. With her method, though, she could put two or three staples into any attacker's body. Then he'd have to stop and decide whether to tangle with her or start getting the staples out of his skin. That gave her a moment to hit back. Last time she'd broken a fingernail. Uncomfortable.

She had had to pack the stapler in her suitcase, which she'd checked in. She was carrying her black jacket in her left hand, and its side pocket sagged where she usually kept the thing. The sight bothered her because it meant there was something missing. Neurotic, her sister Zoe had called her. Rosa decided to fill the pocket with something else. Her glance fell on a stall selling sweets on the edge of the departure lounge. The salesman was leaning against the wall behind it, dozing, eyes half-closed. Except for the family on the walkway, no one had bought anything from him in the last half hour.

Rosa got to her feet and strolled over. Her pale blond hair was even messier than usual; it hung well over her face and hid the outer corners of her eyes. Her minidress had once belonged to Zoe and was too big; the hem came down to her knees. The salesman's glance slid down to her thin legs clad in black stockings. They ended in sturdy boots with metal studs in them, laced tightly around her ankles. If she had to kick anyone, she didn't want them falling off. How embarrassing would *that* be?

"Welcome to Italy, *signorina*," he said in heavily accented English. He wore a cap that looked like a paper boat, and a red and white uniform. Why silly hats would make anyone want to buy more chocolate she couldn't imagine, but someone or other must have told him it would be good for sales.

"*Ciao.* That one, please." She picked out a chocolate bar, the last of its brand, and noticed that the black nail polish on her forefinger was flaking. She quickly put her middle finger over it, but that wasn't much better. She'd obviously been scratching something in her sleep again.

The salesman had a nice face, and there was nothing pushy about his friendliness. He bent down to get another bar from behind the counter. She took her chance to stuff four more into her jacket pocket while no one was looking. Then she paid for the one he was holding out to her, smiled at him, and went back to her place among the crowded rows of seats.

One of the fat tourist children was sitting there now and grinned cheekily at her. She wished she had the stapler handy, but said nothing and looked for a free space on the floor under the window, where she lay down on her jacket with her knees drawn up, straightened her dress, pushed her black travelling bag under her head, and closed her eyes.

When she woke up it was light, and the chocolate had melted underneath her. She threw away all the bars unopened, the one she'd paid for and the four she'd stolen. The boy occupying her seat watched, baffled, as they went into the bin. The salesman waved to her as she passed him. "Nice hat," she said.

At security a flight attendant spoke to her when she reached the gate. North Italian, judging by her accent.

"Rosa Alcantara?" The woman wore too much make-up and looked as if she'd be the first to get herself to safety after a crash landing so she could freshen up her deodorant.

Rosa nodded. "That's the name on my boarding pass, right?"

The attendant looked at the ticket, typed something into a computer, and looked at Rosa with a frown.

"It wasn't me," said Rosa.

The woman's frown deepened.

"The hand grenades in my suitcase. Someone else must have put them there."

"Not funny."

Rosa shrugged.

"We were calling over the loudspeaker."

"I was asleep."

The woman seemed to be wondering whether Rosa was a junkie. A child in the line behind her was bawling. Someone was muttering impatiently. A second flight attendant shepherded the other passengers past Rosa. They all stared at her as if she'd been caught blowing up the plane.

"So?" asked Rosa.

"Your suitcase—"

"I already told you."

"—has been accidentally damaged in transit. Badly damaged."

Rosa smirked. "Can I take your airline to court over that?"

"No. It says so in the terms and conditions."

"So I'm going to land in Sicily without anything clean to wear?" Without music, either. With nothing but 'My Death'.

"The airline regrets your loss—"

Yeah, right, thought Rosa. Sure looks like it.

"—and will of course replace your possessions."

"I had some really expensive things in there." She smoothed

down her sister's old dress. She'd been wearing it for the last two years.

The flight attendant's mouth twisted, her chin wrinkled up until it looked like a peach stone. "We have experts who can check up on that." And almost with relish, she added, "From what's left." She handed Rosa a form. "Call that number and they'll assist you. At the bottom of this form you can give information about the contents of your baggage."

"Can I board the plane now?"

"Of course."

As the woman handed back her boarding pass, Rosa's fingers rested lightly on her wrist. "Thanks."

On the shuttle bus, jammed between other passengers, she opened her hand. A gold bracelet lay in it. Rosa slipped it into a Japanese woman's jacket pocket and put her earphones back on.

*

They had been in the air for three-quarters of an hour when the man beside her pushed the button to call a flight attendant.

Surprise, surprise, thought Rosa when the woman who had stopped her at the gate came down the aisle.

"The *signorina* here won't pull up the blind over the window," he said. "I'd like to see the clouds."

"And lean over to look down my cleavage," remarked Rosa.

"That's ridiculous." The man didn't even look at her.

The flight attendant's glance passed doubtfully over Rosa's black dress.

"Don't worry about it," said Rosa sweetly. "They'll get here."

"I just want to see the clouds," the man repeated.

"My window seat, my blind."

"Wrong. The window doesn't belong to your seat."

"And the clouds aren't part of the entertainment programme."

The man was getting edgy, but the flight attendant smiled with all the charm of a department store mannequin. "There's a window seat free two rows farther forward. I can offer you that, sir, and in a couple of minutes I'll bring you a glass of champagne. Please excuse the inconvenience."

The man brusquely undid his seat belt and pushed his way out into the aisle, muttering to himself.

"Us girls have to stick together," said Rosa.

The flight attendant looked around, slipped into the vacated seat, and lowered her voice. "Listen, kid, I know your type. Give me my bracelet back."

"What bracelet?"

"The one you stole from me. The woman in the back row saw you do it."

Rosa half got to her feet and looked over her shoulder. "That woman with the diamond earrings?"

"Give it back and we'll forget the whole thing."

Rosa dropped back into her seat. "If that woman accused your daughter of stealing rocks like those diamonds of hers, would you believe her?"

"Don't you try—"

"Then why accuse me?"

The flight attendant's eyes flashed furiously. She said nothing for a moment and then rose. "I'm reporting this to the captain. The carabinieri will be waiting for you when we land in Palermo."

Rosa was about to reply, but a voice from the row in front of her spoke first. "I don't think so."

A boy Rosa's own age looked over the back of his seat and stared gravely at them. "I saw a bracelet on the floor at the gate, right where you were standing."

Rosa smiled at the flight attendant. "Told you so."

"Come on, this is—"

"One person's word against another's." He rubbed the bridge of his nose. "As for the police, it's not that easy. The captain will tell you so. Anyway, that gentleman in front of me is waiting for his champagne."

The flight attendant opened and closed her mouth like a fish, stood up abruptly, and walked away.

The boy seemed to forget the woman immediately and looked curiously at Rosa, sizing her up.

"Why don't you worry about your own shit?" she enquired.

Alessandro

He looked good, no doubt about it.

However, the law of probability told her the precise opposite should be true. No one who really helped you out of trouble was ever good-looking. It was never a Norwegian pop star. Or even the acne-scarred quarterback of the high school team. It was guaranteed to be some geek with greasy hair and bad breath.

But this guy was different.

Rosa scrutinised him for two or three seconds, then stood up. "Just a minute."

She slipped out into the aisle and walked slowly to the back row of seats. The woman with the diamond earrings looked up from her magazine.

"If this plane crashes on landing," said Rosa in dulcet tones, "then the chances are ninety-two to eight that all passengers sitting in the back of the plane will burn alive."

"I don't know what you—"

"The rest of us farther forward will probably survive. Particularly the bad guys. Life is unfair and death's a real bummer. But enjoy the rest of your flight."

Before the woman could say anything in reply, Rosa was on her way back to her seat.

The boy had folded his forearms over his headrest and was watching her as she sat down. "What did you say to her?"

"Told her we'd be landing soon."

His eyes were an unusual shade of green. Her own were glacier blue, very light. If he mentioned them, she was going to ignore him. Simply act as if he weren't there.

"I'm sorry about your suitcase," he said, without sounding particularly sympathetic. "I heard what she said. I was standing behind you."

"Did *you* wreck it?"

"Not as far as I know."

"No need for you to be sorry, then."

She examined him at length, since he left her no other choice. And he showed no signs of sitting down again.

He didn't look very Sicilian, even though she could tell from his voice that he'd grown up on the island. Now she remembered seeing him at the airport in New York. Going on vacation to see relatives, maybe. Or back home after a semester abroad. Though he wasn't much older than her, so he couldn't be studying at some Italian university yet. Maybe it was the other way around: He went to college in the States, and was on his way home to visit his family in Italy.

She thought his face looked familiar, though she couldn't have said whether she had ever met him before the airport. Straight, narrow nose, thick dark eyebrows. A touch of cynicism in his eyes and around the corners of his mouth. He had tiny dimples even when he wasn't smiling. His skin was pale gold, unlike her own. Rosa never got a tan, in spite of her Italian father. She had inherited her mother's Irish-American complexion. And that, she fervently hoped, was all she'd inherited from her.

His dark brown hair looked as if he'd just been running his hands through it. The tousled strands surrounded a face that, now that she let her brain study it more closely, seemed to have something aristocratic about it. Not that she knew any aristocrats except from TV. But she instinctively knew that the word fitted him. A touch more symmetry, a little more regularity and perfection, and he'd have been almost too good-looking, although his features still had to develop. Over the next two or three years they'd become harsher, more rugged.

"Am I keeping you from reading?" He pointed to the rolled-up magazine she had jammed between her armrest and the side of the cabin. She didn't even know which one it was. She'd simply picked one up from the stacks of them on the way into the plane, just because they were there. Her usual impulse.

"No," she said, but she took the magazine out and put it on her lap.

"Interesting?"

The amused glint in his eyes drew her glance to the cover. A self-help manual for men. *Ten Tips to Make HER Happy* said the caption above a photo of a couple who looked like waxworks. And in smaller print: *She'll never get enough of it.*

Rosa looked up at him. "I write for them. Tips, first-hand personal stories. Tough job, but somebody has to do it."

"You want me to leave you alone, right?"

"If I did, I'd just say mind your own business."

His eyes darkened. Turning around, he started to sit down.

"Hey," she said.

He looked over his shoulder.

"Why are you flying to Sicily?"

"Family business."

With that he disappeared from view. She heard him settling into his seat. The back of it vibrated slightly against her knee, making her legs tingle gently and giving her goosebumps.

She opened the magazine and studied the ten tips.

They didn't make her any happier.

As they were coming in to land in Palermo, Rosa peered through the small gap between the seats in front of her and saw the veins and sinews standing out on the back of his hand. His fingers were clutching the arm of the seat tightly. He had slender, suntanned hands with neat fingernails. On the other side of his seat, beside the cabin wall, she could see part of his leather jacket. It was no trouble at all for Rosa to reach into the side pocket.

A moment later she was holding his passport. Alessandro Carnevare. He'd be eighteen in a few weeks' time, three months older than Rosa. An intriguing address. Castello Carnevare, Genuardo. No street, no house number. She'd never heard of Genuardo, but that meant nothing. She'd been four when her mother took her to America, and she hadn't been back to Sicily since then.

Alessandro Carnevare.

She was annoyed because he'd brushed her off with such

a brief answer. Family business. She was here on family business as well, and it was complicated.

Instead of putting the passport back in his jacket pocket, she dropped it on a vacant seat near the exit as she left the plane. The flight attendants could decide whether to give it back to him. It wasn't Rosa's problem.

The eyes of the female flight attendant burned holes in Rosa's back as she went down the gangway. She didn't turn around.

Family business.

She wondered whether, for once in her life, Zoe would be there on time.

The opaque glass doors hissed apart, revealing the people waiting beyond them. Behind the barrier stood generations of Sicilian families, with wrinkled grannies dressed in black – Me in eighty years' time, thought Rosa gloomily – and bawling little kids holding balloons. Young women, all dressed up, were waiting for their husbands – or lovers. There were parents looking forward to the annual visit from their grown-up children living in the north. People in dark glasses holding handwritten signs and placards.

But no Zoe anywhere in sight.

Rosa was the first to enter the arrivals hall. She wondered, yet again, what they had done to her suitcase in Rome. Then she found that she'd lost the form with the number to call for compensation. It was a shame, because she'd whiled away the time during the flight by making up a highly imaginative list of expensive items of clothing.

She stepped out into the open air, which was hot, even though it was early October. There was a concrete roof over the entrance area, with taxis parked by the sidewalk. On the other side of the road stood a low-roofed parking garage. She could see the Mediterranean through its latticework structure – white foam and the crests of blue waves. Falcone e Borsellino Airport, Palermo, named after two judges who had been murdered by the Mafia, lay on a promontory of land running out into the sea.

No trace of Zoe here either.

Rosa's sister was three years older than her, and had been twenty for a month now. Two years ago she had moved to Sicily from the States. Zoe had been seven when their father, Davide, died, shortly after their parents had taken them to the USA against the wishes of the Alcantara clan. Unlike Rosa, Zoe could remember a good deal about Sicily. The old family property among gnarled olive trees and prickly pear cacti. Their aunt Florinda Alcantara, their father's sister, who was now the head of the family.

To Rosa, her aunt was only a blurred memory, even more unreal than her father, and nothing but emotions, hardly any clear images, linked her to him.

All around her, people were streaming into the airport and out again. She stood there, lost, in the brooding heat, amidst the exhaust fumes of taxis and buses, her carry-on bag dangling from both hands in front of her knees, and tried to dredge up from her mind some sense of coming home.

Not a thing.

Well, being a stranger would be nothing new; she'd had practice. She was only surprised to feel nothing at all.

A military Jeep was parked on her left, behind the row of taxis, with a couple of armed soldiers in it looking bored. She had heard that in Italy the army was used to assist the police. But seeing them there with machine guns slung over their shoulders was something new to her. One of the young men saw her standing on her own in the sun and nudged his companion. The two soldiers grinned.

"Don't worry," said a now-familiar voice behind her, "they only shoot at Mafiosi."

Alessandro Carnevare, pulling a wheeled suitcase along, had come up to her on the sidewalk. He must have been given his passport back, or he wouldn't have passed through customs so fast.

"Alessandro," he said, holding out a hand to her. His fingers were no longer cramped like they had been during the landing. They were smooth and strong.

"Rosa."

"Anyone meeting you?"

"My sister. If she hasn't forgotten, that is."

"We can give you a lift."

"We?"

He pointed to a black limousine pulling up not far from the entrance. Rosa was just in time to see a 'no parking' sign painted on the asphalt disappear underneath the car. It didn't seem to bother anyone. The soldiers were chewing gum and casting curious glances at the gleaming luxury limo. Cars first, girls second. She was glad of that.

"Well?" asked Alessandro.

"Zoe should be here any moment now."

"Zoe?" He tilted his head to one side. "Are you and your sister Americans?"

"Born here, grew up in Brooklyn." She took half a step back, because being so close made her nervous. Oddly, he made the same movement at exactly the same moment, so that suddenly there was almost a metre of space between them.

"Of course," he said, suddenly catching on. "Zoe Alcantara. Related to Florinda Alcantara, right?"

"Her nieces. She's our aunt."

The door of the limousine swung open. All the windows were mirrored glass. The driver who got out looked surprisingly young. Black hair, rather dishevelled, no older than eighteen. A black shirt hanging loose over his belt, black jeans. Brown eyes that fixed on her and then quickly looked elsewhere. He came over, shook Alessandro's hand, and reached for his suitcase.

"Hi, Fundling," said Alessandro. "This is Rosa Alcantara – Rosa, meet Fundling."

At this introduction the boy with the odd name raised one eyebrow and swiftly offered her a hand, then quickly withdrew it when she didn't immediately take it. "*Ciao*," he said briefly, and put Alessandro's suitcase in the trunk of the car.

She looked at him, surprised, since she thought he seemed like a nice guy, but then Alessandro spoke again. "Don't mind him," he said.

"I don't."

"We can drop you off at your aunt's palazzo if you like."

She fidgeted from one foot to the other, craned her neck, and looked for Zoe, but in vain.

She'd come to Sicily to find peace and quiet. To be alone and think. Meeting new people was definitely not among her priorities. The fact that she now *had* met new people was beyond her control, and she hated that. Inside, she struggled to feel in charge again. *Don't do anything you don't want to do. Don't let them put pressure on you.*

"It's your decision, of course," he said with a smile. He had no idea how that remark made her feel.

The air temperature around her seemed to drop several degrees. "No thanks," she said, her tone dismissive. "No need."

With that she turned around and walked along the row of cars. God, how she hated that expression. *It's your decision.* She'd heard it far too often last year.

Her decision. She wished things had only ever been her decision. Hers and hers alone.

She almost expected Alessandro to call after her. To try to hold her back. But he didn't. And she didn't turn around.

A few moments later the limousine passed her at walking pace. Rosa couldn't help looking at it. But she saw only herself in the reflective panes, with her short black dress and long, tousled hair.

Once the car was past her, it drove quickly down the street and turned off in the direction of the expressway. She felt dizzy.

The soldiers were laughing again.

The Clan

She dropped her carry-on bag and had to steady herself.

At that same moment she saw Zoe. Her sister came hurrying up with a beaming smile and said something that reached Rosa's ears as if delayed, and with a curious echo, like a droning old vinyl record.

Rosa was leaning against the baking-hot side of a taxi, gasping with pain – and then, all at once, the world was back to normal. Traffic moved faster, sounds returned, her dizziness passed.

Zoe put her arms around her sister and hugged her. "It's great to see you here at last."

Rosa breathed in Zoe's perfume, which wasn't the same one she used to wear. Rosa said a few things that she assumed would be expected – she was glad to be here, she'd felt she could hardly wait. They weren't exactly untrue, just a bit of an exaggeration.

They let go of each other, and Rosa had a chance to look more closely at her sister. For the last two years she'd seen Zoe only in photos sent from Sicily. She was half a head taller than Rosa, and nothing was going to change that now. Zoe had the same long blond hair right down her back, but cleverly layered in a way that made it look natural. Rosa could see it had been cut by a good hairdresser. And Zoe's make-up was understated but effective, applied by an expert hand. There was no hint of sweat on her forehead and cheeks, in spite of the heat.

Rosa herself felt she was standing in a puddle, she was sweating so much. "Hey, you're so thin!" she said. Skinny would have been more like it.

"Look who's talking!" Zoe smiled and blew a strand of hair away from her face. Rosa got the impression she did that only to puff out her hollow cheeks. But there were other things to talk about. The flight, jet lag, the wrecked suitcase.

Zoe had always looked like their mother, and now that she was twenty you could see why people always said that Gemma Alcantara – or Gemma Farnham, as she called herself these days – had given birth to her own double. Rosa's resemblance to Gemma was not nearly as close as her sister's. Neither of the girls was particularly proud of it, and as children they had often wished that they took more after their father's side of the family, the Italian side. They had liked to conjure up their roots in faraway Sicily, dreaming of riding their own horses among palm trees and cacti, of magnificent parties in marble ballrooms, of yachting trips.

In the multi-storey garage, Zoe took her to a yellow Nissan. A sticker on the rear window showed that it was a rental, but Rosa was too exhausted to wonder about it. She threw her travelling bag into the back of the car, dropped into the passenger seat and stretched her legs out as far as they would go.

A man in a hideous snakeskin jacket wheeled a suitcase past them and disappeared among the parked cars. As Rosa watched him go by, amused, Zoe shook her head. "Real snakes wear their scales on the inside," she said cryptically.

A few minutes later they were speeding southward along the expressway. To the left, precipitous rocks and steep vineyards rose above them; to the right, the Tyrrhenian Sea glittered beyond the flat shore. Oleanders grew in wild profusion on the central reservation. The sun blazed down from a clear sky, and the absence of shadows robbed the countryside of all its contours. Palms and tall rushes swished past the car windows, merging together in a blur.

Zoe kept on talking, saying how much she liked it here, but Rosa soon nodded off. She dreamed they were being followed, and Zoe was trying to shake off the other car with hair-raising passing manoeuvres. When she woke up, maybe only a few minutes later, the Nissan was driving in the fast lane, and Zoe was still in a relaxed and cheerful mood over their reunion.

"Here," she said, noticing that Rosa had woken up. "This is for you." She handed her a little box with a ribbon around it. Inside there was a gilded cell phone. Tiny gemstones were set into the keys.

"You won't be able to use your old one here," Zoe explained. "The frequencies aren't the same as back in the States. And just so you'll be suitably impressed – I chose it for you myself."

"Wow, and so stylish, too!" Only then did she realise that Zoe meant it seriously. Her sister really did think this thing was beautiful. Feeling slightly remorseful, she leaned over to her and kissed her cheek. "Thanks. That's sweet of you."

She took the cell phone out of the box, turned it on,

and discovered that Zoe had stored a photo of their late father as the background image. He had been a handsome man, black-haired, very Mediterranean.

"Thanks," she repeated.

"There's something else in the box," said Zoe.

Rosa put the cell phone in her jacket pocket and found an ID card and a driver's licence at the bottom of the box. They were both made out in her name. When she glanced sideways at her sister, eyebrows raised, Zoe was smiling. "Look at the date of birth," she said.

January thirty-first, that was right. But the year was wrong. Both documents made Rosa a year older than her real age. That would mean she wasn't a minor.

"Everyone here has them," said Zoe, laughing. "Nothing special about it. You *can* drive, can't you?"

Rosa had qualified for her licence when she turned sixteen, as usual in the US, just before Zoe left. "Yup. I can steal cars too."

"We leave that to other people here," explained Zoe, perfectly seriously. "That and a few other things. The family hardly touches them."

The family. Of course. Their mother had married into the Alcantara family, well aware what she was getting herself into. Only later had there been a rift between Gemma Alcantara and the clan, once she and Davide had begun a new life in the States with their daughters. After Davide's death, her scruples, maybe her wish for independence, prevented her from accepting any support for the two girls from her sister-in-law Florinda, so Rosa and Zoe had to put up with being permanently short of money. Only recently had Rosa found out that Florinda had secretly sent Zoe cheques now and then. Some of the money was meant for Rosa, but she never saw it. She didn't hold it against her sister. As kids they might both have dreamt of the fairy-tale wealth of the Alcantaras, but by now Rosa had lost all interest in money and social status. She'd always been happy enough wearing some of Zoe's better cast-offs, and at fourteen or fifteen she had felt mature and grown-up in them. But a year ago, fate had taken 'grown-up' too literally.

Zoe had gone back to Sicily when she turned eighteen, hoping for a different, more comfortable life. For Rosa, on the other hand, the money and the prospect of luxury held no temptations. She was coming here to find herself, or so she thought on good days. On bad days she knew she was running away.

A honk roused her from her thoughts. Zoe was passing a cattle truck. Ostriches with ruffled feathers looked out through the gratings. "Why don't you text Mom to let her know you've arrived?"

"Later. Maybe."

They had been driving for less than half an hour when Zoe left the expressway, turning onto a country road that wound its way through vineyards and ended in a gravel driveway leading up a bare hillside.

At the top of the hill a helicopter was waiting.

"Does everyone here have one of *those* as well?" asked Rosa.

Zoe left the key in the car and took Rosa's carry-on bag off the back seat. They walked over to the helicopter together. The pilot gave them a monosyllabic greeting and helped them to climb in. Zoe thanked him with a smile, but Rosa was too tired to bother. They were both given ear protectors that looked like heavily padded earphones, and had to strap themselves in before the chopper took off.

When Rosa looked back at the ground below, she saw a long cloud of dust moving uphill from the road. A second car drew up beside the Nissan they had left there. A man and a woman got out, both in leather jackets and sunglasses. The man was speaking on a phone and pointing up to the sky.

"Not taking much trouble to lie low, are they?" shouted Rosa above the noise of the helicopter.

Zoe shook her head. "They want us to know they're watching us. Some new kind of strategy being tried out by the public prosecutor's office. It's worst around Palermo and Catania. They're not quite as obvious about it in the mountains and other places. It's kind of a game – they really know exactly where we're going."

Rosa realised that her pulse had quickened only very slightly. She'd known what she was getting into. The helicopter ride was more exciting than the fact that the police and the public prosecutor's office had their eye on the Alcantaras.

She'd been questioned for the first time when she was twelve, although by then it had been eight years since she'd had any contact with her father's clan. And again at fourteen, and once a year after that. If her mother could have afforded a good attorney, very likely he could have put a stop to that, but as it was she simply let the questioning wash over her, feeling more and more bored each time.

If Rosa really had something to hide, at least that would have made it exciting. As it was, however, she just replied, "No," and "No idea," to all the questions, while someone made squiggly marks on a sheet of paper, someone else translated for the Italian prosecutor, and then they all went their separate ways.

There were more earth-shattering things in life than a family who had belonged to the Mafia for generations.

*

They were flying over a breathtaking landscape of steep slopes, precipitous rock formations, and small patches of yellow, which, as they came closer, turned out to be clusters of square little houses. Mountain villages clung to the rock walls, hanging like eagles' nests above bottomless ravines. In the valleys Rosa saw endless rows of vines, now and then groves of lemon trees, and dried-up pastures. Narrow roads ran from place to place in winding bends, sometimes ending up nowhere.

The farther they went into the interior of the island, the more parched and empty the countryside became. Most noticeable of all were the countless ruins of deserted farms, the remains of a time when the farmers and farmhands working for great landowners had lived there. Today both the farmers and the landowners were gone, and no one went to the trouble of demolishing the last ruined hovels. Wind and weather would do it in the course of time.

Rosa was overwhelmed by the rugged beauty of the landscape. Now and then, on the crests of mountains outside the villages, they saw dilapidated villas, some of them fortified like castles, with battlements and defensive towers, with chapels and their own graveyards. Above the noise, Zoe explained that many of the ancient ruins still showed the influence of the Arabs who had occupied Sicily long ago.

Once they flew over crumbling pillars and the ruins of a temple like a miniature Acropolis, and finally over the stone tiers of an ancient amphitheatre. Nowhere else in the Mediterranean, said Zoe, were there so many Greek ruins so close together. The island had once been a Greek colony, and it was said, on fairly good authority, that many of the adventures of Odysseus had taken place on the Sicilian coast. "There've always been monsters here," shouted Zoe, raising Rosa's ear protectors again. "Not just since Cosa Nostra took over."

After a while the land turned greener again. Gorse bushes, oleanders, and cactus fields gave way to light woodland. The pilot gave them a sign, and the next moment they began their descent. The helicopter flew in a wide curve above a slope covered with olive trees.

"Here we are," mouthed Zoe silently.

Rosa pressed her nose to the glass and saw their destination below. Exactly what she'd been looking for. Somewhere as isolated as possible.

The Palazzo Alcantara.

Predators

"Welcome," said the tall woman as the sisters reached the side of the meadow where they had landed, and the sound of the helicopter blades died away behind them.

Against the background of the baroque house and its grounds, Florinda Alcantara looked like an apparition from bygone days. She was standing in the shade of a huge chestnut tree. There were dozens of them here, forming a dark rampart in front of the gnarled and twisted olive trees.

Florinda had the southern Italian features of her ancestors. Her high, dark brows made her look stern, although there was something very sensuous about her full lips. Her hair, which was black and was pinned up on top of her head, had been tinted light blond. The dark roots were showing.

Her warm embrace came as a surprise. So did the kiss she dropped on Rosa's forehead. "We've been looking forward to seeing you," she said, and her beaming smile startled Rosa. When Florinda smiled, she looked kind and warm-hearted. Only when her expression was serious was there an oppressive darkness to her gaze. Then it seemed as if she had a lot on her mind, and it had been troubling her for a long time.

On the way to the house, Rosa glanced back at the helicopter. Now she noticed that its paint was flaking in many places. The pilot was evidently concerned about a thin plume of smoke rising from the rear engine. He stood on the grass in front of it, legs planted apart, hands on his hips, assessing the damage. A little later she heard the sound of a hammer on metal.

The faded splendour of past centuries surrounded the Alcantara estate. The broad facade of the house cast its shadow on a gravelled front courtyard with a large fountain rising in the middle of it. No water flowed from the mouths of the stone fauns. As she came closer, Rosa saw dozens of empty birds' nests in the dry basin; someone must have removed them from the trees and collected them here.

Wrought-iron balconies dominated the front of the palazzo. The wall was adorned with elaborate stucco work. Statues of pale brown tuff stone watched over the front courtyard from niches. Most of the sculptures were damaged, and almost all were overgrown with moss and lichen.

Florinda led them through a tall, rounded arch. At the end of this tunnel gateway – some ten metres long, smelling of mildewed plaster, and surprisingly cool inside – lay a sunlit inner courtyard. There was a large flower bed in the middle of it, neglected and overgrown with weeds. The main part of the palazzo beyond the courtyard was taller than the other three wings, though it had the same kind of stucco ornamentation, iron balconies, and statues as on the outer facade. Two broad flights of stone steps, one on the left and one on the right, led up to the main entrance on the first floor. Part of the semicircular porch was open.

Florinda asked about Rosa's flight, and the connection in Rome. She herself, she added, thought the whole procedure was an unreasonable imposition. Rosa agreed with her.

"Your sister says you're a vegetarian," said Florinda as she walked up the steps to the entrance with the two girls. The paint on the double door was flaking. A lizard scurried ahead of them over sun-baked stone and disappeared into the building.

"I've been a vegetarian for years."

"I can't remember hearing of any Alcantara who didn't like meat."

"Well, someone here doesn't like birds."

Florinda didn't reply as she climbed the last step.

Zoe shot Rosa a sideways glance. "Florinda hates their twittering. The gardeners have instructions to take all the nests out of the trees, and then once a month they're burnt in the basin of the fountain, so the flames can't get out of control. Forest fires are always a danger in these parts – don't let all the green around here fool you. The whole island is dry as a bone in summer, specially when the sirocco blows over the sea from Africa."

"Sirocco?"

"Hot desert wind. It often brings sand from the Sahara with it." She shrugged. "Doesn't do the skin any good."

"And the nests—"

"*Only* the nests," her aunt interrupted her. "Not the birds." She showed her winning smile again. "I'm not a monster."

Now they were in the entrance hall, which was tall-ceilinged, dark, and again full of faded magnificence. Florinda excused herself, saying she had to see about preparations for supper. Obviously she did the cooking herself. On Sicily, Zoe explained, no one ate a hot meal before eight in the evening.

She took Rosa up a stone staircase with worn-down, carpeted steps, then through long corridors into the back part of the main house. They didn't meet anyone else on the way.

"I thought there'd be servants here."

"Not many," said Zoe. "Florinda doesn't like strangers around the house. It's obviously always been like that with the Alcantaras, even when our grandparents and great-grandparents were alive. In the mornings a couple of women come in from the village near the mountain to do the cleaning, but they don't sleep at the house. The two gardeners come for a few hours in the afternoon, but that's hardly long enough to do more than the minimum necessary."

"Like collecting birds' nests?"

Zoe shrugged.

To Rosa's surprise, her room turned out to be bright and sunny, large enough to be a stately hall anywhere else. It was empty except for a four-poster bed with elaborately carved bedposts and an antique chest of drawers with a marble top that made it a dressing table. A small room to one side appeared to be a walk-in closet. The walls of the bedroom were covered with old tapestries. A tapestry beside the door had come loose, revealing faded wall paintings underneath.

"I'll unpack later," said Rosa, throwing her travelling bag with a sweeping gesture into the small room, where it lay surrounded by walls of empty shelves and cupboards.

Zoe went on talking. About the cook who sometimes did

the cooking on her own, but often just lent Florinda a hand. About the helicopter pilot, who lived in Piazza Armerina and was really a mechanic. And about the guards who patrolled the surrounding olive groves and pinewoods on Florinda's orders.

"Looks as if about ninety percent of the rooms here are empty, right?"

"More like ninety-five percent. It's only at night that it sounds as if they were all occupied. Creaking and cracking noises all over the place."

Rosa whispered, "'...the after-dream of the reveller upon opium – the bitter lapse into everyday life...' Maybe I should go take a closer look at the facade of this place, make sure there are no cracks in it."

"What?"

"Edgar Allan Poe. *The Fall of the House of Usher*. The narrator compares his feelings when he first sees the Ushers' house to the way an opium addict feels waking up. In the end the whole place falls apart... I read it in school. Don't you know it, Zoe?"

Her sister's brow wrinkled. "Well, there are no ghosts here, anyway."

"Madeline Usher wasn't a ghost. She seemed to be dead, so her brother buried her alive. Then she crawled out of her coffin again. Where's the family vault?"

Zoe looked critically at Rosa's black nail polish. "Still crazy about all that horror crap, I see."

Rosa gently touched her hand. "Will you show me Dad's grave?"

*

A granite slab, one among many, laid into a wall devoted to the dead. No pictures, no flowers, just a stone chessboard pattern of carved names.

DAVIDE ALCANTARA. Not even his dates of birth and death.

The vault was in a chapel next to the east wing of the house. There was a connecting door to the main house, but Rosa told her sister she'd like to walk back around the outside.

In the open air it smelled of gorse and lavender. The palazzo was built on a slope rising gently towards the east. On the other side of the chestnut trees, the pinewoods grew all the way up to the top of the mountain. The wide olive groves began downhill, on the slope to the west of the house, below the terrace with its panoramic view, and couldn't be seen from here.

Something drew Rosa's gaze up to the chapel. A cast-iron bell, old and encrusted with black as if it had been hanging in a fire, was mounted in a niche in the facade above the porch.

"Did a bird once nest in there?"

"Florinda doesn't like birds twittering. You don't like other people. So what?"

"Everyone likes songbirds."

"Not her." Zoe waved her off. "And she feels differently about birdsong, believe me."

Rosa looked up at the blackened bell once again, then at the open entrance to the chapel. "I never knew him at all, not like you."

"He was okay, I guess."

"Then why did he marry Mom?"

"She's not as bad as you think."

"You weren't there."

Zoe lowered her gaze. "No, I wasn't. I'm sorry." She said nothing for a moment. "I ought to have been there to help you." But it sounded as if she was still glad that she'd been a long way away at the time.

Rosa took Zoe's hand. "Come on, show me around the place."

Together they walked around the palazzo under the chestnuts. The shining glass of some kind of greenhouse was visible among the trees, like a long glass finger sticking out of the back wall of the house. Rosa had noticed it earlier from her room; it was right under her window.

On the west side, on the outskirts of the olive groves farther down the slope, they met neither the gardeners nor the guards of the property. Rosa was walking in a kind of daze, as if on cotton-wool, but she knew that if she lay down in bed now she wouldn't be able to sleep.

"Florinda wants us to go with her tomorrow," said Zoe.

"Go where?"

"It's kind of an official thing. Has to do with family politics."

"Robbing a bank?"

A vertical line appeared between Zoe's brows. "I told you, we don't have anything to do with all that."

"We just collect what comes in from the people who commit the crimes in our area, right?"

"A lot of the business is… let's say semi-legal these days. Do you know how Florinda's been making a small fortune year after year? With wind turbines. All over the mountains, all over Sicily, she has one of her companies putting up wind turbines. She gets millions from Rome in funding for the project – and so far they haven't produced a single watt of electricity." When she realised that Rosa was hardly listening, she sighed. "Tomorrow is a funeral. Everyone has to go, I mean every family sends its representatives. One of the big *capi* has died. That means we all have to be there at his last rites to show respect, even his enemies… code of honour, blah, blah, blah."

"His enemies?" said Rosa. "Is that us?"

"The Alcantaras and Carnevares have hated each other for ever. But there's kind of a truce that no one will break."

Rosa stopped as if rooted to the spot. "That name."

"Carnevare? They're burying their *capo* tomorrow. Baron Massimo Carnevare."

The cotton-wool under Rosa's feet gave way a little.

Family business, he'd said.

Enemies

Rosa slept until well into the morning. After breakfast in the dining room, she explored the building. On the first floor up, the *piano nobile*, where there were salons adorned with faded frescoes and a dusty ballroom, she met one of the housekeepers who came in from the village, working for an hourly wage trying to get the better of the dust of centuries. The woman gave her a monosyllabic greeting and scurried into one of the other rooms.

At the end of a long corridor on the third floor she found Florinda's study, a spacious room panelled in dark wood. It had no door, only an open, rounded arch that gave her a view straight through to the desk. A wrought-iron balcony looked out on the inner courtyard of the palazzo. The glass balcony door was open. All was still outside, with only a few cicadas chirping in the overgrown flower bed in the courtyard.

There was a computer on a side table. Rosa looked around, and as there was no one in sight to ask for permission, she sat down in front of the monitor. When she moved the mouse, the computer came to life.

She downloaded 'My Death' to Florinda's desktop and made the song the background to her own MySpace page. She hadn't updated her status in over two years, and her list of friends was as dead as the names on the tombs in the family vault. Same with Facebook. She checked out Twitter and her email, found a few from people she communicated with only sporadically over the Internet – and *only* over the Internet – but didn't feel like answering and closed the program again. Then she sent the music file to the recycle bin and emptied it.

She was about to get to her feet and continue looking around the palazzo when something occurred to her. She opened her MySpace page again, looked at her profile, and found the sentence, "Would like to be as self-confident as my sister." It felt like she'd written that a hundred years ago, and she thought of deleting it with all the rest of the nonsense that no longer had anything to do with her. But that felt like killing off a whole person, her old self, the Rosa of a year ago.

It was silly and childish, but she couldn't bring herself simply to delete her profile. It would be like sweeping out a room that no one had entered for too long. She would never open the door to it again, but at the same time something about it fascinated her. The old Rosa would still be alive on the Internet, as if the world hadn't stopped for a moment and then started turning in an entirely different direction.

While Scott Walker sang about death, she stared at the profile of a stranger, and a photo where she was taking a lot of trouble to look melancholy and profound. Shaking her head, she left it as it was, closed the browser again, and felt like she'd just buried herself deep in the Internet under a granite slab without any date of death on it.

Outside, gravel crunched under tyres as a car drove into the inner courtyard. Maybe it was Florinda coming home from somewhere. Rosa hadn't seen her in the palazzo that morning.

She typed the dead baron's name into the search window. Massimo Carnevare. To make sure, she added the name of the place she'd read in Alessandro's passport: Genuardo.

A car door slammed. She heard hasty footsteps.

The screen offered countless sites, mainly connected with the names of all kinds of companies. Most of them sounded straightforward and boring: construction firms, agricultural machinery importers, even a foundation supporting disadvantaged kids in the slums of Palermo and Catania. But there were also press reports of court proceedings, of financial scandals over the construction of government buildings, alleged contacts with North African drug barons. She'd expected all that. She was sure that if she'd entered Florinda's name, similar sites would have come up. Including wind turbines that never went round.

She deleted the name Massimo and replaced it with Alessandro.

She glanced briefly at the archway, which gave her a view through several other rooms to the far side of the wing. No one in sight.

Enter.

A year ago Alessandro had been on a sports team at an American private school in the Hudson Valley. Then he took a course for law students who were going to work in economics. In her mind's eye she saw him in a grey suit standing at a speaker's podium with a laptop, explaining the fascinating attraction of forged balance sheets to other seventeen-year-olds.

She was just losing interest when, ten or eleven links down, she came upon a story about a charity gala in Milan. The article was excruciatingly slow coming up; broadband speeds in the Sicilian backwoods obviously left a lot to be desired. The text appeared first, then, gradually, the pictures.

Alessandro smiled out of the screen at her, hair as unruly as on the plane. He looked unexpectedly elegant in a dark suit. Not even the flash photography could affect him much. He had a small scab on his chin, probably from shaving. Thank heaven there were no photos of Rosa's shins on the Internet.

A man of about fifty was standing beside him, with black hair and a high forehead, dark brows, and a politician's frozen grin.

Baron Massimo Carnevare, said the caption, *with his son Alessandro*.

She didn't meet a soul as she left the palazzo, then walked through the shadowy circle of chestnut trees to the outskirts of the olive groves. She was wearing a short black skirt, a black T-shirt with the words THERE ARE ALWAYS BETTER LIARS on it, and her metal-studded boots. She'd removed the rest of the polish from her nails that morning.

Alessandro's name had led her to another site, and she clicked on it, although there just seemed to be more stuff about his father and his father's businesses on that one as well. But she hadn't had a chance to read more than the opening sentence before it struck her as too risky to go on using Florinda's computer.

Ten thousand people had died in southern Italy because of the Mafia in the 1980s alone – three times more than had died in the Troubles of Northern Ireland over the course of a whole twenty-five years.

She didn't know how many of those victims could be chalked up to the Carnevares and Alcantaras. Today she was going to meet many of the men and women responsible for the massacres carried out by Cosa Nostra. Men and women who had made decisions and given orders back then. It made her kind of nervous, as if she'd been invited to attend a serial killers' convention that afternoon.

My God, what am I going to wear?

She smiled to herself, because that question had probably been on Zoe's mind for days.

By now she was in the middle of the olive groves, and she walked downhill past the distorted tree trunks. Florinda's men must be on patrol somewhere near – the property was surely guarded the whole time – but she saw no one, and was glad of that.

Back at the airport Alessandro Carnevare had offered to drop her off at the palazzo. Not far out of their way, he had claimed. Nonsense. The village of Genuardo, where the Carnevares had their headquarters, was over an hour's journey from here. She knew that now. Had Alessandro just wanted to use her as a pretext for getting to the heart of an enemy clan, so that later he could boast of it to the sons of the other bosses, the *capi*? She didn't trust him a bit.

Which brought up her real problem. She couldn't trust herself any more, either. She'd learned that a year ago, and now she had to come to terms with it, because there wasn't any other option. It was easier to shift her distrust to other people than face herself in the mirror, gaze into those eyes that looked mascara-rimmed even without mascara, and tell herself: It's you. You're the problem.

Something moved to her right.

Rosa stood still and looked at the pattern of sunlight and shadows. A rustling sound hissed through the leaves. Beyond the tangle of prickly pear cacti, she heard a growl.

She tried to make out what it was. But there was nothing. Only dark and light in harsh contrast, as if she had accidentally stepped out of a colour TV programme into a black-and-white photo.

The hissing again. That wasn't the wind.

Out of the striped pattern of light and dark, a tiger came prowling.

Bestiary

His movements were so fast that the next moment he was right in front of her, yellow-and-black head raised, mouth slightly open. He was looking right into her eyes.

Nothing moved. It was as if the world were frozen solid. Everything Rosa had just been thinking was unimportant. The animal dominated her mind and her feelings. She and the tiger were here. Nothing else.

His paws were as big as her head, and his muscular hind legs were broader than her torso. His fangs shone with the saliva that was gathering on his black chops. He smelled like a locker room after a football game.

Something was definitely wrong. She didn't know much about Europe and the world outside the States, but the tiger in front of her didn't belong here. Feral dogs and domestic cats, yes. Not tigers.

A ripple ran through his body. He was crouching, ready to pounce.

That dizzy feeling came back. It was even worse than on her arrival at the airport. This time there was no hot car for her to lean on, so that the pain could clear her head. It's a dream, she thought. It can't be real.

She swayed, almost fell, heard a voice. Zoe's voice. From somewhere or other she was calling Rosa's name.

I'm here, she thought.

Here with the tiger.

But then her vision cleared, and she was alone. Whatever had been standing in front of her was gone. A few olive leaves fell slowly from the lower branches. One settled gently on her hand, but she hardly felt its touch.

"Rosa?"

She turned, still fighting to keep her balance.

"I was looking for you everywhere," said her sister. "What are you doing here?"

Don't say a word, Rosa told herself. Don't say a word about the tiger. Or they'll think you're even crazier than everyone claims and send you straight back to New York.

"Oh, fuck, Rosa – you're not wearing *that* T-shirt to the funeral, are you?"

*

Black limousines followed one another along the narrow mountain road. The deluxe cars made their way around the bends at walking pace, as slowly as if they were part of some huge public spectacle.

Looking out of the window, Rosa watched the endless line of vehicles crawl higher over the brown crest of the mountain, gleaming against the deep blue sky.

"They're coming from all over the island," said Zoe. She was sitting next to Florinda in the spacious back of the limousine. Rosa sat facing them.

"Why don't they come by helicopter?"

"Obviously your mother never taught you anything about piety," said her aunt.

"I'm supposed to learn that from you and your friends."

Florinda and Zoe glanced through their gigantic sunglasses at Rosa. They looked like a couple of devout churchgoers. More than ever, she felt like a stranger who accidentally happened to find herself in this car, in the middle of the wild, ancient landscape. There was no mistaking the close bond between the other two women. Although Zoe looked so like their mother, at that moment she and Florinda, clad entirely in black and with identical pairs of sunglasses, could have been twin sisters.

Rosa saw herself reflected four times over in the black lenses. Her long hair was too unruly for any brush to control it. She had tied it behind her head with a scarf, so that Zoe would leave her in peace instead of delivering lectures about appropriate clothing and respectful behaviour. Respectful – two years ago she'd have thought it impossible for that word to ever pass her sister's lips.

The driver, one of the villagers who had worked for the Alcantaras for generations, steered the limo around the next bend. Genuardo and the Castello Carnevare must be quite close now, but she hadn't seen either yet. They must be behind one of the bare, sun-baked hills, she supposed. There was nothing here but scrubby grass with cattle grazing every once in a while, looking up in surprise as the cavalcade of cars passed by.

They reached the mountaintop in a cloud of dust. Rosa slipped over to the other side of her seat and saw the graveyard.

It was surrounded by a wall about three metres high, and stood on the steep rise like an angular, compact fortress, white and pale yellow like the wide landscape they had been crossing for the last hour. Behind the top of the wall rose the pointed roofs of countless family vaults, a forest of stone crosses and figures of saints. It was a south Italian custom for prosperous families to build expensive chapels as the last resting place of their dead, and many such lavishly decorated buildings stood side by side in this graveyard.

A warm wind bowed the tops of the cypress trees on the other side of the wall. For a rural area like this, the *cimitero* of Genuardo was surprisingly large.

Ten thousand dead in ten years, Rosa remembered. There were probably a whole lot of large graveyards in Sicily.

The procession of cars drove on. Rosa's eyes passed over the flaking plaster of the walls. Now and then there were gaps, gateways covered with gratings through which she could look down the avenues between the tombs. Several of the simpler ones were strikingly decorated with playthings hanging from them, dolls faded by the sun, weather-beaten teddy bears. Apart from the cypresses there were no other trees. The sun drained all colour from the walls and the landscape.

"Look at that," said Zoe.

A figure clad from head to foot in the black clothes worn in these parts by simple countrywomen stood by a grave just beyond one of the gratings. She kept raising a sledgehammer in both hands and bringing it down on the tombstone. One corner of the stone had already broken off, but the woman was not content with that. She went on hammering away without looking up, as the cars rolled slowly by, enveloping her in clouds of dust.

Florinda leaned forward to look past Zoe and Rosa. "I know that woman," she said.

Rosa tore her eyes away from the bizarre spectacle and looked at her aunt.

"Her son was a *pentito*, an informer who gave evidence for the prosecution against the families." Florinda spoke without a trace of emotion. "He didn't take the good advice the judges gave him. Instead of going into hiding abroad under a new name, he came back to visit his mother. His clan's *soldati* picked him up at Messina harbour. A package was delivered to his mother every day for a week, each of them containing a part of his body."

Rosa looked back through the billowing dust. The old woman was leaning on the shaft of her hammer. Then she raised it again, trembling, and struck the tombstone another blow.

"She's begging for her life," said Florinda. "She wants to show everyone she's disowned him, she condemns his treachery to the families."

Rosa touched the glass of the window with her fingertips. "But he risked his own life to see her again."

"Obviously she has more sense than he did."

They had left the gateway with its grating behind; now there was nothing to be seen but the high walls again.

"Will that help her?" asked Rosa.

Florinda shrugged. "Someone will notice her gesture with approval."

✳

An atmosphere of open hostility met them in the graveyard. The expensively dressed men and women waiting in a long line at the main entrance to the Carnevare family vault cast dark glances at the three Alcantara women.

Florinda's bodyguards, who had come in a second car, had been left at the gateway of the graveyard. The heads of dozens of families and the other family members did the same. Out of respect for the dead, the clans refrained from spectacular displays of feeling and unconcealed threats, but many here made no secret of their mutual dislike.

It hardly affected Rosa at all. She still felt like an outsider observing a war-torn area, as if none of it had anything to do with her. But of course she was only pretending to herself. The moment she showed up here with Florinda and Zoe, there was no doubt whose side she was on. Every hostile glance directed at the Alcantaras was as much for her as for Florinda and Zoe.

"Don't worry," whispered her aunt. "No one here will risk breaking the concordat."

"The what?"

"An old word for a truce," said Zoe. "None of these people like the Alcantaras, but no one would risk taking any action against us."

"If there's a truce," said Rosa, "who makes sure everyone observes it?"

She got no answer, because the magnificent funerary chapel of the Carnevares was right ahead of them. It had to be one of the oldest structures in this graveyard; it was taller than the others and not made of marble, like some of the more modern vaults, but of the brown tuff stone used for the baroque palazzi. On both sides of the entrance, carvings of animal figures and faces went all the way up to the mighty gable.

Alessandro Carnevare was standing at the entrance, accepting condolences. His black suit fitted him perfectly. He had combed his hair, but that hadn't done much to control it; it was still tousled, unlike the rest of his family's. Their hair was combed back and kept in place with gel.

The last twenty metres to the chapel were slow going, as the crowd of humanity came to a near halt. Dark, reserved faces. Hostile glances in their direction now and then. Elegant gentlemen, but also a number of thuggish features looking out of place among the expensive designer suits.

Alessandro shook hands with everyone, often using both hands as if it were a fraternity ritual rather than an exchange of condolences.

"The baron was very well respected," whispered Zoe, so softly that Rosa could hardly make out what she was saying. "That's his son. Alessandro Carnevare."

Rosa nodded as if she were seeing him for the first time.

Zoe leaned even closer. "He's going to take over as his father's successor in a couple of weeks' time. As long as nothing happens to him before then."

"Oh?" Rosa clenched one fist.

"The man next to him," said Zoe, unobtrusively pointing, "is Cesare Carnevare, the late baron's cousin and his *consigliere*, his adviser, for many years. He's running the business until Alessandro comes of age."

Rosa narrowed her eyes slightly to get a better look at the man. The hot midday sun laid a shimmering heat haze over the scene. There was an intense smell of cypresses and the musty odour of the gravestones.

Cesare Carnevare was tall and by no means unattractive – you could probably have said that of the whole family. She put his age at fifty, but she wasn't sure, because she would also have thought Alessandro was older than he was in that suit. Cesare had a powerful build, broad shoulders and huge hands, which were particularly obvious when he received the condolences of the mourners filing past. His enormous fingers could have enclosed any other man's entire fist.

Rosa glanced sideways at Zoe, briefly. Her sister went on, "Because everyone knows he'll try to get Alessandro out of the—"

"Hush," hissed Florinda.

They were almost within hearing distance of the family members in front of the chapel now.

Beside Cesare stood a second young man, only a little older than Alessandro, athletic and tanned, with blond highlights in his dark hair. He wore rimless glasses. Rosa was surprised she hadn't noticed him earlier. He was staring at her.

Maybe he'd been doing so all along. So frankly and openly that something inside her turned to ice. She relaxed her fist – so as not to hurt herself if she had to go physically on the defensive.

"Tano," Zoe whispered to her. "Cesare's son."

Florinda led the way. Without hesitating, without batting an eyelash, she gave the three men her hand. Neither Cesare Carnevare nor either of the two younger men showed what he was thinking. Brief, respectful courtesies were exchanged. For a moment Florinda's delicate fingers disappeared in Cesare's great paw.

Zoe was next. She managed to give Alessandro and Tano a fleeting smile, but she could hardly look into Cesare's eyes. Rosa thought her sister was letting her uneasiness show a little too clearly. She hoped to do better herself.

She withstood Tano's stare through the lenses of his glasses easily enough. Shook his hand. Expressed her sympathy courteously. Didn't look away, made no nervous movement. She didn't have to pretend; aggression was her strong point, and the challenge in Tano Carnevare's eyes only made her feel more self-confident.

Come on if you dare, her handshake told him, and from the flash of surprise in his eyes she saw that he'd read the message.

She turned to Cesare, Tano's father and the dead man's cousin. He was a more formidable man, there was no doubt of that even from a distance. At close quarters, she could physically sense the aura of menace that surrounded the late baron's *consigliere*. As she returned his cool, calculating glance, she saw her aunt in a new light, and for that she was grateful to him. Florinda must be an extremely determined woman to have faced an enemy like this all her life without giving an inch.

"You must be Rosa," said Cesare Carnevare.

How did he know her name?

"Welcome home." His voice was deep and pleasant, not at all what she had expected.

She nodded to him and continued on.

Stopped in front of Alessandro.

She put out her hand – and promptly missed taking his because instead she was looking into his eyes, into that unfathomable deep-sea green that seemed even brighter in the sun-bleached graveyard among all the black of the mourners. Finally, after a short, almost embarrassed moment that hopefully no one else had noticed, their hands found each other.

"I'm sorry," she said.

She bit her lower lip and was about to move on when he smiled – smiled at her from beside his father's grave.

"I hoped you'd come," he said quietly.

The Slave's Book

Rosa and Alessandro strolled together down the avenues between the tombs, keeping their distance from the other mourners. After expressing sympathy once again, most of the mourners were making for the exit from the graveyard, where a buffet had been set out in the shade of a tall stone cross, and waiters offered champagne on sparkling silver trays. The priest who had led the funeral procession was standing with the heads of the clans, taking a lively part in their conversation.

Many glances followed Rosa and Alessandro as they moved away from the others and past the monuments. Florinda never took her eyes off them, and Cesare also kept glancing at them. Zoe stood alone with a glass of champagne in the shadow of the archway. With those dark glasses on, Rosa couldn't tell where or at whom she was looking.

"We'll start them gossiping," said Alessandro. "I ought to have warned you they'd talk."

"Let them."

"You don't mind?"

"Should I?" She answered her own question with a shake of her head. "I don't know nearly enough about this place to be seriously worried. I don't know any of these people, so they can think what they like about me."

And that was the truth. She wasn't interested in the others. She was on her guard only with him. Although at the same time she enjoyed the hint of risk in the encounter. Last year in New York she'd been sent to see a therapist who told her, straight out, that she lived in constant expectation of danger, and that she invited many of those dangers herself in order to eliminate the element of the unexpected and stay in control. By showing excessive aggression. Stealing stuff that meant nothing to her. And the high point of her career as a risk junkie to date was this walk with Alessandro Carnevare through the graveyard before the eyes of all the feuding Mafia bosses of the island.

"At the airport," said Alessandro, "I said something wrong. Something that made you angry."

"I wasn't angry, and you didn't say anything wrong."

"I did. And I'd like to know what it was. So I don't make the same mistake again."

"I'm telling you it was nothing." She was brilliant at nipping promising conversations in the bud.

But Alessandro wasn't giving up. "Anyway, now you know why I came back from the States. How about you?"

"I'm on vacation," she lied.

"Your sister's been living here for two years. How long is your vacation going to last?"

"Is this some kind of grilling?"

"Just curiosity."

"That's why you wanted to talk to me?"

He sighed softly and led her off the main path through the graveyard, turning onto a narrow walkway between walls of marble tombs. Five or six long rows of rectangular structures, with framed black-and-white photographs of the dead on them, giving their names and dates of birth and death. Flower arrangements lay on some of them.

"I really wanted to give you something," he said as they disappeared from the view of other mourners among the marble tombs. "A present. And then I wanted to invite you on an outing."

"Me—"

"The present first." He took something out of his jacket pocket.

"Oh," she said without enthusiasm. "A baby book."

It was tiny, smaller than a pack of cigarettes, with leather binding and gilt on the edges of the pages.

"Unlike a real baby, it has the advantage of staying small and cute all its life," he said. "And doesn't cry."

"And smells better, I hope."

He opened it and put his nose between the pages. "Not as good as when it was freshly printed, but it's okay." Her first reaction didn't seem to deter him. "My father gave it to me before he sent me off to boarding school in the States."

She bit back a comment and just watched him. His gaze wandered over the countless faces in the photographs on top of the tombs, most of them old and curiously indistinct, like ghosts. Many of the arrangements on the tombs were dried flowers.

"They die so quickly," she said.

"I can tell you," he replied quietly, nodding in the direction of the Carnevare family vault, "on his tomb they'd wither even without any heat."

She fished the book out of his fingers. "Let me take a look."

His smile returned, wandering from the corners of his mouth up to his green eyes, which momentarily distracted her attention from the little leather-bound book she was holding. But then she examined it more closely and saw there was no wording on the front and back covers, where the leather was scratched. The title was on the spine, in pale gold lettering: *Aesop's Fables*.

She looked questioningly at him, and he showed her that smile again. When she realised that she was returning the sign, she instantly restored her expression to its usual mixture of arrogance and bad temper. She had several variations on it, and this one would make anyone run away. Except train ticket inspectors.

And Alessandro Carnevare.

"Do you know Aesop?" he asked.

"Sounds like an airline."

"He was a Greek slave – lived six hundred years before Christ. He collected stories about animals. Well, really about human beings and their qualities – mainly the bad ones – which he attributed to appropriate animals."

"Like the hare and the tortoise?"

"That's the general idea. Except that one isn't in Aesop." His smile seemed a little arrogant again, but he probably couldn't help it. "He never got to write them down himself; someone else did it a few hundred years later. Only a few of the stories that are called Aesop's fables these days were really by him." He shrugged his shoulders, while his eyes stayed sharp and piercing. "I liked them a lot when I was younger."

"And now you're giving them to me?" She didn't want to sound sarcastic, but there was no way around it. "How sweet."

She opened the little book and touched the binding with the tip of her nose. It did smell good – strange and unusual. At home in New York she'd had paperbacks, but none as old as this. The smell made her think of the library in the Palazzo Alcantara. She'd glanced into it in passing that morning. But still, this book smelled different. Not at all musty, but rather more like it had been opened again and again over many years, as if people had leafed through it and then settled down to read it.

And she realised that the book still meant something to him. Which made it even harder to understand why he wanted to give it to her, of all people.

Aesop's Fables. Stories about animals with human qualities. He was watching her.

"Thanks," she said, closing it again. "I like books. I just haven't ever had many."

"A baby book, you said." His eyes were sparkling. "Let one in and the next will arrive by itself."

She scrutinised him through narrowed eyes, interested but a little irritated. "But that's not all," she said. "Is it?"

"Like I said, I wanted to invite you out. I haven't been in Sicily for years except on vacations, so I'm basically as new to it as you."

"And you think that makes us friends." She said that fast, in a cold, hard voice, and she could see that it had hit home.

But he was trying not to let it show. "Several of us are going over to Isola Luna tomorrow. It's just a big chunk of rock, really. Volcanic rock with a few houses and a landing up on the north coast." He shrugged his shoulders apologetically. "The island belongs to my family. Tano's drummed up a few of his friends for the expedition, but you can believe me when I tell you they're definitely not my friends."

"You're asking me if I'll go with you and your, forgive me, only barely tolerable cousin—"

"Second cousin."

"—and a gang of definitely-not-your-friends who are total strangers to me, out to some offshore island?"

"Don't forget the fabulously showy yacht that'll take us. Another of my father's toys." He pushed his hair back, but it instantly fell over his forehead again. "I can also guarantee that after the first ten minutes a few of the gang will be stepping out of line, probably consuming some kind of banned substance and then sooner or later throwing up on deck." He smiled. "Your aunt will forbid you to come, of course."

She bent her head, looked at him closely, and then glanced past him to Florinda, who had changed position and propped her sunglasses in her hair. She was watching them with eagle eyes as they walked down the path between the graves.

"You'll have to get out of the house unseen." He followed her eyes. "Fundling can collect you tomorrow morning if you like."

✳

Twilight lengthened the humpbacked shadows of the trees. The mountaintops were still bathed in sunlight, falling like golden icing on the tops of the pines, but nocturnal shadows had begun rising some time ago from the inner courtyard of the palazzo and the silent olive groves.

Rosa was sitting at the open window of her room with her knees drawn up, looking out. Two floors below her was the roof of the greenhouse. The glass was clouded with condensation on the inside, and only the faint light of a lamp showed through a tangle of palm leaves and branches. But palms grew outdoors in Sicily, so what else was Florinda growing in there? Maybe orchids?

In the car on the way back, Florinda had been trying to pump Rosa about her conversation with Alessandro. Rosa just said she'd met him at the airport, he had recognised her, and obviously wanted to make friends in spite of the old family feud. She could hear for herself what that sounded like, and it amused her that the reaction of the other two was exactly what she'd expected. Florinda suspected a plot hatched by her archenemy Cesare, while Zoe acted like the big sister and condescendingly warned her against Alessandro's bad influence. The whole thing made Rosa sleepy rather than angry. She blamed it on jet lag; she still wasn't entirely over that. And while the two of them got worked up, she simply dozed off and slept for most of the drive home.

She didn't say a word about the island.

Instead, she waited until Florinda was running herself a bath, then went into her study again. She opened the computer, planning to find out more about this Isola Luna and maybe look at two or three of the articles she hadn't had time to read in the morning. She was also going to Google the name Tano Carnevare.

But a new window opened on the desktop, asking for a password. Florinda must have discovered that she'd been on the computer earlier, and had taken precautions to make sure she didn't do it again without permission. Rosa angrily closed it down, fervently wishing it would get a virus, and wandered out onto the terrace with the panoramic view to the west of the palazzo.

She skirted the swimming pool, fished a struggling moth out of the water, and entered the bay of the terrace, which had a whirlpool set into it. From here you could see the entire slope, the treetops and the lights along the drive up to the house, about a mile and a quarter long from where it left highway 117 and wound through the pinewoods and olive groves up to the palazzo. But the view went on and on, out to the yellow-brown hilly landscape to the west and north. Far away on the horizon, the lights of a small town flickered.

Rosa leaned on the balustrade, listening to the evening wind playing in the trees, and thinking. Only after a while did she realise that she still had *Aesop's Fables* in her hand. She ran her thumb quickly through the pages, lost in thought and humming the tune to 'My Death'.

Finally she went back to her room and put the book in the top drawer of her bedside table. Maybe she'd read some of it before going to sleep.

She and Alessandro had exchanged numbers in the graveyard, and his was the first that she stored in the tacky gold cell phone. Her old SIM card didn't fit it, so her address book was as empty as the menu in her iPod. Alessandro and the mysterious song had replaced the normal details of her old life, and curiously enough it didn't feel wrong.

When she was closing the window, she noticed movement outside among the trees to the east of the house. Someone was hurrying out of the shadows of the chestnut trees and approaching the palazzo.

A moment later she saw it was Zoe. Her sister wasn't wearing the black suit she'd worn that afternoon, but had changed into jeans and a T-shirt. She had tied her blond hair back in a ponytail. From above, she looked almost like the old Zoe, much more natural than the sister who had met Rosa and had been at the funeral.

Maybe she'd just been out for a walk. Or she had something to hide. A boyfriend, thought Rosa, amused. Someone Florinda would disapprove of. From an enemy clan.

Zoe quickly crossed the strip of dried-up grass. She was holding some kind of flat package or bundle close to her as she disappeared from Rosa's view behind the greenhouse. There was a greenish glow inside the building.

Slowly, Rosa withdrew into her room. Somewhere in the darkness a door opened and closed again. Then there was nothing to hear but the chirping of the cicadas.

She briefly wondered whether to wait for Zoe outside her room. But it was none of her business who her sister might be going out with – or why Zoe was doing whatever else she had to do out there. Rosa wanted to be left alone herself, so it was only fair to allow her sister her own privacy.

For a couple of minutes she weighed the cell phone in her hand, running her fingertip thoughtfully over the tiny rhinestones set in the keys.

She opened the menu and called the only number in her address book.

Fundling and Sarcasmo

Rosa stopped at the top of the slope and looked down towards the road. The morning sun was still low behind the hills at her back, but it had already turned the sky blue and was pouring a soft, silvery brightness over the landscape. Even the gnarled olive trees seemed to shine, with dew glittering on every leaf.

The car she was waiting for wasn't one of the showy limousines in which the clans had driven to the baron's funeral. A small Mercedes A-Class pulled up, metallic blue, three doors.

Fundling got out and stood in the open doorway, leaning on the car roof with his arms crossed and his chin propped on them. Looking across the car, he saw her coming and raised his head.

A black dog was standing on the back seat, pressing his wet nose to the glass and wagging his tail hesitantly, but he didn't bark.

Rosa looked around for the guards once more, but again saw no one among the trees. She ran down the slope. She was wearing a black T-shirt, jeans and the metal-studded boots. There was a paper knife from Florinda's desk in her shoulder bag. Just to be on the safe side.

Fundling came quickly around the car and opened the passenger door for her. There wasn't another vehicle to be seen for miles around. Nothing but two lizards crossing the road.

"Good morning," she said.

He avoided her eyes, murmured a greeting, and closed the door behind her. He put the bag with her swimsuit in the trunk.

The black dog was wagging his tail harder, but he didn't come any closer until she turned and held out her hand to pat his head. He enthusiastically licked her fingers and let her tickle his throat.

"What's his name?" she asked Fundling, who was getting behind the wheel.

"Sarcasmo."

"Did you think that up?"

"It's just what he's called."

Fundling cast her a quick glance, and she noticed again how fast his eyes moved. They were brown with a golden lustre to them. He had a broad, strong nose and high cheekbones. His black hair was shoulder-length, and his skin darker than that of most Sicilians. Maybe he had Arab or North African ancestors.

The dog nuzzled the side of her head from behind and panted into her blond mane of hair. She turned around, took his head in both hands, and ruffled up his coat behind his ears. "So you're Sarcasmo. You seem a lot more pleased to see me than your master."

Fundling started the engine and pulled out. "Going to fasten your seatbelt?"

She patted Sarcasmo's head one last time, then turned

forward and adjusted the seatbelt. Fundling switched on the CD player. She thought the music coming softly over the speakers was jazz. The dog let out a resigned snort, stayed in the middle of the back seat, and leaned into the bend in the road with practiced ease. Fundling drove at a steady pace, observing the rules of the road, and she wondered if that was for her, for the dog, or simply out of a sense of duty.

"What breed is Sarcasmo?" She couldn't believe she was actually engaging in small talk. But Fundling's calm manner was a challenge.

"He's a mongrel," he said. "Nobody knows what his parents were like."

The road wound its way through mountains covered with trees. After a quarter of an hour they passed the place where the road branched off to Piazza Armerina, a picturesque little town standing on a hill. The cupola of a domed church rose above the higgledy-piggledy rooftops, golden yellow against the sky.

"Had any breakfast?" he asked.

"Doesn't matter." Her eating habits were catastrophic, as the doctors had told her more than once. She simply didn't enjoy food; she'd always been like that. Her mother rarely cooked, eating school meals could do actual bodily harm, and she hated fast food.

"I have some with me," said Fundling. "You'll find it behind my seat."

She groped around there, while Sarcasmo took his chance to lick her cheek with his rough tongue. She found the handle of a basket, brought it to the front of the car, and looked inside.

Tramezzini, triangular sandwiches made of white bread with the crusts cut off, filled with dark slices of ham, mozzarella cheese and mortadella, and two tiny beakers of coffee.

"All fresh from the bar in your village," he said. "Don't worry."

She scrutinised him. "I wasn't worrying. Why would I?"

"Can't hurt to worry a bit sometimes."

She found she really was hungry, and bit into one of the cheese *tramezzini*. It was delicious. It was as fresh as he had claimed, and after she had eaten it, she ate another right away. Even the coffee was still hot, and very strong.

"Sorry," she said, munching. "You too?"

"Had some already, thanks."

"When did you start out?"

"I got up at four, same as every morning."

"That's pretty early."

"Sarcasmo doesn't think so."

"Hey, Sarcasmo." She took a piece of ham out of one of the sandwiches and offered it to the dog behind her. Sarcasmo snapped it up without chewing and begged for more.

She put the basket down on the floor of the car in front of her feet, and leaned back feeling well fed and content. She had left a note for Zoe: *Back home by tomorrow evening, don't worry*. She didn't bother to wonder how Florinda would take the news. She hadn't come here to answer to anyone, and she certainly wasn't going to get into the habit of feeling guilty just for doing what she wanted to do.

After half an hour the green of the fertile hills around

Piazza Armerina grew sparser, turning to islands of shrubs, cacti and small plantations. At Valguarnera it became the ochre yellow of the bleak landscape of steppes dominating the interior of Sicily. At Enna, they turned onto the expressway and drove north-west towards the coast.

"You're not frightened," commented Fundling after they had been driving in silence for a long time.

"Should I be?"

"Everyone here is frightened of something. Most don't show it, but you can sense it. You could see it in their eyes at the baron's funeral."

"You were there, too?"

He nodded.

"I didn't see you."

"I wasn't at the family vault. I'm only the driver."

"What are they afraid of?"

"The Hungry Man."

"Who's he?"

"You'll soon find out."

She shrugged and didn't reply.

He waited a moment, then glanced sideways at her. "You're not curious."

"No."

They drove on again without another word. Only after a while did Rosa ask, "Are you always like this? Acting like you're not interested in other people, then suddenly trying to feel them out by simply making a statement? *You're not frightened. You're not curious.*"

She could see that she had taken him by surprise. He looked almost angry.

"We don't either of us like to talk about ourselves," he said, matter-of-factly. "You don't like to either."

"What do you want to know?"

"If it's true. That you're not frightened."

She thought of her lost stapler. And what had happened back before that. "Not at the moment," she finally replied.

"I am," he said. "I'm often frightened."

"Of this… Hungry Man?"

He shook his head. "Have you ever wondered who's in the gaps in the crowd?"

She glanced at him in surprise. Maybe she'd been wrong, and he was more than just a little odd.

"Gaps in the crowd?" she repeated.

"If there are a lot of people all in one place, a hundred or a thousand or more, there'll still be some empty spaces. Gaps right at the front. Or in the middle. Or on the outside. You just have to look carefully to see them." He shifted gears as two heavy trucks appeared side by side ahead of them. "Those are the gaps in the crowd. And if you look very closely, you notice that they're moving about. Just like the people around them."

Rosa pressed her lips together and said, "Hmm," as if she understood what he was talking about.

"They're weird," he said.

"The gaps?"

"Because they're not really empty."

"No?"

"No, they aren't. They're always there, and in other places, too. Around us, but invisible. It's only in a crowd you can see them. No one can move into the places where the gaps are." On the back seat, Sarcasmo sneezed. "No dog either."

Her eyes narrowed. "You're making fun of me, aren't you? What is this – some kind of initiation ceremony? Let's see how stupid the little blonde is."

He made a sudden movement as if she had nudged him hard in the ribs. Her old belligerence was back, replacing the contentment that had made her way too friendly and forthcoming.

She waited for an answer. Waited a long time.

"Sorry," he said at last.

Then he didn't say another word for the rest of the drive.

Isola Luna

The yacht ploughed through the sparkling inky-blue water. The Tyrrhenian Sea, the part of the Mediterranean off the north coast of Sicily, was a gently rippling expanse under a cloudless early fall sky. The vapour trail left by a solitary aircraft up there was dispersing like a reflection of the *Gaia's* wake in the air.

The Carnevares' 130-foot yacht was sailing north-east with a ten-man crew. Besides the captain and his men, there was a barman, a cook and a steward. Isola Luna lay thirty miles off the coast; they would be there around midday.

However, there was still no land in sight ahead. Apart from a tiny sail on the horizon, it was as if the *Gaia* had the sea all to itself. It had three decks above the surface and a fourth below. The hollow sound of Europop on the sundeck, with its bubbling Jacuzzi and glazed viewing lounge, floated down to the upper deck, where Tano Carnevare and the five young men and women who had come onboard with him were lounging around, while the barman and the steward were kept busy.

Alessandro and Rosa were one deck lower, sitting on the terrace at the stern of the yacht in front of the open frosted doors of the saloon, which contained a billiard table and a gold-framed flat-screen TV. They had made themselves comfortable in two deckchairs, looking out at the sea and the Sicilian coast far behind them. The sun shone down from starboard, and a warm sea breeze played in Rosa's long hair.

Alessandro wore a white T-shirt, pale summer trousers and trainers. Although his hair was so much shorter than Rosa's, he seemed to have just as much trouble keeping its unruly, curly strands out of his eyes.

"You were right." She breathed in deeply as she looked at him over the little paper parasol in her cocktail. "And I don't like having to say that."

His straw slipped from his lips. "Right about what?"

"This really is the most fabulously showy yacht I've ever set eyes on. We see plenty of them around in Brooklyn, of course. Now and then. On TV."

He smiled. "My father knew how to spend money. My mother hated the way this yacht is decorated. All that marble, and the African wood, half a jungle was probably razed to the ground to provide it."

"How about you?"

"I haven't been onboard often. Only twice, before he sent me to the States."

"You can sell it if you want to. It belongs to you, doesn't it?"

"Not until my eighteenth birthday. If I live that long." He said that without any emotion at all.

Rosa leaned back and listened to the noises drifting down to them through the music from the sundeck. "That bunch up there don't look like killers out to get you."

A shadow flitted over his face. "That's the problem with killers. They never look like what they are." Suddenly he was smiling again. "You're not drinking that cocktail."

She shook her head. "I don't drink alcohol."

"I'll get you something else."

"No, that's okay. I'm still working off the after effects of Fundling's coffee."

He grinned. "He ought to have warned you about that."

"Never mind. Nice of him to think of getting some."

"He didn't scare you, did he? I know what he can be like. Sometimes he says odd things."

She didn't even flush when she said, "Not to me."

His eyes showed that he doubted that. "Did he tell you about himself?"

Rosa shook her head. "He wasn't particularly talkative."

"My mother saved his life."

"She did?" Rosa removed the little parasol from the maraschino cherry and chewed the sharp end of the cocktail stick.

"Fundling wasn't much more than a baby at the time; he could hardly walk. My father's men rescued him from a fire in a hotel near Agrigento… of course they were the ones who'd started the fire in the first place."

"Of course."

"The hotelier hadn't paid his debts. And maybe he told the wrong people who he'd borrowed money from. A lot of the hotel guests and staff died in the fire, and they rescued just that one little boy from the flames. The hotel burned to its foundations; there were no papers left, nothing to tell anyone whose child he was. All reduced to ashes."

"And no one made enquiries? No relations?"

Alessandro shook his head. "No one. Looked like no one missed him."

She fished the cherry out of the glass with the cocktail stick, and after a good deal of hesitation put it in her mouth. Sticky and far too sweet. "Odd, don't you think?"

"Not really."

"How do you mean?"

"The whole thing happened at the time of the big family feuds, everyone against everyone else. Gunmen shooting out of moving cars, whole clans butchered on the street in broad daylight. Children of enemy families were often kidnapped and held hostage to be used in blackmail demands."

She listened in silence as she removed bits of cherry from her teeth with the tip of her tongue.

"Fundling was probably one of those hostages," said Alessandro. "Maybe his kidnappers were just passing through and stopped off at the hotel for the night, but more likely the hotelier was in on the abduction himself. At the time my father assumed that the child's family had been murdered, and the boy would have been the next victim. The arson attack on the hotel saved his life. The men brought him to us at the castle, and before anyone could decide otherwise my mother handed him over to the domestic staff. Between them they brought Fundling up. Later on he helped out in the garages. He can take an engine apart and put it back together again in no time at all; he's pretty good with that kind of thing. For the last year he's been taking messages, acting as a chauffeur, all that."

"And no one ever found out who his parents were?"

Alessandro shook his head again.

She put her full glass down on the deck beside her before she could give way to the temptation to sip it after all. Not here. Most certainly not with Tano Carnevare around.

The thought of him brought her back to reality and the present. She instinctively glanced at the bar. And there he stood between the open sliding doors, a bright green drink in his hand, wearing bathing trunks and an unbuttoned shirt. Up on the sundeck a woman called his name, but he didn't respond. He simply returned Rosa's gaze in the same piercing way he had at the baron's funeral.

"What is it?" she asked sharply.

Alessandro looked over her shoulder, frowned, said nothing but just stared darkly at Tano, his whole body tense – and bared his teeth.

Rosa had caught it out of the corner of her eye, and next moment she thought she must have been mistaken. When she looked straight at Alessandro, his face was still angry, but his lips were firmly pressed together.

Tano turned without a word and strolled back inside the *Gaia*. As he passed the billiard table, he slung a ball over it. The billiard ball struck the cushion so hard that it jumped over the side, came down with a crash on the teak floorboards, and rolled away with a clatter.

"What was that all about?" asked Rosa in a low voice.

Alessandro didn't reply.

*

Isola Luna looked like a piece of moon landscape that had once dropped from the sky and, for some inexplicable reason, had been drifting around the Tyrrhenian Sea ever since. Grey volcanic rock, with flecks of brown and green macchia shrubs. But even the tough furze, oleander and holm oak stopped trying to grow halfway up the mountain, as if all life there was doomed in advance to failure.

The *Gaia* glided into a bay at the south of the island. The fine sand of the beach had presumably been shipped in. At least, from a distance Rosa hadn't spotted such perfect, clean sand anywhere else on the coast of Isola Luna. When they went ashore in two of the yacht's motorboats, Rosa didn't see a single plastic bottle or the slightest scrap of litter floating in the water. Unusual for Sicily.

She and Alessandro were sitting in the bows of the white boat, while Tano's gang filled the other benches. Tano himself was steering the boat toward a narrow pier with the aid of the outboard motor. Rosa felt his eyes boring into her back. Why didn't he stare at one of the three girls who had come aboard with him? One black-haired beauty with the measurements of a model seemed particularly interested in him, but he hardly seemed to notice her.

The two other young men were much less vivacious than the girls with them. They were good-looking southern Italians, both wearing mirrored sunglasses. Rosa thought they were about as interesting as a couple of pretty soaps in a cosmetics department.

Alessandro stretched out his hand to help her ashore.

She accepted the offer not because she needed assistance, but just because she wanted to touch him. However, she took her fingers away from his the moment she was across the narrow channel of water. She had to be careful not to cross any other boundaries between them.

"My family's villa is a little way east of here, farther up the mountain." Alessandro nodded vaguely up in the direction of the lava slope. "You can't see it from here, but there's a flight of steps in the rock."

"Does anyone live in the house?" asked Rosa.

Before Alessandro could answer, Tano got in first. "No. A couple of our employees make sure it's all right when they come to clean up the beach."

Alessandro bent down and picked up a handful of sand, letting it slowly trickle through his fingers. "My mother liked the house. She often came here."

The second motorboat came in. Four of the yacht's crew unpacked all kinds of stuff, spread towels over beach chairs, set up a small music system, unloaded insulated crates of chilled drinks. The steward had come ashore as well and was checking up on the four-course meal the cook had been preparing when they were still on board. Until the full meal was ready to serve, they helped themselves to assorted snacks and antipasti.

The crew went back to the yacht where she lay at anchor in the bay. Only the steward stayed ashore, taking the first orders for drinks. Two of the girls ran out into the surf in their tiny bikinis, while the third, Tano, and the others settled down on the beach chairs.

Rosa was standing there, not sure what to do, when Alessandro took off his T-shirt, but kept his long pants on. He was suntanned like the others, and had a fit, athletic torso. He'd obviously played sports in boarding school. With a silent sigh she decided to copy him and took off her shirt, although she felt very skinny and pale in her black bikini top. She kept her jeans on. Compared with the other girls, her hips were too bony and her thighs too thin. When she'd arrived at the airport, she had wondered whether Zoe had an eating disorder, but now, next to those three Sicilian girls, she thought she must look anorexic herself.

"Want to go into the water?" asked Alessandro.

She shook her head, wondering what the hell she was doing here. *Out of place* was nowhere near strong enough to express the way she felt.

"Let's go for a walk, then," he suggested. His smile was open, but she noticed that he was on edge. She thought of what he'd said before about killers, and looked at the others on their beach chairs. The girl was rubbing in sun cream, but the young men just lay there looking out at the sea. Maybe they were watching the other two girls swimming, but you couldn't see their eyes behind the mirrored lenses.

Tano looked up from the MP3 player that he had just connected to the music system and glanced at Alessandro. There was a cool, calculating note in his voice. "Your father wouldn't have liked to have an Alcantara snooping around on the island."

Alessandro pretended to ignore Tano, but Rosa couldn't help seeing his features harden.

She gave Tano a challenging smile. "Nice to know there are things here that might interest my family."

"Let's go." Alessandro touched her fingers.

"Not too far," said Tano.

Rosa took Alessandro's hand. "Shall we see how far we can go?" And she assumed such a sugary smile that it even stopped the black-haired girl's ostentatious application of suntan lotion for a moment.

Hand in hand they walked away across the beach, taking no more notice of what was going on behind their backs. The music began, something fifties and jazzy, Rosa thought. Not her taste, and she was surprised that it was Tano's.

Alessandro led her up a narrow flight of steps between black lava rocks, then over a fissured embankment, and down to the sea again. From here neither the others nor the yacht could be seen. There was no sand, only rugged rocks where the breakers cast up foaming spray.

"Weren't you going to the villa?" she asked.

"In a minute." He was still holding her hand, and sounded thoughtful. "I want to show you something first."

Only a day ago she wouldn't have trusted him an inch. And now here she was, alone with him, letting him take her around this godforsaken island. But that was the point, she thought, I am letting him do it. Everything under control.

They reached a smaller bay narrowing like a funnel toward the land. A grotto gaped open in the lava rock, black jaws sucking in the sea and spewing it out again. At the edge of the cavern, a few metres above the gurgling surf, there was a tiny plateau with a view of the swirling water below out to the open sea.

Alessandro stopped as if something was holding him back. But Rosa kept climbing, and now she was the one offering her hand to him.

"This was my mother's favourite place," he said as he climbed up to join her. "She often used to sit here painting."

"Was she good?"

"I wish I had one-tenth of her talent."

"You paint, too?"

"Sometimes." He waved the subject aside as if he didn't like to talk about it. "Only for myself."

She looked around her on the plateau, and saw steps cut in the rock and leading farther up the lava slope. Suddenly something occurred to her. "*Gaia*, the name of the yacht, was that—"

"My mother's name, yes. Gaia Carnevare."

She went right to the edge of the plateau and looked down at the current. Steep precipices exerted a kind of pull on her, and the feeling was even stronger here than usual. She thought she could understand why Gaia Carnevare had liked this place so much.

She turned away from the roaring whirlpool and looked Alessandro firmly in the eyes.

"Right," she said. "Why are we really here?"

He hesitated only a moment before answering. "To find out who killed my mother. And why my father let it happen."

Gaia's Secret

They climbed the black steps in the rock and worked their way up to the rugged volcanic cone of Isola Luna.

The villa lay halfway up the mountain, and to Rosa's surprise there was a broad courtyard in front of it, and a narrow road leading downhill.

"There's a second harbour on the north coast of the island," Alessandro explained. "Even large ships can anchor there to unload vehicles and so on."

The villa was an extensive complex of several buildings and annexes. Rosa had expected a comfortable holiday home, a place to spend a few days or weeks. Instead she saw a luxurious building that she could easily imagine in the most expensive neighbourhoods of any big city.

White masonry, a great deal of glass, flat roofs, and a kind of lookout tower that had to have a view over half the island. The sea would be visible from most of the rooms, which had walls that were all windows and glazed doors. Even if you felt shut up anywhere else – or at any other time in your life – here you would be overcome by a huge sense of freedom and space. She began to like Alessandro's mother without ever having met her.

"And no one uses all this any more?" asked Rosa.

"Not as far as I know."

"No curious tourists on their own yachts?"

He shook his head. "Everyone on Sicily knows who owns Isola Luna. And they all know it's better not to tangle with us. The same goes for most skippers in the Mediterranean."

She was impressed, against her will, to think that a name could be better security than barbed wire and walls. And she began to have an inkling of how much more powerful and influential the Carnevares were than the Alcantaras with their wind turbine empire.

"Hardly anyone ever came here except my mother," he said, walking ahead to the barred gate in the wall. She followed him, staying two steps behind and not sure whether she'd be better off watching him or the building.

Crickets chirped in the midday sun; the lava slopes behind both sides of the villa flickered in the heat haze.

Alessandro took a bunch of keys out of his jeans pocket. The tall gate swung open, squealing.

"Tano didn't want us to come here," she said abruptly.

Alessandro glanced at her over his shoulder. Anger flashed in his eyes. For the first time she saw something in him that wasn't just attractive, it was exciting, too.

"If Tano has any objections," he said with deliberate calm, "he's welcome to come and make them."

He was about to walk on, but Rosa took his arm. A fine film of sweat gleamed on his bare torso, and the light reflected off it like gold dust on marble.

"Wait a minute," she said. "If you weren't afraid of Tano, I wouldn't be here, would I?"

He pressed his lips together. Her faint hope that she might

have been wrong burst like a balloon.

"Yes or no will do," she said.

He hesitated for a moment and then nodded.

"Because of the concordat," she stated. "As long as I'm with you, Tano and his friends won't touch you."

Another nod. A cautious one.

"So I'm kind of your guardian angel. They can't do anything to me no matter what happens." This time Rosa didn't wait for confirmation but forged straight ahead. "And they don't want anyone knowing if they do harm you. If they kill you here on the island and get rid of the body. Those men down there aren't Tano's friends at all."

"Depends on how you look at it," he said. "But they're not the killers Cesare has set on me."

"They're not?" She frowned. "The *girls*?"

He nodded.

"All three of them?"

"Only the two who ran into the water. The third one's harmless."

"But they can't do anything to you while I'm around, is that right?"

He sighed. "Look, I don't want you to think I was—"

"Shit, Alessandro!" She prodded him firmly in the chest with her forefinger. "Don't try that emotional shit on me. Cesare and Tano wanted to get rid of you – that was their original plan. They were going to do it here, today."

"My family is split," said Alessandro. The white villa shimmered in the heat haze behind him. "Half of them are on my side, the other half back Cesare. If it got around that he'd had me murdered, that would lead to the final break – maybe the downfall of the Carnevares. He hoped to do it here, without witnesses, so that it could pass for an accident, at least in theory. But *you* – well, you're an Alcantara, so whatever happens he can't touch a hair of your head. As long as you could tell the truth to my supporters—"

"—you're safe." She finished the sentence for him. "Never mind what you find out here in the villa. About your mother's death. And whoever was responsible for it."

He nodded again. "Yes."

She felt deceived and exploited, but she'd be damned if she was going to let him see it. Suddenly she wanted to cover up the bikini top that left so much of her on view, but her T-shirt was down on the beach. She took a deep breath.

"Okay," she said. "Is that all?"

"No," he said. "I like you. It's the truth."

She swung her arm back and slapped his face. Hard.

He didn't move a muscle. "It *is* true."

She did it again. Then she looked at him for a long time without saying a word.

Finally she walked past him to the entrance of the villa. "Come on, then. Let's find what you're looking for."

✳

Ahead of them was an entrance hall with daylight flooding in from all sides through huge windows. Even the stairs up to the next floor were made of thick Plexiglas.

"This way." He led her through several rooms so white that she began to shiver in spite of the sunshine. The furniture was unique as well, with curving bowl-shaped plastic chairs, floor-standing lamps on complicated columns that looked like DNA models, rounded plastic shelving – all of it white with a touch of bright orange here and there. The psychedelic chic of the early Bond films. 'My Death' was echoing in the back of her head again, and it seemed like it had been composed for this place.

The house smelled of musty rooms, warm plastic, and the dust motes hovering in the rays of sunlight that slanted in as if to support the glazed conservatory ceilings.

A flight of stairs led to the upper floor. There was a new smell here – first like wax crayons, and the next moment, more intensely, of oil paint. They walked into Gaia Carnevare's studio. After all the dazzling white, the colours in this room looked brighter.

Here, too, the ceiling was made entirely of glass, and was the only surface not covered with pictures. Unframed canvases hung or were propped everywhere, covered with an inferno of brushstrokes and wild dabs of paint, explosions of colour that at a second glance were faces. Distorted, twisted, disfigured faces.

Rosa said nothing. She turned slowly on the spot and let her eyes wander over the paintings. There were pictures stacked one behind another all over the studio, five or eight or ten at a time; she could only guess how many of those disturbing grimaces were hidden behind the pictures in front.

"Why's all this still here?" she asked.

"Cesare kept my father from taking them over to the castle. He didn't want to have them around him." Alessandro's jaw muscles were working. "He hated her."

"And her pictures?"

"Them, too."

Now she looked him in the eye for the first time since slapping him. "Did he do it? Did Cesare kill your mother?"

"I think so, yes."

"And you're looking for evidence here?"

He went over to one of the paintings, a face with a mouth wrenched wide open, red and black and dark violet. His fingertips gently stroked the surface. "I think she found out that Cesare had been deceiving my father. Cesare knew him better than anyone and was his closest adviser in everything – not just business. But Cesare also likes the old Cosa Nostra traditions. He insists that might is right, and as he sees it, power struggles should be carried out openly. These days the families work more and more like other business enterprises, they run scams just this side of the law, and their quarrels aren't necessarily settled in shootouts between a few stupid, hired henchmen – but all that's passed Cesare by. He can't stand any kind of innovation, everything has to stay the way it always was. That's why he wants the power in the Carnevare clan. He wants to keep what he calls the old values going. And I think that as he saw it, my father had gone too far off that track, with all the deals he did as cover, his facade of charity donations, fraternising with politicians in Rome. Cesare's been putting funds secretly aside to be ready for a change of power, and my father was blind to it and didn't notice. Or maybe he just didn't want to face facts."

"And your mother was different?"

"She and Cesare hated each other from the beginning, even before she married my father. Later on she realised what Cesare was planning. She must have tried to warn my father, but when he wouldn't listen to her she grew more and more withdrawn, and she spent most of her time out here on the island."

Rosa was studying the distorted faces. "Doesn't look like being on her own did her much good."

"That wasn't enough for Cesare, anyway. He couldn't let her know the truth."

"So he had her killed?"

Alessandro's eyes were narrowed, cold, frightening. "I think he did it with his own hands. Here or somewhere else. But he *did* kill her." He walked slowly past more of the pictures, tracing the outlines of the brushstrokes. "My father must have known. Or at least guessed. I'm almost sure Cesare will have talked him into thinking that was the only way. Told him my mother was unhinged, would talk to the wrong people about the kind of business the Carnevares did. And I guess my father just – caved in." Fists clenched, he swung around, and now there was such fury in his eyes that Rosa almost took a step back. But she stood her ground, feeling sure there was something else about him, trying to work it out.Something about his eyes.

As if their pupils were suddenly widening. And for a brief, intriguing moment she thought his hair had changed colour. Was darker, pitch-black. Maybe it was just the strange lighting up here.

"My father went along with Cesare," said Alessandro. "Went along with the murder of his own wife!"

"But you're only assuming that – aren't you?"

"She wrote things down. Put them together. It was what she always did."

"Like a letter, you mean? To you?"

He shook his head. "She didn't trust letters."

Rosa raised an eyebrow.

"I know she wasn't exactly clear in her mind!" he went on. "I *know* that, Rosa! But she wasn't totally crazy, just… confused. There must be notes, diaries, something like that. I'm sure of it. And if there are – "

"Then they're here," she said.

"Yes." He went over to a large, paint-splashed draftsman's desk covered with sketches on large sheets of paper, as if the artist had left the studio only a few minutes ago. He opened the only drawer in the desk, rummaged around in it, and finally brought something out.

A gleaming scalpel.

He turned it over.

She thought of the paper knife that she had taken from Florinda's desk first thing in the morning. She'd left it down on the beach in her shoulder bag.

Alessandro's hair looked nut-brown again, but his pupils

still filled his entire eyes. He went over to one of the pictures and slit it from top to bottom. With a tearing sound, the painting gaped open. A bloodless wound split the distorted face.

He did the same to a second picture.

And a third.

Rosa watched, motionless, as he devastated picture after picture, each with a swift diagonal cut, and she thought instinctively that once, in the time of the great Mafia wars, these faces would have been real people, and the *capi* and their *soldati* would have dealt with them the same way. There was something of that in Alessandro Carnevare. An heir to those times, those men.

She had the same legacy herself. Like a gene firmly anchored inside her. She could sense something stirring. Something in her changing, trying to break out. An eerie fascination joined the tension she had felt just now and the anger that still seethed inside her.

Alessandro stopped and pointed to the open drawer. "There are more in there."

She joined him, looked inside, and saw a muddle of brushes, spatulas, pencils – and blades. Hesitantly, she put out her hand. Took one out of the drawer. Weighed the cool metal in her fingers.

A scalpel just like his. Gaia Carnevare would have used them to scrape paint off canvases. Red paint, by the look of it.

"A single cut," said Alessandro. "That should be enough to show whether there's anything underneath."

She went over to one of the pictures and put the blade against it. Slit open the screaming face. Only a picture. Only paint. She got goosebumps, but at the same time she couldn't help smiling. A tingling ran through her knees, her thighs, her lower body. It reached her rib cage and leaped up into her skull like a flame.

The next picture. And then another.

Once she thought she heard a ringing sound, like tiny bells chiming. Not in her head. Somewhere in the house. But by now she was in a kind of frenzy, and Alessandro obviously felt the same. They were destroying his mother's pictures in search of what might be hidden in them, or under them, or behind them. Cheeks, eyes, mouths gaped open. Where canvases had been stacked behind one another, more distorted faces came into view, more and more grimaces of fear, gaudily coloured glimpses into the depths of Gaia Carnevare's soul.

"Here we are," said Alessandro.

And at that very moment Rosa's blade, too, met a surface harder than canvas and paint, not behind the picture but *in* it.

Alessandro's mother had stuck folders of hard plastic or very thin metal on the canvases, and then painted them over thickly with oil paint, weaving them into her visions and nightmares.

They found ten folders distributed among a hundred or more paintings. And there were documents in all the folders. Bank statements, balance sheets, photographs of Cesare Carnevare with men in dark suits. And sheets of paper handwritten in tiny letters, illegible except with a magnifying glass, probably written with the aid of one as well.

They stood there, breathless, in the middle of the devastation. Alessandro had the scalpel in one hand and the sheaf of papers in the other. Rosa's breasts were rising and falling. Her black bikini top was stretched over them; she felt as if her whole body was in disorder.

Alessandro smiled, while tears glittered in his eyes. Sweat gleamed on his bare skin and the muscles of his forearms.

He took a step toward her, and she could see that he was going to kiss her.

She stepped back, shaking her head.

His smile faded slightly as the reality of their situation gradually made its way back into his mind, and hers as well, and they were both themselves again, realising what the scene around them looked like, and what effect it would have on anyone unexpectedly coming through the door.

Once again Rosa heard the clear, glassy ringing sound.

Closer this time. Out on the stairs.

Alessandro stowed all the loose sheets of paper and the photographs away in one of the paint-stained plastic folders and held it to his chest with his left hand. He kept the knife in his right hand as he spun around in the direction of the door.

Rosa stole over to the entrance of the studio, clutching the handle of her scalpel, which was wet with sweat. With a swift movement she peered around the doorpost, glanced out into the corridor.

In front of all that brightly lit white stood a frail figure, looking lost.

A girl, younger than Rosa herself.

She wore a narrow metal ring on one ankle. A silver chain, pencil-thin, led across the floor and disappeared, tightly stretched, around the nearest corner.

When the girl moved to speak, the links of the chain rang faintly, like little bells.

"Have you come to kill me?"

The Girl on the Chain

Her name was Iole Dallamano. She spoke softly and slowly. She didn't seem afraid of the scalpel in Rosa's hand.

She was fifteen but looked younger, in spite of the shadows under her sad eyes. Her black hair was cut short. One of the men who regularly came here had done that, she said. Otherwise they hadn't touched her. Every few months, when her hair was long again, one of them chopped it short. Iole had asked them why they didn't cut her throat right away, but they never answered that question.

She told Rosa and Alessandro all this even before they reached the bottom of the stairs. Iole was barefoot and moved on the Plexiglas steps without a sound – except for the slight ringing of the chain around her ankle. It had to be eighty to a hundred metres or more long, enough for Iole to walk almost all over the house, but it was too short for her to reach the top of the stairs to the upper floor. Her freedom of movement ended a few metres short of the door to Gaia Carnevare's studio.

Rosa followed Iole down the stairs as she talked. The silvery links of the chain dropped, clinking quietly, from step to step. Alessandro followed them, clutching the folder of documents firmly in both hands. They had left the scalpels up in the studio.

"How long have you been here?" asked Rosa as they

reached the first floor. The stairs led to one of the sitting rooms.

"Over six months on the island," said the girl. "Before that they hid me in other places. A remote farmhouse in the west, then somewhere up in the mountains. There are wolves there, they said."

Rosa looked at Alessandro, whose expression was getting darker and darker. "I didn't know anything about this," he said, seeing the question in her eyes.

"It's been six years," said Iole. "Six years, two months. And seven days."

Rosa swore quietly.

"They took me away from my parents' house." Iole looked at the floor. "They said everyone was dead there. My parents. Both my brothers, all my uncles and their families. All except one person."

"There was a Dallamano clan in Syracuse," Alessandro explained. "I don't know what happened, but—"

Iole interrupted him. "My uncle Augusto… he was helping a judge. A woman judge. They said he'd betrayed the families. A lot of people were arrested because of him; some of them worked for the Carnevares. But the Carnevares think he knows even more – knows about them and their businesses. They took me prisoner to keep him from talking. If he does, they'll kill me, they say. They think he knows that, and that's why he won't tell the police any more."

Her voice made her sound younger than fifteen. It struck Rosa that Iole hadn't been to school for over six years. She had a television set, she told them; she liked the cartoons best. Rosa wondered whether it was only her vocabulary that had suffered from being held hostage so long.

"By *they* you mean Cesare Carnevare and his men?" asked Rosa.

"Yes." Iole dropped into one of the bowl-shaped orange plastic chairs, pulling the chain in after her and putting her arms around it. The metal links chinked softly again. "I've only seen Cesare three times since they took me. Once right at the beginning, then again in the mountains, and the last time was a few months ago. He came here looking for something."

Alessandro pricked up his ears. "Do you know what?"

She shook her head. "But in the end he found a safe behind one of the pictures in the strawberry room." She smiled apologetically. "I called it that because there's a picture hanging there with a big red blotch that looks like a strawberry. I've given all the rooms names. And the animals outside the windows."

Rosa gazed at the front of the room, which looked out on the rough surface of the lava slope and the inky blue sea. No animals anywhere in sight.

"What was in the safe?" asked Alessandro.

Rosa looked at him accusingly. He did seem to be sorry for Iole, but his wish for revenge on Cesare was stronger than any other feeling he might have. Rosa sensed his rage coming back. The strange, turbulent emotions that had come over them both in the studio were gradually disappearing. She had let herself be carried away, she'd lost control. That was bad.

Just as he'd used her, now all that really interested him

about Iole was what she knew about his enemy, Cesare. Rosa stepped between him and the girl on the chain. "Leave her alone. We have to think how to get her out of here."

He stared at her as if that were completely beside the point. Then he shook his head. "If Cesare finds out we've met her, he'll know we found something."

Rosa took a menacing step closer to him. "So we just leave without her? You can't be serious!"

"Papers," said Iole behind her back. "There were papers in the safe. And photos. Cesare looked rather pleased."

Alessandro swore.

"They were useless," said Rosa. Even before he looked at her in surprise, she realised she'd spoken without thinking properly, but in fact it was only logical. "Your mother didn't even bother to hide them. I mean, in a *safe*? She probably wanted him to find something. So that he wouldn't keep searching and find the important files – the folders hidden in the pictures. They were for you."

Alessandro nodded. "Yes, that's possible."

"You have what you wanted now," she said coolly. "So let's make sure she doesn't have to stay here any—"

"Of course!" Suddenly the grim determination she'd heard when he had the scalpel in his hand was back. "Tano will know about Iole. I'd better start with him."

"It's not so bad here," said Iole. Her fingertips were circling one another in the air in front of her drawn-up knees, like a pianist's fingers. "This is a lovely house. And it's always light here in the daytime. It's only at night, when the animals come—"

"I'll see to it," Alessandro interrupted her. "Rosa, you stay here with her." He was hurrying out, but at the last minute realised that he was still holding the folder of documents. After a moment's thought, he came back and handed it to Rosa. "Watch this, will you? Just while I get things sorted."

She couldn't figure him out at all. The only thing she did know was that he made her furious all the time, never mind what he did. First he made use of her, then he put on airs and left her standing. All the same, she was still supposed to do as he said. *You stay here with her*. And *Look after this*. She never did anything for other people. Not if she could help it. She had surprised herself by standing up for Iole.

"It's all right, you run along after him," said the girl, looking even smaller and more vulnerable, as if the horrible dish-shaped chair were holding her in a plastic fist. "Don't worry about me."

Run along after him? Rosa almost choked as she got her breath back. Then she nodded briefly. "You wait – we'll be back here soon, okay?"

"Are you really going to do it? Get me out of here?"

Rosa wanted to leave at once with the wretched folder, but she stopped for a moment, hesitated – then went up to Iole, stroked her hair, and said, "I promise. We'll get you out of here just as soon as we possibly can."

Iole looked at her, wide-eyed like a cartoon character in one of the TV shows she liked so much. "Remember to watch out for the animals… they come at night. Always at night."

Rosa forced herself to give Iole an encouraging smile before she raced away. Holding the documents close, she left the villa, crossed the front courtyard, and followed Alessandro down the steps to the beach. He was either extraordinarily fast or extremely angry or both – anyway, he had a considerable start on her. She caught a glimpse of him down by the grotto, then he disappeared from her view.

When she finally reached the beach, she stopped dead at the scene in front of her.

Alessandro had flung himself on Tano. The two of them were fighting so hard that even the young men with the mirrored sunglasses had retreated and were making no attempt to stop the fight.

Rosa slowed down and stopped twenty metres away. She'd seen plenty of fistfights in Brooklyn. But what intrigued her here was that neither of the combatants uttered a word. As if there were nothing more to be said between them, as if the opponent wasn't even worth abuse. Slowly, she moved closer, softly putting one foot in front of the other on the churned-up sand.

Tano wasn't wearing his glasses; one of Alessandro's blows had knocked them off. But that wasn't the only thing that made him look unusual. There were his eyes. They were filled with darkness, with two huge pupils swallowing up the world. Just like Alessandro's eyes earlier, in the studio. And now that she looked at Alessandro again, she realised that his eyes too were deep black once more, and his hair seemed even blacker than before.

The two girls who had been into the water were standing

on the beach a little way off to one side, beside the crates of provisions. The third girl was sitting up on her beach chair, following Tano's nimble movements with a fixed gaze. The young men were still watching, motionless. Only the waiter tried to do anything, shouting something meant to calm everyone down. A hiss from Tano's throat silenced him.

The two combatants circled each other warily. Waiting for whatever kind of attack the other would decide to launch.

Rosa's eyes fell on Tano's bare back. It was hairy. She had thought that was the effect of the sunlight glinting on it, but now she saw a thick line of pale yellow hair running from the nape of his neck down his spine.

Tano uttered an angry bellow, and the two of them clashed again.

No one was taking any notice of Rosa. She hurried over to her bag and stuffed the folder with Gaia's documents in it. As she straightened up again, she heard a droning noise over the sea, coming toward the beach.

The sound of helicopter blades.

Blinking into the sun, she saw a chopper coming in over the water, racing past the anchored yacht and heading straight for the beach. Its outline was blurred by the glittering of the sun on its fuselage.

Alessandro threw Tano to the ground and dropped with both knees brutally on his adversary's ribcage.

The two girls tore open one of the crates, and next moment they had machine guns in their hands. *Machine guns!* The sight was so unlikely that Rosa blinked again.

One of the boys took his sunglasses off. The steward looked as if he were turned to stone.

Alessandro crouched over Tano on the ground, threw his head back, and uttered a triumphant howl like a beast of prey. Shadows raced like wildfire over his body, turning it black as pitch.

Tano howled as well.

Alessandro opened his mouth wider, even wider. He looked as if he were going to sink his teeth into Tano's throat. Or was he calling something out, something that Rosa couldn't hear through the noise of the rotor blades?

Sand swirled up and hid her view.

I promise you, she'd told Iole, *we'll get you out of here.*

The skids of the helicopter touched down.

Family Feud

The pilot left the blades turning as he ran from the cockpit, bending low, and opened the sliding door in the side. Sand blew over the beach; the girls' hair danced on their bare shoulders.

Rosa already knew who she was going to see.

Florinda Alcantara slipped out, ducked under the noisy scythe of the rotor blades, and straightened up. Two armed men jumped out of the helicopter behind her.

Her henchmen were carrying light machine guns, like the girls in Tano's party. The pilot drew an automatic from his jacket, too. The whole thing was like a scene from a third-rate action movie – made on a low budget that didn't allow for crowds of extras.

Bikini-clad girls toting machine pistols, Mafiosi with mirrored sunglasses. A pilot in an artificial leather jacket. She'd have liked to call "Cut!" to stop the action. Then they could all go home while the movie people swept the set.

Instead, her aunt called, "Come along, Rosa, the party's over." Even her dialogue belonged to a villain in a B movie.

Florinda was halfway between the helicopter and Rosa. Her dyed blond hair whipped around her face, while the two men with guns took up their position on either side of her.

You had to hand it to Florinda, thought Rosa. This might be a silly scene, but she was as elegant as ever in a black suit with a short skirt and a fitted jacket. The clearest sign that she didn't seriously expect violence was her high-heeled boots. In a fight, she couldn't have run three metres over the sand in those things.

And suddenly Rosa saw what was going on. All this was pure theatre. Every gesture, every word, every look was part of a secret language that only members of the families understood. The concordat protected them from each other, and the whole macho show was nothing but the icing on a cake with a flavour they all knew well. It was like the Mafiosi were sticking to a tradition based on what they'd seen in films about themselves. They could probably all reel off the dialogue of *The Godfather* and *Scarface* along with the actors.

Alessandro was still kneeling on Tano's chest, with both hands around his cousin's throat. The strange darkness that had come over his body just now had disappeared. Rosa couldn't see his eyes closely; they still looked very dark, but that might be because of the shadows. When he glanced at her, she thought she saw sadness in his gaze.

Only seconds had passed since Florinda's arrival. Tano used the moment of surprise to rear up – and this time he succeeded in throwing his opponent off balance. Alessandro's attention had been distracted just a moment too long, and now he was paying for it. Tano flung him off and jumped to his feet, but didn't try to attack Alessandro again. Instead he stared at him with hatred in his eyes, then ostentatiously turned his back on him and walked slowly up to Florinda and her men. He knocked the sand off his bare torso, entirely unaffected by the storm of the rotor blades, and planted himself three metres from Florinda.

"This island is private property. You know that. But you come here anyway, bringing your henchmen with you, waving guns about – which could very quickly lead to a breach of the concordat – without caring at all about giving my guests a hell of a fright." He had to shout to be heard over the howling of the chopper.

Alessandro got to his feet. Rosa pressed her lips together and stared him down. She still didn't understand exactly what had just happened, but whatever it was she could handle it.

She picked up the bag with her things and set off for the helicopter. It was better this way. For everyone here, probably even for the lonely girl up in the villa. Rosa joined Florinda, who didn't even deign to glance at her.

Alessandro walked over to Tano.

The four of them stood facing one another in the middle of the swirling clouds of sand.

Florinda was staring at Alessandro as if looks could kill, but her remarks were for Rosa. "You have no idea what you're getting mixed up with. They could have taken you hostage. It probably wouldn't even have meant a breach of the concordat."

Tano grinned. "We'd have to look that up somewhere, right?"

"No bloodshed, no kidnapping," said Alessandro. "That's the agreement."

"Always useful to have a budding lawyer in the family," remarked Tano derisively.

To Rosa's indignation, Florinda's anger seemed to be aimed solely at Alessandro, not his arrogant cousin. What would happen if she left him alone with the others now? Would Tano really kill him? Not after all this fuss, she hoped. Especially since it wasn't a secret now that those two girls knew their way around automatic guns a little too well.

But she couldn't be sure.

Come with us, her eyes pleaded with him.

An imperceptible shake of the head. If he turned his back on his family now and went with the enemy clan, he'd have no one left on his side. He'd lose face. Maybe Tano was speculating about that very possibility. His problem would solve itself if Alessandro showed weakness.

Florinda gripped Rosa's upper arm firmly to lead her to the helicopter. Rosa shook her hand off so energetically that the reproach in her aunt's eyes gave way for a moment to an anger and dislike that almost turned Rosa's stomach. That only made her even angrier herself.

"Don't do that again," she snapped at her aunt. "Ever."

And with that she turned and marched to the sliding door of the helicopter, carrying her bag, with Gaia's documents in it.

She glanced at Alessandro once more. She was looking for the darkness in his eyes, the shadows she had just seen. Nothing left of that. The sand pattered against his bronzed skin, but he didn't move a muscle.

Florinda got into the seat opposite her, and finally the two gunmen followed. Rosa wedged the bag between her knees and held it tight with both hands.

The helicopter took off. Its slipstream carved a trail of spray though the surf. Then it gained height again and flew a circuit in the air around the yacht.

Rosa looked down at Isola Luna one last time through the window. She thought she saw the topsy-turvy white structure of the villa bright among the lava rocks, and thought of Iole, who might be still crouched in that plastic chair, waiting for her to come back.

She avoided looking at Florinda for the rest of the flight. She had nothing to say to her anyway, so they sat in silence until the olive groves were moving past below them, and the palazzo rose in the golden light of afternoon.

The next day Zoe took her for a drive to the north in her convertible. They cruised a few miles along the expressway to Catania, but soon left it again and drove farther into the bleak, mountainous country of the Sicilian interior. At first the landscape was one of undulating ochre hills, but then it became harsher. The few fields were uncultivated, or charred black where farmers had burned the stubble after harvesting their crops. The smell of smoke was everywhere, though there was none to be seen. Sometimes there were broad bays at the side of the winding road where containers crammed with rubbish stood; generally the local people had just left their rubbish bags beside the bins. Plastic bottles and empty packaging had collected in the ditches along the roadside, too.

"I've never seen so much garbage all in one place," said Rosa as they passed yet another blackened field with charred remains of plastic scattered all over it.

"It's better than it used to be," said Zoe. "But you're right, it's hard to imagine that it ever *could* have been worse."

"I thought Cosa Nostra made a bundle by getting rid of trash illegally."

"Not on their own doorsteps. A few of the families really are big in the garbage business, yes, but they ship it off to Calabria or other places."

"Which doesn't make it better, right?"

Zoe gave her a serious glance before she had to concentrate on the next bend. "Better not start thinking you can afford a guilty conscience. Or you're in the wrong place here."

"What do you do to fight it off?"

Zoe seemed surprised by the question. "I go shopping," she said at last. "Retail therapy is good for a lot of things."

"But it's not what you're about to do now, is it? Go shopping, I mean."

"No."

"So where are we going?"

"I want to show you something. We're nearly there."

"Was this Florinda's idea?" Rosa made a face. "To get me back on the straight and narrow? I mean as far as the family's concerned?"

"She was too angry to say anything at all."

"She'll get over it."

"She doesn't have it easy. Hardly any women are heads of

families. Dad was going to be the next *capo*, but then he and Mom took us back to the States. Suddenly Florinda was alone in her palazzo, having to manage it all."

"But surely she doesn't manage the family business on her own?"

"She has her *consiglieri*, her advisers," said Zoe. "But they're in Palermo and Catania, a few of them in Rome and Milan. Some of them are second cousins of ours. They run the firms and advise Florinda, but the final decision is always hers. They come here regularly to report back to her, and Florinda often goes to see them. The Internet and the phone aren't secure enough. Most of the business is still done privately, face-to-face, and no technology, however advanced, is going to change that."

Rosa looked at her sister's beautiful but thin profile. She was beginning to realise that there were two sides to Zoe. There was the wayward, fashion-crazy, pleasure-loving Zoe she'd known in the past. But there was also another Zoe, who had obviously thoroughly studied the family and its business ventures. This was a new and unexpected side of her, until Rosa remembered that she had already met that Zoe at the beginning of her stay here – on the way to the funeral, when she and Florinda had sat opposite her, looking like two queen bees.

That mental image paled when she found herself, against her will, thinking of Alessandro again. She thought it unlikely that Tano had simply given up on his plan. Had something else happened on the island after Florinda had swept her away? She felt like a child dragged away from the playground, and it made her furious.

"You like him?" Zoe suddenly remarked.

"Alessandro?"

"You know who I mean."

"I don't even know him."

"Exactly, and that's the problem. The Carnevares aren't like us. Their family and ours—"

"Oh, don't start with all that Romeo and Juliet crap!"

"Then you really do like him." It wasn't a question this time.

"He invited me to the island with him. I went. That's all. We didn't make plans to have five kids and topple Cosa Nostra."

"Don't take it so lightly."

Rosa's hand clasped her bony knee more firmly. "We wanted to go swimming, that's all."

"Sure."

The convertible was crossing the plateau of a flattened mountain peak. Once again a wide panorama of mustard-coloured hills opened out in front of them. Below was a large expanse of water. At first Rosa thought it was a broad river, but then she saw that it was a long lake winding its way through several valleys. To the right of them, in the east, she saw a huge dam. It looked out of place in this deserted yellow landscape.

"Nearly there." Zoe steered the car down around several bends, until the two-lane road led straight across the dam. To their right yawned a valley full of ravines, to their left the water of the reservoir glittered.

Zoe parked the car by the roadside, right in the middle of the reservoir. There was no other vehicle in sight, nothing but a flock of birds soaring above them in the cloudless sky.

"Lago Carnevare," said Zoe, mockery in her voice. "That's not really its name, but it belongs to them."

Rosa shrugged her shoulders. "They own a lake. So?"

"So they earn a pile of money with an asset like that. Building projects for the state serving no real purpose. No one here needs a reservoir. Hardly anyone around here grows any crops, so there's no need for irrigation. Take a look – this is a wilderness, mountains where nobody goes, deserted farmhouses."

"We build wind turbines that don't generate any electricity. They build dams. What's the difference?"

"That's not what I'm talking about," replied Zoe, shaking her head. "What you ought to know… why you're here…" She hesitated, and began again. "It's about what's *in* the lake."

She opened the driver's door and slipped out into the open air. Rosa joined her sister at the waist-high parapet. For one or two minutes they looked down on the smooth surface of the water in silence. The sunlight sparkling on the reservoir dazzled Rosa.

"So what *is* down there?" asked Rosa at last.

"Ruins," said Zoe.

Rosa shrugged. "Sicily is full of those." There was no missing that fact, any more than you could overlook the piles of rubbish by the roadside. Whichever way you looked on this island, you'd soon see at least one deserted farmhouse, at least one ruined barn. No one bothered about them, so why start here?

"There's a whole village under the water there," said Zoe. "Giuliana. The signposts on some of the roads near here still point to it. If you went that way in the dark and didn't watch out, you'd end up in the lake. They didn't even build barriers over the roads."

Rosa blinked hard, trying to see something under the surface, but it was useless. The water was much too deep, the light too bright.

"The Carnevares moved heaven and earth to land that building project," Zoe went on. "Mountains of fake reports, expert opinions, surveyors' plans. Huge amounts of hush money paid out, up to and including the highest political levels in Rome and Brussels. But what they spent on that they got back a hundred times over: European subsidies, state financing, and of course the wages for an army of engineers, construction workers, and so on."

"It still doesn't sound to me any different from what Florinda does with her wind turbines. Except that the Carnevares are clever enough to do it on a larger scale."

"Wind doesn't kill anyone. Water does."

Rosa looked askance at Zoe. A gust of cool wind from the lake ruffled her blond hair. Zoe didn't return her glance, but kept looking out over the water.

"What happened?"

"The inhabitants of Giuliana protested. They did what you'd expect people to do when the village where they live is going to be simply wiped off the map. Meetings first, then public rallies, even a demonstration outside the Parliament building in Rome. No one showed the faintest interest in it. And then nothing more. That was four years ago."

"Nothing more?"

"No more protests, no resistance."

Rosa guessed what this was leading up to, but all the same she asked, "They were bought out?"

"Resettled, apparently." The corners of Zoe's mouth twisted into a bitter smile. "Given new homes somewhere in Calabria, on the other side of the Strait of Messina. As if you could just put eight hundred Sicilians in a boat, ship them off across the water, and leave them somewhere else for the rest of their lives." She wasn't smiling any more when she said, "That didn't even work with us."

"So what's the truth?"

"Officially they're all living over there raising sheep or cattle. It'd be closer to the truth to call them the sheep themselves. The wolves came and tore them to pieces. Well, the lions and tigers, to be precise."

Rosa suppressed her memory of the tiger in the olive grove. "The Carnevares killed them? You know what that sounds like, don't you?" Then she thought of the girls on the island with their machine pistols. "They drowned them in the lake?"

Zoe picked a tiny pebble off the parapet and threw it over. Rosa couldn't hear it hit the water. "They didn't drown. Or not as far as I know. Officially they simply went away. Overnight. The dam was almost finished by then. Giuliana lay in the valley down in its shadow." Zoe pointed to the depths of the lake. "And there it lies today. So, probably, do its people.

If you ask me, I'd bet that their bodies aren't the only ones down there. Did you know that the Carnevares are kind of grave diggers for Cosa Nostra? If the other families want someone to disappear, they turn to them for help. Roads, airport runways, even administrative buildings in Catania and Palermo. Cesare Carnevare's labour force builds concrete into their foundations – and not *just* concrete."

So this was the inheritance that mattered so much to Alessandro. He was fighting Tano and Cesare so fiercely for the chance to dispose of corpses under buildings and expressways. Leaving depopulated villages at the bottom of quiet lakes.

Rosa clambered up onto the stone of the parapet wall and took a step forward, until she was directly on the edge of it. The surface of the lake lay some twenty metres below.

"Come down from there."

Rosa brushed her sister's hand off her calf. "No, you come up to me."

For a moment Zoe looked furious, then she took a deep breath and managed a smile. She took the hand that Rosa reached out to her and climbed up on the wall. They stood there side by side, just a finger's breadth from the edge, while the wind blew through their clothes and ruffled their hair.

"Why did you tell me that?" asked Rosa quietly. "I mean, really why?"

"Because Alessandro Carnevare is not—"

"Because Florinda told you to? Did she think up this story herself?"

"It's true, Rosa."

"Well, maybe it is. But is that supposed to scare me? Am I supposed to hate him now? I knew exactly where I was going when I boarded the plane for Italy. Do you think I'm so naive? Does Florinda think so? I know who and what our family is. And I know it's no better than the Carnevares and the Riinas and all the rest of them. You and I are a part of it."

"You don't know just *what* we're a part of," Zoe whispered into the wind.

"I think I do." Rosa felt for her sister's hand, something she hadn't done since she was little. "But other crimes have been committed in other places, crimes for which we're responsible. Our family, anyway. Probably our father. What does Florinda expect? Does she want us to fall in love with nice boys from respectable, law-abiding families in Turin or Milan? Or live alone all our lives just like her?"

Zoe's hand was very cold. "You can't understand it. Not yet."

"You know," said Rosa, depressed, "I don't have a guilty conscience, I don't have scruples about what may have happened to the people of Giuliana. Because I'm an Alcantara and I can't change that. Just as Alessandro can't change what *he* is."

Zoe opened her mouth to say something, but no sound came out. She moistened her lips with the tip of her tongue and said no more.

"Nothing happened on the island," said Rosa, blinking again as she looked at the dazzling surface of the water. "It's not what you think."

She said nothing for a while, gazing at the far bank of the reservoir in the distance.

"Nothing," she whispered again, and this time it wasn't Zoe she was trying to convince.

Tiger and Snake

It was already dark when they got back to the palazzo. Alone in her room, Rosa tried calling Alessandro, but a recorded voice told her that the number was no longer in service. Annoyed, she tried again, with the same result. She flung the gold cell phone down on her pillows, where it landed softly as if in a snowdrift.

The plastic folder containing Gaia Carnevare's documents also lay on the bed, with *Aesop's Fables* beside it. Both of them evidence that Alessandro trusted her. So why couldn't she reach him? Had something happened to him on the island? But if that were the case, would Cesare have blocked the cell phone straight away? It seemed unlikely.

She had to admit she was worried. Even though she had every reason to be disappointed in Alessandro after he'd taken her to Isola Luna only for his own protection. She could handle that. It wasn't like her to sulk just because someone wasn't nice to her. In fact there were few things she could excuse as easily as *not being nice*. After all, she herself never apologised to other people. But why was she worried about someone when she ought to be furious with him?

He liked her, he'd said. But you could also like puppies and guinea pigs. It wasn't any reason to go worrying about a changed phone number. She wasn't even sure whether *she* liked *him*.

She tried his number a third time. Not from speed dial,

but typing in each digit separately. She'd stared at the number long enough to know it by heart. She didn't have a delete key in her brain.

She got the same recording again.

The cell phone landed in the cushions once more. Impatiently, she jumped up, opened the window, and took a deep breath. The air smelled pleasantly like pine needles.

Below her the greenhouse shimmered. The glass was covered with condensation on the inside. Again she wondered what the point was of a greenhouse on an island where palms grew outdoors. There were even some here at the palazzo, along the huge panoramic terrace on the west side, where they cast their shadows over the pool at sunset.

She couldn't see anything through the condensation on the glass.

She saw a movement just around the corner of the house, and knew at once that it was Zoe.

Her sister moved out of the shelter of the building and crossed the strip of open land, stopping halfway. Rosa quickly stepped back into her room until she could no longer see whether Zoe was looking up at her window. When she next dared to look outside, her sister was moving into the shadow of the chestnuts.

Rosa was wearing black jeans and canvas trainers, with one of the dark T-shirts that Zoe had given her. She had the key to the front door in her jeans pocket. That was all she needed; a torch might give her away.

She quickly left her room and crept along the high-ceilinged, dim corridors to the stairs, until she reached the back door and was out in the open. Florinda was usually in her study at this time of day; the domestic staff had gone home to the village or to Piazza Armerina long ago. Rosa just had to take care not to run right into the arms of one of the guards patrolling the grounds.

Her sister had been heading up the slope. Beyond the row of chestnuts, pinewoods rose toward the top of the mountain. Although Zoe had not looked as if she were in a hurry, she had a considerable head start by now.

Rosa had noticed exactly where Zoe disappeared among the trees. The sky was still clear, the moon, half-full, gave a little light. Soon Rosa found a small trail leading up the mountainside.

Pine needles muffled her footsteps as the path wound its way past hollows and steep slopes. Just before she reached the top of the mountain, she saw her sister, a shadow among the tree trunks. Zoe was about fifty metres ahead of her. She was walking briskly, but not with any great haste.

Once, Rosa looked back over her shoulder and saw a few isolated points of light beyond the trees. The palazzo windows. Why hadn't the motion detector light outside the house come on? Had Zoe switched it off? And if so, whose eyes was she hiding from? Florinda's? Rosa's?

Zoe disappeared down the other side of the mountain, and Rosa quickened her pace. More pine trees, more shadows. Somewhere ahead of her Zoe was walking through the darkness. Wind rustled in the needles of the trees.

And then the slope came to an end as suddenly as if someone had chopped a piece off it with a gigantic spade. A sharp edge, and below it a rocky, wooded ravine. Maybe ten metres deep, no more. The opposite slope was also wooded, with the clear, starlit sky above it.

Rosa stopped at the edge of the drop. Now she could see that the path, after bending sharply, led along the side of the ravine, and she thought she could see Zoe again, a slender figure between the rocky edge and the trees. Rosa followed her more slowly now, which kept her from being seen when her sister stopped abruptly and looked around. There was no time to look for a hiding place farther in among the trees. She stood where she was, in the shadow of a pine, and hoped the darkness would hide her. Zoe was looking straight at her now. But she turned her eyes first to the ravine, then up to the sky, as if expecting airborne pursuers.

When Zoe continued, Rosa stayed put a little longer before finally moving again herself. The path led on for several hundred metres farther along the edge of the drop, not more than a couple of steps from the ravine below. Somewhere in the distance, an owl hooted.

The bulky outline of a farmhouse emerged from the darkness. Rosa thought at first that the run-down place was empty, but then she saw a faint light inside. The tiles on the roof were crumbling, the pale walls were dilapidated. There were no shutters on the windows any more, but someone must have hung black curtains inside. A thin strip of light showed through a narrow gap in the dark fabric.

Zoe shouted something that Rosa couldn't make out. The back of the house came right up to the edge of the rock, and the front of it faced the woods. The door opened, creaking, and yellow light flooded out onto the ground. Zoe was silhouetted against the bright rectangle, in which a figure appeared, thickset and broad-shouldered. The man beckoned her in, and the door closed again.

Rosa took cover among the trees on the edge of the pinewood, choosing a place that would be out of the light when the door opened again. She wasn't sure what to do now. Stealing over to the window seemed childish. Why would she be interested in what Zoe was doing inside the house? But then, why else had she followed her sister? She felt almost ashamed of it now.

She was about to simply turn away, leaving Zoe to go about her own business, when the door creaked again and swung open. There had hardly been time for the two people inside to exchange greetings.

Her sister came out with the sturdy man, both of them black silhouettes against the brightness of the doorway. Zoe leaned forward, kissed the man on both cheeks in a friendly farewell, and hurried back along the path at the edge of the ravine. She was holding a flat bundle of something in one hand, as she had the first time Rosa saw her out like this. She looked back over her shoulder once, waved to the man, and disappeared into the darkness.

Rosa held her breath as the outline of the man lingered in the doorway for a few moments. He seemed to be looking around. His gaze wandered over the outskirts of the wood, including the place where she was hiding. He paused several times, as if he had noticed something, but then went back into the house and closed the door. Rosa bit her lower lip, hardly daring to move.

As she hurried back to the path, she realised there was no real reason for her to be nervous. This was Alcantara land, the palazzo was quite close, and her aunt's armed guards were patrolling on the other side of the mountain. Florinda must know about the man living in this ruin. Rosa assumed Zoe was visiting him on her aunt's behalf. But what did she come here to do?

Ahead of her the path above the ravine was empty. Zoe must have made good time. Rosa quickened her pace too, and was soon climbing the slope, following the narrow trail to the mountaintop.

Something growled among the pines.

First on her left, then behind her, then on her right.

She didn't run away, but instead stopped in her tracks.

Slowly, her eyes moved over the tree trunks. No undergrowth blocked her view, and the trees grew far apart.

There was no missing the tiger. She had always thought that big cats were elegant and supple, but the animal standing there in the dark was powerful, a mighty mountain of muscle and fur striped black and orange, with white markings around his muzzle. The tiger bared his canine teeth.

She ought to have been surprised. Or scared to death.

But she was neither.

They come at night.

The growl turned to a deep roar.

Always at night.

The tiger completed a loop around his prey, while she turned with him, never taking her eyes off him. A few metres up the slope he crossed the path and slipped between the trees to her left again. He was approaching her, not directly but in a spiral, gradually decreasing the distance between them.

Another circuit, and then another.

When he crossed the path for the third time, he was only a few metres away. There was something hypnotic about his threatening aura. Rosa stopped turning and stood there facing the ravine. She couldn't even fathom the thought of making a break for it.

He was ten times faster than her. She didn't have a chance.

The stealthy sound of his paws padding over dry pine needles died away. He was right behind her, just behind her back. So close she could smell his breath. He smelled of the wild. Of animal power. Of the confidence that he could do anything he wanted to her, and there was nothing she could do to stop him. And although she knew he was far more dangerous than the human beasts of prey she had met earlier, she still felt no fear. All her senses were paralysed, including whichever one set off the panic instinct.

Very slowly, she turned to face him.

He stood about a metre farther up the path, his gigantic body tensed, his head lowered. Staring at her.

She remembered that look.

She recognised his eyes.

She still felt no urge to scream and run away, but she began to move anyway, cautiously, nudging backward step by step. And wondering why she hadn't recognised him before.

He was going to kill her. That was why he had come here.

She'd had bad things done to her once before, and since then she'd been ready to defend herself. Against anyone or anything. But why was a strange chill spreading through her body, instead of hot rage?

The tiger followed her. Slowly, crouching low, he prowled down the path, still keeping the same distance between them. As she walked backwards, her feet felt for support on the springy forest floor. The path was steep here. The slightest wrong step and she would fall. The ravine wasn't far behind her, perhaps ten steps away.

She could see that he relished having the advantage of his superior strength. He was watching her, and seemed to be waiting for something. Waiting for her to finally panic? The ice in her veins prevented it.

She began to tremble as the unnatural chill took possession of her whole body. The tiger narrowed his eyes. She expected him to pounce on her at any minute.

Rosa opened her mouth.

There was a hiss. For a moment she thought she had uttered it herself.

Behind the tiger, the dark path came to life. Its winding bends quivered; the ground was moving. Shadows were gliding down the mountain.

Rosa stopped, but the tiger kept on coming. He was crouching, ready to leap.

All at once the darkness lifted from the ground, a black ribbon rose in the air behind the great cat, and it looked like the path itself was changing course, flowing over the tiger and seizing him.

The beast of prey uttered a high snarl as he realised that he was being attacked from behind. The darkness wrapped itself around the tiger's body. Its front end gaped open, two golden almond-shaped eyes glittered in the moonlight. The mouth that had just been hovering in the air above the nape of the big cat's neck shot down.

The tiger was faster by a fraction of a second. He threw himself aside, his back hitting a tree, and squeezed his attacker between his heavy body and the trunk. The thing had been about to bite, but the force of the impact left its jaws snapping at empty air.

It was a snake. A snake several metres long, with silvery black scales, a skull the size of a crocodile's, and fangs as long as Rosa's fingers.

It had coiled itself tightly around the tiger's body and was crushing his ribcage, while its head whipped back and forth in the darkness to keep out of reach of his snapping jaws.

Cold-Blooded Creatures

The tiger and the snake rolled on the ground, hissing and growling in a life-and-death struggle, colliding with tree trunks. The big cat tried to pounce but staggered, and the beasts landed back on the path again still entwined. This time they were on the slope just below Rosa, who swung around and tried to keep her eye on the chaotic tangle of yellow and black, claws and sharp fangs.

She still felt the chill inside her, but it had stopped spreading. Her whole body was pulsating as if her heart had swollen to many times its normal size and was threatening to break through her thorax. She was in pain; something was tugging at her limbs, trying to twist and break and then reshape them.

But all that was in the background, because the struggle between the two creatures demanded her full attention. Rosa, struggling to keep her balance, could not take her eyes off the raging tiger. He was trying to summon enough strength to throw off the giant snake, which had now coiled itself several times around his body. Once again he stumbled, then fell and rolled away down the path, taking the snake with him in a swirling cloud of dust and pine needles. He got to his feet again only when they reached the outskirts of the wood, and through a daze Rosa remembered what lay beyond it. The edge of the rock. And below that the ravine.

The snake's skull, half stunned by the impact, swung back and forth above the tiger's back. Once again the wide mouth gaped open, the curved fangs shining like ivory daggers. The tiger passed one paw over his head and shoulders, almost clumsily, as if a troublesome insect had settled there. He caught the reptile below its head; the supple body bent, elegantly absorbing the force of the murderous blow. But still the snake couldn't manage to sink its fangs into the tiger's neck – and it saw, just a moment too late, that the tiger's blow had also served a second purpose. Its swift evasion had brought its body within reach of the tiger's muzzle, only for a moment, but that was long enough.

With a roar, the big cat attacked, sank his jaws into the snake's body, and pulled. The reptile screamed, but instead of giving in, it continued to fight back. Its curved fangs disappeared in the tiger's fur, digging in until they met flesh. Its bite couldn't be venomous, or the cat probably would have collapsed at once. Now the two were more closely intertwined than ever. The tiger tried to free himself, but with his neck twisted he could exert only a fraction of his strength. The snake was throttling him. Its fangs were in his body, and it was nothing short of a miracle that he could still stay on his paws.

Rosa staggered against a tree near the path, about a metre from the two combatants. She pushed herself away from it with one hand, convulsively rubbing her eyes with the other. She could see the tiger and the snake only as a confused blur now; her own body seemed to be shimmering. Maybe the chill was now affecting her vision as well, or maybe it was real.

The tiger roared with rage and let go of the scaly body. The snake let out a sharp hiss, muffled by the fur and flesh in its mouth. At last its pressure on the big cat's body seemed to have an effect. The tiger ran out of breath and stumbled aside.

His feeble leap carried him to the very edge of the rock. The snake, too, knew what was going on, but was much too tightly coiled around his body to escape in time.

The entangled tiger and snake lost their balance and were carried over the edge. Rosa heard the cracking of dry twigs, followed by the sound of a dull thud at the bottom of the wooded ravine.

Their images faded before Rosa's eyes, like a nightmare brought halfway out of sleep before reality finally extinguishes it. The path and the edge of the rock lay deserted again, a patch of wilderness in the pale light of the half-moon.

Down in the ravine, something was stirring.

Rosa swung around and staggered up the slope.

The lights of the Palazzo Alcantara danced in the darkness ahead of her, vanished behind trees, reappeared. She stumbled along the path, fell, braced her hands on fallen pine needles, and hauled herself up. The outlines of the trunks, grey splinters of the night sky, and the shining dots of the windows all turned into a whirling dance in which she could distinguish nothing. She was chilled through and through and couldn't stop shivering. The cold was radiating from her heart, forcing the blood out of her veins.

Broader tree trunks. The chestnuts.

Her breath was racing, and in her own ears it sounded like reptilian hissing. She couldn't feel her fingers any more. Her knees gave way again and again; she had hardly any control left over her legs. Her lips felt dry and cracked, and she moistened them with her tongue. She stumbled again, fell over, almost bit the tip of her tongue. Struggled up and continued.

Suddenly there was someone in front of her, a human figure. Rosa tried to push it away – *Not me, not again!* – but her hands met a void. Then she was picked up and lifted in the air. A man was talking to her. One of the guards.

While he carried her along as if she weighed nothing at all, he asked many questions, but she couldn't understand any of them. She was still struggling in his grasp. A stranger's eyes, a stranger's hands. A body so close to hers, much too close.

Then another voice.

Florinda.

She was giving angry instructions that Rosa didn't understand. Her trembling died down slightly, and she was still cold, but not quite as cold as before. There was light all around her. Visions of angels and devils – the paintings on the ceilings of the palazzo. She was in the house, still in the man's arms, and she looked up as he carried her down the halls. Grave, round-cheeked, pale faces. Among them the thin, bony heads of holy men. Intertwining ornamentation and patterns. She had never before noticed the pictorial power of the frescoes.

The paintings were superimposed on Florinda's voice as sight and hearing became one, freezing and sweating, the rattle of her breath and the hissing of the giant snake out in the forest.

Then a door creaked, and Rosa heard Florinda again, this time sounding furious, beside herself. She felt hands on her body. She wasn't being carried any more, she was lying on something soft. Her bed? No, not a bed. She felt grass. Or earth. Was she outside again?

Not back into the forest! she wanted to cry, but only a faint snarling came out, a hissing as if through breathing holes. Her tongue ran over her dry, rough lips in a compelling rhythm, again and again. She tried to move her fingers and her feet, but if she succeeded she didn't feel it. Her body reared up, formed a bridge, collapsed again.

The man had left long ago. Florinda had fallen silent. Was she still there with her? Rosa didn't care one way or the other, because nothing meant anything any more. Not where she was. Or what she was. In the staccato interplay of waking moments and darkness, none of that played a part.

It wasn't as bright as it had been a little while ago; now her surroundings looked pale and cloudy, a mingled green and blue. Like the light in an aquarium, she thought, dazed. Underwater, like the drowned people of Giuliana. But she could breathe more easily now, she could breathe without taking water into her lungs. There were sounds around her, rustling and a faint cracking, as if something heavy were being dragged through dense undergrowth. Not Rosa herself, because she was lying quietly on the ground. Still not in bed, but on warm earth.

A scream rose in her throat. A scream like the one she had uttered a year ago. Someone had undressed her then, too.

She felt her bare skin, stroked her torso, her bony hips, her thighs. She could feel her hands again.

Her eyes got used to the dim light. She saw plants everywhere, dense, tropical vegetation. Like a jungle. The air was moist and sultry. Diffuse light was reflected in the glass panes above her. There must be lights among the plants.

Now she knew. It wasn't an aquarium. This was a *terrarium*.

She raised her head, saw movements. Snakes, dozens of them, but none as large as the snake in the forest. She wasn't afraid of them. She'd rather have them crowding around her naked body than humans.

The snakes nestled close to her, crawled over her, but they didn't seem to mean her any harm. They seemed almost afraid of her. When Rosa looked down at herself, they swiftly slid off her body and away into the dense vegetation, hissing.

Not a dream. She was in Florinda's greenhouse.

The snakes withdrew respectfully, hiding in the shadows, staring at her out of the darkness with eyes like jewels.

Rosa sat up and brushed dry scales off her skin.

Wild Dogs

Rosa slept until early afternoon. Even when she woke up she still wasn't sure just when reality and dream had merged last night.

Her body was clean and smelled of soap, although she didn't remember showering. Her pillow was damp, probably from her wet hair. Remnants of foam were left around the drain in the tub in her bathroom. That was more unsettling than the blurred images of giant snakes and big cats in her mind. Ever since last year, having gaps in her memory had been her greatest fear. She shuddered, and her fingers wouldn't stop trembling.

She was wearing pyjamas with a gold flower print. Probably Zoe's. Neutral black clothes, found for her by her sister in Piazza Armerina a few days ago, lay on a chair, along with the dress she had worn on the plane, which had now been cleaned.

Somehow she managed to brush her teeth as if nothing had happened. Even after she combed her hair it still looked as wild and tousled as before, but she tried desperately to pretend everything was normal. *Do everything the same as usual. Don't show any weakness. You're in control.*

The problem was that, yet again, the past was eluding her control. What had happened in the woods, the way she had woken up in the greenhouse half-buried under snakes – *none* of that had been under her control. She didn't even know what had really happened.

She made it to the toilet bowl just before she threw up and stayed there on her knees, feeling so weak she didn't know if she could ever get on her feet again.

Somehow she hauled herself up, washed the tears from her face, brushed her teeth again, and gargled until she was out of breath. Finally she put on the minidress, a black T-shirt, and black stockings. As she laced up her metal-studded boots, her fingers shook. She thought she'd never finish.

There was a knock at the door of her room.

"I'm dead," she said.

Zoe came in. "I'm even more so." And she was right. She looked terrible. Evidently she had tried to cover some of her swellings and injuries with make-up, but was about as successful as if she had set about making a car from the junkyard look brand new with nothing but some paint and a brush. She had a black eye and a split lip, and Rosa saw the edge of a white bandage under the neck of her shirt.

"What on earth happened?" Rosa jumped up, which wasn't a good idea. Her knees gave way, and she immediately dropped back onto the edge of her bed again.

"Look who's talking," said Zoe.

"You're injured, I'm only crazy. So you start."

Zoe managed a thin smile. "I was outside yesterday evening." She hesitated, obviously not sure whether Rosa had followed her or had just happened to be in the woods by chance. She had to have guessed the truth, but she wasn't about to broach the subject. "I went for a walk, and something attacked me. A wild dog, probably. Or a whole pack of them.

I don't know any more, it's a total blackout. The guards picked me up. I have you to thank for that, by the way – if you hadn't crossed their path earlier, and if they hadn't been searching the whole mountain for you, they wouldn't have found me so quickly."

Rosa looked at her hard. "Seems like going for walks around here isn't a great idea."

Zoe returned her gaze. "Seems like it isn't."

How much of her calm composure was just for show? And how much was real coolness?

"What's the matter with your shoulder?" asked Rosa.

"Looks worse than it is. A bite. The doctor from Piazza Armerina gave me an injection. He was here last night – for you, too, by the way."

There was a lump in Rosa's throat. "I can't remember anything."

"He gave you a tranquiliser, Florinda says. When they found you on the outskirts of the woods, you were distraught. She put you to bed and then sent the guards out searching. And when she went up to you again, you'd disappeared. You walked in your sleep and ended up lying in the green-house, she says. Then the doctor arrived and put you out for the count."

Rosa didn't say a word, but her glance must have spoken volumes.

Zoe misinterpreted it. "Doctors who treat the families don't dither and ask questions. They usually have much worse to deal with than a few scratches and bites. They simply do what has to be done and never say a word about it later. Better for all concerned, and they're well paid for it."

"The law of silence," whispered Rosa.

"This is Sicily. *Omertà* is part of it, like the smoke over the burning stubble and the litter in the roadside ditches."

"How poetic."

Zoe shifted from foot to foot. Probably to hide the uncertainty that she obviously felt, she went to the window and looked out.

Rosa waited to see if her sister was going to say anything. But she just stood there, looking out in silence.

Rosa frowned. "There's something else, right?"

Zoe sighed, turned around, and tried perching on the windowsill, but it was painfully obvious that in her present condition she'd better stand. It was clearly difficult for her to answer Rosa's question, but not because of her injuries.

"He was here," she said.

Rosa had expected something quite different. For a moment she was thrown off balance. "Who was?"

"Alessandro Carnevare."

"Here, in this house?" After Florinda's ostentatious rescue operation on Isola Luna, he could hardly have done anything more stupid than to turn up here.

"Not exactly in the house," said Zoe. "On the doorstep."

"How did he get past the guards?"

A shrug of the shoulders. "He asked permission over the intercom to come up."

"And Florinda let him?"

"She even expressly invited him, she says. To tell him face-to-face that she'd break the concordat if he didn't take his filthy fingers off her stupid, naive, ungrateful niece. Her words, not mine."

Rosa jumped up. To her surprise, this time it worked quite well. "That was when we were out in the forest, right?"

Zoe nodded.

"Was he alone? Or was Tano with him?"

A shadow crossed her sister's face. "Florinda didn't mention anyone but him."

"What did he want? Fuck, Zoe – don't make me drag every word out of you."

"What do you think? He wanted to talk to you."

"And Florinda threatened to murder him?" Rosa's eyes sought the plastic folder that had been on the bedside table. Had anyone looked inside it? Whoever had put Rosa to bed, Florinda or the doctor or one of the guards, must have cleared away the folder and the book.

Gaia's documents were still there, but the little book of *Aesop's Fables* was missing. Or no: it was lying open on the floor a little to the left, beside the skirting board. As if it had been thrown there.

Obviously someone around here didn't like animal stories.

Zoe followed the direction of Rosa's eyes, frowned, and went over to the little book, limping slightly. She gasped with pain as she bent down to pick it up. Rosa would have bet that the Zoe who'd lived in the States until two years ago had never heard of a Greek slave called Aesop, but now a fleeting glance at the title was enough to send her into a fury.

"Did Alessandro give you that?"

Rosa clenched her hand into a fist among the bedclothes. "That's none of your business. Or Florinda's either."

"He's playing with you."

"What, by giving me a book?"

Zoe flung the little leather-bound volume down on the bedspread, shook her head vigorously, and limped to the door.

"What the hell is this all about?" Rosa yelled at her.

Zoe stopped with her hand on the door handle and looked at her. "He's interfering in matters that have nothing to do with him. And don't go thinking it's for your sake."

She opened the door, but stayed there with her back to Rosa, as if expecting another outburst.

Rosa's voice was icy. "Maybe the Carnevares sink dead bodies in lakes," she said, "but what were *you* really doing out in the woods?"

Zoe froze, and looked like she was about to turn around again, but she stayed where she was. The seconds passed by.

Rosa stared at Zoe's back. "You have to help me."

"So?"

"I need the Porsche."

Zoe let out a sharp breath. "The key's in the ignition," she whispered as she walked out.

Castello Carnevare

The GPS led her to Genuardo. She had intended to ask the way to Castello Carnevare there, but that proved unnecessary. The clan's fortress rose on a peak above the village, a medieval colossus of yellowish-brown rough-hewn stone walls, looking about as homely from the outside as a collection of monuments.

The winding road led up the mountain. On her way, even before she reached the village, she noticed several guards posted. A biker with a motorcycle at the side of the road, pretending to check his exhaust. A man with a pair of binoculars, sitting on the hood of his car in a parking lot making a show of bird-watching. Probably even the teenager taking a dog for a walk near the fork in the mountain road, talking on his cell phone and surreptitiously scrutinising her car at the same time. There'd certainly been a few others who'd escaped her notice. But no one stopped her.

She drove Zoe's convertible to the gateway of the castle. Close up the facade looked just as uninviting as it had from down below, but now she saw that the historic walls were deceptive. The roofs were covered with glazed ceramic tiles, and modern window frames had been set into the ancient stone masonry. No one could get past the iron gate to the front courtyard without being watched by several cameras. The fact that it stood open was the final proof that they were expecting her.

She drove through the arched gateway at a crawl. Twice her

wheels jolted over the beds of lowered steel spikes that could be raised in an emergency. More cameras followed her as she rolled into the inner courtyard of the fortress.

The extensive open space had a garden where palm trees, climbing roses, and orchids grew. Huge topiaries had been pruned into the shape of seated animals. At first Rosa thought they were meant to be dogs, but when she looked more closely she saw that they were actually cats as tall as men. She had expected a gloomy ancestral home, something out of a horror novel. Instead she saw signs of good landscaping, with fountains running and an aviary full of songbirds on the far side of the courtyard.

In the dim light of the open garage doors, well-polished vintage cars gleamed. Something was scurrying among them – a black dog. Sarcasmo! He recognised her, wagged his tail – and suddenly shot around as if someone had called to him from the shadows. Maybe Fundling, but she couldn't see him anywhere.

Several men were sitting on balconies behind stone parapets, their eyes hidden by sunglasses. Rosa was sure they were all looking down at her.

She turned off the engine, and was about to get out when the big door at the top of a flight of marble steps swung open. Alessandro came out, wearing trainers, a pair of faded jeans, and a T-shirt with a band logo on it. He looked furious. Glancing briefly over his shoulder and back into the building, he called something that she couldn't make out, then hurried down the steps and leaned over the passenger door.

"Leave the engine on," he said without any greeting.

She put her fingers on the ignition key again, but didn't turn it. She was preparing a not particularly friendly reply, but he grimly shook his head and swung himself over the door and into the passenger seat. He did it so casually that one of her eyebrows shot up in sheer surprise.

"Wow, I'm impressed!" Her irony was merely meant to hide the fact that she really was.

"Drive."

She waited a moment longer, looking at the darkness beyond the open portal, and noticed the men on the balconies rising from their chairs as if on command. As if an invisible puppeteer above the rooftops were pulling the strings that worked them. Only now did she see that they all wore headsets.

She switched the engine on and turned the car.

"What about the gate?" she asked.

"Don't worry. I'm with you."

This was such a wrong answer it left her speechless. She was tempted to stamp on the brake and throw him out of the car.

Except for that undertone to his voice telling her that he wasn't showing off. He really was convinced that his presence was keeping her from harm.

She sighed. "Go on, say it. I shouldn't have come."

"You shouldn't have come." He looked sideways at her and gave her a fleeting grin. "But I'm glad you did."

She steered the convertible through the arched entrance, waiting for the metal spikes to rise. Her tyres rolled over the first barrier with a slight jolt. Then the second. The dark eyes of the cameras watched the car leave. There were loud voices in the courtyard behind them. When she glanced briefly in the rearview mirror, she saw someone approaching the balustrade of the marble stairway, leaning both hands on it, and looking at them as they drove away. The jolt as they passed over the second barrier prevented her from seeing him clearly.

"Cesare?" she asked.

Alessandro nodded.

They left the tunnel and passed the cameras and microphones on the outside. Out on the winding road, Rosa stepped on the gas harder than necessary. Alessandro turned pale as she raced around the next bend. She smiled, satisfied.

"Your aunt was right," he said.

"I bet she wasn't."

"Right to take you off the island, yes. Tano was furious when Cesare discovered you'd been there and he hadn't even… given you a fright."

It was Alessandro who had given her a fright when he changed into a different person during his fight with Tano. Or she thought he had changed.

He smiled suddenly.

"We'll just act as if you've come to pick me up for an outing."

"If you say, 'Let's start over again,' I'll scream. My tolerance for scenes from bad movies is pretty low since I met Tano's bikini babes."

He laughed, and briefly touched her hand where it rested on the gearstick, but his fingers were gone again so quickly that it could have been a warm breath of air. "How are you?"

Rosa shrugged her shoulders. "My sister turned into a giant snake last night. And your cousin Tano—"

"Second cousin."

"He was there too. He was a tiger. I recognised him from his eyes. Then I fainted." She looked at him. "How does that sound?"

"Like *Aesop's Fables*. The one about the snake and the tiger."

"Is there really one?"

He laughed. "No, but it would fit."

"The other possibility is that I just imagined the whole thing." She was still driving way too fast as she passed the sign for the village. "I sometimes do that. I imagine things."

"Well, you're not imagining that speed trap ahead."

She braked sharply and managed to slow down to fifty kilometres per hour just in time. "Who puts up a thing like that in your village?"

His eyes fell on the plastic folder of documents. It was on the floor of the car in front of the passenger seat. "You brought it with you!"

"That's what you were after when you came to see us yesterday."

"Mostly I came to see you."

She frowned. "I happened to be lying in my aunt's greenhouse in delirium, with something in my blood that the doctor had injected me with, and I saw some crazy things. Believe me, I wouldn't have missed that for any visitor in the world."

"What did they do to you?"

"What anyone would do to someone who has hallucinations of giant snakes and tigers. In the woods. In the dark. They tranquilised me. I was out of it."

He looked at her, frowning, and finally took a deep breath.

"It's okay," she said. "I often have funny dreams. I don't usually need a shot for them."

"Sounds like you have experience with those."

"Plenty, yes."

They passed the sun-baked piazza at the centre of the village. The Porsche glided through the shadow of a stone statue of a saint. A dozen old men sitting outside a bar watched silently as they drove by.

As they left the village again, Alessandro bent down and picked up the folder. "Did you look at it?"

"No," she said, shaking her head. "None of my business."

"Seriously?"

She shrugged her shoulders. "How about Iole?"

He took the documents out and leafed quickly through them. "I've spoken to Cesare about her. He'll see to it."

Her jaw dropped. "And that's all?"

"Officially he has to do what I say. There were other people there when we talked, enough of them to make sure he can't afford to ignore my orders."

"Your orders! He wanted to kill you, have you forgotten?"

"It's complicated," he said, putting the papers back in the folder.

Her voice was icy. "Don't you talk to me like I'm too stupid to understand."

"This whole thing is a mess. Cesare and Tano and my father, even if he's dead, and—"

"And your mother." She meant that to hurt.

"Yes," he said quietly. "Her, too."

"The family lost its leader when your father died," she commented, when he didn't continue talking at once.

"The clan's split. Some of the family support Cesare, some support me. And neither can risk offending the other."

She raised an eyebrow. "Because then the Carnevares' all-powerful Mafia empire would fall apart?"

"That's the best-case scenario. Worst case, one of the groups might try getting the protection my father used to give them from the public prosecutor's office instead. It's not like the old days, when everyone stuck together and going to the police was considered dishonourable. Now anyone will weigh his personal advantages. Two or three years in prison, with cable TV and visiting rights, sounds more appealing than risking life and limb in guerrilla warfare between two *capi*."

She could tell where this conversation was going. "So neither Cesare nor you can openly challenge the other? And because you'll come into your inheritance in a few months' time, Cesare is keeping up appearances and obeying you."

"At least about unimportant things."

She struck the steering wheel with her hand. "That girl has been shut up for *six years*!"

"That's unimportant to him," he corrected himself.

She looked into his eyes. In the background, bare hills were gliding past.

"You don't trust me," he said.

She laughed mirthlessly. "Of course not."

"Because I took you to the island with me?"

"Because you didn't tell me the truth about why you did it."

"Would you have come if I'd told you?"

"Maybe." She thought about it for a moment. "Yes, I would."

She sensed that he was still watching her, but she had to concentrate on her driving. The road was winding again.

"Would you make a right just up ahead?" he asked.

"And then?"

"I'll show you something."

"More mysteries."

"There's nothing mysterious about it."

"You're the mystery."

He smiled. "Me?"

Rosa nodded, and brushed her hair back from her face. But she didn't say any more, and turned off to the right the next time the road forked.

They came to a dusty barrier across the road, made of wooden planks nailed together crosswise. Alessandro indicated that she should drive around the blockade. And the next two as well.

They were the only people in a bleak landscape of burnt stubble fields and wild olive trees. A cloud of dust billowed in their wake, dividing the landscape behind them like a brown wall. On the hills, cacti reached their arms to the sky.

Ahead of them lay an expressway access road. Except that

there were no guardrails or markings. No road signs either. And no other vehicles at all. Yet the road, following a narrow curve, led to a broad ribbon of asphalt tracing a straight line all the way to the horizon. Again, it had no lines painted on it and there were no signs. Rosa thought there would have been space for four traffic lanes on it, but it was covered with the dust and loose soil that had blown over it.

No other sign of life. Just the two of them, the car, and a forgotten road to nowhere.

"Where does it go?"

"To the end of the world," he said.

He was right about that.

The End of the Road

Rosa couldn't drive as fast as she would have liked because there were cracks in the asphalt of the road surface. It had risen up in many places, where one tiny plant had found its way through to daylight, followed by a hundred others. There was something unsettling in knowing there was so much life seething under the dead grey ribbon of road, eager to break the bars of its dungeon and burst out into freedom.

"What is this road?" she asked.

"An expressway that was never completed. It was supposed to link the A19 right across the interior to the A20 up on the north coast. My father landed the contract and let his construction gangs loose in this area – until a new government in Rome put a stop to it."

"And now it simply stays the way it is?"

"Tearing up the finished part would cost almost as much as building the whole thing in the first place. The provinces of Sicily have no money. There were protests years ago, but after a while the organisers just moved on to the next scandal, the next ruined building that made someone or other rich."

"Not someone or other. The Carnevares."

He was looking straight ahead. "My family, yes."

She concentrated on the road, staring at the ugly, now useless, construction ahead of her – and suddenly realised that she liked it here. Maybe because nothing like this existed anywhere else – its charm lay in the totally unique nature of the place. Of course there were deserted roads elsewhere. But in front of her stretched mile upon mile of empty asphalt over which hardly any vehicle had ever driven apart from bulldozers. It gave her goosebumps all the way down her back.

"And under it?" she asked.

"What do you mean?"

"Is this just an expressway that no one uses, or is something hidden underneath it?"

He'd understood her at once, she was sure of that, and it was to his credit that a trace of shame made him hesitate to talk about that part of his family's business.

"I don't know," he said, "and that's the truth."

"I saw your lake. And the dam."

He waved a dismissive hand. "That old story? Not a word of it is true."

"Who told you so?" she asked contemptuously. "Your father?"

He pressed his lips together and didn't reply. "Children of the clan", he said at last, "are lied to from the moment we're born. If our mothers and fathers pretend we're leading a perfectly normal family life – well, that's the first big lie, and after that it never stops. They try to make us think everything's the same as for other people, other families. But *nothing* is the same." He shifted restlessly in the passenger seat. "If we grow up and have kids ourselves, and then grandchildren, we keep finding out stuff we'd never have thought possible. Finding out—"

"Crimes," she suggested, with a shrug.

"Business deals. With all the inevitable consequences, going beyond anything we can imagine. And it'll be just the same for our kids, and their kids – because after a while we lose any real sense of our own behaviour. We don't even realise we're no better than our fathers and grandfathers."

She slowed down and glanced at him. "And I thought *I* was a pessimist."

"We're born into this life. Into the clans and their tradition. We didn't ask for all that, did we?"

"I ought to have stayed in the States." She reflected for a moment. "You too, come to think of it."

"I don't think those stories about Giuliana and the dam are true," he said, unmoved. "But do I know for sure? And do I know what I may find out sometime, maybe just by chance, in some old file somewhere?"

She was still thinking about that when the horizon ahead suddenly got much closer. She swore quietly, took her foot off the gas, and braked. The car stopped less than twenty metres from the end of the world.

Alessandro got out. "Did I promise you too much?"

She was still staring ahead over the wheel, so he came around the car and opened the door for her, not with exaggerated gallantry but as a matter of course. "Take a look up close."

"Up close?" she murmured. "But there's nothing to see there. Nothing at all."

"You just have to look hard. Then you'll find what you're after."

It sounded almost as if he were trying to help her in her search for the unique, awkward magic of the place. And she realised he must have thought the same, the first time he ever drove along this road to nowhere, maybe every time he returned. Even today. Maybe everyone, in the face of this void, was searching for something to cling to. Alessandro perhaps even a little more than other people. In the last few minutes she'd discovered more thoughtfulness in him than she'd have thought possible, more desire for answers. Thinking this, it was difficult to look away from him and turn her eyes on what lay ahead of them again.

The trail, overgrown with weeds, ended in a jagged edge of splintered asphalt, as if a mighty mouth had bitten off the road. Beyond it yawned a deep abyss with a drop of ninety metres or more – a wide rocky ravine with steep walls that had countless openings in them. At first Rosa thought they were a strange natural feature, a curious structure in the porous stone. Then she saw that they were caves.

"Tombs," said Alessandro, "several hundred of them. About three thousand years old. They were made by the Siculians, one of the original peoples of Sicily. The Arabs exterminated them later. They left no trace behind but their necropolises, the cities of their dead. There are several more of them on the island, and this one isn't even the largest. The Pantalica ravine down south is—"

"Do you ever keep your mouth shut just for a moment?" She didn't mean to snap, and he didn't seem offended. But she couldn't listen any more; she had to walk on for a little way and see the place alone, with her own eyes, before getting any explanations.

She walked up to the edge where the road broke off, impressed but not afraid of the height and the wind blowing up from below. At the bottom of the ravine lay large chunks of concrete rubble. The gorge was about half a kilometre wide, possibly more, and the opposite edge looked as abrupt and jagged as this one. Beyond were the humped backs of hills, and dusty valleys, and somewhere beyond the horizon no doubt traces of civilisation again. At the moment, however, she and Alessandro seemed to be alone in the world.

"The bridge to the other side was the last part finished," said Alessandro, breaking the silence. "But after the construction work stopped, the government said the bridge had to go. My father's firms were commissioned to destroy what they'd only just built. But after that the provincial government in Enna didn't have the money to take the rubble away, so it all stays there just as if it fell from heaven. Thousands of tons of concrete in the middle of the Siculians' valley of death."

There was a note of respect in his voice that startled her. He was always surprising her, and she had to admit that she liked that.

She sat down cross-legged on the hot asphalt, not caring that her minidress had ridden up. The edge of the gorge was only a foot and a half in front of her, and gusts of wind kept blowing up from below to try to drag her down into the depths. She was strong enough to resist the urge to let herself go with them.

Alessandro sat down beside her and splayed his fingers on the asphalt. It was as if he could sense something under it, the heart of this secret place. Suddenly she, too, felt it, beating like her own.

"You don't really think it was a dream, do you?" he asked abruptly.

"The snake and the tiger?"

He nodded.

"So what? That doesn't mean anything."

"I don't understand you."

"I was in therapy for almost a year." How easy it was to say that. Maybe for the very reason that she hardly knew him. "They're always telling you that none of what you see and hear is real. Or none of the interesting things anyway. Never mind what you believe or don't believe, they say, it's all in your head. Because you're crazy."

"But you're not crazy," he said.

"I could be crazy as hell and you'd have no idea of it. I could be an axe murderess. Fucking Freddy Krueger from your worst nightmares." She slowly turned her head and looked at him. At his attractive, open face that could turn dark and reserved within seconds. The curve of his lips. The green eyes that looked into her a little too far and that she couldn't defend herself against.

It could have been so simple. But she was who she was, and *simple*, in her case, meant on the other side of the globe. Probably somewhere beyond Australia and down at the South Pole.

She had problems getting too close to anyone. And she

couldn't even trust herself any more, let alone anyone else. She avoided meetings and conversations, without knowing why. Inside, she guessed she was as twisted as one of the wild olive trees on this island.

She was a nightmare, more particularly her own nightmare, and everything in her cried out to her to put up barriers and barricade the gates at once.

It would have been only fair to tell him so. To explain, right now, that she was the bloody *Titanic* whose wake would carry him under, if he didn't jump into the lifeboat and head for the open sea.

Instead, he leaned over to kiss her.

She waited. Hesitated. Then withdrew her head before their lips could touch. For a split second he looked offended, but then he smiled, blinked at the sun, and said, "Well, when it gets to that point, I want to be there."

"When what gets to what point?"

"When you're not looking at everyone else as if they'd just declared war on you. And when you realise" – he pointed across the ravine – "that things may look like the end of the world but the world still goes on, over there on the other side. Maybe just one really large step would cross it."

"Right now I'm glad of any small step I can take without stumbling." She spoke softly, almost to herself. "That's why I came to Sicily. I'd been standing still long enough."

Alessandro looked at her and nodded thoughtfully. He knew when to keep quiet, that was something else she liked about him.

"Change the subject?" she suggested.

He'd probably seen it coming. "Iole?"

She nodded, jumped up, and reached her hand out to him. "We'll do it ourselves. Just you and me. We'll get her out of there."

He clasped her fingers, not so she could pull him up but clearly because he wanted to touch them. She wanted it too, way too much, and then he stood there right in front of her, the abyss beside them, and she could smell his skin and his hair, and let go of his hand, even though she secretly wanted something quite different.

"Right away?" he asked.

She nodded.

Rain Shadows

Isola Luna rose from the sea, enveloped in grey-blue mist. The first stars were shining in the sky, and the two of them had been sitting in the bow of the yacht for a while doing nothing but searching for the next bright point in the darkness.

From time to time their eyes met, only briefly, before returning to the horizon.

After a while Rosa had begun to talk again. About New York and the first storms of fall, and the leaves in the streets around the parks. About the mothers with their children by Turtle Pond, bundled in scarves and caps and lined hoods.

Then she said, "A year ago I killed my son."

She wasn't sure why she said that. To challenge him? To provoke one of the usual reactions: horror or pity or stammering uncertainty? So that she could check him off as *one of them*, one of the others?

He was looking at the rise of the hill to the north gradually getting larger. "What was his name?"

No one had ever asked her that. Most people assumed that aborted children didn't have names.

"Nathaniel," she said. "I wanted to give him something special. Something to make him different from all the others who… who have to stay there in the hospital."

The *Gaia's* engine was humming down in the depths of

the hull. Spray flew up from the bow. There was something soothing about the monotonous sounds.

"They said it was my decision to make." She scratched her thumbnail with her forefinger and then couldn't stop. "They said: We're sure you know what you're doing." Her voice was level. "But I didn't know. I was afraid no one else would be glad when the baby was there. I thought then I'd be really alone, alone with him. But it isn't other people who decide if you feel alone, it's yourself. Only I didn't know that yet. That's why Nathaniel is dead now."

Alessandro said nothing. The island was getting closer. So was the darkness.

"Giving him a name helped," she said. "And imagining what he would have looked like later on. Because that way he turned into a person, and a person can forgive you for making a mistake. However bad it is – they can forgive you."

The island lay like a black portal in the twilight, moving inexorably towards the yacht. Rosa turned her head until she couldn't see Alessandro out of the corner of her eye any more.

"But a time came when you did make a decision," he said.

"There's only red or black."

"Red or black?"

"Like in roulette. One is no more right or wrong than the other. You can think as long as you like about which colour's more likely to win, but it doesn't help you. You think it over, back and forth, but in the end you don't have any influence over it."

He hesitated for a moment. "But if you think only of

yourself and not of him for once – are you sorry then?"

"Since then I've thought of *nothing* but myself."

"And is that good or bad?"

"It's just the way it is. You can't evaluate it."

On the edge of her field of vision she saw him give a tiny nod, and once again she had the feeling that she was letting him get far too close to her.

"How about the father?" he asked.

"No idea."

He gave her time, waited until she finally continued of her own accord.

"I was at a party," she said. "Someone spiked my drink. That's all I know. Not at all spectacular, is it?"

For the first time he showed emotion openly, and it did her good to see that it was anger. Pure, seething anger very like her own. "He raped you."

"One, several of them – anyway, it wasn't any immaculate conception. They found traces in me from only one man. But I don't remember anything about it. Someone found me lying on the sidewalk and called an ambulance. They told me that later. When I woke up I was lying in a bed and everything was clean and sterile, and my mother was holding my hand and crying her eyes out." She smiled bitterly. "You know what my first thought was? I thought I must have been in a coma for years, like in a movie when people wake up after a long time, and while they were out of it, China has conquered America. My mother looked really, *really* old. But soon I realised it was only from crying so much, and nothing had changed at all.

It was only a few hours later, and everything was back to what it had been. Except for that one tiny difference inside me."

"Who told you to get rid of the baby? Your mother?"

"Her. And the women doctors, and the psychologist. *It's your decision*, they said, and there was a big 'but' after it, only none of them said it out loud. The only person who had a different suggestion was Zoe. *Why don't you just fly out here and take things as they come*, she said. She'd been in Sicily for a year by then."

"No one just takes a thing like that as it comes."

"That's Zoe all over. She's like that. And I think it's what she'd have done in my place: she'd have waited until the decision made itself and she had no choice but to have the baby." She picked at the nail bed of her thumb, although it was already bleeding. "But I'm not Zoe. I did something, and it was the wrong thing to do."

"I don't think so."

She thought it was brave of him to say that. She'd talked to far too few people like him, people who simply said what they thought, never mind whether it sounded uncivil or unfeeling. They all just wanted to soothe and comfort her. Wanted her to stay packed in cotton-wool for ever so that she'd have no reason to bang her fist on the table and scream and shout, and maybe become a bit unhinged.

Alessandro made a movement as if to put his hand over hers, but then he bent forward and took hold of the yacht's rail. His knuckles were white. "I don't think you did the wrong thing."

She waited. Watched him. But he just looked over towards the island.

"Maybe none of us ought to bring children into the world," he said. "None of our kind, anyway."

*

It began to rain as they reached their destination. Storm clouds were gathering around the extinct volcano of Isola Luna, looking more menacing from minute to minute. The captain of the *Gaia* tried to persuade Rosa and Alessandro to stay onboard, but they wouldn't hear of it.

The yacht had half rounded the island to come into the north coast. Here it didn't have to anchor at sea, as it did in the bay off the sandy bathing beach, but could put in at a grey concrete landing. Through the driving rain, and in the beam of the yacht's lights, Rosa saw a solid, squat building with a flat roof, hunched among the rocks close to the landing. It looked like the foundations of a now demolished lighthouse.

Rosa and Alessandro reached land from the *Gaia* over the landing. There were only three sailors on board as well as the captain. At Alessandro's wish they all stayed on the boat.

Rosa and he had put on dark Gore-Tex raincoats; drops of water ran off them like quicksilver. Two heavy torches had enough battery power for several hours. In addition, at the captain's insistence Alessandro had taken a flare pistol. He told Rosa that the man belonged to the half of the Carnevare clan that still supported him. Alessandro had fired his predecessor, one of Cesare's men, and the new captain had been on the yacht only for the last week.

The end of the long landing to which the *Gaia* was moored was blocked by a high barred gate. Alessandro tapped a numerical code into a keypad on the gate. The security lock snapped open.

In front of the squat building there was an asphalt front courtyard, with a narrow road leading from it up into the volcanic rocks of the slope. Alessandro had told her about it on her first visit to the island. There was no view of the villa from here.

Thunder rolled in the distance. White lightning twitched over the underside of the clouds like wildfire. Seen against the sudden bright light, the peak of the volcano looked three times as high and inhospitable.

The beams of their torches moved over the front of the squat building by the shore. There was a broad doorway at ground level, its two halves wide open in spite of the bad weather.

"We used to keep equipment for cleaning up the beach and the shoreline in there," said Alessandro. Water was dripping from the peak of his hood. "There was a motorboat for excursions around the island, and diving and paragliding gear."

Rosa shone her torch beam over the front courtyard and into the building. They were about thirty metres away from it. In the light of the beam she saw a bare concrete wall, and a low opening in it leading down.

"Looks empty," she murmured.

"It was a weapons emplacement against the Germans in the Second World War," Alessandro explained. "My mother always wanted my father to demolish the building, but he thought it was still useful for sheltering machinery and vehicles. It's completely stormproof, anyway."

Now she knew what the structure had reminded her of – old wartime bunkers that she'd seen on TV. Or rather, it looked like the part of a bunker above ground. The idea that there might be a network of rooms and corridors below the building sent a shiver down her spine.

"Do you think Iole's in here?" she asked.

Alessandro shook his head. "She can't leave the villa on her own. And I don't see why they'd have brought her here." He turned to her. "Listen, this is really important. You must keep as close to me as possible. Whatever you do, don't go running around here on your own."

"I thought there was no one here but Iole."

"That's how it should be. Most of the time the island's left unguarded."

"Isn't that odd? I mean, they're keeping a *hostage* here."

"No one who knows the coast in these parts would dock here just like that."

"Let's go straight to the villa," she suggested. "The sooner we get there, the sooner we can leave again."

The open door of the old weapons emplacement seemed to be weighing on his mind. But then he slowly nodded and set off with her. They crossed the front courtyard and followed the narrow road uphill.

Rosa had not forgotten what Iole had said about wild animals outside the villa windows at night. She could still see the eyes of the tiger in front of her. Human eyes. Tano's eyes.

Again and again she shone the beam of her torch into the darkness on both sides of the gravel path. To the left, the slope fell away to the shore. The roar of the surf rose to their ears, as rain and darkness blurred their vision. The yacht down at the landing was visible only as pale dots of light at the portholes. And the bunker was sunk in the night as if the past had reclaimed it.

The storm still hung over the other side of the mountain, but it was raining without stopping. Thunder rolled at earsplitting volume. Flashes of lightning came thick and fast, illuminating the sky on the other side of the volcanic cone.

They had been walking for some time, struggling up the winding path, when Rosa abruptly broke the silence. "You think he's going to kill her too, don't you?"

Alessandro sighed softly.

She stopped, rivulets of rain washing around her shoes, and turned the beam of her torch on his rainproof hood from behind. He turned and blinked at the light, but she studied his face in its brightness for a moment before lowering the torch. "That's why you were ready to come up here right away," she said.

"I think..." he began, and then stopped, searching for words. "It probably wasn't a great idea for me to mention it to Cesare. I ought to have known better. I know him, and I know how he solves problems. I can only hope he's racking his brains about something else at the moment, and we get there in time."

What was she going to do if they found Iole's corpse in the villa? This idea hadn't even crossed her mind before. An unaccustomed sense of responsibility stirred in her. "Let's go," she said huskily.

He adjusted his pace to hers and stayed beside her for the rest of the way. Their hands touched several times, but only through the sleeves of their raincoats. The winding road was steeper than she had thought at first, and it was tempting to take shortcuts and clamber over the rocks. But that would probably cost them too much strength, and ultimately take even more time.

Finally they rounded the last bend. The villa lay just ahead of them. In a rapid series of lightning flashes, the complex looked like even more of a jumble than it had by daylight. In its way, it came from another era as much as the concrete bunker down by the shore. The huge windowpanes reflected the lightning and magnified the raindrops leaping up in the glare. But as soon as the bright light faded, darkness reigned.

Alessandro opened the barred gate. He closed it carefully again behind them, shone his torch once more back through the iron bars, scanning the front courtyard and the slope, then hurried toward the house with Rosa. They brought the wet weather in with them, and stood dripping in the entrance hall. The front door latched shut with an echoing crash.

Rosa took off her raincoat and let it fall to the tiles. "Iole?" she called. Only now did she notice that their powerful torches were still the only light in the place.

Alessandro walked over to the switch near the corridor leading to the rooms and flipped it several times. The house stayed dark.

"Was it working when we were here before?" he asked in annoyance, but he seemed to be talking to himself.

Rosa mopped rainwater off her forehead. "The sun was shining outside. We didn't need to turn on any lights."

He crossed the wide hall to another switch and tried that one. Nothing. Through the opaque glass of lamp shades like curved bowls, you couldn't see whether the lightbulbs had been damaged or removed.

He swore, and tried the next room, with the same result.

The rain pattered against the windows in front of the house; its dull drumming came from all directions at once. The streams of water running down the glass left a marbled pattern of rain shadows on the interior of the rooms.

Rosa let the circular beam of her torch wander around. "Iole?" she called again, louder this time. "Iole, it's us. Rosa and Alessandro." Suddenly she wasn't sure whether she had ever called the girl by her name.

When there was still no answer, she tried to remember which way the chain on Iole's ankle had led. Not to the salon with the steps leading upstairs, but to one of the rooms on the right side of the hall.

Alessandro was there already, looking around him. As he walked he stripped off his raincoat. The stiff, rubberised fabric dropped onto the yellow and red carpet, only half collapsing, and lay there like a hunchbacked gnome. "Maybe she's hiding."

She looked darkly at him. "Maybe."

"Cesare would never have sent anyone out here that fast."

"How about Tano?"

Images like lightning flashes. The tiger with human eyes. Yellowish fur on Tano's back while they were fighting on the beach. And the black colour spreading over Alessandro's body. His huge pupils.

She wasn't going to leave this island until he told her the truth.

Alessandro steadily met her questioning gaze. "No, I don't know what happened here. It's possible they came to take Iole away. Maybe worse. Or she might be hiding somewhere in the house."

"She was kept on a chain. How hard can it be to find her?" Impatiently, she moved away. Even the hood hadn't kept her mane of wet blond hair from sticking to her shoulders and forehead. She pushed strands roughly out of her eyes. She was beginning to feel cold, because the black stockings she wore under her minidress were also drenched.

"Let me go first." He moved past her. "I know where to start."

"We ought to have tried getting that bloody chain off her right away."

"Without tools?"

"Yes, I know. It's just that… we shouldn't have left her behind."

"Let's keep searching."

She followed him, running the beam of her torch over any

places he forgot. Mostly, she searched the floor. That chain had been thin, but anyone was bound to see it. Iole couldn't hide behind furniture or in a corner without her silver shackle giving her away.

They walked through several salons and reception rooms, all full of retro seventies furniture, from beanbags to transparent plastic sofas and lava lamps. And everywhere those huge windows ran from floor to ceiling. Beyond them were only the night and the pouring rain, illuminated by flashes of lightning. Shadowy streaks flowing from the walls opposite the windows, making their way over the floor.

Outside, something moved. She thought at first that it was her own reflection in the windowpane. Then she saw that there was something behind the glass, something crouching low. Not *small* in itself, just staying down. On all fours.

Instinctively, she looked around her, back through the corridors from room to room, and saw at a distance the black gnome of Alessandro's raincoat.

"Rosa!" Alessandro's voice was alarmingly far away. He hadn't noticed that she was lingering behind him. The beam of his torch showed that he was already two rooms ahead. She couldn't see Alessandro himself, only the sporadic movement of his torch.

"Over here," he called. "Here – come look at this."

Hunting Instinct

It was a small room on the first floor. Probably the only room in the whole house to have no window, just a barred skylight.

The room lay beyond the spacious kitchen that Rosa had crossed earlier, and must once have been a larder.

Now it was a prison cell.

Against one wall stood a bed with tumbled sheets and greasy pillows. The bedclothes hadn't been changed in a long time. Rosa felt a pang, because although she herself had so often felt all alone, only now did she understand what being alone really meant.

There were a few old magazines lying around. Some books, carefully stacked. Crumpled garments that looked as if someone had emptied a rack in a department store, buying the same thing over and over again just as long as the size was right. Plain dresses that the prisoner could put on over her head, because the chain on her leg kept her from climbing into them.

The longer Rosa looked around, the more details she noticed. Alessandro was standing beside her, one hand clenched into a fist, his lips pressed together so tightly that all the colour had drained out of them.

Two iron rings were set in the wall beside the door. The chain lay on the floor, a little heap of silver. The empty ankle ring emerged from it like the head of a snake.

"She's gone," whispered Rosa.

Alessandro was staring at the chain as if he were paralysed.

"Or dead," she murmured. She had rarely found it so difficult to say two words.

"I'll murder him," whispered Alessandro.

"That won't help Iole."

"The bastard!" He spun around and walked past her and into the kitchen, where he opened several drawers. They were all empty.

"She won't be in there," Rosa pointed out.

Another drawer. Then the cupboards. All empty, except for one containing packs of microwave dinners.

"What are you looking for?"

There was an animal roar outside.

"A knife," he said. "For you."

In a few swift steps she was beside him, a hand on his shoulder. "What's happening here?"

"You heard that, didn't you?"

"I'm not deaf."

"They've been prowling around the house for some time."

"They?" Rosa tried to suppress her thoughts of Iole and think only of herself again. She had so much damn practice in that, why didn't it work now?

"Animals," he said. "Big cats."

She held on to his shoulder more firmly; it had to be painful for him, but he didn't shake her hand off. "Tano?" she asked tonelessly.

"I don't think so. No."

She struggled against her anger, against her helplessness. "What's going on, Alessandro? Why did that tiger look at me with Tano's eyes? I didn't just imagine it, did I?"

"I'd hoped your aunt would explain that to you. Or your sister."

That roar again. It was answered at once, at closer quarters, from right outside the kitchen windows. Rosa tried to make something out, but all she could see was the rain beating against the panes.

"I'll tell you all about it," said Alessandro. "I promise. But first we have to get away from here."

"Take a stroll out there, you mean?" she asked sarcastically. "Oh, sure."

The sound of heavy movement came from several rooms away.

"One of the glass doors opening," whispered Alessandro. "Hell, I knew it."

"Knew what?"

"There's someone else on the island. Someone who keeps the animals shut up during the day, then lets them out to wander free at night. Someone has to feed them and get them back into their cages. A kind of overseer."

"What *is* all this?" She let go of his shoulder. Her arm felt as heavy as lead. "Your family's private zoo?"

"It's like your aunt's snake house, I'm afraid. Only not with snakes." He went to the doorway. "I didn't know about this. They used to be kept somewhere else. Cesare dares to use my mother's island to—" He cut his sentence short when he saw that there was no door ahead for him to close. Rosa too realised, at that moment, that she had seen nothing but open rooms and corridors all over the house. All the doors had been taken off their hinges.

"Come on," whispered Alessandro.

Reluctant as she felt, she still followed him, because something in his voice made her feel blind trust in him.

Made her feel blind trust in him. Later she'd taste those words with relish on her tongue – if she ever got the chance.

There were so many reasons not to trust him. He had kept a great deal hidden from her, might even have lied to her. And yet he was the first person in a whole year whom she'd told about Nathaniel of her own free will. It hadn't even been difficult. But now she was sorry again.

The sound of roaring once more.

Inside the house this time.

"He's let them in." Alessandro stood still and listened, his posture strange. Leaning slightly forward, waiting. Like an animal picking up a scent.

She was feeling colder. Shivers ran through her limbs.

"Whoever's looking after the animals here is one of Cesare's men," he murmured. "He probably called him, let him know we're here."

"And Cesare told him to let those creatures loose on us?"

"Perhaps to scare you. Or to kill both of us." He looked at her, a question in his eyes. "Do you have your cell phone with you?"

"No." She'd left it on her bed in the palazzo that morning.

"Then there'll be no helicopter coming to the rescue this time."

"What do you mean—?" She fell silent as the truth dawned on her. "You think *that's* how she knew I was with you and the others?"

"I'll bet it was a present, right? The moment you arrived." He snorted bitterly, nodding towards a staircase to the upper floor and heading towards it. "Up here, come on!"

"They… you mean there's a *transmitter* in the bloody thing?"

"Of course." He came back, took her hand, and impatiently led her over to the stairway. "It's nothing unusual in the families. Children of the clans are often kidnapped or try to run away. Many parents even have tiny transmitters implanted under their sons' and daughters' skin so they can find them in an emergency."

For a moment she followed him as if in a trance. The narrow stairwell wound around and around. She felt that Zoe and Florinda had betrayed her. Had he, too? She was less and less sure of her own feelings.

Alessandro stopped when he reached the upper floor. He put his forefinger to his mouth. His lips silently formed the words: *No talking.*

They were in a corridor. Faint grey light filtered through open doorways. Rain hammered on glass.

Something moved at the far end of the corridor, then froze and stood there. Rosa saw only a black silhouette. It was impossible to see exactly what it was. A tiger. A lioness. As if exactly what kind of animal tore her apart made any difference.

The big cat was listening intently, ears pricked. A long black tail swung slowly back and forth, a sign of pent-up tension.

Neither she nor Alessandro moved from the spot. The drumming of the rain must be irritating the animal as well. It obviously hadn't yet recognised the two of them as potential prey.

Now the cat began to move again. Came down the corridor with a flowing, silent elegance that was both majestic and murderous.

Alessandro let go of Rosa's hand.

The animal disappeared through one of the open doorways. It wouldn't stay long in the room beyond the doorway if it found nothing there.

Alessandro signalled to her, but she was faster. She was already racing down the corridor the other way. He followed her into a guest room with no door to its en suite bathroom. Strange that the doors had been removed from all the bedrooms. It reminded her of a zoo enclosure. A playground where animals could hide and chase one another. Was that what this house had been used for, before Iole was hidden here?

"The window," whispered Alessandro.

She didn't expect it to open, but he had only to press a lever down and the pane swung in. Rain pattered into the room, along with the smell of wet stone. They were in a side wing of the villa. Rosa saw rough lava rock below the window. You couldn't see the perimeter wall here, as you could from the front of the house, but it was probably farther away, hidden in the dark.

"Can you jump down?" he asked quietly.

She looked back at the doorway over her shoulder. If there was something approaching on velvet paws, the deep darkness meant that not even a shadow would give advance warning.

She nodded vigorously. This was the upper storey, and bare rock gleamed below. But the window came almost right down to the floor of the room, so it was less than three metres to jump in all.

"I can go first and try to catch you," he suggested.

The idea of landing in his arms like some captive fairy-tale princess was so silly that she almost smiled. She shook her head, climbed out on the narrow windowsill and past him, looked around for any animals stalking closer – and jumped.

The impact was much harder than she'd expected. She felt as if her legs had been rammed up inside her body. She lost her balance, fell forward, hands first, and landed on her knees. Rough lava rock tore her stockings, grazing her skin. At first she felt nothing, then it burned like fire, and she knew without having to look that she was bleeding.

Once the animals picked up that scent, there'd be no way of distracting them.

"All right?" whispered Alessandro from above.

Her face distorted with pain, she pushed herself up, swayed for a moment, and then stood upright. Her feet hurt, so did her legs and her hips. But when she cautiously moved, she decided that nothing was broken or sprained.

Blinking, she looked up at the window and stood aside. Alessandro glanced behind him and suddenly seemed to be in much more of a hurry. He took off from the sill, drew his legs up as he jumped, stretched his arms downward and landed neatly, crouching on all fours, his knees out at an angle. He didn't even wince as he stood up, smiled at her incredulous gaze, took her hand again, and tried to drag her along after him. Her fingers, wet with rain, slipped out of his grasp, but she followed him anyway, stumbling slightly and gritting her teeth. At least she could still run.

They hurried past the facade of the villa, along a kind of ditch that ended on one side at the wall of the house and at the other against rocks. Somewhere in the darkness a big cat roared again; two others answered. At least one of them was out here. The roar had sounded very close.

They reached the end of the side wing. The lava rock to their left no longer rose as steeply. When Rosa looked cautiously around the corner, she saw that they had reached the front of the house. The perimeter wall surrounding the grounds rose ten metres or so ahead. Alessandro had closed the gate to the front courtyard when they arrived, but it stood open now.

Rosa looked at him. Their eyes met. He seemed uncertain of himself, and she wondered whether that was because of the injury to her knees. The warm blood seeping through her torn stockings. He raised a hand. Before she could flinch back, he stroked her wet hair back from her face, leaned forward, and kissed her on the mouth. It was hardly more than a fleeting touch, but the protest inside her refused to pass her lips.

"Sorry," he whispered. She thought he meant about the kiss, but he added, "For bringing you here."

"I wanted to come," she said tonelessly. "What about Iole? Do you think she's still here?"

He shook his head. "If she's alive, they've taken her away. Maybe I was wrong and Cesare kept his word. Something new, but not unimaginable."

"That'll make us look rather foolish if his animals tear us to pieces."

"They won't. Trust me."

Through the rain his hair looked very black again, as it had down on the beach. His eyes seemed darker, too.

She pointed to the barred gate. "Is that the only way?"

"It's the quickest. Just follow the road. Run, and don't turn around."

"What about you?"

"I'll follow."

"But why…?"

"Please," he said urgently. "Just go on ahead. And wait – you have to memorise the number code for the gate down at the landing." He told her a sequence of six figures. Only after a moment did she work out that it sounded like his mother's date of birth. That would fit, if the two final numbers stood for a year.

Then they ran. Out of the shelter of the wall of the house, into the space between the villa and the perimeter wall, while the rain whipped into their faces and the roar of the big cats rose again.

A moment later something crashed into the armoured glass of the windows from inside.

"Faster!" Alessandro was no longer trying to keep his voice down.

They ran through the gate, crossed the front courtyard, and turned onto the winding road. On the way up it had seemed endless to Rosa, but now she could see the shore below through the darkness and the rain. However, the landing was a few hundred metres farther north along the coastline. And there were all those bends, and pursuers behind them who wouldn't bother to follow the road but would take shortcuts over the rocks.

Alessandro stayed a little way behind her, though he could run faster than she could. Her knees hurt, her legs felt strange. He could easily have overtaken her, but he hung back. She heard his footsteps and thought of what he had said: *Don't turn around.*

All the same, she instinctively glanced over her shoulder. Asking Rosa not to do something was a surefire way of getting her to do it anyway.

Alessandro kept looking back himself, even now. There was something thirty metres or so behind them on the road, a blurred shape in the rain, moving much faster than they were and just on the verge of catching up.

Rosa looked ahead again so that she could stay on the road. She would fall at once among the rocks. She had to stay on the asphalt road surface and try not to slip in the rivulets of water.

When she glanced back once more, Alessandro had disappeared.

Shredded clothing was scattered on the road. The sight was like a hard blow in her back, making her stumble, and when she somehow caught herself up she stood there, swaying.

"Alessandro?"

Their pursuer, too, had stayed beyond the dark rocks at that last bend in the road. For a moment, even the pattering of the rain seemed to fall silent. Rosa stood in the middle of the road, eyes narrowed, staring up the mountain and hearing nothing but her own heartbeat and fast breathing. The raindrops seemed to fall from the sky in slow motion. She felt as if she could pluck each of them out of the air with her fingertips, one by one.

Rigid, she looked back up the road. At the clothes lying in the rain as it ran downhill. Reluctantly, she searched the ground for other traces. For blood mingling with the water.

A deep growl, unexpectedly close, reached her ears. She smelled the hot breath of a beast of prey. Not like the tiger in the forest, wilder.

Slowly, she turned her head to one side. Looked at the rock rising not three metres away from the roadside.

A full-grown lion with a dripping mane stood there, mighty muscles visible under his wet, gleaming coat. His eyes were burning. He looked at her, the scent of her warm blood in his nostrils, his mouth half-open to bare the teeth that would be tearing at her any moment now.

She spun around and ran on, although she knew it

was useless. She ran as fast as she could. Only when nothing pounced on her did she look back.

The blackness of the night was coagulating into a solid, supple body that leaped up the rock and rammed into the lion. The beast roared, lost his balance, and fell heavily to one side, snapping at his attacker and carrying the other animal down with him.

The lion crashed sideways onto the road with a furious roar. The second big cat landed on him, striking out with claws and fangs, shredding fur and flesh. Then it leaped over him, whirled around again, and turned to its opponent. The lion rose too, mad with pain and rage, and lost no time in counter-attacking.

When a flash of lightning lit up the night, Rosa saw the second animal more clearly. The sight was still flickering before her eyes while she ran down the mountain, feeling numbed.

A panther, black as pitch, almost as large as his adversary, but slender and more supple. His open mouth full of gleaming teeth.

She carried the images and sounds of the fighting animals down the slope with her. She hardly felt the road beneath her feet, and saw the landing and the barred gate only when she had almost reached them.

A man barred her way. Rosa had no time to feel surprised. She rammed her shoulder into his chest with a groan and, running full tilt, leaped past him before he could grab hold of her, and reached the shore. Waves broke against the rocks, sending the surf a metre high.

Behind her, higher up the slope, the panther and the lion

were locked in battle. The man called something that she couldn't make out.

At the far end of the concrete landing, the lights of the *Gaia* shone through the driving rain.

Now only the barred gate stood between Rosa and the yacht. The numerical combination would open it – if she could tap it into the keypad in time. Water made the gleaming surfaces flow together like liquid steel.

Once again the man behind her called out. Heavy footsteps were coming closer. And she heard something else through the rain – the roars of several big cats.

She looked back. The figure was coming closer across the open space. Three shadows moved away from the black mass of the rocks.

Rosa found the flap by the gate and opened it. A red light shone above the keypad.

NUMERICAL CODE DELETED, said the words on an illuminated panel. NEW COMBINATION ACCEPTED.

The man had changed the bloody code. She couldn't get back to the yacht.

Cursing, she turned around, avoided her pursuer's hands, and saw the three big cats racing up. Her one escape route led to the old weapons silo.

She ran through the broad entrance into the bare concrete room behind. Bent low to slip through the opening in the back wall.

The rank smell of beasts of prey surrounded her.

The Cages

Neon lighting shone down from a grey ceiling, one of the tubes flickering and humming louder than the others. Insects crashed against the glass.

Rosa looked around, her breath coming fast and her heart thudding; she could hear it behind her eyes. Her head ached, and her vision was blurred.

The stench in the rectangular concrete room was terrible. Straw covered the floor and there were several grates over openings in the walls that led to individual cages. Four of the grates were open, two closed. If there was anything alive in there, it wasn't showing itself. The room outside the cages contained a wide water trough and huge bowls with shreds of dried meat on their rims.

Rosa looked back at the space outside the room. The three big cats had crossed it and were approaching slowly, relaxed and confident. As they did so, they passed the man without even looking at him. They knew him; he fed them and looked after them. All Rosa could see of him was the outline of his figure and the woolly cap he wore.

The opening through which she had entered the straw-covered space was a short tunnel about two metres long through the massive concrete wall. Only one of the animals could fit through it at a time. There was a barred door closing the tunnel off, but it lay at the far end, and she couldn't get at it from her side without moving closer to the creatures. That would have been suicide, since all three were prowling into the building now. They'd be on her in a few minutes.

She hastily looked around her. An iron door at the back of the room might be the zookeeper's way in when he came to feed the animals. She walked over, and almost slipped and fell on the big cats' droppings. What a lovely death that would be, she thought. Landing with your bum in tiger shit while the beast itself bites your head off.

One of the big cats let out a roar. It was already in the tunnel. Rosa reached out to the iron door but couldn't turn the doorknob, even with both hands.

With a cry of rage, she kicked the door. It didn't even shake. She heard the rustle of straw behind her.

To her right, one of the cages stood open. Without thinking, she took three steps towards it, seized the grating and pulled it shut after her as she ran in. Iron crashed as the door struck the frame – and rebounded off it. Rosa was thrown backward, but she didn't let go of the grating. She closed it again, a little more slowly – and this time the barred grating latched into place.

Groaning, with a dry mouth and burning eyes, she looked out through the bars.

A white lioness stood on the other side, staring at her. Her fur was wet and dirty, her paws black with mud. She growled and came closer, raised one paw, and struck the barred door with it.

Rosa retreated, stumbling farther into her voluntary prison, and only now did she realise that she wasn't sure whether it was really empty. Expecting the worst, she spun round.

Here, too, a neon tube shone from the cement ceiling. Straw covered one side of the cage, sand the rest of it. In the back wall, at eye-level, was a horizontal gap that had probably once been a loophole for gunners. It had been closed from the other side with some kind of yellow substance sprayed into it, bulging like a sore into the interior of the room. A water pipe also ran through the slit and into a trough.

The lioness struck the door again. Rosa jumped. When the zookeeper came in with his keys, she wouldn't be safe here any more. But there was no way out. She had manoeuvred herself right into a trap.

Outside, she heard a human scream. Wild roars and growls reached her ears, muted by the concrete. The lioness paced restlessly back and forth before deciding to stand by her companions. She disappeared back down the tunnel.

Rosa took a deep breath. She felt like she was about to throw up. Not just because of the stench. Images flickered through her mind, but she couldn't pin any of them down. The lion up on the rock. The panther who had come to her aid. Alessandro's wet clothes scattered in the rain puddles. It was clear to her now what it all meant, and she stopped trying to shut the idea out.

But she had guessed long ago, hadn't she? The tiger with Tano's eyes. Zoe's injuries and the lies she'd told about them. But it was one thing to imagine people turning into giant snakes, something else entirely to actually see it happen.

A howl rose outside, interrupted by a hoarse roar. Then silence. Finally the whimpering of an animal in retreat. Maybe two. Someone called out, but the voice ended in a dull sound of pain.

Step by step, Rosa retreated from the barred door until she could see only a small section of the room outside the cage. A strip of straw, the closed iron door. Her calves backed into the water trough against the wall, and she stopped. She pulled at the metal pipe sticking out of the wall, but it wouldn't budge. There was nothing else she could use as a weapon.

She was sweating, but at the same time she felt terribly cold. When she looked at her forearm, she saw that the veins were standing out in a blue network, as if her blood had been exchanged for ink. Her skin was dry and scaly as if she had eczema.

She'd felt this once before, waking up in the greenhouse in that strange state between trance and a hyperawareness of her surroundings. She was trembling, sweating, with tears in her eyes. She felt sick, but she stayed on her feet, one hand on the iron pipe, the other clutching the drenched fabric of her minidress. Something was trickling into her eyes like sand. But when she wiped her face, the back of her hand was white with the scales of skin peeling from her forehead, sticking to the bridge of her nose and her cheekbones, gluing her eyes shut.

"You don't have it under control," said a voice at the entrance to the room.

Alessandro was now wearing jeans much too large for him. His bare torso shone with a mixture of rainwater and blood.

"You have to suppress it. It's the best thing to do right now."

But how could she suppress it when she didn't even know what it was?

Alessandro set to work on the lock of the cage with a bunch of keys. The third one fitted, and the grate swung open.

Stumbling, Rosa supported herself on the rough concrete of the wall with an outstretched arm. Exhausted, she let her head drop forward, looked at the floor without seeing anything, and tried to concentrate on her breathing. She still wasn't entirely successful, but she imagined warm air streaming into her ribcage, pushing away the icy cold, forcing it out of her. It worked.

He rested his hands gently on her shoulders from behind. Warmth seemed to flow out of them and spread through her whole body. The trembling died down, and now it came only in short bursts of shivering.

His fingertips carefully felt their way down her ribs, held her waist, closed around her flat stomach. He held her very firmly, pressing his upper body to her back, burying his face in her wet hair. Warming her until the last of the shivering went away. She was still shaking slightly, but for a different reason, one that frightened her almost as much as the big cats.

They stood like that for a long time, her back to his chest, and she didn't ask what had happened outside because no words would pass her lips, only a hissing that sounded strange and alarming even to her own ears.

The Arcadian Dynasties

Rosa and Alessandro sat wrapped in blankets in the saloon on the top deck, among the shiny gold fittings and expensive wood panelling. Artificial flames flickered in the fireplace; a hidden fan wafted gentle warmth with a pinewood fragrance through the air.

"I've never in my life seen anything so awful," said Rosa, and she didn't mean the animal cages on the island.

"Not everyone can afford it," said Alessandro, "so it must be something special. At least, that's what my father thought."

They were sitting opposite each other in two big wing chairs in front of the fire. The *Gaia* was on her way back to her home harbour on the north coast of Sicily and would be underway for more than another two hours. The sea was rough, but the storm was over.

Rosa wore a fluffy bathrobe much too large for her, and fur slippers. Her own clothes were in the dryer on the lower deck. She had snuggled deep into the chair, drawing up her knees, which now had bandages over the scrapes. The blanket came right up to her chin. She was still freezing, but that was partly because she was so tired.

"Go ahead," she demanded.

Alessandro was wearing a Norwegian sweater, borrowed from a member of the crew, and an old pair of jeans that he had found in one of the cabins. The zookeeper's jeans that he had worn in the cage were back with their owner somewhere belowdecks, where the crew had locked the man in. Alessandro was wrapped in a blanket as well, and he held a steaming cup of tea. Rosa hated tea.

"You really don't know anything about it?" he asked.

She stared at him over the blanket and shook her head. Her old impatience was returning.

"That book," he said, "*Aesop's Fables*. I gave it to you because I wanted to know how you'd react. To find out what they'd told you. If you'd known, then you would have said something. Given yourself away."

"What makes you think so? You didn't know me at all."

He grinned. "I got to know you on that plane."

She sighed softly.

"The fables are about animals with human qualities. And all of us, your family, my family, many of the others – we're the same. Or maybe the exact opposite, depending on how you look at it."

She briefly considered acting stupid so that he'd finally put it into words. Human beings turning into animals. Tigers and snakes and panthers.

"Have you ever heard of the Arcadian dynasties?"

She shook her head and thought, Here we go again. This must be the Alessandro who'd been taught rhetoric at boarding school.

"A country called Arcadia keeps coming up in ancient Greek mythology. In fact there's still an Arcadia today. It's a province of modern Greece, but it's only taken on the old name. The *earlier* Arcadia, the one in the old stories, was a Greek island kingdom in the Mediterranean. Over thousands of years it acquired a few more names, too."

"And they taught you all this stuff at Hogwarts?"

"One of the names is Atlantis."

She looked at him sternly. "Panthers, Alessandro. And lions. Not little green men, okay?"

He drank some of his tea, made a face, and went on. "In the earliest Greek legends, only the gods could take on animal form – never human beings. But that changed when Zeus, the father of the gods, visited the kingdom of Arcadia one day. It was ruled at the time by a king called Lycaon, and more than anything else he was a criminal."

"Same as us," she said gloomily.

"Lycaon wasn't only a tyrant, he was also a cannibal. He ate human flesh. When Zeus dined at his table, King Lycaon had large chunks of meat on spits served to him. Zeus tasted them and instantly knew what they were. In his anger and disgust he cursed all of Arcadia, starting with its ruler. He turned Lycaon into a wolf, so that everyone would know what a beast he was, and what he fed on."

"Clearly we have all the time in the world," she said crossly. "Feel free to start way back with the dinosaurs – just as long as you get to the Carnevares and Alcantaras sometime."

"Hang on! Lycaon was the first human who could take on animal form. He was both man and wolf. The curse of Zeus spread all over Arcadia, and later, when the island sank into the sea, the few survivors scattered to all corners of the world.

But at heart they were still Greeks, and at the time Greece was the mightiest realm in the Mediterranean. Its seafarers had founded colonies on all the coasts of the known world. The surviving Arcadians settled in Europe and Africa and Asia, and many of them rose to fame in new city-states and provinces. Have you seen all the ruins on this island? Sicily was one of the most important Greek outposts."

The warmth of the fire ought to have made her sleepy, but Rosa was wide awake now. She nodded silently.

"The Arcadians quickly became very powerful. Their families acquired more and more land; they were governors of the island, or influenced the governors' decisions. When the Greeks were finally driven out by the Carthaginians, many Arcadians negotiated with the new rulers for the right to stay. They were far too comfortable in the nests they had made for themselves to simply leave Sicily. That was about two and a half thousand years ago, and nothing has changed to this day."

"And all that time they were turning into big cats and snakes and so on when the moon was full—"

"It has nothing to do with the full moon," he interrupted her, smiling. "We can control it – at least, we can with a bit of practice. But sometimes strong outbursts of emotion trigger the change. Anger and hatred, even love, can make us lose control, and then it simply happens."

She rubbed her eyes with both hands. When she took her fingers away from her face again, there were no scales clinging to them. The change had stopped long ago; her skin was smooth and almost back to normal, it just looked slightly sunburnt.

"With everything I've been through in the last year… wouldn't you think I'd have felt a few *strong outbursts of emotion*?" She had meant to sound scornful, but with Alessandro she somehow couldn't quite succeed.

"It doesn't happen until our bodies are ready." The corners of his mouth stretched into a smile. "I know what that sounds like… usually it happens around the time we come of age, if not exactly on the day. It will probably take a little longer for you." He put his cup down and leaned forward. "By the way, did your aunt invite you here, or was it your idea?"

"Zoe's idea, really." Even as she said it, she realised what he was getting at. "You mean Florinda persuaded her to do it? Of course Florinda and Zoe always kept in touch with each other – and two years ago Florinda asked Zoe to come here. And then, when I was in such a state, she must have made Zoe… " She groaned in annoyance. "Florinda planned it all. To have the two of us close to her."

Alessandro nodded. "It's much easier to keep the whole thing secret here. And so much dirt has been swept under the rug in Sicily over the last hundred years that we have plenty of experience covering things up." He frowned, and his dimples deepened. "Can you imagine how tricky it was keeping something like that secret in an American boarding school!"

"Didn't anyone warn you in advance?"

"Yes – Tano, of all people, but I didn't believe him. The first time it happened to me I was captain of the track team. I'd broken my leg, there was some kind of contest and

I couldn't take part, so I lay in bed furious with myself… Don't look at me like that, it's the way things are in a boarding school! Anyway, it would have been even more of a shock if Tano hadn't told me anything at all."

Rosa thoughtfully wound a strand of damp hair around her finger. "Arcadians," she said slowly. "So they're everywhere?"

"In other areas and other countries the dynasties went underground or simply disappeared. The Russian bear clans, the Hundingas – dog-headed people of ancient Germania – even the fox families in China were originally descended from Arcadians. But here on Sicily it was particularly easy for them to maintain the power of the dynasties and still look like a federation of clans to the outside world. The Carnevares are Panthera – big cats of several kinds, not just panthers – and you Alcantaras are Lamias, snake women. For some reason it affects only the women among you, never the men."

Why didn't that surprise her?

"I was told," he went on, "that boys born to the Alcantaras seldom get old. And when one of them does grow to adulthood, the change stops."

"Seldom growing old meaning that they die young? Or… or they're killed?"

"I don't know," he said. It didn't sound convincing.

She tried to work out the connection for herself as well as she could. Her father had died young. And her own child, her son… No, she wasn't going to follow that train of thought to its end.

"So the Mafia," she asked, trying to come up with something

else, "is really nothing but a front? A masquerade to give the Arcadian dynasties a kind of official cover?"

He shook his head. "No, when the Mafia started up in the nineteenth century – secret societies of large landowners in Sicily – the Arcadians were drawn into it by chance at first, because of their history. Many of them belonged to the old landed nobility, your family and mine and several others, so they became part of something that at first they didn't even want. They were afraid that attention paid to their documents and files would bring far more to light than just a few illegal business deals. But in the end the dynasties realised how easy it was to use Cosa Nostra for their own purposes – and that if they weren't part of it, they would lose their influence over the politics and society of Sicily to the Mafia. It's only three or four generations ago that the Arcadian dynasties merged entirely with Cosa Nostra. Only a few of the Mafia clans are Arcadians, but all the Arcadians of Sicily belong to the Mafia."

A heavy swell lifted the yacht. Rosa almost slipped out of her chair, then snuggled even farther back in it. "Those lions and tigers on the island… were they—"

"No, they were ordinary animals," he interrupted. "Like the snakes in your aunt's greenhouse. The dynasties once believed that after death the soul of an Arcadian passed into an animal related to the same species, so they kept live specimens as totems. They venerated the creatures and offered them sacrifices."

Rosa wasn't sure she wanted to know what kinds of sacrifice.

"Many Arcadians, mostly the older people, still believe that the spirits of all their dead live on in animal form. And when the animal dies, the Arcadian's soul passes into the nearest newborn baby. If that were true, then every descendant of Lycaon would still be alive somewhere in the world, in some species of animal."

"So would Lycaon himself."

"Many think he is. Some even believe he may have been reborn to take command of all the dynasties."

She vaguely remembered what Fundling had said to her on that first drive to the yacht.

"The Hungry Man," she murmured.

Alessandro blinked. "Then you've already heard of him?"

"Only in passing."

"Yes, that's what Lycaon was called, not in his lifetime but later, when the myth of the cannibal king of Arcadia was passed on from generation to generation."

"And the dynasties are afraid of his return?" Fundling had suggested that, as well. Was he an Arcadian himself? Was that why the Carnevares had taken him in?

"You have to distinguish," said Alessandro, "between the original legend of the Hungry Man and what was made of it later."

"Meaning what?"

"For many years the *capo dei capi*, the boss of bosses, the supreme head of the Mafia, has also come from the Arcadian dynasties of Sicily. And the predecessor of the present *capo dei capi* called himself the Hungry Man as an honorary title, bolstering his claim as head of all the dynasties and Cosa Nostra as a whole."

Another heavy wave met the *Gaia* on the starboard side. Alessandro adjusted his position in his chair. "The police arrested him almost thirty years ago. He's still in prison, not on Sicily, on the mainland." He shrugged his shoulders. "But for some time there's been a rumour that the new government in Rome may pardon him. And that's exactly what most of the families fear: the Hungry Man coming back to Sicily to reclaim his old powers. No one knows how many are still on his side and will support him as soon as he sets foot on the island. That could lead not only to a power struggle within the Mafia but also a war between the families."

Rosa threw back the blanket and pulled the bathrobe together over her knees. She wasn't freezing any more; now she felt hot. Alessandro's glance lingered on her bare legs for a moment.

"There's only one problem," he went on. "The origin of the dynasties... well, it's only a myth. And unfortunately myths aren't necessarily true. They tell us what people thousands of years ago thought was possible. But not much more... Do you believe in God?"

"What's that got to do with it?"

"You don't, do you? Nor do I. So how can we believe there really was a god called Zeus who laid a curse on the Arcadians?"

She was finding it hard enough to accept the existence of human beings who could take animal form. But of course he was right. Believing in something totally crazy that she'd seen with her own eyes was one thing. Believing in the gods of ancient Greece was quite another.

"But if the story of Zeus's punishment of Lycaon is only a legend," he said, "what *really* happened? How did the Arcadian dynasties come into being in the first place?"

"Well, if you don't know…"

"I've no idea," he admitted, shaking his head. "And I don't know anyone who's ever found another explanation."

She slowly shook her own head. This was too much all at once. She could only listen, and at most absorb it all. Particularly as there was another and much more pressing problem.

"What's happened to Iole?" she asked quietly.

The House in the Forest

It was too late to regret anything now.

Too late to get on the next plane and fly home to the States.

Too late to take the new life she'd hoped to find on Sicily back to the New Lives store and exchange it.

Instead, she decided to go on the offensive. The course she didn't take was the obvious one of asking Florinda and Zoe to explain themselves. She wasn't ready for that yet. They could have told her all kinds of things – so could Alessandro, if she was honest with herself – things that might be the truth or might be another lie, or a mixture of the two intended to reassure her.

But only real answers could do that. She had a right to know about her family and her origins. About what might happen to her over the next few weeks or months.

She had come back to the Palazzo Alcantara, deathly tired, in the early hours of the morning, stealing quietly into her room and closing the door. Still, she hadn't escaped notice, and inevitably there'd been trouble out in the corridor: Florinda working herself up into the expected fury, Zoe – of all people – saying she wanted to have a serious talk with her.

To make sure she was left alone, Rosa had wedged the back of a chair under her door handle, and put the pillow over her head. After that she slept soundly.

When she woke late in the morning there was a breakfast

tray outside her door. A note in Zoe's handwriting told her that Florinda had flown to Lampedusa, an island between Sicily and North Africa, on urgent business. Zoe herself had an appointment, she wrote, and wouldn't be back from Catania until the afternoon. Next to that she had drawn a smiley face surrounded by sunbeams.

All forgiven and forgotten? That was hard to imagine. Rosa went down to the kitchen with the tray, brewed herself another coffee so strong it would have made even Fundling blanch, and was just taking her second bite of a sweet pastry when she had an idea.

After she had showered, put on fresh bandages, and buried the golden cell phone deep in the drawer of her bedside table, she set off along the path into the forest.

Still feeling exhausted, but curiously euphoric, she climbed the mountain above the Alcantara property. The sun shone through the branches, and a warm wind wafted up from the plain below. The air smelled of resin and warm pine needles.

Even when she passed the place where the tiger had threatened her, she felt only a slight sinking in her stomach. Had Tano intended to kill her, even at the price of breaking the concordat? Or had he just wanted to scare her so that she would go back to where she'd come from as quickly as possible?

She suppressed the thought of him, of Alessandro, even of Iole when she finally reached the ravine in the forest and continued eastward along the edge of the rock.

Beyond the trees the run-down farmhouse came into sight. Its yellow walls lay in shade, and there was an outbuilding entirely covered by dense undergrowth and climbing plants. The place looked even more dilapidated by day than it had in the darkness. Only when she looked more closely did she see that half of the sagging roof was a little higher above the crumbling walls than the other half, and was probably propped up inside. The shutters over the windows were closed, and hadn't been broken off their rusty hinges long ago, which also suggested that someone lived here. Not to mention the electric cable that she'd noticed even in the dark.

She didn't try to hide her presence, but walked straight up to the house, knocked on the door, and hoped that no one was going to blast her head off with a shotgun the moment it opened.

But it stayed closed. No one answered her knock.

She tried again.

The stained wood was smooth and solid under her fingers. It had been treated with something to make it look old and weather-beaten.

"Good day, Rosa," said a voice. Not on the other side of the door, but among the trees to her right.

She turned around, very slowly. No sudden movements. Nothing hasty. The gun she had expected to see in the doorway emerged from the shadows. Double-barrelled, a sawn-off muzzle. Hands marked by brown age spots, sinewy and dark-veined under skin like parchment. A brown woollen sweater fraying at the hem and neck. A pair of dirty jeans worn with boots.

His hair was white as snow, tied back behind his head.

She had always felt that old men with ponytails were suspect, even without a gun. This one also wore a patch over one eye, and she instinctively wondered if it was just for show, like the artificially weathered door and the ruin where he lived.

"You know who I am," she commented.

"You're Rosa. Zoe's sister."

She was wearing one of Zoe's leather jackets with her jeans and T-shirt. He could have recognised it and drawn the right conclusions. But something told her that he hadn't needed to do that. Because he knew not only her name, he knew her face and God knows what else about her. Suddenly she felt like the piercing gaze of his eyes was stripping her naked.

"Are you going to shoot me?"

"No," he said, but the gun was still pointing her way. "You're not afraid of that. Good. From all I've heard of you, I felt sure you were a real Alcantara."

"Wouldn't my passport have told you that?"

He lowered the gun, came over to her, and gave her a resounding slap in the face. Her hand shot up to hit back, but he had already seized her knuckles and was holding them firmly. His fingers were surprisingly strong and their grasp painful. Her cheek was burning, but its heat had more to do with her fury than the slap.

"I apologise," he said, but he did not let her free herself when she tried to jerk away. Only a full minute later did he let her go. She took a single step back. He smiled, not in an unfriendly way. His face was thin and wrinkled. In his mid-seventies, she guessed. Maybe older.

"What was the slap for?" she asked calmly.

"I've already apologised."

"I'm not deaf."

"Don't you accept my apology?"

"Is that the way you act here? Hitting people first, then apologising?"

"Only if there's a good reason for it. You were impertinent to your *capo*. You have learned that that's a serious offence. However, you should also know that I don't hold a grudge, even against an Alcantara. And finally: apologising for something is not a sign of weakness. Any more than accepting an apology is."

"'I'm not looking for a friend,'" she quoted. "'I'm looking for a Jedi master.'"

He looked at her in surprise. "What?"

"*Hamlet*." She offered him her hand. "I'm the stupid American girl from the house down the mountain. My passport just happens to say Alcantara by chance. I guess I was switched with some other baby at birth. My real parents were probably tourists passing through. First time ever in Europe, no map, travel guide falling apart, all very exciting. If I had my way I'd be in line to inherit a doughnut stall in Taylor, Arizona."

The old man stared at her, astonished. But then his harsh expression softened, and he burst out laughing. He took a step towards her and raised his hand again, but this time he only patted her other cheek and stroked her hair. "Your sister has never made me laugh!"

She lowered her voice conspiratorially. "Well, she's a criminal. No laughing in Cosa Nostra."

"More than you think, my dear. More than you think." He produced a key and unlocked the door. "Come in," he said, going ahead. "You look half-starved. I have bread and sausage and cheese. Your aunt and your sister care for me well."

He had a house inside the house. Below the collapsing roof of the ruin a new ceiling of wooden beams had been fitted, about two metres high. Walls had been built inside the crumbling outer walls. They made the single room less spacious, but they insulated it. There was a rough, sturdy wooden table, two chairs, an unmade bed, and an old chest of drawers with tarnished brass knobs. A mirror with a crack running through it. A tiny washbasin with an old-fashioned faucet. A few framed family photographs, most of them yellowing, hung on the walls. The men and women in them looked as if they'd lived around the time of the Second World War, maybe earlier. Rustic scenes in the fields or in narrow village streets, a couple of posed group photos in front of a painted landscape.

There was a rancid smell in the air, and she hoped that it came only from the dried sausages and the ham dangling from the beams on strings.

No books, but there was a tiny TV set. Its satellite dish must have been hidden in the ruined roof. Beside it stood a refrigerator, on top of that a clock radio. No phone, definitely no computer.

Not exactly the HQ of a supervillain. But the old man hadn't had to say the word *capo* to give Rosa the right idea.

"You're the *capo dei capi*," she said, looking around her. The boss of bosses. Head of the Sicilian Mafia. "Is that why the other families hate the Alcantaras so much? Because Florinda and Zoe run errands for you?"

The gun landed on the table with a clatter. He opened the refrigerator, took out a wooden board with cheese on it, and placed it beside the firearm. There was also a sausage and a loaf of bread. "Sit down," he said, pointing to one of the chairs.

She chose the other chair, which was closer to the door. He registered that with a smile, sat down on the first chair himself, and brought out a pocketknife. Very much at his ease, he cut the sausage into finger-thick slices. Rosa watched him. He drew the sharp blade through the firm meat again and again with practised ease.

"I am Salvatore Pantaleone," he said, without looking up. "If you were to go to the police and tell them that name, there'd be more carabinieri than trees in this forest in no time at all. They've been after me for nearly thirty years, and in that time I've lived in many dilapidated hovels. But this one, I trust, will be the last."

If there was melancholy in his words, he hid it well. It sounded more like the voice of a man on the verge of a great triumph.

"I told your sister to bring you to me."

"Well, she didn't."

"Oh yes, of course she did. You think it was just chance that she passed beneath your window every time she came here?"

"Why didn't she just take me with her?"

"I told her not to."

"But—"

"You have courage. And a strong will of your own. I'd hoped that would be the case, but I wanted to be perfectly sure. Zoe told me what happened that night. The attack by the tiger, that Carnevare bastard. But you came back anyway. I like that."

"So Zoe was only a decoy?"

"She carries out other tasks. You said so yourself. She works as a messenger for me, just as Florinda and others did before her. I had to disappear from the view of the authorities very early, and since then the Alcantaras have been my link with the outside world. I put my life in your family's hands, Rosa. So far they haven't disappointed me."

"That package Zoe had with her – it was letters to the other families? With instructions?"

Pantaleone nodded. "I am not the first *capo dei capi* forced to spend a lifetime in hiding. The world out there has changed, technology has developed – but some things never lose their usefulness. Paper and ink. Messages may travel faster by these newfangled methods, but everyone understands a note with a few sentences on it, whether he's the *capo* of a clan or a man from a mountain village. Even the stupid can read these days, but not everyone gets along with a computer. What's more, data files can be traced back, but a sheet of paper?"

She thought how easy it had been for her to wave goodbye to her own online existence, to Facebook and MySpace.

If she'd sent any of her digital friends a handwritten letter, most of them would probably have thought it was a joke.

"You wanted to meet me. Why?"

"You're an Alcantara. You will be an important person someday."

She laughed. "Sure."

"You're Florinda's heiress, didn't you know that? She has no children, no other close relations. The Alcantaras are dying out, and who can blame their menfolk?" He grinned in a knowing way that sent a shiver down her spine. "There's only Florinda, your sister and you left. With an empire of companies – it's quite easy to assess their value, and they can be kept going by a few trusted employees and some distant cousins."

"In a couple of weeks I'll be flying back to the States. And that will be it as far as I'm concerned."

"I doubt it," he said, and pushed a piece of bread, some slices of sausage and the cheese across the table to her. "Eat that."

She didn't touch it. "None of this has anything to do with me. I'm only here because…"

"Because you lost your child. I know."

Zoe. Of course. "Go to hell," she spat, and did not retreat an inch when he leaned over the table. "And if you try hitting me again, I'll defend myself."

He grinned. "You're right. It has nothing to do with me."

She didn't for a moment think he meant it seriously.

"I apologise again," he said in friendly tones.

"I'd better go now."

"Eat." Just the one word, calm, without emphasis.

She hesitated. There was something Alessandro had said that she couldn't get out of her mind: the *capo dei capi* came from the Arcadian dynasties. So Salvatore Pantaleone was one of them, but for the life of her she couldn't imagine what animal might be lurking inside him. And she wasn't anxious to find out. Certainly not here and now.

She tore off a piece of dry white bread and chewed without pleasure.

"The sausage is good," he said.

"I'm a vegetarian."

Whatever else he might be, he was a Sicilian who had spent his whole life in the country. The idea of someone not eating meat seemed to annoy him.

"Then eat some of the cheese. You're too thin."

"It runs in the family."

He sighed softly. "Yes, so it does."

To satisfy him she ate a piece of cheese. It didn't taste bad, but she didn't feel like eating.

He watched her chewing, both elbows on the table, his mottled hands clasped in front of his chin.

"You don't often get visitors," she commented.

"Only your sister. Even Florinda hasn't been here for a long time. I wouldn't let her."

"Wouldn't let her?"

"Waste of time, talking to Florinda. She's not the future, you are."

She was going to contradict him again, but something kept her back. His keen eyes, his firm tone of voice. He seemed perfectly sure of himself.

"Never forget who you are," he said. "You Alcantaras are my voice and sometimes my eyes. My hand is over you, protecting you. No one will dare to touch a hair of your heads while I'm watching over you."

"Tano Carnevare obviously didn't see it that way."

His fist crashed down on the table. "That boy has no idea what he's done! The entire Carnevare clan are nothing but trouble. Make sure you don't get too close to them." So Zoe hadn't told him about *that*. "The baron was a weakling who listened only to what his advisers whispered. God knows what plans Cesare's thinking up. I'd have given orders to exterminate the whole brood long ago if their influence on the mainland hadn't been so extremely useful to us all."

This was the time to ask the question that had been on the tip of her tongue for ages. "And who makes sure the concordat's still in force? You?"

He snorted softly. "The concordat protecting the Lamias is too old for anyone to break it."

"But who makes sure that peace is kept? And who will punish Tano Carnevare if he ignores the agreement again?"

"You know more about the Arcadian dynasties than Zoe and Florinda think. Who told you?"

"Oh… I overheard them talking. They thought I was asleep, but I picked up a few things."

His glance became more penetrating.

He doesn't believe me, she thought. He can tell I'm lying.

Brusquely, he pushed his chair back. "Maybe you really should go now."

She put the rest of the bread on the table and stood up. Being careful to walk slowly, she went to the door.

"Over there, the letters." He pointed to a bundle lying on the floor near the doorway. "Take them with you. And tell Zoe she needn't come up here any more. I want you to do it in future."

Everything in her cried out to tell him where he could shove his letters and his orders. But then she only bent down in silence, picked up the package, and opened the door.

"Why do you trust me?"

"You're one of us."

"So are the others. Even Tano."

He smiled. "But I know your destiny. And it's waiting for you here, not in America."

She stared at him for a moment longer. Then, without a word, she closed the door behind her and headed home.

Rome

She didn't know which surprised her more: that her sister had a best friend here, or that Zoe hadn't breathed a word about her before.

Lilia was pretty, red-haired – and stoned to the eyeballs. Zoe too was in an unusual state of euphoria, acting as if nothing had happened last night. She didn't say a word to Rosa about the furious scene in the hall outside her room. She didn't even want to know where Rosa had been with her car when she was gone for almost twenty-four hours.

"You *will* come, won't you?" It was the third time she'd asked, although Rosa had already said yes.

Zoe and Lilia were flying to Rome for two days, to shop and have a good time, they said, and they wouldn't give Rosa any peace until she agreed to go with them.

In fact she had no objection at all. She wanted to turn her back on Sicily for a while. She needed time to catch her breath. Time to think. And she needed new clothes. There were hundreds of things she had to discuss with Zoe. Although not while her sister was running frantically around the room like a spinning top. And definitely not while this Lilia was present. Maybe there'd be a chance for a private conversation with Zoe on the way to Rome.

Lilia – red-headed, beautiful, stoned Lilia – clapped her hands when Rosa asked, "When do we leave?"

"Right now!" cried Zoe, delighted, laughing along with Lilia as if someone had cracked an incredibly funny joke.

"You're planning to go to the airport just like that?"

With a flourish, Zoe produced three tickets from her bag. "Ta-da! All booked. The chopper will take us to Catania, and Catania—" She interrupted herself, exchanged a startled, wide-eyed glance with Lilia, and then burst out laughing again. "Well, not Catania, but the plane – from Catania, I mean – will take us to Rome. After we've taken the chopper to—"

"Yes," Rosa interrupted her. "You said that already."

"Did I?" Genuine surprise, and then a giggle. "Pack your things and let's go!"

"Does Florinda know?"

"She won't be back from Lampedusa before this evening. I wrote her a note." She thought about it. "Or didn't I?"

Lilia nodded. "Yes, you did."

Zoe hugged Rosa. "I'm so glad you're coming."

"That's okay."

"*Really* I am."

"Okay, okay. I'll fetch my stuff."

Zoe grasped Lilia's hand and pulled her to her feet jubilantly.

They're like a couple of cheerleaders on ecstasy, thought Rosa.

*

They landed in Rome late that evening, took a taxi into the city, and moved into a suite in a grand hotel not far from the Pantheon. It was one of those old, plush hotels that Rosa knew only from pictures, with high ceilings, a lot of stucco, gilded decor, and heavy, dark red curtains.

Zoe had stayed here several times. The receptionists greeted her by name, shaking hands, and Rosa noticed, morosely, that Zoe introduced her to perfect strangers as *my little sister*. To cheer herself up she stole a gold fountain pen from the doorman, then didn't know what to do with it and left it in the potted plant just outside the elevators. As the other two were getting ready in the bathroom, she lay on her bed without any make-up on and immersed herself in 'My Death'. After a while she tried calling Alessandro but only got his voicemail. She hesitated for a moment, and listened to the silence after the tone, then she hung up.

Zoe and Lilia came out of the bathroom on a wave of high spirits, enveloped in clouds of sweetish vapours. This was a no-smoking suite; they were lucky the smoke alarm hadn't gone off. All they needed, thought Rosa, was to have the whole hotel evacuated just because those two couldn't go ten minutes without their next joint.

"Ready?" asked Zoe.

Rosa lay where she was. Iole's face came before her eyes, and for a moment her conscience pricked her. La dolce vita for her in Rome, while Iole – yes, what had become of Iole? Dead? Torn to pieces by beasts of prey?

Reluctantly, she sat up. "Yes, I'm ready. Can't you see that?"

"You haven't even brushed your hair."

"Are we going out to eat or exhibition skating?"

"Both," said Lilia. "We want the audience to look, but not touch."

They ate in a small, comfortable trattoria near the hotel. Rosa didn't talk much, but she couldn't help watching Zoe all the time. Her scratches and bruises had healed astonishingly fast. She wondered how her sister had explained her injuries to Lilia.

And then there was Lilia herself.

After a while Rosa concentrated entirely on Lilia, looking for anything to show whether she, too, belonged to the Arcadian dynasties. But she had no idea how to tell.

Lilia's red hair tumbled to her shoulders in profuse ringlets. She was wearing a black leather jacket, a tight-fitting top, and a short skirt with flat shoes. She wasn't as heavily made up as Rosa had expected, considering the hour she and Zoe had spent in front of the mirror.

After dinner, the two of them dragged her off to an expensive club near the Spanish Steps. They were escorted past the people standing in line to get in, and Rosa felt uneasy under their glances. Zoe went ahead, gave the doorman a kiss on the cheek, and was the first to plunge into the droning, noisy darkness beyond the heavy iron door. Rosa followed the other two down a stairway to the lower floor, where it was even darker, more crowded and noisier. She didn't want anything to drink, but Zoe brought her something from the bar anyway – it was more ice than drink, and so colourful that

Rosa assumed her sister had ordered it just because of the pretty decorations.

She found herself a place to sit with her back to the wall, then held her glass up to eye-level, but didn't drink. No one had come close enough to it to mix anything with its contents, but she couldn't help it. She'd probably never shake off her distrust.

After a while the droning basses and the dim light were confusing her far more than the cocktail could have done. She stood up and went slowly towards the dance floor. Since the party a year ago she had avoided large crowds. On the flight here, she had hated the crush at the airport. All this was like her worst nightmare, but this time she let herself simply sink into it. She danced until her clothes were damp with sweat, until she felt almost intoxicated by the heat, the volume of sound, and everything she had avoided for months. Her mood was somewhere between panic and euphoria, her heart was racing to the rhythm of the music, and soon she felt as if she were in a bubbling cauldron with individual faces bobbing up to the surface again and again and then disappearing.

She stopped only once, looked for Zoe and Lilia, saw them at the bar with two other young women, and plunged back into the crowd. The noise level was still rising, and with it the temperature. Laughing faces whirled by in a blur, human bodies became a colourless mass. Sometimes she thought she heard sounds that were not voices or part of the music, a howling and screeching, and then she saw glowing eyes among all the others, saw fur on faces and sharp fangs, saw figures bending down and racing away on all fours amid all the confusion. Hands turned to claws, noses to muzzles, ears grew longer and pointed, eyes shone green and yellow and fiery red.

Someone took Rosa's arm and drew her aside. She started, was going to resist, came up against a wall, and realised that she had reached the edge of the dance floor.

"That's enough," said Zoe. "Let's go now."

Lilia was beside her. They both looked sober and serious, and Rosa gradually came back to herself. When she looked over her shoulder at the crowd, she saw only dancing human figures. No beasts of prey, no curved fangs. Only their eyes still glowed in the flashing artillery of lights.

She felt a strong pulsing in her ribcage, then in her hips. That was how the phantom pain in her lower body announced itself. She had to get out of here, fast, and suddenly realised that Zoe had noticed already. Lilia, too, was looking concerned.

The two of them manoeuvred her out of the crowd, up the stairs, and into the fresh air. Rosa made it to the nearest corner, just out of sight of the people waiting to go in, and then collapsed against a wall in one of those terrible crying fits that she could never explain and never control.

Zoe and Lilia stayed with her, giving her all the time she needed, and after that they helped Rosa back to the hotel, put her to bed, and stayed with her until she fell asleep.

*

She was up early, watching the sun rise over the roofs of Rome. The suite was on the top floor of the hotel. From the balcony, she could see red-gold light flowing over the jumble of gables and terraces, making its way into narrow ravines of masonry, while antennae on the rooftops cast shadows like charred skeletons.

As she leaned against the balustrade of the balcony in her knee-length T-shirt, images of the previous night came back into her mind. She wasn't sure what had happened to her. She had enough hours of therapy behind her to analyse her behaviour and talk about stuff like *emotional compensation* and *freely chosen confrontation*. But ultimately that was all nonsense. She had collapsed long before she got out into the air again, and instead of simply falling down, her body had become part of the crowd, drifting with it of its own accord.

Some memory that she had obviously suppressed had surfaced. She wasn't perfectly well yet; a part of her was still sick and would stay that way.

At breakfast, Zoe and Lilia handled her with velvet gloves. Only when they realised that Rosa was not going to explode at the first wrong word they said did they relax and tell her their itinerary for the day. They wanted to initiate her into the mysteries of the city and – above all – its boutiques. Rosa put a damper on these plans by saying she was going to stay in the hotel that morning, and neither their long faces nor their objections could make her change her mind.

After the other two had left, she studied a map of the city that she had found among the other brochures in the room.

She had no intention of hiding away in their suite, but a shopping trip with Zoe and Lilia was the last thing she needed right now. Instead she was going to explore the streets around the hotel on her own, letting herself wander around the district for a while.

She was just about to set off when there was a knock at her door. "Rosa Alcantara?"

"Who is it?"

A short pause, and then a second voice. "Police," said a woman. "Open the door, please."

Ironically, the first thing she thought of was the stolen fountain pen, and only then did her family's businesses cross her mind. But instead of making a rope of sheets and shimmying down from the balcony, she put out her hand, like a sleepwalker, and opened the door slightly.

She had it open just a crack when she thought of the peephole in the door itself, and the fact that anyone could say they were the police.

She slammed the door shut again.

"Please, *signorina*, what was that for?"

Standing on tiptoe, she looked out and saw a man and a woman, both in leather jackets, hers short and waisted, his long, with bulging pockets. Not uniformed officers, then. Both were quite young, thirty at the most.

"Do you have ID with you?"

The two of them exchanged a glance, then took out small folders, opened them, and held them up to the peephole. Through its circular eye, Rosa could see only their photos.

They might just as well have been student IDs.

"I could call reception," she suggested, playing for time.

"We'd rather you didn't. It would only cause unnecessary agitation."

"But I *am* agitated."

"No one wants to do you any harm. At least, we don't."

Keeping the police waiting worked on TV shows, but here and now it struck her as childish. "Okay," she finally said, and opened the door.

"Thank you," said the man, and he held out his ID to her again. "Antonio Festa. This is my colleague Stefania Moranelli. Please come with us."

"Where to?"

The young woman, dark-haired and wiry, with slightly Arabian features, pointed down the corridor. "Only a few rooms down, don't worry."

Sure enough, there was a door open down the corridor, with light spilling out of it.

"Do I need a lawyer or anything like that?"

The man who had introduced himself as Antonio Festa smiled. His nose was so large that for a moment it was as if she were still seeing it through the magnification of the peephole. In an angular way, he was almost attractive. His hair was very short, and a narrow scar ran through one eyebrow. He might indeed be a police officer. Or a contract killer.

"You're not going to be accused of anything," he said with a crooked grin. "Apart, perhaps, from the theft of several chocolate bars, a bracelet, and a gold fountain pen that turned up in a flowerpot in the lobby here."

Her heart missed a beat. "How long have you been following me?"

"Since you landed in Italy. But don't worry, only while you were out in public. Your private sphere has been respected throughout your stay."

"I'm an American citizen."

"We know that you hold two passports. And our laws also apply to tourists."

Here the young woman, Stefania Moranelli, intervened. "Listen, no one's trying to set a trap. At the moment our superior officer would like a word with you, that's all. I promise it won't take long. After that you can go and meet your sister and Lilia Dionisi in the city if you like."

"I was twelve when I was interrogated for the first time," Rosa said. "If it's about my family, then I know exactly what my rights—"

"Just follow us," said the policewoman, nudging her colleague. "We don't want to discuss this kind of thing out in the hall."

Rosa gave herself a little shake, took the key card out of its slot in the lock, and let the door lock behind her. The carpet in the hallway felt deeper and softer the closer she came to the open room.

The man went ahead. The woman stopped outside the room, waved Rosa in, and followed her. Then she closed the door.

A second woman was standing at the window, with her back to the doorway, and turned around as Rosa entered the room. She was smaller than the two officers who had escorted Rosa here, not much more than five feet tall. She had short brown hair, a tousled fringe, and looked as if she'd bought her clothes in a department store years ago and had never given a thought to refreshing her wardrobe; she wore beige trousers, a dark sweater, and over it a thin silver chain with a pendant the size of a thumbnail hanging from it. Rosa suspected it opened to show a photograph of her child. She probably saw him or her only at weekends on visits to her ex-husband.

"My name is Quattrini," she said, offering Rosa a slim hand. "Judge Quattrini. I am leading the investigation into your aunt Florinda Alcantara."

"Are you arresting me for three stolen chocolate bars, or can I go now?"

"I know quite a lot about you."

"What do you want?"

The judge had a dark birthmark on her left cheek. Her eyes were surrounded by tiny folds, and she looked as if she didn't get enough sleep. "I'd like to ask you to work with me."

Rosa almost choked. "You want me to spy on my aunt for you? You must be out of your mind!"

"No." Quattrini gave her a mirthless smile. "Not your aunt. I know more than enough about her. In fact that's part of the deal I would like to offer you. I'll hold back the evidence against Florinda Alcantara if, in return, you will cooperate with me."

"I have no idea what you're getting at."

"The person we would like to know more about is not your

aunt." The judge took a step towards her. Rosa wasn't tall, but she stood half a head above this woman. "There's someone else I'm interested in. I believe you know him well. His name is Alessandro Carnevare."

Sisters

The plane from Rome landed at Catania around nine in the evening. A little later Rosa, Zoe and Lilia were racing west down Expressway 417 through the twilight in a black Mercedes. Florinda was still on her way back in the helicopter, so the three girls had called an Alcantara limousine to pick them up. They dropped Lilia off in Caltagirone, a little mountain town where she lived with her father and a younger brother.

Half an hour later, around eleven, the limousine turned into the long drive of the Palazzo Alcantara, and finally stopped at the foot of the double flight of stone steps in the inner courtyard. The driver took out the baggage, a good deal more of it than when they'd set off. Zoe had shopped for both of them, and gave instructions for which designer logo shopping bags belonged in which room. Rosa stood there in silence, watching her sister.

When the man had disappeared into the house with the first load, Rosa touched Zoe's arm. "Can we go for a little walk around the house? I need to talk to you."

"If it's about all that in the club—"

"It's about the family."

Zoe looked at her, surprised, as if until now she had successfully suppressed all thought of where the money she had been spending so freely in Rome's Via Condotti came from. "Can't it wait till tomorrow?"

"Florinda will be back tomorrow. She'll spend hours tearing me a new one because I went out with Alessandro."

"In my car."

"It doesn't have a scratch on it."

Zoe suddenly looked grave. "I don't care about the scratches on my car. But what about my little sister?"

Rosa smiled. "Call her that once again and never mind the car, she'll scratch your eyes out."

They strolled out of the gateway of the inner courtyard. Ahead of them, in the car headlights, stood the dried-up fountain. The stone basin was still full of empty birds' nests. Something rustled among the dry leaves and twigs.

"Mice," said Zoe.

"Or snakes," suggested Rosa.

Zoe said nothing. They walked past the western side of the palazzo, below the huge terrace. A cool wind blew down the slope, carrying with it the scent of lemon trees and lavender. Whenever they came within the sphere of the next motion detector, another light came on; there were several in the tall palm trees on this side of the property.

"I talked to the old man," said Rosa. "You could have just told me he wanted to see me instead of staging that game of hide-and-seek in the forest."

"He wanted it that way," replied Zoe. "In these parts you obey when Salvatore Pantaleone gives an order. Did he tell you who he is?"

"The *capo dei capi*."

"One of the most wanted men in Italy – maybe in all Europe.

Our people guard the mountain for a long way all around. He himself is… he's the last of his clan. All the other Pantaleones have died, one way or another. It's a privilege that he picked the Alcantaras to convey his orders to the other families. He treats us as if we were his family now."

"That sounds as if you learned it by heart."

Zoe sighed. "Florinda drummed it into me for months after I arrived here. Pantaleone insisted that I was to take over running the errands – and I assume it's going to be you in future."

"Did he tell you so?"

"No, but he's curious. And the fact that you're here in Sicily—"

"That was his idea?"

"He never said a word about it to me. Florinda suggested it after she heard what had happened to you, and I thought it was a good plan. But now I'm inclined to think it was his order in the first place." Zoe stopped. "I'd have told you, Rosa, except…" She shook her head. "It's not so simple here. And there are rules you have to obey, even where your own sister's concerned. I'm sure you're thinking terrible things about me now, but—"

"You saved my life up there in the forest."

Zoe walked a little faster, as if she didn't want to look Rosa in the eye. "Tano… I don't know whether he really wanted to kill you. Normally no one dares go that far into another clan's territory. Others would hardly have got past the guards."

"Oh, a tiger would."

Zoe slowed down again, and this time she did meet Rosa's eyes. "How did you find out? From Alessandro?"

"I'd rather you had told me."

"I wanted to. Especially after that stupid book of animal stories turned up. When I saw it, I realised why Alessandro had given it to you. And I knew there was a danger that he'd be the first to tell you. I told Florinda we had to do so before him, and I said you ought to know the truth. But she wouldn't listen. She thought you wouldn't believe a word of it anyway until you yourself had—"

"Turned into a snake for the first time."

"How do you think *I* found out? I woke up one night in the greenhouse among all the snakes, and I was in such a panic that it happened right then." She grimaced. "And I always thought I *hated* snakes."

"Is that why Florinda had me taken there that night?"

"She wanted to find out if you'd reached that stage yet."

"But I hadn't."

"You weren't afraid of the snakes, they weren't enough to trigger the change… we were watching you."

Zoe sounded ashamed. Rosa wanted to get angry with her, but she couldn't. Instead she simply listened, while the tangled threads of everything that had happened gradually came together.

"When I was there with the snakes, I was in such a state that the transformation began," Zoe went on. "That was about three months after I arrived here. But the whole thing didn't affect you at all."

"Of course it did."

"All the same, it wasn't enough to trigger that first change. You need furious rage for that, or fear."

"I felt as cold as if my blood had suddenly frozen."

"That's how it begins," said Zoe. "You had… It had begun. But then it just stopped and you were human again."

None of this really shook her. She thought it was fascinating, and felt a slight tingling inside her. "Did Mom know?"

Zoe shrugged her shoulders. "If so, she never mentioned it to me."

"She must have had some reason for staying in the States after Dad's death. When the two of them married, you—"

"They did it in secret. Did you know that?"

Rosa stared at Zoe. "In secret?"

"They ran away together. The Alcantaras didn't want him marrying an American. He was different from the others, and they—"

"Different because they left him alive, instead of killing him at birth?"

"You don't want to believe everything you're told. It's not like that. No Alcantara woman has ever killed her son."

"Yes, they have," said Rosa. "One of them, anyway."

Zoe took her hand. "Rosa, you don't even know it would have been a son. It was at such an early stage…"

"I felt it. I knew it was a boy."

Zoe was sensible enough not to contradict her. "You didn't kill him."

"No, the doctor did that. But she was only doing her job,

and I should have done mine—" Rosa was struggling to find the right words. "You know, it's not as if I want a child. I mean, for God's sake, a *child*… but I could have given him up for adoption after he was born or something like that. Instead of just… oh, how do I know what I should have done? Not listened to other people, anyway. I definitely shouldn't have listened to Mom."

"You can't blame it on her."

"You know what I've been wondering ever since I knew about this… this snake thing? Did Mom want the baby out of the way so there wouldn't be another of us come into the world? Another Alcantara. Another—"

"Arcadian?"

Rosa nodded. "After Dad's death she must have been terrified of them. Of Florinda."

"If Florinda had wanted something to happen to her, she could have fixed it much earlier."

"Perhaps she did want it. But then she dropped the idea because of us. Because then she wouldn't have had any heirs. Did Florinda ever mention that she can't have children? I thought about that half the night. Look at it that way and it all makes sense. She left Mom in peace because without us the Alcantara clan would die out… and it suited her for Mom to look after us until we were old enough to move back here." She gave a derisive little snort. "To the bosom of the family."

"But Rosa, all this, here… it's good for us! It's where we belong. We're a part of it. We're Alcantaras."

"And is that why a Carnevare and I can't—"

"Have sex?"

"Talk to each other."

"You saw what happens. Tano comes here and is on the point of breaking the concordat. They almost killed each other out on that island because of you. And as for the other day, whatever the two of you were up to—"

"We weren't *up* to anything,"

"It only makes trouble."

They walked on in silence, passing the north facade and the greenhouse now. The dim green light came through the clouded panes.

"Once you're used to it," said Zoe, "you'll enjoy it."

"Enjoy crawling through the dirt?"

Zoe stopped. Anger flared in her eyes, and for a fraction of a second Rosa thought she saw her sister's pupils narrow to slits. "Can't you see what this is, Rosa? We're not the same as ordinary people… we're human beings *and* Arcadians. We are the superior species. Our ancestors ruled Arcadia. They dominated the Mediterranean and the countries on its shores."

"Until two years ago you didn't even know where the Mediterranean was."

Zoe let out her breath sharply and walked faster again. Rosa kept up with her from one circle of light to the next. The chestnuts on the outskirts of the forest were rustling. The cicadas had struck up their nocturnal concert long ago.

"What will happen if the Hungry Man comes back to Sicily?" asked Rosa after a while. "Pantaleone says there could be a power struggle between the dynasties."

"They're all afraid of him."

"Does he really think he's the reincarnation of an ancient king? That Lycaon?"

"Some of the others are sure of it."

"He must be quite old."

"About the same age as Pantaleone. Mid-seventies, I think."

"How great can it be to belong to a... a *species* that would commit murder just because an old man tells them to?"

"No one knows what he's really planning. But he must have powerful allies."

"Doesn't the Mafia already exert an influence on the government?"

"Pressure must have been applied in the very highest places to get a man like that set free." Zoe stopped as they entered the front courtyard again. They had walked all around the property. "It's still no more than rumours. No one knows exactly when and why the Hungry Man will be let out. Or what's going on behind the scenes. But the *capi* are uneasy, and Pantaleone... well, some say he isn't strong enough now to keep the dynasties safe from prying eyes when he's been living underground for decades."

"Maybe that's why someone is spreading rumours – to weaken Pantaleone's influence and prepare for the return of the Hungry Man."

Zoe uttered a mirthless laugh. "Do you think you're the first to think of that? Florinda's always going on about the possibility, and Pantaleone doesn't seem to know what to think. It would be much simpler if half the families weren't at odds with the other half. But as things stand?" She shook her head.

Rosa leaned against the parapet of the fountain. She took a deep breath. "There's something else I have to tell you."

Zoe looked at her expectantly, more anxious than curious.

"In Rome, at the hotel," Rosa began, "when you were out and about in the morning with Lilia…" She hesitated, and then told her about Judge Quattrini.

Zoe compressed her lips. "Did she ask you questions about our family?"

"Yes. I didn't say a word, and finally she let me go again." She scrutinised her sister. "Did they try that with you, too?"

Zoe shook her head. "Not so obviously. Sometimes at first, when I went out, I had a feeling… well, that people were throwing themselves in my way, people I thought were new friends. I figured it was because of all the money at first, and I told Florinda about it. She warned me against the police, undercover officers who'd try to pump me. But for a judge to approach anyone so openly and so soon… Are you sure you didn't tell her anything?"

"Absolutely sure." Rosa didn't mention that the conversation in the hotel room had been all about Alessandro and the Carnevares. She was afraid that Zoe would tell Florinda, and then her aunt really would move heaven and earth to make sure Rosa didn't see him. "She lectured me for a while. Why it was important to oppose the Mafia, the whole works, drug trafficking and contract killing and so forth."

Zoe took her hand. "We should have prepared you for something like this."

"She seemed to know a lot about Alcantara business. And she wasn't just talking about wind turbines."

"No," said Zoe quietly, "of course not."

"Florinda's flights to Lampedusa… they have to do with people trafficking, the judge said."

"Refugees from North Africa coming to Europe of their own free will." Zoe sighed. "They try to cross the Mediterranean in tiny boats, and if they're lucky they make it to Lampedusa. Anyone who lands on the island can't be sent back. One of the largest reception camps for refugees is there. And Florinda sees to it that a number of them get a reasonable chance of—"

"Nonsense," Rosa interrupted her. "Florinda picks the strongest men and sends them to building sites all over Europe, where they work for starvation wages."

Zoe avoided her eyes. "You've always known wind turbines aren't the only way we earn our money."

That was true. And she had never felt like a criminal. No one who saw their modest apartment in Brooklyn could have thought that they or their mother had profited from the Alcantara wealth. But here she was today in this palazzo, with the fast cars, and the bags full of designer clothes from Rome waiting for her in her room.

Zoe was staring at her in astonishment. "She didn't really manage to do it, did she? Give you a guilty conscience? My God, Rosa, you never used to have problems with that kind of thing."

"I told her to go to hell and leave me in peace, that's all."

She looked Zoe in the eye. "You have to promise me something."

Zoe swore under her breath. She clearly guessed what was coming.

"You can't tell Florinda and Pantaleone anything about this," said Rosa. "Not a word. I don't want them thinking I'm a risk to them. Or sending me home again."

Zoe looked at the ground. Rosa's hand shot out and seized her arm, forcing her to look up again.

"Promise, Zoe."

"That—"

"You owe me. I know about the transmitter in that cell phone. It was a mean trick to play, and you know it."

Guiltily, Zoe bit her lower lip before she uttered another sound. "Florinda—"

"As if I give a damn. And it's okay. *Once* it's okay. But not again. I didn't have to tell you all that. But… well, you're my sister."

Zoe nodded slowly. She didn't seem to be happy about it, but she looked Rosa in the eye again. "I can keep my mouth shut when it matters."

"You swear?"

"Oh, come on, you want me to spit on my palm, turn in a circle three times, and—"

"I want to have you on my side, that's all."

Zoe swallowed, then threw her arms around Rosa. "I won't say a word, I swear. And I'm really glad you're here. I've missed you."

Rosa hugged her back. "Missed you, too."

They stood beside the fountain for a little longer, close together, saying nothing, and only when the limousine rolled out of the courtyard gate and turned on its way to the garages did they let go of each other, as the beam of the headlights moved past them, and the rumble of the engine drowned out the sounds of the Sicilian night. They walked back to the house together.

That was the night she first dreamed of the panther's kiss.

Kiss of Darkness

She knew from the first moment that it was a dream.

She was lying in her bed, and the bed was surrounded by jungle. Moisture dripped from fleshy leaves. Orchids flowered in the twilight, the glowing eyes of the flowers watching her. Gigantic pod-shaped fruits pulsated in the shade like lungs, swelled, and then collapsed. A breath of hot air wafted through the undergrowth, stroking her hair back from her bare shoulders.

There was something missing, and only after a moment did she know what it was. Animal noises. The jungle was almost totally silent. Only the swollen lobes of the pods rattled and rustled, while a quiet squealing and cheeping came from among the leaves. It was a few more minutes before she realised that it came from the orchids as they discussed her with one another.

Something stirred behind the nearest trees; a black outline moved through the thickets, soundless, prowling quietly on soft paws. Rosa watched him, waited for him, because she knew he wanted to find her.

As he came closer she was amazed by his supple beauty. He moved out of the shadows like a blot of ink, and only in the twilight did he take on the shape of a panther. Keeping low as the big cats do, he prowled once around the bed before stopping at her feet and placing one black paw on the snow-white bedclothes. The orchids whispered faster, in frenzied excitement.

She was sitting upright now, the bedspread a high white cloud. She could hardly see over the edge of it. The panther's eyes were glittering, and there was a silvery sheen on his black fur. She noticed everything about him: his quivering whiskers, his gleaming teeth, the pink tip of his tongue.

With a fluid movement, he jumped up on the bed and pushed himself under the bedspread at the foot end. It seemed much longer now, surely a good twenty metres long, and the panther was moving under it, a slight mound under that white cloud. Only now did she see that the jungle had vanished, and the bed had grown even larger, reaching to the horizon in all directions. The mound was coming closer, perhaps ten, perhaps a hundred steps away from her now, a wave that would soon reach her bare legs.

She was breathing faster, and the hoarse sound that the plants had been uttering a moment ago now came from herself, came warm and rhythmically through her lips. As she sat she braced her upper body on her arms, the palms of her hands firmly on the bed. Her blond hair fell from her shoulders as she laid her head slightly back, eyes half-closed in expectation of his touch. She felt him approaching under the covers, felt the mattress shaking slightly, as big as the whole world, and senses she had never guessed at stirred in her.

She dared not look down at herself, because she was afraid of waking up. Afraid that he might suddenly be gone, leaving her alone. But the shaking of the bedspread was more marked as he made his way towards her.

First there was a new kind of quivering, very close to the soles of her feet, then a gentle touch on her toes, her ankles, moving up her calves. He was there, very close to her, and the bedspread rose even higher, pushed up from below into her field of vision, although she was still looking up, and her eyes had become narrow slits.

She had to fight the impulse to pull back the covers and look at him, the growling, hissing beast of prey pushing himself towards her. His fur touched her skin, and every single pore sensed that he was close. He filled her with his presence.

Enormous warmth radiated from the panther as he lay on her, robbing her of air. Sweat stood out on her brow and ran into her eyes. Her lips tasted salty; muscles and sinews stretched taut on her neck. His breath had reached her hips; its hot vapour was creeping over her stomach, pressed through her rib cage, touched her breasts and her collarbone, then her throat.

She had closed her eyes long ago, sensing him only through his touch. His paws brushed along her thighs, his claws punched holes in the sheet.

Very slowly she lowered her head again, looked down at her body leaning back and at the edge of the bedspread. It had risen, forming a dark cave above her torso. Cat's eyes flashed in it.

He ran his tongue over her, rough and warm and supple, licked the sweat off her skin, licked her up to her armpits and then down again, over every part of her.

She shifted her weight to one hand and pushed the other

under the bedspread, felt the soft, silky fur between his eyes. Slowly, she raised her arm, carefully pushed the covers aside, and saw him crouching over her in all his impressive elegance, a shadow that had become a beast with glowing eyes.

He pricked up his ears, seemed to wait, only for a couple of heartbeats. Then he lowered his panther's head, licked the white human skin off her body like milk, and revealed the golden scales of her serpent self.

Cat's Heart

"Iole's safe," called Alessandro, jumping out of his red Ferrari in the inner courtyard of the palazzo. "For now, anyway."

Rosa ran down the stone stairway from the terrace. She was relieved, but also surprised to see him suddenly turn up on Alcantara property. "What are you doing here?" she said. "If Florinda finds out—"

He had stopped on the bottom step. "She knows already. The guards at the end of the drive told her."

"That's not possible. Florinda isn't here. She won't be back until later."

Alessandro shrugged. "Well, they called the palazzo, and someone told them to let me through. So if it wasn't you—"

A window opened above them. Looking up, Rosa saw Zoe.

"Hurry up," she called down. "If Florinda gets back and sees the two of you together, it won't be fun for any of us."

Rosa gave her a smile. "Thanks."

Zoe winked and closed the window. The blue sky was reflected in the glass, so they had no way of knowing whether she was still watching them.

"That was nice of her," said Alessandro.

"Zoe's always surprising me." She looked into Alessandro's eyes. "So what about Iole?"

"She's at the castle with us. Cesare really did have her removed from the island just before we got there. He knows what happened. He's furious, but he doesn't dare move openly against me yet."

"Did you speak to Iole?"

"Only briefly."

"And Tano hasn't hurt her?"

"Cesare seems to be keeping him on a tight rein. Right now he's more cautious than usual. I'm sure Cesare is planning something, but he'll wait until it suits him before letting trouble break out between his supporters and mine."

Rosa was exhausted. After waking up from her dream she'd had difficulty even getting out of bed. Her skin felt hot and irritated, and she had muscle cramps. She'd also bitten her lower lip, and it throbbed slightly.

"Looks like a cold sore," she said awkwardly, when he looked at her mouth, "but it isn't."

"You had a bad dream," he commented.

To change the subject, she pointed to the gate. "Let's get out of here. If we take two cars you don't have to bring me back later. Drop me off outside our garages and then I'll follow you."

"Where to?"

She smiled. "To the end of the world," she said. And thought, *What the hell do you think you're saying?*

But before she could change her mind, he was holding the door of the Ferrari open for her. She sank into the black leather upholstery.

Alessandro let her out when they reached the palazzo garages. One of the boys from the village came in regularly to wash and wax the six sports cars that were lined up side by side. None of them was brand new – Florinda had obviously lost interest in her expensive hobby over the last few years. Rosa didn't know much about cars, so she opted for a black Maserati Quattroporte. Aside from Zoe's Porsche, it was the only automatic. The boy looked a little nervous as he handed her the key, and went white as a sheet when the engine howled as she drove away.

Forty-five minutes later they got off the A19 at Agira and continued north along dusty country roads. This time Rosa made sure to memorise the way. The hills they passed showed no sign of life, and in another thirty minutes they reached the barricaded access road to the unfinished expressway. Here they drove side by side – they had all four lanes to themselves – and Rosa adjusted the speed of the Maserati to Alessandro's Ferrari.

The steep ravine where the expressway ended was just coming into view when Alessandro slowed down, driving in the middle of the highway. It was another half mile to the fallen bridge, but he switched off the engine and got out. Rosa slipped out of the driver's seat of the Maserati and looked at him across the roof of the car, through the flickering heat haze.

"Let's go the rest of the way on foot," he suggested.

She looked around. There wasn't a soul in sight, but she locked the car anyway. The car was too old to have a remote control, and for a moment she wondered whether her father had driven it. The idea moved her more than she liked to admit.

After a few steps, Alessandro bent down near a dandelion

that had fought its way through the cracks in the road surface.

"Oh, don't pick it," begged Rosa. "It's tried so hard to reach daylight."

Alessandro shook his head, cautiously reached out his fingers, and picked up a beetle from the shady side of the plant. He gently placed it on the palm of his hand. As the insect explored his skin with its feelers, its wing case shimmered with all the colours of the rainbow.

"Look at that," he said, "it isn't at all afraid of me."

Rosa looked up and met his eyes.

"So why are you?" he asked.

"What makes you think I am?"

"You're trying to hide something from me. Exactly what," he said, smiling, "well, I was only guessing."

"Maybe you guessed wrong?"

"What is it, then?"

"This whole thing – this place, the island, you, being here with you – it makes me nervous. But I'm not afraid."

He put the beetle carefully back on the ground, watched as it scuttled away into the shade of the solitary dandelion, and walked on.

Just then a single cloud covered the sun, and the hilly ochre landscape on both sides of the empty expressway lost its brilliance. Under the shadow of the cloud, they walked over the asphalt, kicking aside pebbles. Tiny lizards ahead of them scurried off.

"I've looked at the files from the studio," he said. "My mother's notes, the documents, all of it."

"So?"

"So it's exactly what I thought. She knew all about the way Cesare went behind my father's back. Obviously she even tried talking to my father about it, more than once." There was a note of bitterness in his voice. "But he wouldn't listen to her. He wouldn't hear a word against Cesare; he'd trusted him and his advice all his life. My mother hadn't wanted me to go to that boarding school, either, but Cesare told my father that getting a good education in the States was important for my future as *capo* of the Carnevares. So that got me out of the way, and Cesare had only my mother to deal with."

As they walked she surreptitiously looked at him: his perfect profile, his supple way of walking. It reminded her of her dream, and this time she let herself enjoy the memory without feeling ashamed.

"In the end she must have withdrawn almost entirely to Isola Luna. She spent more and more time alone at the villa. Clearly my father didn't mind. She says in her notes that he told her she was out of her mind if she thought Cesare was a threat. He just refused to see it, the idiot! Didn't *want* to see what kind of game Cesare had been playing all those years."

"And finally she gave up?"

"No, she kept trying to convince him. In the end she had all the evidence she needed to expose Cesare. Evidence that not even my father could have ignored. Copies of secret agreements, even recorded conversations between Cesare and politicians in Rome and Brussels… In the notes she wrote not long before her death, she says she called my father and asked him to come out to the island to see her. In those last weeks she seems to have been afraid to leave Isola Luna herself. She barricaded herself in the villa – and he couldn't have cared less."

She touched his hand with her fingertips. "I'm sorry."

"But she also writes, on the very last page, that he did at least agree to come and look at what she had. My God, she was so proud of that. Thinking that he would finally have to believe her, that she hadn't gone to all that trouble for nothing…"

"But Cesare went out to the island instead of your father."

"She must have suspected something. She hid the important documents in her paintings, and left a few harmless papers in the safe for Cesare to find. But she didn't write anything else about that. Her last few sentences sound…" He swallowed. "They sound almost happy. She still loved my father, in spite of everything, and she writes about me… she writes…" He fell silent, and turned away for a moment. Rosa waited. She longed to put her arms around him and comfort him. But then she saw the line of black fur creeping up the back of his neck, and she hesitated.

A moment later he was in control of himself again. He gave her the ghost of a smile and took her hand to walk on.

The cloud moved past the sun, and sunlight flooded the dry landscape again. In the distance, the edge of the asphalt turned to a flicker of silver.

"I can't help it," he said, after a short silence. "I mean, sometimes the change just happens…"

She knew what he meant. At that moment it was all clear to her. There was something in his voice. And the feel of his hand. The little hairs she suddenly felt beneath her fingers.

She didn't look at him.

"It's not so bad," she said softly. "It's not bad at all."

He sounded different now, as if he were finding it difficult to get the words out. "It's not... not because of my mother," he said with difficulty. "Or Cesare..."

She looked straight ahead, couldn't bring herself to look at him. She didn't know just why. But she couldn't.

Not while it was happening.

"It's only because of *you*," he whispered hoarsely.

Then why, she wondered, numbed, isn't it happening to me? I feel just the same, damn it. Why don't I change?

His hand slipped out of hers. The fine hairs brushed her fingers once more. An affectionate caress, then they were gone.

The end of the road was coming closer, its shape forming in the bright, flickering light, against the blurred background of the ravine.

He stayed slightly behind her. There was a rustle of fabric as he stripped off his jeans and T-shirt before the change could wrench at the seams and fibres. She heard it, and still she didn't look. She kept walking.

A scraping noise, then the sound of paws on the asphalt. Stepping lightly, on all fours, speeding up, catching up, yet still a little way behind her, just far enough not to enter her field of vision. But she sensed him, heard him, even smelled him.

She reached the jagged end of the road, sat down, and swung her legs over the edge, looking into the depths below, trembling, her mind in turmoil.

Why not me? she wondered. Don't I feel enough? Do I *still* not like him enough?

Or was something else bothering him? Fear of something? His hatred of Cesare? Maybe a sense of guilt had brought on the change?

The paws were coming closer. Purring in her ears. The feel of his fur rubbing against her back, her upper arm. The hot animal smell, the wildness radiating from him. Sleek muscles under the pitch-black fur. An elegance that made her tremble.

He sat down beside her, very close, and leaned his beautiful panther head against her shoulder.

Night Ride

When she had taken the Maserati back to the garage, she went down to the front courtyard as if in a trance. The baroque facade of the palazzo was visible beyond the pine and chestnut trees: its tall windows, the gargoyles, the stucco overgrown with green moss.

The sound of an engine was coming up the drive, chugging through the olive groves below the property. It sounded like a lawn mower.

In fact it was a motor scooter, with Lilia riding it. She stopped the Vespa beside Rosa, right in front of the stone fountain, took off her helmet, and shook her dark red hair loose over her shoulders. It stood out like fire against her black leather jacket. Through the tumbling locks at the back of Lilia's neck, Rosa thought she caught a glimpse of a tattoo.

"*Ciao*," said Lilia, beaming.

"*Ciao*." Rosa tried to return the smile. She was feeling melancholy, and most of all confused. The smell of the warm panther fur was still with her.

Lilia frowned. "What is it?"

"I...oh, I only went for a drive. In the Maserati. Very exciting."

"I can imagine that. Any scratches or dents?"

Rosa shook her head.

"That was your father's car, did you know?"

She sighed softly. "I wasn't sure, no."

"Zoe told me. She sometimes drives it herself. Because you Americans can't cope with a manual gearshift."

"Does she know you're here?"

Lilia shook her head. "I was going to fetch her. Go for a ride together. We do that quite often, especially at twilight. Have you seen her Vespa?"

"There isn't one in the garage."

Lilia patted the broad saddle behind her. "Hop on and I'll show you."

Rosa climbed onto the scooter and held Lilia tightly around the waist. The next moment she was jerked backward as Lilia stepped on the gas too hard. Then she rode the Vespa out through the gate and into the inner courtyard of the palazzo. Once there she honked a few times, rode in a circle around the weed-grown flower bed in the middle, and finally stopped in front of a narrow door on the east side of the facade. A way into the cellars, maybe? Rosa hadn't explored the underground part of the palazzo yet.

Lilia was looking around impatiently. "Where is she?"

Rosa shrugged and dismounted. "No idea. She was up there this morning." She pointed to the second-floor window. "Maybe Florinda's back, putting Zoe through the wringer."

Lilia took out her cell phone. "Let's see."

Silence lay over the inner courtyard. No ringtone could be heard behind any of the windows. Lilia shook her head and put the phone away in her jacket pocket. "Only her voicemail."

"She must be out with Florinda."

Lilia kicked the support of the Vespa down and slipped off the saddle. She firmly pushed the old-fashioned bolt of the door aside and looked back once over her shoulder. "I'm just so jealous of this thing."

When she opened the door, Rosa saw that she had been wrong. There was no way down to the cellars behind it, only a dimly lit storeroom. Garden tools hung from hooks, or stood against the walls; the place smelled of earth and peat. When Lilia flipped a switch near the door, several lights came on. Something rustled in a corner, but whatever had made the sound was hidden behind an assortment of brooms and rakes.

Lilia pointed to a brightly polished motor scooter covered with transparent plastic film. She pulled this cover off to reveal a dream of a Vespa, all chrome and gold. The surfaces shone like mirrored glass. "Even the tuning cost a fortune!"

Rosa dutifully joined her. "Lovely," she said, without much interest.

"Don't be such a spoilsport! Sit on it."

Rosa shook her head. "No, thanks."

"Go on!"

"Zoe will kill me."

"Sure, but only if she knows." Lilia grinned. "And I don't know who's going to tell her."

Rosa sat on the soft saddle, placed one hand tentatively on the handlebars, and with the other traced the curve of a wing mirror. The key was in the ignition.

"Well?" asked Lilia. "What do you think?"

"What do I think about what?"

"Going for a little spin. Anyone can ride one of these. Even you."

She had once ridden an old motorcycle a few times around an outdoor basketball court in Brooklyn. The bike had belonged to a boy she hardly knew, but he loved to show it off. Rosa had managed better than expected, and finally he let her ride it once around the block. She brought it back again two hours later. The boy had been furious with her, but it had been worth it.

"Well?" said Lilia expectantly. "How about it?"

"I should at least ask Zoe."

"She'd say no."

Rosa raised one eyebrow. "That's meant to convince me?"

"We won't be out for more than an hour, maybe two. The landscape looks its best at sunset. I'll show you a couple of places that'll take your breath away."

Maybe a little risk was just what she needed now. Kind of like shoplifting. She smiled to herself. Why not?

Lilia was already outside, running to her own Vespa. Rosa started Zoe's scooter and followed her slowly out into the front courtyard. She glanced up at the windows once more, then rode around the bushes and weeds in the middle of the courtyard, trying the scooter out. It rode surprisingly well.

For the first time she felt at ease on her aunt's estate. Probably because she was about to leave it.

*

In the evening twilight, they rode along the winding highway 124 to Caltagirone. Rosa kept seeing feral dogs on the side of the road, and once, when she came around a bend, she avoided hitting one only by lurching to a stop as it casually trotted across the road ahead of her. She had already noticed the skinny dogs, often seen sniffing around the rubbish bins, from her drives in the area. She felt sorry for them, especially after seeing the first few lying dead by the roadside. It would have broken her heart to hit one herself. After that she drove more cautiously, and was on her guard every time she rounded a turn.

At first Lilia was challenging her to keep up, but when Rosa didn't go along with that idea, she rode ahead at a more leisurely pace. Halfway to Caltagirone, she turned right on a narrow road that wound its way north.

There were no houses here. Wild olive groves and cacti covered the hills. Darkness was rising like black mist from the valleys and the dried-up streambeds. Once, when the road forked, they passed a sign saying MIRABELLA 5, but Lilia turned right again. Rosa saw no more road signs for the next half hour.

She was riding without a helmet, and Lilia's own was dangling from her handlebars. The air was full of the fragrance of olive and lemon trees, and Rosa's long hair danced wildly over her shoulders. Once again she noticed the tattoo on the back of Lilia's neck, and she thought she could tell what it was: the head of a snake rising from the collar of her leather jacket and reaching up to her hair at the back of her head.

Rosa stepped on the gas for a moment, until she drew level with Lilia on her left. The headlights of any vehicle coming towards them in the dark would alert them to its approach from a long way off.

"What's that tattoo?" she called.

"I had it done in Gela, down on the south coast. Horrible town, but teeming with sailors."

"Sailors!"

Lilia laughed. "Not what you're thinking. Where there are sailors, you find the best tattoo studios… if those dirty holes can be called studios."

"Why a snake?"

"And no anchor?" Lilia's knowing smile was framed in her swirling red Medusa locks. "I know about it, Rosa. About the Alcantaras. And what you are."

Her glance told Rosa she didn't mean the Mafia. "Did Zoe tell you?"

"She kind of *had* to give some kind of explanation after I woke up in bed with a snake."

"Oh."

"Then Zoe hasn't told you?"

"I didn't know that you two were—"

"Florinda can't know. She'd be beside herself."

"Are you sure she hasn't guessed?"

"Guess that the heiress to the Alcantara fortune likes women? If she did, all hell would break loose." Lilia pushed her hair back from her face. "But you asked about the tattoo… I did it for Zoe. I'm not like you and her, but I… I *would* be if

I could, if you see what I mean." She laughed again, a little nervously this time. "If she were a vampire, I'd want her to bite me so that I could be like her. But it doesn't work that way with your kind. So I had that snake tattooed over half my body, to show her that I... oh, hell. Rosa, you know what I mean." She shrugged her shoulders. "Sentimental nonsense."

"No, not at all."

"If you say you think it's romantic, I'll force you off the road."

"But it is romantic."

With a grin, Lilia swerved and drove towards her. Rosa easily avoided the other scooter and sped up slightly, until she was driving in front of Lilia through the deepening twilight. The first stars showed faintly in the darkness, and now and then Rosa saw a bat fluttering over the steep, fissured rocks.

She was touched, although she had thought she was beyond that kind of emotion. *Sentimental nonsense*, sure – although not what Lilia had done, but Rosa's own guilt about it.

Lilia had gone to great lengths to show Zoe how much she loved her. Rosa herself had never considered tattoos proof of love, but the snake was more than a gesture, much more than a name inked on someone's upper arm. Lilia had tried to turn into a snake herself for Zoe's sake by the only means available to her, so wholehearted was her love. She had left a permanent symbol of her feelings on her skin, a proof of her love that Zoe would never have demanded, but had been given willingly.

Go ahead and cry, Rosa thought, furious with herself. But she smiled all the same as a single silly tear ran down her cheek, and she was glad that Lilia was behind her and couldn't see it. If she, Rosa, could change shape like the other Alcantaras, then why hadn't her stormy feelings when she was near Alessandro been enough to start the transformation? Instead, she had sat on the edge of the abyss in human form with him, feeling inadequate and terribly helpless.

Finally she had just got to her feet and driven away, leaving Alessandro behind at the end of the world, hoping he would understand and know what was troubling her.

"Rosa!"

Lilia's call brought her back to the present. Several headlights appeared behind them in the darkness, disappeared around a bend, and reemerged on the next straight stretch of the road. Four single lights – motorcycles, then. They were much faster than the Vespas, and they were steadily catching up.

She wasn't sure what warned her. The same strange, sinking feeling that Lilia obviously had, too.

"Do you know who they are?" called Rosa.

"No." Suddenly all trace of Lilia's carefree mood had gone.

"Suppose we simply let them pass us?"

Lilia shook her head. She accelerated and took the lead again. "Stay right behind me. And step on it."

Around the next bend, Lilia swerved onto an asphalt path just wide enough for a single car. It led up the mountainside, winding in hairpin turns. They left the olive trees behind; the macchia grew as high as a man on both sides of them.

The motorcycles roared as they overshot the place where

Lilia had turned off the road, then came back and followed the two girls up the mountain.

"Fuck, Lilia – who the hell are they?"

"Can't you guess?" The path was even steeper here, and Lilia had to look ahead. "They like to hunt in packs."

"Carnevares?"

The very next moment Tano caught up with them.

The Amphitheatre

He pulled up beside her on his motorcycle, leaning far forward and wearing black leather and a black helmet. When Tano turned his face to her, Rosa recognised him by his eyes.

She couldn't avoid him. There was nowhere to turn off the mountain path. The slope fell steeply to her right, and Tano kept pace with her on her left. His three companions were riding close behind her, all in dark leather, with their faces hidden under shiny helmets. Their bikes made a horrible noise as they revved the engines for fun.

Lilia was still ahead, going farther and farther up the mountain. She looked back over her shoulder several times, stone-faced. It would have been easy for the four Carnevares on their motorcycles to force the two Vespas off the trail and down the slope. But they weren't attacking the girls yet, just following them, and Tano's eyes showed Rosa that he was laughing behind the visor of his helmet, enjoying his power over her.

Rosa gripped the handlebars more firmly. Over and over again, in her nightmares, she had relived what might have been done to her after that party in the Village while she lay unconscious somewhere, to this day she had no idea just where. She had seen men's distorted faces in her mind's eye, she had felt their sweaty bodies, heard laughter and hoarse groaning.

Secretly, however, she thought it could have been quite different. Teenagers feeling bored after a party. Maybe a dare, or a gang initiation. And suddenly she didn't know which would be worse: these four Carnevares doing what the unknown strangers back in New York had done, or Tano tearing her to pieces with tiger claws.

He's trying to scare you, she thought. Just like that night in the forest. He wants to frighten you into getting out of Alessandro's life, that's all.

But then she saw his eyes again, with that greedy gleam in them, and she recognised it as the look of a wild beast who saw her only as his prey. They could have stopped here to get it over and done with. But Lilia was still riding on ahead, and Rosa herself wasn't ready to give in, however pointless her flight might be. She and Lilia hadn't the ghost of a chance, and every yard they rode only postponed the inevitable.

The trail forked again. To the left it led still higher up, and on the other side it ran in a wide curve that disappeared on the other side of the mountain. Lilia turned right, and Rosa followed. Behind her the others revved the engines of their motorcycles, but Tano wasn't bothering with their games. He stuck close beside her, and every time he glanced at her, his eyes were laughing: cold, silent, pitiless laughter.

Ahead loomed a high wall of rough-hewn sandstone. A single olive tree, hunched and twisted, stood in front of it.

They raced past the wall and the tree in a close-knit, noisy group, and found themselves in a wide, open space, a huge notch cut out of the mountain ridge. From up here, you could catch a swift glimpse of the moonlit landscape, and to Rosa's left, tiers of seats rose up the slope in a semicircle.

An ancient amphitheatre.

One of the many Greek ruins on Sicily, most of them now restored and open to visitors, but some, like this one, neglected and fallen into oblivion. Weeds grew on the tiered stone seats, as tall bushes swayed in the wind like expectant spectators.

Lilia raced to the bottom row of seats, where she braked sharply and started towards the tiers on foot. But one of the motorcycles accelerated, and the rider slammed on his own brakes, cutting her off as dust and pebbles sprayed up under his tyres. Lilia swore.

Rosa gritted her teeth, took a deep breath, ignored Tano – and stepping on the gas, she rode straight for the bike barring Lilia's way. She braked at the last moment, but the Vespa hit the motorcycle hard enough to knock it aside. The rider yelled inside his helmet as he fell under his heavy bike. Rosa was flung out of her own saddle, grazing her elbows as she fell, but got to her feet again at once.

Lilia took her chance and ran past the fallen motorbike, and then up the steps between the tiers. Rosa was going to follow, but Tano and one of the others had already caught up with her. The other boy barred her way, while Tano put down the kickstand of his bike and got off. He grabbed Rosa by the arm. He was still wearing his helmet, and so were the others.

"Leave her alone!" shouted Lilia, halfway up the auditorium, a small, dark figure among the rows of seats. The fourth rider had dismounted from his bike now, and began to follow Lilia, but Tano gestured to him to stay where he was.

"She's not important." He pushed up his visor, swung Rosa around by her arm, and sniffed the blood on her grazed elbow. "We have the Alcantara slut, that's enough."

Rosa kicked him as hard as she could between the legs. But he was too close, and her foot made contact mainly with his thigh. He staggered back a step anyway, swearing at the top of his voice and letting go of her. Rosa spun around and ran – only to collide with the second biker. He hit her in the chest and she stumbled back with a cry and was caught by the fourth man. His arms went around her torso, squeezing the air out of her. She tried to fight back, hitting the back of her head against his helmet, struggling and kicking as he held her in front of his knees, but she realised that she had lost. He was a head taller than she was, and a lot stronger, and his eyes and face were protected under his helmet. Panic tightened her throat, but she got herself under control enough to stay still and save her strength for a better opportunity.

Up among the tiers of seats in the empty amphitheatre, Lilia was shouting threats, but the men ignored her.

When Tano reentered Rosa's field of vision, he had taken off his helmet and leather jacket. The T-shirt he wore under it was drenched in sweat, and was the next item to land in the dust of the arena. His hands went to his fly next. In a matter of seconds he was undressed and standing before her in nothing but his shorts.

He was taller than Alessandro, and even fitter, with bulging muscles that shimmered in the light of the rising moon.

When she'd first met him at the baron's funeral, he had been wearing glasses. He had none on now; his cat's eyes saw better than the eyes of any ordinary human being. They glowed as yellow as amber. His hair had changed colour, too, and was lighter and coarser. Stripes of yellow, brown, and white downy fur were rising from his hips up his naked torso.

Rosa avoided his pitiless gaze and stared past him, over the arena, out into the dark landscape. Mountain ridges merged with the darkness in the east. Even more stars had appeared in the sky. Rosa began counting them.

There was an earsplitting explosion, followed by a rolling echo.

"Take your hands off her!" shouted Lilia. "I have a gun."

Tano's transformation was already too far along. The adrenaline pulsing through him drained the last vestiges of humanity from his body, as if his bones and muscles were changing shape. His torso fell forward, and he landed on all fours. When his paws met the ground his joints shifted, his limbs grew shorter, and fur covered the last bare patches of skin. His face was now a muzzle, and he had fangs and fiery eyes.

Lilia fired into the air for a second time, shouting a warning. Her voice sounded closer. She must have come part of the way down the steps.

Rosa's perception was clouded, as if someone were holding her head under water. Her body temperature had dropped, her sweat was cold as ice. Once again she felt that pulling and tugging sensation, and it wasn't because the two bikers were now holding her arms.

But something still prevented the snake from emerging. She couldn't do it deliberately. She felt numb. She was gripped with panic, fear that the same thing was happening all over again. Part of her recognised the situation as familiar, even though she had been unconscious that night in New York. She was alone and defenceless again, and there were men around her, ready to do whatever they liked to her.

The tiger prowled closer.

Suddenly her arms were free. The other two bikers had let go of her and retreated. Certainly not out of fear; they must have seen Tano's transformation many times before.

A third shot cracked through the amphitheatre like a whiplash.

Someone behind Rosa screamed. One of the men collapsed, hit by a bullet. His companion howled with rage and ran. Another dragged himself away, limping. He must be the one Rosa had ridden into on the Vespa. They were going to surround Lilia and capture her.

The tiger was licking his lips. A cruel growl rose from his throat as one of his paws ground the torn remnants of Tano's shorts into the dust.

Rosa shivered with cold and tried to begin her own change through willpower. But her panic still paralysed her, and obviously also the part of her that she didn't know, that was entirely new to her, although it had always been there.

Another shot. Another scream. Someone was running down the stone steps of the tiers, shouting.

The tiger roared furiously in the dark. Rosa smelled his

breath, not at all like the panther's, but hot as a jet of fire. Then she noticed something else.

The trail leading to the amphitheatre was suddenly bathed in glaring white light. The shadow of the distorted olive tree wandered over the ground, turned this way and that, and grew denser. Then car headlights came around the corner.

The tiger's head swung around.

He crouched to pounce.

This time the gunfire sounded so close to Rosa's ear that it deafened her for a second. In a flash of flame she saw Lilia, her eyes wide with fright, with a figure flinging itself on her from behind – and the tiger, half his skull torn away in an explosion of fur and blood.

Lilia screamed. So did the man throwing her to the ground.

Rosa, able to move again, staggered back.

The tiger – Tano – collapsed. The bullet had blown his forehead apart, destroying much of his face.

More headlights, their beams lighting up the ancient tiers of seats. Car doors were flung open. Men shouted in wild confusion.

But the loudest voice of all was Cesare Carnevare's, as he rushed forward out of the bright light and fell on his knees beside the tiger's body.

Lilia's little revolver was torn from her hands. It landed at Rosa's feet. She bent like a sleepwalker to pick it up.

Cesare howled, inwardly already more beast than man, and leaped over his dead son, his suit tearing apart as he sprang and fell on Lilia in the form of a gigantic lion.

A Vow

The lion threw Lilia to the ground and stood over her for an endless moment – then lowered his open jaws to her, bit, tugged, tore, raged.

Within seconds her body moved only when the lion dug his fangs into it and shook her lifeless limbs.

Rosa couldn't breathe as she watched what Cesare was doing to Lilia. Still holding the gun in her shaking hand, she stepped back, aimed it at the huge lion, and pulled the trigger. The bullet missed by more than a hand's breadth and fell in the dust beside him. Stumbling backward, Rosa stumbled over the body of the biker whom Lilia had shot, recovered her balance just in time, and pulled the trigger again. The gun clicked. Once, twice. The six bullets had already all been fired.

The next moment she was seized and swung around. A hard blow struck her arm, sending the revolver flying through the air. Someone came down heavily on her, while the agitated voices around her grew louder. Suddenly the arena was full of men in dark suits, shadowy figures hurrying around in the beam of headlights. Several vehicles were standing in a semicircle on the edge, their lights aimed towards the seats.

The lion was still raging. Rosa couldn't see Lilia any more. Her head was being pressed down to the ground, and the body of the dead biker mercifully spared her from the sight of what was happening. But she heard the sounds as Cesare savaged the body, and vomit shot up through her throat and out of her mouth. The man holding her head let go in disgust. She just barely managed to turn her face away.

Vaguely, she saw two men bending over the dead tiger. One of them was shaking his head. The animal was gradually returning to human form.

The man on top of her suddenly let out a scream. He was abruptly knocked aside as a fist struck his skull, and then his assailant kicked him hard in the ribs. There were yet more voices, more shouting; the whole arena was full of turmoil. All of a sudden she was free, as someone gripped her upper arm and helped her to her feet.

"Alessandro?" she managed to gasp.

He put an arm around her waist and pulled her firmly to his side. "Leave this to me."

Several men approached them menacingly. The guns they were holding were not aimed at Alessandro yet, but the expressions on the faces of Cesare's followers left no doubt that they were ready for anything, and just waiting for a chance. Other men, however, were now moving towards them with drawn pistols.

The lion paused in his fury, threw his head back, and uttered a terrifying roar. Blood gleamed on his muzzle and stuck his fur together, covering his face from the eyes all the way up to his mane.

"She broke the concordat," cried the man who was still kneeling over Tano's body, one hand going to the pistol in the shoulder holster he wore under his jacket.

"So she did," said someone else. To Rosa's horror, he was one of the men who had been protecting her and Alessandro from the others. He stared at her, then pointed to the revolver on the ground. "She fired a shot. An Alcantara has shed Carnevare blood."

That's not what happened! she wanted to cry. But what difference did it make in the end? Lilia had killed Tano to save her. Rosa might just as well have pulled the trigger herself.

The lion left the mutilated pile of Lilia's remains lying on the ground and turned to Rosa and Alessandro. Cesare's men made way as the huge cat stalked through the middle of the crowd, stopping not three metres away from the two of them.

Alessandro fixed his cold gaze on the lion. "Don't even think about it, Cesare. She didn't do it, you saw that as well as I did."

Rosa didn't know why he was here, or why they had all arrived so suddenly. She hurt all over; her bruises and abrasions from Isola Luna were aching again, and now she had new ones to join them.

The lion retreated, but Alessandro did not. He kept one arm around Rosa and gestured towards his followers with the other.

"Rosa Alcantara did *not* shoot him," he called to them.

"Protecting one of *them*, are you?" one of Cesare's men spat. "Your father would have killed you for that."

Alessandro glared angrily at him. "My father was your *capo* because he had strong nerves. He didn't let grief and anger lead him to do anything foolish. In a few weeks' time I'll be succeeding him. And I won't drag his reputation through the dirt by standing by to watch Cesare kill an innocent woman."

"He's right," said one of the men who had come with him. "I saw it myself. It was the other girl who fired the gun."

"I knew her." The man beside Tano's body spoke up. "She hung out with Zoe Alcantara all the time. She's one of them, so it makes no difference which of them pulled the trigger. The Alcantaras murdered Tano, that's what counts."

A terrible roar came from the lion's jaws, but now a cry of human rage was mingled with it. The beast's features were shifting, the proportions of his body changing, and slowly, with a crunching sound, he stood upright. His body was still densely covered with fur, and his mane was slow to change back.

Somewhere in the darkness, a suitcase snapped open, and a man hurried up to him with a snow-white bathrobe. Perhaps that was the most bizarre sight of all – the moment when Cesare Carnevare, stained red all over, had the white bathrobe thrown around him as if he had just climbed out of a bath full of blood.

Then Cesare pushed the man aside and came to within an arm's length of Rosa and Alessandro. His facial muscles were twitching. The blood covered his features like a samurai's war mask.

"The concordat is cancelled," he said, with some difficulty, as if his vocal cords had not yet fully returned to human form. "It has clearly been breached, and we may now strike back by every means available to us."

A horrifying suspicion surfaced in Rosa's mind. Had Cesare

allowed Tano to provoke her and Lilia into breaking the peace treaty? Had Cesare even *told* him to do it? Their meeting with Tano and the other three this evening couldn't possibly have been mere coincidence.

Alessandro gently pressed his fingers into her waist, sensing that she was about to say something. Maybe he was right, and she'd be better off keeping quiet.

Not that that was going to stop her.

"You planned this from the start!" she accused Cesare. "You *sacrificed* Tano to give yourself a reason to attack my family."

The blow came quick as lightning, but Alessandro was quicker. He caught Cesare's fist with one hand, still keeping a firm hold on Rosa, and at the same time pushed him away with all his might. Cesare swayed for a moment, took a step back to recover his balance, and opened his mouth in fury. It was the threatening roar of a beast not yet fully aware that he had returned to human form.

The men at Alessandro's side drew closer together. But Rosa saw doubt in the faces of some of the *soldati*. There were a number who questioned Alessandro's judgement, she suspected, however much they opposed Cesare's claim to leadership. Alessandro might well be gambling away all his chances of ever being accepted as his father's successor.

In that white bathrobe, Cesare was an incongruous sight among the men in dark suits toting guns. He had wiped his hands on the white towel, leaving bloodstains. For an endless moment, he looked at Alessandro and Rosa wordlessly, then turned slowly towards his son's dead body. He kept his back to them as he crouched down and gently stroked fur that was only gradually turning back into human skin.

"Come on," said Alessandro quietly to Rosa, "let's get out of here."

She was going to object, but then just pointed in the direction of Lilia's body, and let him lead her gently away and over to the cars. Several of the men covered them. Rosa could tell from their footsteps, though she didn't look back.

A cry of anguish broke from Cesare, echoing back from the stone tiers of the amphitheatre and down the valley, following Alessandro and Rosa as they reached a black Mercedes. Alessandro helped Rosa into the passenger seat, hurried around the car, and got into the driver's seat himself a minute before the chauffeur, who was about to get behind the wheel.

"I'll do this," he told the man briefly. "You go with one of the others. Tell them to give us two minutes' start, okay?"

Now Rosa did look back through the window, and saw the two groups facing each other, increasingly baffled, while Cesare crouched over Tano's body with his head bowed.

"What's going to happen now?" she whispered as Alessandro started the engine.

"I won't let anyone hurt you."

"What will *he* do?"

"Stir the others up against me. This is his opportunity to swing it his own way."

"Because you protected an Alcantara?"

He did not reply.

"I *would* have shot Tano," she said quietly. "And if that meant breaking the damn concordat – well, too bad."

Alessandro drove the car out of the amphitheatre and onto the narrow mountain track. "Tano got what he deserved. He was a bastard, and Cesare knew it. It wasn't a coincidence that we came here. Someone tipped Cesare off about Tano's plans. But you were wrong to accuse Cesare of planning the whole thing. He followed Tano to stop him."

"How about you?"

"I was afraid something like this would happen."

"If they don't accept you as their *capo* any more, then what?"

"We'll see when it gets to that point," he said. She saw black fur on the back of his hand on the wheel, but this time he had it under control. He was staring grimly through the windshield and out into the darkness. "No one will hurt you. I swear it."

Shaking, she reached over to touch his thigh. "How much time do we have?"

"What do you mean?"

"Cesare will take his chance. He'll send men after me at home… and after Zoe and Florinda, too. If there was ever a good time for him to eliminate the Alcantara family, then this is it, right?"

He still wasn't looking at her. "I can't take you home."

"What?"

"You're not safe there."

"I have to warn my sister!"

He took his cell phone out of his pocket. "Call her. Tell her whatever you like. But I'm not taking you there."

She leaned forward to look him in the face. "*Of course* you are."

"No."

She struggled to find words, and then all the anger she had been damming up for the last few minutes broke out. It made no difference that none of what had happened was his fault. Nor did the fact that he'd saved her, or what he had sacrificed to do it. He was a Carnevare. He was one of them. And he was preventing her from going to her sister's aid when Zoe needed her.

"The girl that Cesare killed," she snapped, "her name was Lilia. She… she loved my sister. Do you understand that? Zoe has just lost the person who probably meant more to her than anything else. And Lilia sacrificed herself *for me*. How can you think that—"

"I'd have done the same thing," he interrupted her calmly. "I'd have died for you up on that mountain."

That took her breath away. For a moment it deprived her not only of her self-control, but of the ability to utter another syllable.

After endless seconds, she stammered, "That – that's nonsense."

"It's the truth." He turned his head and looked at her. "I'm in love with you, Rosa."

She hesitated, fighting for composure.

"Oh, hell," she whispered.

He smiled sadly.

Then neither of them said anything, until finally she took his cell phone and called Zoe.

Iole

No one answered.

Rosa left Zoe a message and tried not to think of Lilia. She couldn't bring herself to tell her sister about her girlfriend's death over voicemail. Instead, she left a confused, breathless warning about the Carnevares, who would try to avenge Tano. She didn't say who had fired at him. After that she tried the landline in the palazzo several times, but there was no one there either.

Alessandro was looking straight ahead, biting his lower lip and driving the Mercedes through the night way too fast.

"No one's answering," she said at last. "We'll have to go there. The guards down at the gate have to be warned—"

"They've been waiting for years for our men to make the first move," said Alessandro. "They won't need any warning. They'll be prepared for something like this, that's their job." He sighed softly. "Aside from that, I hardly think Cesare will set out at once to—"

"But you saw him. Did it look to you like he was going to think the whole thing over calmly?"

"That's exactly what he'll do. For one thing, he's satisfied his thirst for blood for now. And he'll have to calm down – the men won't follow a raving lunatic, not in the long-term, and he knows it. The one advantage Tano's death gives him is that he can lay part of the blame on me. That's something he'll exploit."

She stared at him blankly. "But this isn't about you. He's killed Lilia, and he'll do the same to my sister and my aunt."

If her words hit a sore spot, he didn't show it. "Only when he's positive that the Carnevare clan is behind him. And when he feels sure the other dynasties also consider the concordat broken. Cesare will take care to get justification for his plans, or he could soon have *everyone* against him. So he'll summon a tribunal to decide the question."

"The question of my guilt, you mean," she said coolly.

"He'll make it seem as if you fired the shot."

As she stared at his hands on the wheel, with the downy black hairs that were thinning out faster and faster now, finally disappearing, she remembered that those hands were the first thing she'd noticed about him. The way his fingers tensed while the plane was landing.

Alessandro raced across an isolated crossroads. In this nocturnal no man's land there wasn't another vehicle anywhere in sight. "If he can stir up the men against me—"

"Stop that!" she spat. "If your claim to leadership is all that matters to you – well, you might as well let me out of the car right now."

This time she could see that she'd hurt him. "I'm not going to let Cesare take over as the new *capo* of the clan," he said quietly, without looking at her, but in a tone of dogged determination.

"Lilia is *dead*!" she said furiously. She didn't understand how that couldn't affect him.

"Like my mother."

She closed her eyes for a moment, but behind their lids she still saw the beam of the headlights probing the blackness ahead. When she opened them again, litter from the roadside was blowing past. An animal's dead body lay in the ditch, was lit up briefly by the car lights, and then faded like a spectre.

She pressed both hands to her face, let her head lean against the back of the seat, and tried to breathe regularly. In her therapy sessions she had learned breathing techniques to use in stressful situations, but they were no good at all here. The regular breathing turned to a sob, and she felt moisture trickling through her fingers. It was a little while before she realised that she was crying.

"Hey," said Alessandro gently. He took his foot off the gas for a moment and reached out his hand.

She flinched away. "I don't want you feeling sorry for me."

"Didn't you hear what I said back there?"

What could she say to that? Her knees felt shaky, and she had an urge to go and steal something.

Taking her hands away from her face, she pressed them down on her legs to keep them still, and hated herself because she felt her lower lip quivering. She couldn't come up with any answer, except a long look at him through her tears. In the icy blue of the dashboard lighting, he could have been a ghost.

"Where are you going?" she finally got out.

"Somewhere they won't look for you." He pointed ahead into the night. The peak of a mountain blotted out the stars. "I'm taking you to Iole."

*

She had guessed even before the castle on the peak came into sight. Castello Carnevare.

"He'll think you might be anywhere," said Alessandro, "but not right here under his nose."

At that moment she felt strangely indifferent to what might happen to her. As the Mercedes drove along the winding road up to the fortress, Alessandro looked down at the valley. "There they come."

She wiped her eyes, but still she saw flickering stars around the column of tiny pairs of lights far below on the plain.

Alessandro turned off the headlights and drove on with side-lights only. The darkness instantly moved to within a metre of the front of the car. "Don't worry, I can drive this road blind if I have to."

She doubted that, when he unexpectedly swung the wheel around and turned right off the road. But they drove halfway around the mountain on a bumpy gravel path, until they were at the back of the fortress. There he stopped and pointed to some narrow steps cut into the rock. "Can you make it up those in the dark?"

She nodded, bemused.

"It's not far. The steps lead to a small wooden door. It's one of the old escape routes from the castle. Wait there until I let you in from the inside, okay?"

She nodded again, but didn't get out.

"I have to get the car back to the castle courtyard before

the others arrive. They have to see me arriving on my own."

She pulled herself together and pushed the car door open. Alessandro took her arm. "Rosa…"

She turned hesitantly.

"I mean it. This is the worst possible time, I know, but…" He ran out of words, just cursed quietly and looked down.

"You meant it about being in love with me?" she asked.

"I meant it about being ready to die for you."

"You want to be *capo* of your clan," she reminded him, with a sad smile. "*That's* what you really want."

He looked downcast. "I can't let Cesare win, Rosa. He can't ever get what he tried to buy himself by murdering my mother."

"No one has to die for me," she said, slipping out of the car. The cool night wind caught her hair and swirled it around her face; she hoped it would blow a little sense into her fogged brain.

He said nothing for a moment. Then he asked, "You will wait up there, won't you?"

"Where else would I go?" She looked up at the rocks. She couldn't see the top of the steps from here; she would have to hurry, because her pursuers would soon reach the castle.

"Okay," he said, and straightened up behind the wheel again.

She closed the car door. Her eyes turned to the empty nocturnal landscape. Carnevare country.

She heard the gravel crunch under his tyres as he pulled quickly out on the narrow drive, to head back around the mountain and reconnect with the road. Only when his rear lights were out of sight did she turn around. She wiped her eyes and swept her hair back.

In the dark, she found the steps and began to climb.

*

She counted the stairs to reassure herself a little. At every other step she breathed in deeply, and then out again. Felt the air in her ribcage, concentrated on the cool of it in her lungs.

The door at the top of the steps was wide open. A single candle stood on the ground, flickering, casting light on part of the stone portal. Someone was sitting on the rock in front of it, wrapped in a blanket and looking at her.

"I knew you'd come," said Iole. "I knew it when I saw the lights. From the car. They weren't very bright. Not as bright as usual."

Rosa sniffed, wiped away the last of her tears, and crouched down in front of the girl. "A *candle*? Is that all the light he gave you?"

"Alessandro?" Iole grinned suddenly, and much too cheerfully for a night like this. "I found the candle for myself. Matches, too. I think it's much prettier than the torch."

Despite herself, Rosa had to smile. "You're not afraid of the dark, are you?"

"There aren't any animals here, like on the island," replied Iole, shrugging her shoulders. Her short black hair smelled as if it had just been washed with apple-scented shampoo.

She wore jeans and a turtleneck sweater much too large for her, with faded trainers. She was holding a can of soda.

"Is he going to hide you here, too?" she asked.

"Alessandro?" Rosa grinned, realising that she had given his name the same intonation as Iole had a moment ago. "Yes, I think so."

"He's gone to a lot of trouble. He's very nice."

"Sometimes."

"You like him."

Rosa pricked up her ears. "I do?"

"I knew that right away. Even on the island when you both came there. Before they took me away."

"Where did they take you?" Maybe it was a good idea to change the subject.

"To a farmhouse not too far away from here. Alessandro got me out and brought me here. He says the others are looking for me." Her voice sank conspiratorially. "I'm sure he wouldn't like me to be sitting out here on my own."

"You're not on your own now."

"That's right."

At fifteen, Iole was only two years younger, but Rosa felt as if she were speaking to a small child.

"Is he coming?" asked Iole.

"In a few minutes."

"The other men mustn't know we're up here."

"It's better if they don't."

"But sooner or later they'll find us." Iole's tone was so matter-of-fact that it gave Rosa goosebumps. "Sooner or later they always find you. Alessandro says not this time, but I know better. I've had to hide from them before."

"All that will be over soon."

"Is that another promise?"

Rosa felt everything inside her tighten up. "Another promise that I won't be able to keep, you mean?"

Iole shrugged. "Alessandro told me you both came back to the island to fetch me."

Rosa nodded. Images came back to her of the empty villa, with the doors taken off their hinges, and the big cats fighting each other. She tried to put them out of her mind, but it was no good.

"The animals were there. I warned you about them."

"Yes, it was stupid of us not to listen to you."

"But you came back because of me." It wasn't a question. Iole smiled, and looked past Rosa at the night sky, lost in thought. "You two like each other, and you came back because of me. That's nice." She crossed her arms and rubbed her shoulders, shivering. "That's very, very nice."

On the Sea Floor

Half an hour later the three of them entered Iole's hiding place in the castle cellar. It was a small apartment with no windows, but it was clean and well lit, and furnished like a hotel bedroom, if a rather shabby one. The open door to the bathroom gave Rosa a glimpse of grey marble with silver fittings.

Two closed-circuit cameras hung from the ceiling. Their cables had been cut.

"What are those for?" asked Rosa.

"Sometimes family members have to disappear for a while, to keep out of the way of the police," said Alessandro. "Coming from the castle, you go through two secret doors to get here. It's been a long time since this room was last used. I think the Hungry Man once hid here, years ago. It must have been just before his arrest."

"They arrested him here, in the castle?"

He shook his head. "In Gela, as far as I know. But this was one of his last hiding places."

"Then he was close to your family?"

"To him, they were what the Alcantaras are to Salvatore Pantaleone now." He looked unhappy about this answer.

She worked it out. "So that's why Cesare hates us. Because the Alcantaras took your family's special status as the closest allies of the *capo dei capi* – snapped it up from under their noses."

"That wasn't the only reason."

She waited, but he offered no more explanation.

"If you Carnevares knew him so well, why are you as frightened of him as everyone else?" she asked at last.

"Because he blames us for his arrest. He thinks a Carnevare turned him in." Alessandro grimaced. "If he really does come back, and if his supporters among the clans are still loyal to him, we'll have a problem. Another one."

Bouncing a little, Iole sat down on her bed, drew her knees up, and clasped her arms around her legs. "Mine!" she announced, as if someone had questioned it. It didn't seem to trouble her that she had only exchanged one prison for another.

Alessandro saw Rosa's expression, and lowered his voice. "I wanted to get her out of here, but I didn't know where to take her. She has one last surviving relative, and if I can find out where he is, I can get her to him. Until then she'll have to stay here."

"What about the police? Couldn't they help her?"

"Cesare would find out about it. He pays hush money to police officers all over the island. And he wouldn't let Iole go running around free, talking to judges and state prosecutors. Right now he thinks she just got away without help from anyone else. His people are still looking for her in the Madonie Mountains. They kept her hidden in a hut up there after they took her off the island."

"And you got her out?"

Iole spoke first. "All by himself. It was very brave of him."

Rosa put her head on one side and scrutinised Alessandro. "Yes, it really was."

He avoided her eyes and closed the apartment door. "I cut the cables of the cameras to be safe, but no one's going to notice. It's been so long since there was someone hiding here, it's unlikely anyone would think to check up on the place now, of all times."

Rosa fidgeted uncomfortably. "I know you mean well… but I can't stay here. I'll go out of my mind if I don't hear from Zoe soon."

"There's no cell signal down here," he said regretfully. "We're deep in the rock, and even on the upper floors the castle walls are almost a metre thick."

"Wonderful."

"I'll try to reach Zoe," he promised. "At least stay until I know what Cesare is planning. He'll be in a hurry to summon the tribunal. Just now, when he and the others arrived, he simply stormed past me, didn't even ask where I'd taken you."

She wrinkled her nose. "Maybe he was tired of walking around in public in a bathrobe."

The corners of Alessandro's mouth twitched. "That's always possible."

As she was wondering about her best course of action, her eyes fell on a framed photograph on the table next to Iole's bed. There was a crack across the glass. When she went over to look, Iole snatched up the photo and clutched it to her breast.

"It's okay, I don't want to take it away from you," said Rosa.

Iole nodded sheepishly, but she still held the picture close.

"Are those your parents?" asked Rosa. She had seen only two outlines against a blue background.

"My father and my uncle Augusto."

"He's the one who helped a judge, isn't he? A woman judge."

Iole nodded.

Rosa sat down on the bed beside her and looked at Alessandro, who was standing there rather awkwardly with his hands in his pockets. "Is that the family member you're trying to find?" she asked reproachfully. "A man protected by the police as a witness? Living under a false name goodness only knows where in the world?"

"It won't be easy," he admitted.

"So is Iole just supposed to stay here until you find him?"

"Can you think of a better solution? I know it's not ideal. But we can't bring the police in."

"Because Iole would give evidence against your family?" Rosa's eyes narrowed. "And because that would endanger your inheritance? Shit, Alessandro, this is more important than—"

"If Iole gives evidence," he interrupted, "Cesare will find a way to kill her. Even if he goes to prison, he'll hire a hit man to do it. Is that what you want?"

Rosa took a deep breath. She was torn between her suspicion and the feeling that what he said made sense. She turned to Iole again. "May I see it?"

Hesitantly, the girl held the photo out to her.

"Thanks." Rosa took it carefully and pointed to the man on the left. "Is that your father?"

"He's the other one."

"Ruggero Dallamano," said Alessandro, who had come over to them and was crouching down in front of the bed. "The *capo* of Syracuse. He… died a few years ago."

"Your family killed him," said Iole, in such a matter-of-fact tone that a cold shudder ran down Rosa's back.

The men in the photograph were wearing diving suits and gleaming with moisture. The open sea lay in the background. They were probably standing by the rail of a ship, but she couldn't tell for certain; the photograph showed only their heads and shoulders. Ruggero Dallamano had taken off his diving mask and was laughing cheerfully. His brother Augusto, the informer, was removing the mouthpiece of his oxygen supply with one hand, so that the lower half of his face was covered. However, behind the diving mask his eyes showed that he was laughing too. The hood of his neoprene suit covered his head, and his brother's hair was also hidden. The photograph must have been taken just after the two of them climbed back onboard. Their oxygen cylinders were still strapped to their backs.

"If all the pictures of your uncle show so little of him, it shouldn't have been too difficult for him to disappear," said Rosa sceptically.

"There were better ones," said Iole. "But I didn't take this photo with me because of Uncle Augusto, I took it because my father looks so happy in it. He wasn't often happy. He didn't laugh much. Only in this picture." She ran her fingertips over it; her voice sinking to a whisper. "Only in this one."

Rosa blinked slightly as if it would help her to make out more of the man with the diving mask. "Did they go diving together a lot?" She was asking only to delay the moment when she would have to turn to Alessandro again and broach the subject of what she was going to do now. Or what he was going to do now, if he had his way.

"That was their profession, diving," said Iole.

Rosa wrinkled her brow. "Really?"

"The Dallamanos owned the biggest specialist construction company in Italy for building structures in and under the water," Alessandro told her. "They didn't often go diving themselves, but they knew their way around the sea. From harbour complexes to bridges to drilling rigs in the Atlantic, they built all kinds of things, of course with—"

"State subsidies," she finished the sentence for him.

He nodded. "In the end, none of the projects could be finished without them. But it's said there were attempts to break their monopoly."

"Your family did a good job with that, then," she said dryly.

He didn't take her bait. "Their firms were dissolved. None of the other *capi* bothered with them because... because of the informer. I think the Japanese took over a good deal of the Dallamano technology. The rest... who knows?"

Rosa was about to give the picture back to Iole when she noticed something. "What's that?" She pointed to a narrow strip at the left-hand edge of the photo, which had slipped a fraction of an inch in its frame. There was something else behind it.

"Another picture," said Iole.

"Does it give a better view of your uncle? Maybe it would help Alessandro" – Rosa gave him a meaningful look – "to track Augusto down."

He made a face, as if to say *Don't start that again*, which she rather liked. She preferred it when he went on the attack, rather than expressing doubt. Defensiveness didn't suit him.

She quickly turned back to the photo frame.

"There's nothing interesting in the other picture," said Iole. "Who's it of?"

"No one. Only an old stone statue."

Alessandro crossed his arms and raised a sceptical eyebrow. Rosa noticed out of the corner of her eye that he was looking at her, not the picture.

"May I see it?" she asked Iole.

The girl nodded, took the frame from her, and undid the back of it. Sure enough, there was a second photograph behind the first. Iole couldn't get hold of the thin edge properly with her bitten fingernails, and Rosa's own were not in much better shape. Alessandro leaned over them and removed the photo with thumb and forefinger. His green eyes darkened as he turned it over.

"What is it?" she asked.

He took a step back and tilted the picture slightly under a ceiling light.

"Alessandro?"

Iole was talking faster, breathlessly. "I thought it was pretty, so I took it. It was with lots of others on my father's desk, and when Cesare's men came I grabbed the framed picture of Papa and this other one. But they didn't notice, and I hid it. Later, when no one was watching, I put it in the back of the frame."

She would have gone on chattering if Alessandro hadn't been looking at her with such concern. Rosa jumped up and went over to him. She took the photo carefully and turned it so that she could see it too.

It did indeed show a statue, just as Iole had said. A figure carved from some kind of porous stone, lit by the beam of a torch, showing it against a bleak underwater scene. Swarms of particles were drifting through the image, and a silvery fish swam at the edge. In the background, the indistinct outlines of angular shapes were visible. They might have been rocks, or ruins on the sea floor. All that could be seen clearly was the brightly lit statue.

It was of a big cat standing on its hind legs as if ready to spring. The scaly body of a snake, as broad as the muscular throat of the feline, wound around it in a spiral. The panther – for it was obviously a panther, not a tiger or a lion – had its mouth closed and was staring as if spellbound at the head of the snake just in front of its own. The big cat and the reptile were looking into each other's eyes, but neither of them seemed aggressive. The scene that, at first sight, had looked like the depiction of a fight, turned out to be something quite different when you examined it more closely. The two animals were observing each other, silently communicating. Even the way the snake twined around the body of the big cat didn't look like a stranglehold.

"Are they *embracing*?" whispered Alessandro.

Rosa's pulse raced and pounded in her temples. The hammering noise grew louder and louder, but it was a moment or so before she noticed that the others could hear it as well.

Only it wasn't coming from her.

Someone was knocking on the door.

TABULA

"**O**pen up, Alessandro!" Cesare's voice came through the door, muted by its thickness but as commanding as ever. "I know you're in there." And after a moment he added, "All three of you."

Alessandro spun around, dropping the photo. Rosa slipped it into her jeans pocket. Iole, on the bed, moved back until she was up against the wall, clutching her father's picture.

Alessandro exchanged an anxious look with Rosa.

"Someone's given you away," she said quietly. "Looks like they're all on his side now."

His cheek muscles were twitching with anger. He strode quickly over to the door. "This is still my house, Cesare."

"The men have decided against you. Taking the little Alcantara witch under your wing was a mistake."

"Tano would be touched to know how long you spent mourning him."

For a moment there was silence, then Cesare's fist struck the door. "You're hiding an enemy of your clan here, boy!"

"She's not to blame for Tano's death. You know that as well as I do."

"That's for the tribunal to decide."

Rosa touched Alessandro's shoulder. She lowered her voice to a whisper. "This tribunal… will it listen to what I have to say?"

"Cesare will muster a dozen witnesses to swear on their mothers' lives that you're responsible for the death of Tano. And the worst thing is, they'll start to believe it themselves. In the end it'll make no difference who pulled the trigger."

There was more knocking, then the sound of several men's voices on the other side of the entrance.

"Do I really have to break this door down?" asked Cesare. "If you want to save face, don't skulk in there like a coward."

Rosa made the decision for Alessandro. Her hand went out to the key in the lock. She turned it and opened the door.

Cesare was accompanied by five of his men. Rosa recognised their faces; they had all been on his side in the amphitheatre.

He wore a silver-grey designer suit with a handkerchief in his breast pocket. His hair was still wet, and the blood was gone from his face. Only under his left eye did she detect a dark mark that didn't belong there, not much larger than the head of a pin. A splash of dried blood, a tiny reminder of Lilia. Her stomach muscles tightened.

"We can settle the whole thing like civilised people," he said. From a man who had killed a woman in a frenzied rage only two hours before, this astonished her. "Or then again, maybe not."

Alessandro was about to step in front of Rosa to shield her, but she moved to stand beside him. Together, they blocked the doorway. Behind them, Iole started crying quietly.

"Never mind the big talk," said Alessandro. "Just tell me what you really want."

"Me," said Rosa. "That's obvious."

The corners of Cesare's mouth moved, but he didn't actually smile. "What would I do with you, Rosa Alcantara? The tribunal of the dynasties will decide your fate." He pointed to the hallway behind him. "You can go. Once you're sentenced, we can find you anywhere, so don't bother trying to hide. Until then, however, no Carnevare will hurt a hair on your head."

She glanced quickly at Alessandro.

"I've promised the men a hunt," Cesare went on, "and a hunt they'll have. Chasing a quarry that many of them have wanted for some time."

Iole's sobs were loud and desperate now.

"You can't allow this!" cried Rosa, looking at Alessandro.

At the same moment, the five men made their way past Cesare. Four of them moved to seize Rosa and Alessandro, while the fifth crossed the room to Iole.

Rosa screamed with rage. She hit one of the men in the face and kicked the other man's knee. The pain made neither of them handle her any more gently.

Alessandro's opponents, larger and stronger than he was, had overpowered him, too. Rosa was hauled away from the door and Alessandro. Cesare didn't even look at her. He was staring expressionlessly at the bed.

Iole was pressed back against the wall, knees drawn up, holding the photograph of her father to her with both hands. Tears were pouring down her face.

The strange sensation of cold that Rosa had felt a couple

of times before was rising up her body. It affected her calves, her thighs, spread through her lower body. Suddenly she was aware of every square inch of clothing on her skin. The fabric scratched and itched; she wanted to be rid of it. Her eyes met Alessandro's, the eyes of the wild beast that, if that shadowy black fur went on growing over his body, would break out of him at any moment now.

Suddenly she felt a prick on her throat, not even especially painful, and saw that a needle had also been inserted into the muscles at the back of Alessandro's neck. She had no idea what was in it – only that the substance immediately spread through her, dispelling the cold.

"It will last about fifteen minutes," said Cesare. "Until then you'll stay as you are."

Alessandro's transformation had also been stopped in its tracks, but he still struggled like a captive animal as the two men held him in an iron grip. The fifth man picked Iole up, pulled the framed photograph out of her hands, and threw it carelessly aside. The glass shattered on the floor. Iole cried out, but she couldn't fight the man off. He hauled her away from the bed and dragged her past Rosa and Alessandro to the door. Cesare stood aside to let the two of them pass, watched for a moment as they went down the hallway, then turned back to Alessandro.

"You know the tradition," he said. "A hunt in honour of the new *capo*. The men expect it."

"You can't just kill her," cried Rosa.

"We can do much more than that, as your own family will

soon find out. And then word will get around about what it means to sell yourself to TABULA."

"Leave her out of this!" hissed Alessandro. A fist punched him in the face, and he almost collapsed. Rosa flinched as if the blow had struck her instead. But Cesare's baffling words had hit home.

"What do you mean?" she asked.

"Don't play the innocent little lamb with me."

"Let Iole go, and I'll do anything you want."

Alessandro groaned. "She doesn't know," he gasped.

"You didn't tell her?"

Alessandro was silent.

Cesare turned to Rosa. "Didn't he tell you about it?" He gave a snort of derision. "You really have no idea what your family did? What kind of allies they've made? Who they're in league with, against their own kind?"

Rosa spat at him. The saliva hit his cheek, but it only made her feel even more helpless.

Cesare wiped it away with the sleeve of his jacket, shaking his head. "You think I'm doing this just because I want power, don't you? You're wrong. *That* is not why Tano died."

"Tano died", she cried, "because he was a bastard who got what he deserved." Tactically unwise, but it came from the heart.

Cesare's glare became several degrees colder, increasing her fury. "I assume", he said, "that someone has at least told you about the dynasties. You must surely know something about that."

"Leave her alone, Cesare," groaned Alessandro. He could hardly breathe; one of his two guards had put an arm around his neck from behind to keep him under control more easily.

"TABULA," repeated Cesare. "Does that mean anything to you?"

She stared at him without replying.

He sighed. "You tell her, then," he told Alessandro.

"There's an organisation," Alessandro said after a moment's hesitation, "an international group that takes an interest in the Arcadian dynasties. It's known as TABULA to its members. No one seems to know anything definite about them. They play many different parts, pretending that they're employees of governmental authorities, or politicians, or public prosecutors."

Rosa was listening, but she had difficulty concentrating on his words.

"TABULA has been trying to find out more about the Arcadian dynasties for years," Alessandro went on. "At first everyone believed it just had to do with the clans' business activities – the usual anti-Mafia campaigning. But for some time now there have been rumours that one of the dynasties based in Sicily is working with these people, feeding them information."

"Why would anyone do that?" Rosa's voice was husky.

"Promises. Money, power, that sort of thing."

Cesare spoke again. "It's no rumour. One of the clans is certainly working with them. *Your* clan, Rosa. The Alcantaras are traitors. They've sold themselves to TABULA."

"That's only what he suspects," Alessandro put in. "He has no evidence."

"I won't need evidence once sentence has been passed on the Alcantaras," said Cesare. "The problem will solve itself then."

"Tano's death must have been very convenient for you," said Rosa.

Cesare took a quick step towards her. In the downlighting from the ceiling, his eyes glowed like a cat's. "Tano was my son," he cried, only centimetres in front of her face. "And someone has already died for what was done to him. Others will follow. None of you Alcantaras will be left, none of those who were loyal to you. You'll pay for his death and your treachery. There's nothing more valuable than the camouflage under which the dynasties have existed for centuries, and I will not allow anyone to endanger it. I maintain the tradition. I preserve our security. And I will punish anyone who breaks the Arcadian laws!"

He fell abruptly silent. A vein was pulsing at his temple, and his features were shaking, but he got himself under control again. Finally, almost casually, he took his cell phone out of his jacket pocket, typed something on the shining surface, and held it in front of Rosa's face.

"Look at that," he ordered.

On the tiny screen, no bigger than a pack of cigarettes, a video appeared. The camera, swaying, moved past bars and out into a corridor, passing rows of cages stacked on top of one another. Heavy breathing could be heard over the camcorder's loudspeaker, along with background animal sounds of many kinds: spitting, growling, hissing. Whoever was filming seemed to have been in a state of panic, afraid of being discovered.

Animals crouched or huddled in the cages. In the dim light, Rosa saw several big cats. An unusually large fox. A gigantic bird, taller than a heron or a stork. A monitor lizard darting its tongue in and out. A couple of wolfhounds and a hyena. Then the camera passed a trembling creature that Rosa couldn't see properly in the dim light, but it seemed to have too many legs to be a mammal. Shortly after, the screen showed tigers and lions again, a wild boar with curving tusks, a man-size rat with a shaggy coat. They were all shut up in the endless rows of cages, looking undernourished and half-crazed with fear. Some appeared to have mutilated themselves.

"TABULA," whispered Cesare, as if the word filled him with unspeakable horror. "And that's only a part of what they do. That's why I hate the Alcantaras so much. And why you will all soon die. But until then," he added, breathing out sharply, "until then do as you like."

He slipped the cell phone back into his pocket, cast a last glance at Alessandro, shaking his head, and left the room. He walked slowly, shoulders bowed, as if in spite of everything he had suffered a defeat.

"Keep them down here for a few more hours," he called back to his men, "until you're sure they've calmed down. And then you can let them go. We'll be able to find them as soon as the tribunal has passed judgement."

Allies

Rosa put the cell phone down. Outside the car windows, the landscape of Sicily was racing past in the light of dawn.

"Who were you calling?" Alessandro gripped the wheel of the black Mercedes very firmly. At this speed, a moment's lapse in attention could kill them both.

Rosa deleted the last number in the menu and put his cell phone into the glove compartment. "Can you take me to Catania?"

"I thought you wanted to go home."

"Change of plans."

"Rosa – who was that on the phone?"

She didn't reply. There was a good reason for her silence. Several, in fact.

"You still don't trust me," he commented.

She looked straight ahead, through the windshield, at the flame-red sky above the road. "No one ever said anything about a hunt. And why didn't you tell me my family were working with this – this TABULA, and—"

"Cesare is convinced they are," he interrupted her. "I'm not. Oh, damn it, Rosa… I know almost nothing about TABULA. Who these people are, what they want… no one knows, and that includes Cesare. They capture Arcadians and keep them in cages. Obviously they have some way of keeping us in animal form. They carry out experiments, or so people say, but whether that's all—"

"What was that stuff that Cesare's men injected us with?" She clenched her fists and added, icily, "Forgive me, but I'm just a teensy bit sensitive about injections that I didn't ask for."

"Only a tranquiliser. The prescription is as old as the hills, said to date from classical times… but I don't know if it's true. Maybe that's just talk, too. I've even injected myself with it. As long as you don't overdo it, it doesn't do any harm."

"Says who?"

He glanced sideways at her. "All we know about ourselves and our kind is what we've been told. Traditions are passed on through stories. If we started questioning them, we'd have to doubt everything."

"You already do. That story about King Lycaon being punished by Zeus… you said you didn't believe it."

"It's a myth. Probably. But I've used that drug on myself, more than once. It stops the transformation for fifteen or twenty minutes. I even had a couple of doses with me in the States."

Resigned, she shook her head. "And what about Iole? When he mentioned a hunt, did he really mean—"

"Yes."

"And you didn't see fit to mention this to me?"

He angrily stepped on the gas. "What do you think I should have said? 'Oh, and by the way, when a new *capo* takes over as head of the family, tradition says we spend a night hunting human beings'?"

Speechless, she stared at him.

"As it happens, I wouldn't have had to do it myself," he went on, "because I'm my father's heir. If a *capo* dies and is succeeded by his son, there's mourning and not a celebration. But if someone else, someone who isn't a direct heir, takes over as boss, then that's a victory guaranteeing him and his supporters prosperity for many generations – and *that* is something to celebrate."

"And this celebration," she said tonelessly, "means that the Carnevares go hunting human beings? Hunting and killing a fifteen-year-old girl who's been through more than we can even imagine? Is that what your family calls a *celebration*, for God's sake?"

"I didn't make the rules."

"But you don't question them." She gave an angry snort. "And you accuse me of not trusting you!"

His knuckles on the wheel were white; blue veins showed on the backs of his hands. "I've always told you the truth about everything."

"But this is about what you didn't tell me," she replied forcefully. Then, after a moment, she asked, "How much time do we have left?"

"There'll be an election. The highest-ranking members of the clan will gather to vote. Then, afterward, there'll be a ceremony in which Cesare takes his oath as the new *capo*. All that will take a little time, particularly if he wants to convince the tribunal first that you're to blame for Tano's death."

"When will they kill Iole?"

"The hunt comes right after the swearing in of the *capo*. In two days' time, I should think."

"Not any sooner?"

He brought his hand down on the wheel so hard that the car swerved. "How the hell can I know for sure?" They were both ashen-faced as he got the Mercedes back under control. More quietly, he added, "I don't think he can manage to discredit me with all the others any earlier."

"Discredit you because you protected me?"

He nodded. "Iole ought to be safe until then."

"And you have no idea where they'll take her?"

He shook his head. "Cesare's obviously hunted humans on Isola Luna before. That's why the animals were kept there – he used to enjoy hunting side by side with real lions and tigers."

Rosa uttered a sound of disgust. "So maybe he'll decide to go there again."

"I don't think so. The *capi* of other clans are usually invited to a swearing-in ceremony, and they all distrust one another so much, they'd never follow someone like Cesare to a remote offshore island. No, I think he's picked somewhere on Sicily. I just have to find out where. If I know where the hunt's going to take place, I can try getting Iole out."

"By yourself?"

"It's enough for one of us to risk life and limb."

"We need help."

"From the other clans? Forget it."

"That's not what I meant."

"Who from, then? Your aunt?"

She shook her head. She didn't even know where Florinda was. And Zoe? It was best not to think about it. She could cope well enough with the risk, not nearly so well with anxiety.

"Well?" he asked.

The road ahead led straight into the sunrise.

"Take me to Catania," she said again.

An hour later they left the expressway and were racing through ugly industrial estates to the city centre, when Alessandro noticed that they were being followed. Rosa was as unsurprised as he was. Cesare had let them go – probably to avoid any eventual accusations that he had anticipated the decision of the Arcadian tribunal – but he was no fool. He had clearly told his people to put her and Alessandro under surveillance.

But it took Alessandro less than ten minutes to shake off the other car in the dense rush-hour traffic.

"Where did you learn to do that?" she asked.

"Manhattan. I used to drive down to the city from the Hudson Valley, with a couple of other guys." He didn't have to say just what kind of pursuer he had shaken off in the chaotic traffic of the streets of New York. She was sure that he, too, had had plenty of experience with police questioning.

"You made it look easy," she commented as he glanced in the rearview mirror again, and she saw his frown clear.

"That wasn't all."

"You mean there are more of them after us?"

He shook his head. "I'll bet this car is crammed to the roof with tracking devices."

"Wonderful."

"Not to mention it's probably bugged."

"They're listening in on us?"

"No." He fished his key ring out of his pocket with his right hand. It clinked as he waved it in the air. Among the dangling keys, there was a small silver rectangle. In other circumstances she would have thought it was a lucky charm, or maybe a memory stick.

"Is that a jammer?"

He nodded.

"Where did you get that, Mr Bond? From Q?"

"From eBay." His smile was almost cheerful. "All they can hear is distorted noise and static."

She pointed to his pockets. "Any more secret weapons I ought to know about in there?"

He smiled. "Just tell me where we're going."

She gave him the name of the street, but not the number of the building. "Drop me somewhere near there. I'll go the rest of the way on my own."

"What are you planning?"

"The less you know, the b—"

He rolled his eyes. "Oh, come on, Rosa."

"It's enough for one of us… and so on."

He looked at her in annoyance and programmed the

GPS with one hand. "You don't trust me an inch – but you want me to trust you."

"That's because I'm honest."

She avoided his eyes when the light turned red, and he stopped and looked at her. "Once again: I didn't lie to you. I truly thought Iole would be safe there. How could I have guessed that—"

"Green."

He sighed, and drove on. "I'll find out where they've taken her. Cesare won't pick a place he doesn't know. If he's really going to invite other *capi* to join in, he'll want to play it safe. He has to know his way around wherever she is."

Now they were driving down the winding streets of the city centre, past little supermarkets, with wooden pallets outside stacked high with condensation-covered bottles of water. Past pharmacies with barred windows. Past teens on motor scooters. Past bars with the inevitable old men sitting on plastic chairs outside their doors.

The woman's voice on the GPS announced that they had now reached their destination. Rosa pointed to a street sign high on the corner of a building, among a tangle of power and telephone lines that ran together up there.

"I'll get out here," she said.

Reluctantly, he pulled over by the sidewalk. His eyes scanned the facades in vain for some kind of clue. "Are you quite sure? First you were dead set on going to your family, then you changed your mind. What suddenly seemed so important?"

"We need someone to help us. Not just because of Iole, also because of Zoe and Florinda. You know as well as I do that Cesare will never leave us in peace, whatever that tribunal decides."

He scrutinised her, and she realised that he guessed her plan, had maybe guessed it all along. "If this is what I'm afraid it is, then you're on the verge of doing something massively stupid."

"Better stupid than dead." She opened the car door and swung one leg out. Her metal-studded boot crunched a piece of broken glass.

"I'm coming with you," he said.

"No. If you do that, you'll lose the rest of your supporters."

"You think that would change anything? Maybe it's better if I look after you."

"It's *important* for me to go alone. Trust me."

He said nothing, but returned her look with anxiety in his eyes.

"This photo," she said. "You want to know what it's all about, too. Where it was taken."

"You really think that's the key?"

Rosa took the picture out of her pocket. "Maybe this is proof that our families didn't always hate each other."

"It's only a statue, Rosa. Some ancient artefact down on the sea floor." But his expression said something else. He seemed uneasy and at the same time hopeful, as if the picture of the panther and the snake had touched him, too, far more than he wanted to admit. "We don't even know how old it is. Or where the Dallamanos took the photo."

"That's exactly what I want to find out." She put it away again, trying to summon up a smile, but unsuccessfully. "I'll call you when I'm through here."

His gaze lingered on her. "Promise?"

She nodded, and was going to get out, but then thought better of it. Her eyes were burning. Her heart was beating much too fast. She brought her leg back into the car, took his face between her hands, and kissed him hard. His arm came around her waist.

When she took her lips off his, he was smiling with a bitter-sweet determination that almost made her waver in her own decision.

"Okay," she said, briefly returning his smile. "I have to get going now."

"No, you don't."

"Yes, I do." With a lump in her throat, she moved out of his embrace and slid into the open air. On the sidewalk, she bent down to him once again. "See you soon," she said.

"Take care of yourself."

"You too."

He shifted the car into gear, but never took his eyes off her. Rosa closed the door, stepped back, and collided with an overflowing rubbish bin. When she turned to look at the street again, the Mercedes had already threaded its way into the traffic.

She took a deep breath, got her bearings from the nearest building number, and started walking.

The lookout man was leaning with his arms crossed in the graffiti-sprayed entrance to a stairway, next to a dilapidated pet supply store. She felt uncomfortable at the sight of the animal cages behind the grubby window.

"Signorina Alcantara," he greeted her.

She nodded to him.

"Come in," said another figure, standing in the shadows behind Antonio Festa.

Rosa's eyes narrowed. Stefania Moranelli smiled at her. "The judge is expecting you."

The Pact

"You need help," said Judge Quattrini. "Otherwise you wouldn't have come to us. You weren't too cooperative last time we met."

Rosa crossed her legs. She was sitting on a chair opposite the judge's desk, and could sense the eyes of the two bodyguards fixed on her back. Festa and Moranelli were leaning against the wall behind her. She was sure they had chosen that position on purpose to unnerve her. The whole thing was just like all the other interrogations she'd undergone. She had hoped to handle the situation better this time.

"Let's get one thing clear right away," she said. "I'm not telling you anything about Alessandro Carnevare."

The judge ran her fingers through her short hair. Its colour was fading, and grey roots showed at her hairline. She wore the same clothes she had at that hotel in Rome: beige slacks and a brown sweater. Rosa supposed that Quattrini had a whole wardrobe full of them, or maybe just a travelling bag: the same outfit a dozen times over.

"So what do you want?" asked the judge, as she perched on the edge of the desk opposite Rosa. She was a small woman, and the tips of her toes barely touched the floor. "Why did you call me?"

Rosa had been racking her brain for an answer to that very question. What should she say about Cesare and Iole? Or about her own family? It intrigued her to realise that she didn't feel like a traitor, although she had just committed what, to the Mafiosi, was a mortal sin. In the annals of Cosa Nostra, thousands had been executed for that same offence; shot in the neck or stabbed before their bodies were sunk in water, cast in concrete or dissolved in vats of acid.

This was a high-stakes game, she knew. If she wanted to get any information from the judge, she would have to offer something substantial in return.

"Out there in the city," said Quattrini, "there are probably half a dozen young men, no older than you, who have orders from their *capi* to shoot me or blow me up with a bomb. We have a whole series of safe houses like this apartment, hideouts where we manage our operations and take shelter from the vengeance of the clans. But first and foremost they're exactly that: *hideouts* – and who likes to hide behind drawn curtains, with a fake nameplate by the doorbell? Second, there aren't so many that we can afford to lose one for no good reason. But that is exactly what we'll have to do when you leave. Because although I trust you enough to ask you to come here, I don't know whether someone might be able to force you to give this address away later." The judge sighed quietly. "What I am saying is this: you're costing me one of my safe houses, and whatever you have to say had better be worth that loss. So don't waste our time with whatever fictional story you were about to tell me. Why are you here, Rosa?"

"You say you trust me. Why?"

"I know your records from the United States. I've read

the transcripts of your interrogations more than once – and the files dealing with your mother, your sister and your father. I know your previous history." She let that sink in, as if making sure that Rosa thought about it. "You were not a straightforward child, and these days you're *really* complicated. And guess what? I like that. Not because I have a weakness for rebellious seventeen-year-olds, but because most of the Cosa Nostra girls I've dealt with are half-wits. But you, Rosa, are unusual. And the young man you don't want to talk about is also unusual. Except that he's planning something, and it would be extremely foolish to trust him while he's devoting all his efforts to becoming the next *capo* of the Carnevares."

Rosa smiled mirthlessly. "Go ahead, try manipulating me – it won't work."

Behind her, Stefania Moranelli took a step forward.

"Why are you here?" Quattrini asked again.

Rosa pulled herself together. "I want to talk to one of your Mafias witnesses, a man who turned state's evidence and has been living under your witness protection programme for the last six years. In return I'll give you information about my aunt Florinda Alcantara's business affairs."

Quattrini laughed. "You know nothing about her business affairs. Certainly no more than I do."

"But unlike you, I can get into Florinda's study without permission from Rome, pack a bag with her files, or copy documents and smuggle them out of the house."

"You'd do that?"

Rosa nodded. "Or simply answer your questions if I can. As long as they're not about Alessandro."

"How do I know you won't tell me a pack of lies? Or that Florinda didn't send you here herself to palm me off with a set of forged documents?"

Rosa smiled coldly. "If you thought that was a possibility, you wouldn't have given me this address."

Antonio Festa gave a little laugh, earning a dark look from the judge.

"I know I'm asking you for the impossible," Rosa went on. "I also know what witness protection means. False names, new faces. And I know you'd be crazy to give the niece of a Mafia boss access to someone like that."

Now even the judge was smiling, which worried Rosa more than her earlier impatience. "Who is it we're we talking about?" asked Quattrini.

"Augusto Dallamano."

"Why him?"

"That's my business."

"As far as I know, the Alcantaras and the Dallamanos have never had any—" She stopped short, and her face cleared. "You're doing this for the boy? He didn't send you here, did he?"

Rosa kept her face expressionless. "You really don't know anything about me."

The judge got off the edge of the desk, went over to one of the windows, and pushed the curtain back a little way. At once Moranelli hurried over to her, one hand on the gun in her shoulder holster. With an abrupt gesture, Quattrini sent her back to her place.

"Do you like cats?" she asked, looking at Rosa.

"They're okay."

"I love cats. I really do. If I still had a house and a family, the place would be full of cats. Over the course of all the ops I've carried out these last few years – pursuing criminals, taking flight a couple of times – I've run over seventeen of them. Seventeen cats, Rosa. And those are only the ones I counted. That brief shock when the tyres catch them, or the noise when they rebound off the hood of the car. And do you know what? I didn't feel sorry about a single one. Because they died for something I believe in. The struggle against the Mafia. For victory over your family and all the others. For an Italy where no one will have to live in fear any more."

"I don't give a shit about Italy," said Rosa.

"Then why are you here?" The judge sounded neither offended nor impressed. "You feel it too, Rosa. Don't tell me it's just your grief for your child. Or Alessandro Carnevare. There's something more keeping you in Sicily. There's no place like it."

She let the curtain fall back, sat in the chair at her desk, leaned forward and looked intently at Rosa over interlaced fingers. "They laugh at us in other countries. When foreigners come here, they're only interested in where to find the cleanest beaches, the best restaurants, the most chic boutiques. They laugh at us because the country is ruled by cynics, most of whom have been charged with fraud or tax evasion or cooperating with the Mafia. Because our judges can be bribed, and every few years there's an amnesty on a grand scale, and the worst criminals are let out of prison and claim compensation. Men I've hunted down and seen convicted. Others laugh at us because our politicians laugh at us themselves. Because they pass laws preventing me from questioning families like yours and placing most of the evidence I have against you before a court. Laws that won't allow me to search your houses and properties unless one of you has gone so far as to shoot the prime minister. And that's not all. Other countries laugh at us because a glamour model can get appointed minister of equal opportunities, while the police close down harmless sex shops. Because our politicians may stand in line to kiss the Holy Father's hand in the Vatican, but at the same time there are seventy offenders with previous convictions sitting in Parliament." The judge took a deep breath. Her forehead was glistening with sweat. "All that is part of Italy. And although other countries may laugh at it – I think it's a country worth fighting for, all the same. I think it's worth all the deaths, and the poor damn cats I hit with my car. And if you think otherwise, Rosa, then you can get out of here, and never call me again." She leaned even farther across the desk. "But if you think that I'm right, at least to some extent, if you admit that within a few days of arriving you'd fallen head over heels in love with this country, then you can stay and talk to me."

"Augusto Dallamano," Rosa whispered. "I just want to speak to him. Only once. That's all."

"And what do I get out of it? Don't try that line about

a few files and photocopies from your aunt's poison cupboard again. That isn't your *real* bargaining chip."

Rosa blinked. Sunlight fell through a crack between the curtains. She put all the determination she could muster up into her voice.

"Salvatore Pantaleone," she said.

Stefania Moranelli uttered a sound of surprise. Antonio Festa whistled through his teeth.

The judge, however, didn't move a muscle. Her face stayed composed as she looked into Rosa's eyes. "The boss of bosses," she said, as if reading from a courtroom file. "Has been living underground for decades. Rules Cosa Nostra with the aid of handwritten notes and letters; they turn up now and then and are confiscated, but they've never led us to his hideout. He's changed it at least a hundred times over the past thirty years, or so we suspect at least. And he certainly has a Mafia family close to him that enjoys his confidence – maybe several."

"I can help you to find him."

"Where is he?"

"I want to speak to Dallamano first."

"He's one of our most important witnesses."

"The cases in which he gave evidence were over long ago. He's no more use to you. But he is to me."

Quattrini shook her head. "That's not good enough."

"I can hand you Salvatore Pantaleone on a plate. And another thing: you have your eye on the Carnevares. You're not getting Alessandro. But maybe I can tell you something about Cesare Carnevare that you don't yet know."

"He's only a bookkeeper."

"Soon he'll be the new *capo* of the Carnevares."

The judge pricked up her ears at this. "So your good-looking boyfriend has fallen out of favour?"

Rosa's hand went to the photo in her pocket: the picture, taken underwater, of the embracing Panthera and Lamia. "Well, how about it? Will you arrange a meeting with Dallamano for me?"

Later, Rosa went to a news-stand in the neighbourhood and bought one of the used cell phones that the owner kept under the counter. In the shade of a building entrance, she called Alessandro.

She didn't let him hear her relief at the sound of his voice. There were distorted background noises that could have been the grunting and screeching of animals.

"Can you pick me up?" she asked. "We have to get to the airport. Our flight to Portugal leaves in an hour and a half."

The House of Stone Eyes

Rosa slept like the dead during the flight. Even when they stopped over in Rome to board their plane to Lisbon, Rosa could hardly keep her eyes open, and once she and Alessandro were finally settled in their seats, she couldn't fight her exhaustion any longer.

When turbulence finally woke her, they were already coming in to land. At first she felt as if she would never be able to think straight again. After two or three hours of sleep she felt even more tired than she had been earlier. It was a few minutes before she was clear-headed enough to see that Alessandro was smiling at her.

"You laughed in your sleep," he said

Her tongue tasted like a dishcloth. "Never!"

"Yes, you did."

Her face stayed expressionless. "Probably because my sister's disappeared, her girlfriend's been murdered, and soon I'm going to be on the Mafia hit list myself."

The flight wasn't fully booked; the row of seats behind theirs was empty, as well as several others.

"You missed out on the airplane food," he said. "Here, I kept this for you." He held up a flabby dinner roll. It looked the way her tongue felt.

"Did I really laugh?"

He nodded.

"I'm so mixed up right now."

That made him smile again. "Otherwise we wouldn't be here, right?"

The underwater photograph was lying in her lap, and the slight vibration of the plane almost made it seem like the snake and the big cat were alive. Rosa picked the picture up and looked at it.

"The Dallamanos found out something about us," she said. "About a link between the Alcantaras and the Carnevares. Something that most people obviously don't know."

"Or maybe it's just that no one talks about it."

She lowered her voice so she wouldn't be overheard. "The judge says that the first Dallamano murders happened *before* Augusto went to her. If that's true, then there must be some other reason why Iole's family was butchered."

"But there could be hundreds of reasons," he replied. "Infringing on territorial borders. Some kind of insult. Even a quarrel over a woman, who knows? Cosa Nostra has never been particularly squeamish about those things."

Rosa tapped her index finger on the photograph. "But this is no coincidence. I mean – a panther and a snake?" She swept her hair back from her face. "Iole says this photograph and others like it were spread out in her father's office when Cesare's men kidnapped her. They were the last things he'd been looking at before his death. If they were lying on his desk, they must have mattered to him."

"If they were lying on his desk," he repeated, "and they were as important as you think, Cesare would have taken them. He certainly wouldn't have let Iole pocket one."

"Well, maybe something distracted him. Or else" – she raised her hands helplessly – "or else he wasn't looking closely. How do I know… oh, hell!" Her card house of assumptions was beginning to teeter. So Cesare had ignored the photos and hadn't kept Iole from taking one – yes, that was a stumbling block. But there had to be some explanation for it.

Alessandro leaned over and kissed her. "They'll kill you if they hear that you've talked to that judge. There's no greater crime than giving information to the police. If Cesare had no good reason to want all your family dead before – well, you've given him one now. And no one's going to be happy with us for boarding a plane and flying abroad, either. Certainly not the tribunal."

"We'll be back in Sicily tomorrow. I'm not running away from them."

"Running might be the most sensible thing to do."

"Leaving Florinda and Zoe to answer for Tano's death?" Shaking her head, she nibbled at a hangnail, then felt annoyed with herself and let her hand drop. "If Augusto Dallamano can tell us anything about the place where the statue was found, and if I'm right that Cesare's hatred of us is somehow involved, then we may have something we can use against him."

At Lisbon Airport they were met by a man in dark glasses

holding up a pink sign with no words. He wore jeans and a leather jacket and spoke no Italian, only broken English. They were taken to a Peugeot parked outside the entrance. On the way, Rosa noticed the man's shoulder holster.

A few minutes later, they were turning onto the expressway. They quickly realised that they weren't driving towards the city centre.

"Where are you taking us?" asked Rosa.

"Sintra."

"What's that?" She wasn't sure whether she had understood him correctly.

"Is a town. Thirty kilometres. Much traffic, maybe one hour."

Alessandro raised an eyebrow. He was sitting beside Rosa in the back seat, holding her hand and looking from her to the chauffeur and back.

"Sintra is very beautiful," claimed the driver.

Rosa leaned forward between the head supports in front of her. "You're a police officer, right?"

"In a way."

She nodded, as if that explained everything.

"I know Antonio," he said. When she did not react at once, he added, "Antonio Festa? Good man. On mission with him in Gibraltar. Three years ago."

She leaned back. "Okay."

Alessandro whispered, "Who's Antonio Festa?"

She laughed quietly, then worried that she sounded slightly hysterical. "A Mafia hunter."

Alessandro tightened his lips, nodded slowly, and looked out the window, lost in thought.

✳

They turned onto a narrow road past high walls, with huge and ancient trees on both sides. The branches reached out to one another, weaving a canopy high above the uneven road.

The drive had lasted an hour and a half; heavy traffic on the last stretch of the expressway had held them up. Twilight was already gathering when the driver brought the car to a halt outside a black, barred gate in a wall that must have been around five metres high.

A bus passed them, honking as it went by. After that they had the road to themselves.

"I wait here," said the man. "The drive back go faster. Last flight leaves just before ten." He pointed to two printouts on the passenger seat beside him. "Your tickets."

"Thanks," said Rosa. She and Alessandro got out.

The driver's window opened with a soft hissing sound. The light was really too dim for him to need sunglasses any more. He gestured towards the barred gate and the villa standing on a steep rise beyond it. "Quinta da Regaleira," he said. "Is a strange house. Closed this time of day." He looked at his watch. "Tourists should be gone since two hours. Dallamano said to meet you here."

"The gate's open," Alessandro noted.

"Of course," replied the driver.

Alessandro took Rosa's hand. They nodded to the man and exchanged a brief glance as, despite saying he'd wait for them, he started the engine and drove off. However, he was only turning to park the Peugeot on the other side of the road.

Rosa went first, squeezing through the narrow gap between the two halves of the heavy gate and entering the grounds of Quinta da Regaleira. Only then did she notice the fantastic structure that rose before them.

It was a three-storey palace of greyish-white stone, adorned with stucco and pointed turrets. Towering behind the trees, the building was flamboyantly romantic, and was surrounded by a walled veranda, balconies with carved balustrades and elaborate stone edging.

"If you could crochet a house," said Rosa softly, "this is what it would look like."

Alessandro was examining the winding path leading up the hill. Dense ferns grew on both sides, fleshy rhododendrons, weeping willows with branches hanging low. They passed a hut that was the ticket office, now closed for the night, and listened for voices, but they heard only the whispering of the foliage and the twitter of birds.

The path forked several times under the shady canopy of trees. They saw elaborately designed fountains, statues of goat-legged flute players, grinning gargoyles. Delicate stone nymphs stood in niches. A devil with spiral horns leaned over a wall. Naiads with their arms outstretched greeted them from the middle of a pool.

"What *is* this place?" Rosa whispered.

A deep voice behind them said, "An alphabet of alchemy in stone. The dream, made reality, of a Freemason, a student of hermeneutics, and a magician."

They spun around.

The man was standing less than a metre behind them. With his enormous stature, he would have impressed even a more powerful adversary than Alessandro. His black hair was long and shaggy, his beard a wild tangle. In curious contrast to his mane of hair, he wore a well-cut pinstriped suit.

"You know who I am, and I know who you are," he said. Under his thick brows, his glance went to Alessandro. "You're a Carnevare."

"Alessandro Carnevare." There was a challenging glint in his eyes.

"Rosa Alcantara," she said. "Thank you for coming."

"I had no choice."

"Your niece is in danger," said Rosa. "She needs your help."

"*You* need my help. Iole is dead."

"No, she's been held prisoner for six years," she contradicted him. "Ever since she was kidnapped. She's been a prisoner all that time. And I think you know it. You didn't tell the judge the whole truth in order to keep Iole alive."

Dallamano came a step closer. "I have told her what I know. There are more than twenty men convicted on my evidence, now serving life sentences."

Rosa's chin jutted out. "But no Carnevares among them. Although they're the ones who killed your brother and his family."

The man's eyes moved to Alessandro again. "Which is why you deserve to die."

"Alessandro tried to save Iole."

"Oh yes?" said Dallamano ironically. "Of course." He paused for a moment, and then told Alessandro sharply, "You clear out."

"No," said Rosa. "He's staying."

Dallamano shook his head. "Quattrini didn't say anything about that. I was to talk to you. Not to any Carnevare bastard. You really think he's your friend?" He spat contemptuously. "He's soon going to be one of the leading Mafia bosses of Sicily. He's no one's friend."

Beside her, Alessandro stiffened. Suddenly there was an eerie silence. After an endless moment, Alessandro said, "I'm not leaving Rosa alone with you."

"Just as you like." Dallamano turned away and walked up the path.

"Wait!" Rosa called to him.

The man had stopped in the shadow of a faun with ivy clambering around its dancing body.

"He's not going to hurt me," Rosa whispered to Alessandro.

He stared back at her as if he wanted a fight. "I can't leave you alone with him."

"I only want to talk to him."

"And what does he want to do?"

"Cesare and your father have his whole family on their consciences. What do you expect?"

"Your friend," called Dallamano, "is afraid I might tell you things about him and his clan. Might warn you against him, and what he'll soon become once he's the *capo* of the Carnevares. None of his promises will be worth anything then."

Alessandro didn't even glance at Dallamano; he looked only at Rosa. "He's lying."

"I know that," she said softly.

"He wants to play us against each other."

"What he wants is revenge. At this moment words are his only weapon." She stood on tiptoe to kiss him. "And trust me, I'm immune to that." Then she turned around and hurried up the path.

"Rosa."

She looked back once more.

"You mustn't believe everything he says. Take care."

"We'll see. Don't worry."

Dallamano was smiling when she reached him. "You have him eating out of your hand, don't you?"

"He's doing what you ought to be doing. Trying to save your niece."

His eyes wandered darkly from her to Alessandro. Then he said, "Come on," and went ahead.

"Where to?"

He sounded as if he were smiling. "To the Initiation Well."

The Riddle of Messina

Rosa followed Dallamano uphill, past an artificial grotto from which a waterfall cascaded into a pool. Soon they reached several rocks under a tree with a mighty crown. The sky above was dark blue now, and the separate branches stood out only in the glow from a lamp-post beside the path.

"Along here." He led her to a space between the moss-grown rocks where a spiral stone staircase began winding its way down. Rosa waited until Dallamano was past the first turn before leaning over the balustrade to look.

She saw a round shaft. The staircase ran along its walls behind a pillared arcade. It was as if, long ago, a complete tower had been rammed into the ground by force. Faint light showed the tiled pattern of an eight-pointed star at the bottom.

"Do you expect me to go down there with you?"

"Yes." He reappeared behind the pillars on the opposite side of the shaft, and then disappeared from sight again when the spiral staircase took him directly under her. "Watch your step," he called up. "The steps are wet and slippery."

"Why can't we talk up here?"

"This shaft goes twelve metres down into the rock," he replied. "There's no cell phone or radio reception at the bottom. We're safer from bugging there than anywhere."

She cautiously took her first steps down. "You seriously think I have some kind of bug planted on me?"

"I'm only making sure." The echo of his words was getting louder and louder. "This was once a place of initiation, long before the villa and the park were open to visitors. Anyone who joined the secret society of Freemasons had to walk down this staircase, from the light into the darkness. The initiation ritual occurred at the bottom."

She liked the word 'ritual' even less down here than up above.

"The man who built the palace was a crazy millionaire who made a fortune in business in Brazil. Early in the twentieth century he bought four hectares of land from the barons of Regaleira, and commissioned an Italian architect to build the main house, the chapel, and all the other structures. They had the whole place finished within six years, complete with artificial ruins, grottoes, underground passages. There's even an amphitheatre. But to me this well has always been the most fascinating part of it."

As Dallamano talked, Rosa slid and stumbled down the wet steps, and the way it was getting darker and darker the lower she went did not improve matters. Plus, she was still exhausted.

When she reached the bottom of the shaft, Dallamano was waiting in the centre of the tiled star. The twilight sky above was reflected back only faintly from the damp stone slabs. The black semicircle of the mouth of a tunnel opened in one of the walls.

Dallamano was still standing in the middle of the star, looking at her. "Come over here," he said. "I have to pat you down."

"You *what?*" She almost turned back.

"I'm sorry," he said, "but I can't take your word for it. You could be wired from head to foot for all I know."

"Don't touch me!" She retreated until she was standing back among the pillars marking the entrance to the bottom of the stairway.

Dallamano didn't move. "I won't force you, of course. We don't *have* to talk to each other."

She took a deep breath, gritted her teeth, and slowly walked over to him. Back came memories that might not be memories at all: strange hands on her skin, fingers exploring every part of her. She felt a strong instinct to retch, and suddenly she tasted bile. She quickly turned her head away and spat it out.

"I'm sorry," he said again.

She turned back to him, trying to seem as impassive as possible, and stepped forward. Hesitantly, she raised her arms. Held her breath. Waited for his touch.

He went about it quickly and professionally, like the security staff at airports. It took him only a few seconds to reassure himself that she was not set up to record their conversation.

"Thank you," he said, and took a couple of steps back into the dark mouth of the tunnel. "You can stand there if you like, or come over here if you don't want to risk being seen from up above."

She stayed where she was.

"How is Iole?" For the first time his voice was gentler.

"Doing pretty well, I think, for someone who's been held prisoner for six years."

"Those bastards."

"The last place where they held her was an empty villa on an island. Alessandro and I got her away from there by ourselves. She told us she has only one last living relation – you, Signore Dallamano – and Alessandro was planning to take her to you."

"Not a good idea," he whispered.

"You don't want to see her?"

In the darkness she couldn't make out his face, only the outline of his wild head of hair. "I'd give my right hand to see her, but it's no use. There are a few people who know my real identity – not many, but I don't trust anyone. Except Judge Quattrini." He paused for a moment. "I really died long ago. Augusto Dallamano no longer exists. I don't even look like him."

She thought of the photo of him and his brother, the two laughing men in their diving suits. First he had lost his family, then his honour, his name, his face and his past.

If the clans found out that Rosa had been to see the judge, it would be the same for her. Even if the tribunal found her innocent, and she could prevent Cesare from eliminating the entire Alcantara family – even then her deal with Quattrini would be a sword of Damocles hanging over her head for the rest of her life. Treachery to Cosa Nostra was blood-guilt that never faded.

"You're afraid the same thing might happen to you." It was like he had read her thoughts. "Because you are here, and talking to me."

She didn't reply.

Dallamano was still standing motionless in the entrance to the tunnel. "We are both running a great risk. And you're not doing it only to tell me about my niece, are you?"

"Iole was abducted a second time yesterday," she said. "Cesare Carnevare found out where Alessandro was hiding her, and this time he's going to kill her if we don't stop him."

Now it was he who remained silent.

"Cesare is going to kill not just Iole but me, too, and my entire family, Florinda Alcantara, my aunt… you know her. Then my sister. And probably everyone who works for us." She cleared her throat. "If we don't find a way to stop him, the Alcantaras will be wiped out, just like the Dallamanos six years ago."

"And why would that interest me?"

"You know something that Cesare is afraid of," she said. "By kidnapping Iole he silenced you when you were giving evidence in court… Yes, I know you told them a lot, but not that *one* thing. And nothing that would incriminate the Carnevares."

He took his time answering. Maybe he was thinking. Or maybe fighting back anger. When he finally spoke, his voice sounded strained, and deeper than before. "But why is he going to kill Iole? He had six years to do it, but you say he didn't."

What was she to say to that? Did he know about the Arcadian dynasties? When he made those finds on the sea floor, had he drawn conclusions from them about the secrets of many of the Sicilian Mafia clans?

"He's going to sacrifice her," she said, and remembered the

fictitious story that she had concocted during the drive from the airport. "He's assuming you're no longer alive because he hasn't found you in all these years. So now he intends to show the other bosses that he's disposed of the Dallamanos once and for all. That's why he plans to execute Iole in front of them. To prove that he's consistent and to gain their respect. Cesare has convinced the Carnevares that he would make a better *capo* than Alessandro. Now he needs the support of the other families, and finally eliminating *all* the Dallamanos will get him that." Did it sound credible to a man who had been a high-ranking member of Cosa Nostra himself for decades?

An icy draught of air blew out of the tunnel behind Dallamano. She could smell the aftershave that, to her surprise, he used in spite of the beard covering his face.

At last he asked, "What exactly do you two intend to do?"

Her entire body was tense, her limbs, all her senses, even her eyes hurt. "If I know what Cesare is so anxious to keep secret from the others, I can suggest that he make a deal with me."

"He'll kill you."

"Maybe he'll try. But he may not succeed."

"Are you brave or terribly naive?"

She took a step closer to him in the dark, and was even more intensely aware of his presence. Under the aftershave, he had an animal odour.

"What did you find back then?" she asked. "What was it that you and your brother discovered?" Her hand felt for the picture in her pocket, but he wouldn't be able to make it out in the dark anyway. "It has to do with the photographs of the sea floor, doesn't it? The pictures that were on your brother's desk." She was on thin ice here. But there was no going back now.

"I've seen the statue," she said. "A photograph of it, a panther and a snake. Iole took it off her father's desk just before Cesare's men dragged her away. She says there were more like it."

He nodded, almost imperceptibly. "What else do you know?"

"Nothing else," she replied truthfully. "Only that you and your brother took those pictures."

"It wasn't just one statue."

Disappointment muted her excitement. If there were statues of all the Arcadian dynasties on the sea floor, what linked her and Alessandro might not be anything out of the ordinary.

"Remnants," he said. "The remains of several statues. Snakes and panthers in various positions."

"*Only* snakes and panthers?"

Dallamano nodded. "After our dive, my brother was elated. He obviously knew more about those figures than he ever told me. He packed up some of the pictures, twenty or thirty photos, and took them with him when he went to see the Carnevares. For some reason he assumed they'd be interested in our find." He snorted bitterly. "They came the next day. Killed the family and kidnapped Iole."

"All the family except you."

"I was out at sea on one of our ships. Ruggero sent me a message. He gave me Judge Quattrini's name and said I was to get in touch with her – and he wouldn't have done that if the whole affair hadn't been deadly serious. I never went back to Sicily; I actually tried to disappear from the face of the earth. But I soon found out what had happened. I went to Quattrini and turned state's evidence for her. It was only when I was in remand prison that I heard about Iole's survival. They sent me pictures of her in chains and told me she would die if I either testified against the Carnevares or said anything about the photos. They also wanted to know the precise coordinates of the site we found on the sea floor. So I withdrew my evidence against the Carnevares, but I stuck to what I'd said about all the other accused."

"What about the coordinates?"

"I didn't tell them. To keep Iole and myself safe."

"How about the crew of the ship? The one you and your brother were on when you made your dive? Didn't the Carnevares go after them?"

"It was too late by then."

"Too late?"

"That was the first thing my brother dealt with after we were back on land."

"You mean he… his own people?"

Dallamano shrugged his shoulders. "He sent some of his bodyguards to the ship that same evening. The crew members were still on board. And that's where they stayed."

After a moment, Rosa said, "Then no one but you knows precisely where you made that find? That was how you managed to save Iole's life."

"Even if that were so – do you imagine I'd tell you the place? You and that Carnevare up there?"

"But you said you knew where—"

"No. I only made sure that the Carnevares thought I did. The truth is that only my brother knew the exact coordinates."

"Then it was all just bluff?" she exclaimed.

"Almost all."

She quirked her head to one side.

"We had a civil engineering contract at the time," he said. "The biggest we'd ever been given. For a very long time there had been plans to build a bridge between Sicily and the mainland. Several miles long, a suspension bridge on gigantic piers, about a hundred metres above the water. We got the contract and started by investigating the sea floor. It was on one of those trips that our geologists' instruments showed distinctive features. Ruggero and I went down with a couple of our divers and took a look around."

"Is the sea shallow enough there for divers in ordinary scuba gear to reach the bottom?"

Dallamano laughed softly. "Where everyone else planned to build the bridge, between Messina on the Sicilian side and Villa San Giovanni on the mainland, the water is three hundred metres deep – only a submarine can reach the bottom there. But Ruggero had a different plan: he was going to build the bridge in a shallower part of the sea. It would have to be almost twice as long, but because the water isn't so deep it would be much easier to construct. So at that point we were looking for a place farther south. There's an underwater ridge of rock there above which the water is just forty metres deep. An experienced and reasonably skilled amateur diver can do that."

"You really don't know the coordinates?"

He shook his head. "Not exactly. And without them you could spend decades searching the bottom of the sea for a few unusual stone formations. The Strait of Messina has steep rocky ravines running through it. The sea floor has many fissures, so there are extreme variations of height and depth. Without the precise coordinates, no one will find anything there. Except by chance – as we did."

"So that's why you've never tried to make a deal with the Carnevares. Without that data you had nothing of value to offer them." She cursed. "Then all this has been for nothing. They'll kill Iole, and my family, too…"

"You're really going to try it, am I right?"

She looked at him even more suspiciously than before.

"You'd make a deal with a man like Cesare? To make sure that nothing happens to Iole?"

She nodded, hoping he could see it in spite of the darkness.

He said quietly, "There could be a way of getting those coordinates. Maybe – and I mean maybe – my brother's documents still exist."

"Cesare would have found them," she objected. But then she also remembered her conversation with Alessandro during the flight, and the question she had asked herself. How had Iole been able to take the photo without letting Cesare discover all the other pictures on Ruggero Dallamano's desk?

And suddenly she realised what she really should have asked. Where, for heaven's sake, was that desk now? Somewhere in the Dallamanos' house that Cesare still didn't know about? Iole must have been there right before she was kidnapped.

At that moment there was only one person who could answer the question.

"Do you think the documents are still there?" she whispered. "In your brother's villa?"

"Yes. But I can never go back there. I'd be found and killed almost immediately. Otherwise don't you think I would have returned to look long ago?"

"I could go," she managed to say. "I could look for your brother's papers. And for the coordinates."

"Yes," he said, after a long silence. "Yes, it's just possible that you could."

Promises

On the flight back they had to stop over in Rome again, only to find that their connection to Catania was cancelled. The pilots' strike was still on, and there was no way of getting back to Sicily that night.

When dawn came, Rosa woke up in the airport lounge. Voices over the loudspeakers roused her from confused dreams. She was lying across two chairs with her knees drawn up, her head resting on Alessandro's thigh. He had slept sitting up, and he was already awake, smiling down at her, dark rings under his eyes. Then he kissed her hair gently and murmured something unromantic about disposable toothbrushes available from vending machines over by the toilets.

Three hours later they landed in Catania and didn't even look for the Carnevare car in the multi-storey garage. They set out at once in a rental car.

The drive down the coast to Syracuse lasted just under an hour, and after dozens of attempts, she finally reached Zoe on the phone.

Her sister sounded terrible. Her voice was only a whisper, and for a moment Rosa was afraid that she, too, had been dragged away by Cesare's men.

"Are you okay?" asked Zoe. "What happened?"

"I'm okay."

"Is Alessandro Carnevare with you?"

She saw no point in lying. "Yes."

"Lilia is dead."

Rosa clenched her fists. She couldn't get a sound past her lips.

Memories of another time, another place. Then, too, they had spoken by phone. Zoe had called Rosa after she left the hospital. She'd said how terribly sorry she was, but she assured Rosa she'd soon forget the pain and the grief. Everything would be all right again.

But nothing had been all right. Rosa had hated her sister for her superficial consolations, the way she'd hated everyone who offered her good advice. Sympathy. Pity. It all had such a stale taste that, ever since, she had wanted to spare other people such remarks.

"They're claiming that you shot Tano Carnevare," said Zoe.

"No. Lilia shot him. For me. That's why Cesare killed her."

A long silence at the other end.

"Zoe?"

Her sister began to cry.

"Lilia told me all about it," said Rosa gently. "I know everything." She listened to her sister's sobs and cursed herself for being unable to comfort her. She felt Alessandro's fingers on the back of her hand, and reached blindly for them.

Florinda's voice could be heard in the background, low and alarmingly harsh. With an effort, Zoe pulled herself together. "Florinda wants to speak to you," she said, then hesitated for a moment before adding, "You mustn't come home. The tribunal of the dynasties will—" She broke off, and there was a loud rustling noise, then Florinda's voice.

"Rosa, are you all right?"

"Yes. Lovely weather."

"Zoe says she told you everything. But the fact is, she did not. Not quite everything. There's still something you have to know."

"TABULA," said Rosa huskily. "Am I right?"

"I know what Cesare says," Florinda replied, after a moment's silence. "He's been making the same accusations for years. His dislikes are so incredibly unimaginative."

"Is it true?"

"Cesare tells lies the moment he opens his mouth. He makes a great many wild claims – for example, he says you shot his son."

"I would have killed him, if I'd been holding the gun instead of Lilia."

"Where are you now?"

"Why do you want to know?"

"*Where*, Rosa?"

"In a car. There's still something I have to do before I come home."

"You trust Alessandro Carnevare more than you trust me?"

Rosa sighed. "How often have we really talked, Florinda? Three times, four times? I know the cleaning ladies in the palazzo better than I know you." She was expecting her aunt to interrupt, but Florinda said nothing. "As for Alessandro, he's explained something to me that I ought to have heard from you. That says a lot for him, don't you think?"

"You wouldn't have believed me if I'd told you everything right away. And in your state at the time—"

"I let my baby be killed. If I can cope with that, then I suppose I can face the fact that I'm likely to turn into an enormous snake at any moment." It came out sounding less laconic than she'd had hoped.

"You could *not* cope with it. That's why you came here to us, remember?"

Rosa closed her eyes to calm herself. Deliberately cool, she said, "There's something I still have to do. But if this tribunal is making decisions on rules that I'm supposed to have broken, I'd better be there."

"No," said Florinda firmly. "We'll do it for you. Now, listen to me, Rosa. Cesare's influence has its limits. This is what will happen. The tribunal will declare us innocent because the concordat was broken by an outsider, not an Alcantara. Lilia is not on our payroll. Or not on any of them that I was aware of."

Rosa clenched her hand into a fist. "You didn't really just say that, did you?"

"Will you keep—"

"Bitch."

Florinda took a deep breath, hissing dangerously down the line. "So we can't be held responsible," she went on. "Cesare doesn't know it yet, but a couple of the men who were there will speak up in your favour."

Rosa knew what that meant. "Pantaleone has a finger in the pie."

"He's still the *capo dei capi*. And a friend of the Alcantaras."

Alessandro laid his hand on her thigh and pointed through the windshield. The car was turning into a well-tended avenue lined with oak trees. Baroque villas came into sight behind the branches, their facades lavishly adorned with carvings. His lips silently formed the words, *Almost there*. She nodded.

To Florinda, she said, "I ought to be there, all the same. If the tribunal doesn't believe your paid witnesses—"

"Then he's never going to believe you. But the two of them will be very convincing. And what's more, we have proof that the gun belonged to Lilia."

"What kind of proof?"

"You explain, Zoe." Florinda handed Rosa's sister the phone.

"Lilia had a license for the gun," said Zoe a minute later. "She bought it legally. She never wanted anything to do with our business." Zoe's voice was getting unsteady again.

"You mustn't come here for the time being," said Florinda, joining the phone call again. "Not until this business is over. The tribunal of the dynasties will meet at dawn tomorrow. Zoe and I will go and defend our family. Cesare will have to accept defeat, but the tribunal will sweeten it for him by recommending that the Carnevares elect him their new *capo* – which is what, in effect, he has been for years anyway, although neither the baron nor your friend would admit it."

"They'll be declaring Cesare the *capo* tomorrow? Is that absolutely certain?"

"It's the most likely outcome."

If the human hunt, with Iole as quarry, was really going to

be held in honour of the new head of the clan, thought Rosa, then they didn't have much time left.

"I have to hang up now," she said.

"Please, Rosa – don't come here. Promise me that."

"What would my promise be worth," she said cuttingly, "when we're all so honest with each other all the time?"

"I've given my word to Pantaleone you'd stay out of danger. And I intend to keep *my* promise."

"Okay," she said quietly. "If that's what you really want, then for now I won't come home."

Florinda breathed a sigh of relief. "I just don't want anything to happen to you."

"Is that what *you* want, or Pantaleone?" And with that she hung up and put the cell phone down on her lap. She felt exhausted.

"We're here," said Alessandro.

The Dallamano villa stood at the end of the avenue, on a small hill overlooking the coast and the glittering Mediterranean. The drive led them through the garden and up to an impressive porch. Tall palms and pines cast a pattern of shadows over the handsome house, which seemed to have been renovated recently.

The gate down by the road was open. There was a brass plate fitted to it.

"A scientific library?" asked Rosa, surprised.

"That's the kind of thing that happens to Mafia property

when the courts turn it over to the state," Alessandro explained. "Usually they're requisitioned for community purposes. As there were no heirs, the Dallamano villa was handed over to the provincial government. Not a bad catch for the local politicians. The site alone must be worth a fortune."

Two elderly men were talking outside the entrance. One of them held a stack of papers, the other was carrying several books.

She groaned softly. "They're never going to believe that we want to do scientific research here."

"Then we'll come back when it's dark. Easier getting into a library than a bank. The building won't be all that secure."

She gave him a sceptical look.

He smiled. "We're gangsters, remember? That must come in handy for something."

He turned the car outside the entrance, drove back down the avenue, and took the road to the city at the next junction.

On their way, Rosa repeated what Florinda had said about the tribunal, and Cesare's appointment as *capo* of the Carnevares. "Which means," she finished her account, "that time's running out."

"Tomorrow night," he murmured, with a grim nod. "Cesare likes to hunt in the dark."

"How will you find out where the hunt's going to take place?"

After a moment's hesitation, he said, "The man from the island, the zookeeper. He's still in the hospital, and I know which one."

Rosa's eyebrows shot up. "I didn't think he was that badly injured."

"He wasn't when the captain and his men took him onboard the *Gaia*."

"You mean you gave them orders to—"

"He was trying to *kill* you." He spoke with such contempt that her mouth felt dry. "If anything had happened to you on the island, I wouldn't have just had him beaten up. I'd have strangled him with my own hands."

She had realised by now what it meant in Sicily to be a member of Cosa Nostra, but she still wasn't used to it.

"I'll find out where she is," he said. "You discovered where we have to look for Dallamano's papers – I'll find Iole."

In Syracuse city centre, he stopped by one of the last public phone booths, near the Piazza Duomo. He asked Rosa to wait for him in the car.

"Who are you going to call?"

"The captain of the yacht. I want him to see about the man in the hospital."

"Is he still on your side?"

Alessandro shrugged. "Honestly? No idea. But we're starting to run out of allies."

His phone call lasted almost ten minutes. Thoughtfully, Rosa watched him through the glass: his handsome face, looking so grim, his untidy brown hair, his angular profile. He seemed to be strained and edgy, but at the same time he radiated a self-confidence that both surprised her and made her feel slightly afraid. Not *of* him, but *for* him. He was going to have powerful enemies all his life, enemies just waiting for him to make a mistake.

At last he came back to the car. "If the zookeeper does know where the next hunt is to take place, then we'll hear about it, too, first thing tomorrow at the latest."

A shiver ran down her back. But she hid her feelings behind a nod, leaned back, and waited for nightfall with her heart pounding.

The Hidden Room

Once it was dark, they climbed over the fence and approached the villa under cover of bushes and weeping willows. There were no lights on inside; the last member of the library staff had left just after eight, and no other vehicle had passed the end of the oak-lined avenue in the two and a half hours since then.

Silently, they crossed a narrow strip of lawn and reached the palm trees growing around the villa. They headed for the back of the building, where there was a broad terrace with a view of the rocky coastline. The lights of a freighter flickered out at sea, on the invisible horizon between the ocean and the starry sky.

The Dallamanos' swimming pool had been drained years ago. Huge terracotta pots contained dead plants, and a pile of old shelving was stacked against the wall of the house. Once, when the clan still lived here, the building must have been well guarded; today there wasn't even an alarm system. Presumably no one was seriously expecting thieves to break in and steal collected editions of scientific works and encyclopaedias.

A dog barked somewhere farther down the road, on the grounds of one of the neighbouring villas.

Alessandro had bought a long screwdriver, a rubber hammer and a torch in the city that afternoon. Now he easily levered open one of the tall windows on the first floor.

"Not the first time you've done that, huh?" whispered Rosa.

"When you grow up in a castle full of Mafiosi, you learn a lot of strange stuff."

"Very practical."

"You told me you can break into cars."

She shrugged her shoulders. "That's Brooklyn for you."

They cautiously climbed inside. Rosa closed the window after her.

The only lights in the place were the illuminated emergency exit signs over the doors. Alessandro turned on the torch. Its beam passed over tall bookcases, frescoes on the walls, and a few busts and statues on stone plinths.

The two of them quietly walked through the rooms on the first floor. A pleasant smell of old paper lingered in the air.

They followed the directions to the cellars Augusto Dallamano had given to Rosa and soon found the door they needed. At the foot of the stairs a passage led to several storerooms crammed full of books, dusty folios and cartons. In the third room, the torch beam revealed a grate over the drain in the floor. Alessandro undid the screws, removed the grate, and unhesitatingly put his hand inside the dark rectangle. Rosa watched as he felt around the walls of the narrow shaft, and finally found an opening with a lever inside it, just as Dallamano had said. Once there had been a remote control for the mechanism, but it had disappeared along with the rest of the family's possessions. What Rosa and Alessandro had here was only for emergency use, but it would do.

The lever stuck, and Alessandro swore quietly. He tried it again several times before he thought of using his foot. Sure enough, the mechanism turned out to function like a pedal. From above, he could reach it with the toe of his shoe and push it down.

There was a crunch, then a motor hidden in the wall hummed to life. Moments later, a door-sized rectangle in the back of the room slid aside.

There was darkness behind it, of course; they were underground. Only a glance at the steel core of the mechanical door showed Rosa that this was not just the entrance to a secret room.

It was a bunker. A private bunker built as a wartime shelter, the kind of refuge that rich people all over the world had had erected in the 1950s and 1960s. Later, when the fear of nuclear war gradually receded, Ruggero Dallamano must have converted it into a second office. He would not have run his legal building company from here, only the business that had made him one of the most influential *capi* in Sicily.

Nine-year-old Iole must have known about this place. She had probably hidden down here during the massacre of her family. Rosa could only guess how and why she had left this refuge again unseen, taking the two photographs with her. Perhaps she had thought that her parents' murderers had left, but ran straight into their arms. The Carnevares had certainly not found the bunker, or else they would have looted it.

Alessandro shone the torch into the darkness. "Do we go in?"

The first of the two rooms beyond the door was full of

cabinets containing hanging files from which documents, newspaper cuttings, and paperwork spilled out. Rosa glanced briefly at a few of the papers, recognised none of the names on them, and walked ahead of Alessandro into the second room.

Her hand found a switch on the wall, and several neon tubes on the ceiling came on, filling the sparsely furnished place with bright light.

There were more filing cabinets, many of them open, a leather reading chair, and wood-panelled walls with a few old family photos on them, including one of a child with big eyes and a happy smile. A large desk stood in the centre of the room.

"It really does look as though no one's touched anything here for years," whispered Rosa.

A swivel chair lay toppled on the floor. There were more photographs on the desk, of Ruggero Dallamano and his family in narrow wooden frames, just like the photo of the two divers behind which Iole had hidden the picture of the statue. In the middle of the desk lay a thick notebook with a heavy cardboard cover. It was closed; the end of a ballpoint pen stuck out from between the pages. Photographs were scattered everywhere, dim, sometimes underexposed snapshots, many of them showing only pale, faded patches against a black background.

The neon tubes crackled. Their humming suddenly stopped short. The lights went out.

Rosa swore. Alessandro shone the flashlight at the doorway. Dust motes danced in its yellow beam. It was pitch dark again in the front room of the bunker and the storeroom outside it.

"The fuses," Rosa whispered.

"There should be a generator down here. It probably hasn't been serviced for years, or the lights would have come on again right away."

Rosa took a deep breath. Only now did she notice how stale the air was here. Wasting no time, she picked up the notebook and a handful of random photographs. Although Alessandro had the beam of the torch turned on the door, its light was not enough to show any details on the pictures.

"Let's get out of here," she said, holding the notebook and photos against her and moving around the desk. Alessandro walked ahead to the door, listened for a moment, and went into the front room, then out of the bunker and into the cellar. Rosa followed. She was about to go on when Alessandro stopped, put his foot down into the drain outlet, and activated the pedal. The sliding door closed almost soundlessly behind them.

"There's someone up there in the house," he whispered.

She had heard the noises herself.

Alessandro crouched down. With his free hand, he put the drain cover back into the opening. There was no time to get it back in place. Instead, he dropped the screws into the shaft through the bars of the grate and dragged one of the cartons of books up to stand over the outlet cover. "That'll have to do."

Rosa wondered for a moment whether to leave Dallamano's documents somewhere down here in the cellar, but decided to keep them with her. Not only was she eager to find out what he had discovered on the sea floor, but she also needed the information to exchange for Iole. Whoever was sneaking around the villa couldn't be allowed to hold them up now.

Alessandro switched off the torch and took Rosa's arm. Feeling their way, they went out into the passage. The cellar stairs at the end of it showed dimly as a rectangle of diffuse stripes. Faint nocturnal light was reflected on the marble steps.

Above them, a shadow hurried past.

Rosa held her breath and pressed close to the wall. She expected someone to expose them at any moment.

But no one came down into the cellar. Whoever it was had passed by the door to the stairs.

Cautiously, they stole on. Alessandro stuck the torch, still switched off, into his waistband, and took out the screwdriver he had used to break open the window. He held it in front of him like a knife. Rosa put the photos between the pages of the notebook, so that she could hold everything with one hand. She took the rubber hammer from Alessandro and hefted it, weighing it in her hand. It wasn't as good as her stapler, but it was better than nothing.

He cast her a quick glance, but she could hardly see him in the dark. Once again they listened for sounds from above, then cautiously began to climb the stairs.

They would have to walk through several rooms to reach the window through which they had entered the house. Moonlight cast deep black shadows between the bookcases.

There was a clicking sound, like switches being hastily pressed up and down. Someone was working on a fuse box. That must have been why the lights in the cellar had gone out.

Unnoticed, they reached the room with the window that

they had broken open. It was just as they had left it. Whoever else was in the house had probably come in another way.

Rosa pulled the window in by its handle. A cool draught of air from the sea came in. She put the papers and the hammer on the sill outside and clambered out, followed by Alessandro.

They heard a voice somewhere in the house. Then a short, dull sound. A second voice swore, saying something about moving shadows.

"Was that a shot?" Rosa groaned.

In the moonlight, Alessandro looked paler than usual. "Come on," he whispered, ducking low and taking her wrist. It was good to feel his hand: a touch of warmth in the glacial cold that once again had taken hold of her body. But she couldn't run like that. She moved out of his grasp with a quick shake of her head. Then they both took off, past the palm trees that offered little cover, over the dried-up turf of the lawn.

There were voices behind them again, outside in the open air now.

The bushes on the boundary of the property rustled. There was a barred fence beyond them.

All at once they saw something else there as well. A long, black outline, winding its way through the dry grass like a rivulet of viscous oil.

"A Lamia!" whispered Alessandro.

The sound they had heard in the house was repeated. Twice.

Right in front of them, two fist-size craters were torn into the ground. Grass and dust went swirling into the air.

"Stay where you are!" said a man's voice.

Rosa spun around and threw the hammer.

Treachery

The gunman wore a black ski mask with slits for his eyes. He must have noticed Rosa's movement, but it was too dark and the hammer flew through the air too fast for him to avoid it. The hard rubber head hit him in the face – a horrible noise – and threw him backwards to the ground. The revolver dropped from his hand; he let out a groan as if half-dazed.

A second man, also masked, swore, fired into the grass in front of Alessandro again, and strode quickly over to the two of them.

"Get away from the girl!" he snapped at Alessandro. "Quickly!"

It was possible that Rosa had smashed the first attacker's skull with the hammer; at the very least she had broken his nose, yet she felt nothing. None of this fitted together: the shadow flowing through the grass, the gun pointed at them.

Alessandro stepped in front of Rosa, protecting her with his body. He made no move to obey the man's order. "Stay behind me," he whispered over his shoulder. The panther's short, dark coat was creeping up the back of his neck.

"What's that you're holding?" asked the man.

"Screwdriver," growled Alessandro.

"Not you – her!"

"Nothing," said Rosa, hoping he was only bluffing and hadn't seen anything.

"Hand it over."

"No." If she gave up Dallamano's papers, Iole would die. That was what mattered. Not herself, not Alessandro – only this one, thin thread from which Iole's life dangled, and which must not break.

On the ground, the injured man felt his face with his hand and screamed again. He was trying to take the ski mask off, but that must have made the pain even worse.

The other man was standing about three metres away from Alessandro and Rosa. "Give me those," he demanded again, "or I'll shoot your friend in the knee."

Rosa moved a little way out of the cover Alessandro was giving her and shook her head vigorously when he tried to get in front of her again. "No," she said.

Behind them, there was a hissing and a rustling among the bushes.

Rosa didn't look back. She was keeping her eyes on the man with the gun. The slithering sound came again. "Florinda."

She'd been so stupid. Her aunt had kept her talking so that the cell phone could be located. Easy enough for the telephone company.

"Florinda!" she said again, adding, "I know it's you. And he won't shoot me."

"Not you," said the man, with an unpleasant smile, "but I'll shoot young Carnevare if he moves so much as a muscle."

Rosa moved in front of Alessandro. He was still in human form, but she sensed the coat growing under his clothes, thrusting at his jeans and T-shirt.

She took a step towards the man, carefully staying in the line of fire between him and Alessandro. She calmly held the notebook out to him.

"You won't do anything to him."

The man put out his hand to take the documents. Behind him, his companion was getting to his feet with difficulty, both hands to his face. "Bitch," he muttered in a low voice, and peered through his fingers, trying to find the revolver he had lost.

"You two belong to *my* clan," she said coolly. "And Florinda won't always have the last word."

Impatiently, the man beckoned her closer. Another step.

Behind her, Alessandro let out an animal roar.

The man jumped with surprise, his revolver jerking to one side – and Rosa rushed him.

A shot was fired. The notebook and photographs fluttered through the air. Rosa went for the man's face with her nails, knocking him backwards with the sheer force of her impact. At the same time she rammed one knee between his legs.

None of it would have worked if he had really intended to shoot her. But for that he needed explicit orders. He doubled over, howling with rage and pain. Rosa let go of him and brought her knee up a second time, this time under his chin. Not with any particular accuracy, but hard enough to make him cry out as it struck his jawbone.

Alessandro swept past her, still human, but covered with black fur – including his face – and threw himself on the second man. Out of the corner of her eye, Rosa saw him bring

Alessandro down with him as he fell. At the same moment, however, her own adversary struggled up, swung his arm back – and hit her so hard on the temple that everything went black before her eyes.

When she was conscious again, just a few seconds later, she was lying on the ground while the man in front of her gathered up the notebook and the scattered photos. She couldn't see Alessandro, and tried to sit up, but her head hurt like hell. She heard the sounds of fighting, and then that hissing and slithering again, getting louder, coming closer and closer.

Alessandro cried out in alarm, and Rosa forced herself into a crouch. The man with the gun had collected all the photos now. He put them back inside the notebook, turned, and ran.

"No!" she cried. Reptilian cold filled her from head to foot, but it still wasn't enough to change her, damn it.

Then her eyes fell on the revolver that had been carried by the first man, who was now lying helpless on his back. Alessandro was kneeling over him, half human, half panther, his head flung back, his mouth wide open – too wide, full of too many sharp teeth – to sink his fangs into his victim's throat.

Rosa called out his name as she crawled forward on all fours, and managed to grasp the revolver. The sight of his prey's blood seemed to enrage Alessandro even more. She saw his T-shirt split down the back.

"Alessandro, don't!"

She wasn't sure why she wanted to stop him. The men had threatened them and shot at him. Killing them both seemed only right, even more so as the cold of the snake inside her took over her mind as well, forcing out all ideas of morality. She crouched there on her knees, the revolver lying heavy in her hands, and now she aimed it at the man with the papers. In the moonlight, she saw him running for the bushes and the fence, right in front of her weapon. Its barrel and muzzle were heavily encased in a silencer.

Rosa's finger quivered on the trigger. The cold was driving out her scruples, but a last remnant of reason still told her that it was wrong to shoot anyone in the back.

But she *wanted* to kill him. To save Iole, and because of what he had done. The blow he had struck her, her pain. What he had wanted to do to Alessandro. And most of all because she *could* kill him, while the person she was really angry with was gliding invisibly through the shadows in the form of a snake.

And then, once again, she registered the rustling of the dry grass over which something was moving towards her, and she realised that only two or three seconds had passed, and the snake was coming closer.

She abruptly turned around, held the gun out in front of her – and aimed it between the amber eyes of the snake's huge head.

Time stood still. Her body felt frozen; her blood was ice water. The gun did not move a fraction of an inch. Even her trigger finger stopped shaking.

The snake stared at her out of sparkling slits of eyes. The split tongue touched the muzzle of the revolver, licked along it and all the way around it, and Rosa thought: I can do it. I can do it now, and then everything will be different.

But out of the corner of her eye, she saw something else.

Alessandro tore the larynx out of the injured man with his teeth, held it triumphantly between his panther jaws. Finally he flung his trophy away from him, uttering a deafening victory roar.

Rosa's hatred disappeared instantly. She lowered the gun. The snake shot away across the grass, following the second man, and merged into the shadows.

Rosa crouched on the ground, the revolver in her lap, her head bent, unable to think straight. Minutes passed as she stared at the gun in her white fingers, waiting for warmth to come back into her – waiting for what she had rejected for so long, her plain, vulnerable humanity.

He came up behind her and gently touched her shoulder. When she looked up, she expected to see his panther's jaws smeared with blood. Instead, she met his green eyes, full of guilt and very sad. Once again she shivered, but not with cold, only with fear, and misgivings, and helplessness. He was himself again, his T-shirt torn, his lips bleeding.

"They've gone," he said as he knelt down, put his arms tightly around her, and drew her head down to his shoulder. "They took it all with them."

She wept into his torn T-shirt, feeling the hot tears between her cheeks and his skin. Listening to the pulsing of his veins, feeling his racing heartbeat.

The Heiress

Alessandro turned into the driveway of the Palazzo Alcantara. The two guards at the gate looked at him suspiciously when they saw Rosa. She was huddled in the passenger seat of the car, her hair untidy and her face dirty, while her throbbing forehead was bruised where the man had struck her. Rosa indicated to them that everything was all right.

The revolver still lay in her lap. Its weight gave her a distressing sense of security – distressing because it reminded her that soon she had to make a decision. She had to get the stolen photographs back. But how far would she go to do it? Would she pull the trigger? She could have shot the huge snake, and she hadn't. But if what happened last year had taught her one thing, it was that she couldn't make the same mistake twice.

They did not talk during the last mile or so to the palazzo. The car headlights lit up the rows of trees lining the road; darkness covered everything beyond them.

Rosa didn't know what the next hour might bring. Or the next day. She didn't even know what she was going to say to Alessandro when they reached the front courtyard outside the house: how she could ask him to let her go in alone.

She still understood very little of what had happened. Florinda must have spent the afternoon driving to Syracuse with her men. Which left the question of just how much her aunt knew about the Dallamanos and their find on the sea floor. Was there a link between Lamias and Panthera, between Alcantaras and Carnevares, one that both clans desperately wanted to keep secret at any price?

More and more, she was realising that she could take only one step at a time. The first was Florinda herself. Or alternatively – and it was hard to admit this – Rosa's own sister. All she had seen was a Lamia, a member of her dynasty. It hadn't necessarily been Florinda. And yet…

"Something's burning," said Alessandro.

Farther up the slope a fire was blazing, hidden every once in a while by the trees, then flaring again.

When they drove into the front courtyard, the basin of the fountain was aflame like a torch or a pyre, the fire bathing the facade of the palazzo in its glowing light, bringing the statues in their niches to life.

Alessandro drove slowly over to the blazing fire. "What is that?"

"Birds' nests."

He gave her a sidelong glance. "Who's burning something here in the middle of the night?"

"Well, who would hate birds enough to have their nests knocked out of the trees?" Florinda was a mystery to her. From the start there had been an invisible wall between them.

The flames blazed high, a crackling signal fire on the dark mountainside. You could probably see it from miles away.

The same thought occurred to both of them. They looked westward over the olive trees, out into the moonlit landscape, but saw only the tiny lights of farms and villages far away.

At the entrance to the inner courtyard, Rosa said, "I'm getting out here. Will you wait for me?"

He pointed to the revolver. "What are you going to do with that?"

She weighed the gun indecisively in her hand, felt awkward, and almost left it in the car. But then she pushed it into the waistband of her jeans. The cold metal pressed uncomfortably against her hipbone.

"I'll be right back," she said, climbing out. Sparks flew above the front courtyard, and the air was filled with the smell of burnt branches and leaves.

"Rosa," he began, and she guessed what was coming next. "I can't stay here. You saw what happened. You saw *me*. And there will be others worse than me at this hunt. Cesare is only one of them." He shook his head. "I have to go there alone."

She took a deep breath. Wondered how she could stop him, and knew at once that he wouldn't let her. In his place, she would probably have done the same.

The engine roared as he suddenly stepped on the gas. The door slid away from Rosa's hand. Dust and pebbles spurted up. The car moved forward in a curve, completed a circuit of the fiery fountain, and raced away towards the drive.

She stood motionless, watching him go. He was driving much too fast.

About fifty metres away the brake lights came on – then the car stopped. Her body tensed. For a moment she thought of following him. But Alessandro was only closing the passenger door from the inside, and he drove away again.

If the zookeeper does know where the next hunt is to take place, then we'll hear about it, too, first thing tomorrow at the latest, he had told her in Syracuse. But now she wondered if the captain of the yacht hadn't already told him on the phone. If so, Alessandro must have known all along, and yet he hadn't mentioned it to her. Because he wanted to protect her, for God's sake!

Behind her, glowing drifts of sparks rose to the night sky. "You stupid idiot," she whispered.

The rear lights of the car finally disappeared behind the olive trees. Rosa turned, hurried through the heat of the flames to the gate, and entered the dark inner courtyard.

✳

"Zoe? Florinda?"

There was a melancholy silence in the halls and corridors of the palazzo, as well as the charred smell of the fire. Rosa's footsteps echoed back from the walls. As she explored the rooms, she didn't need to switch on any of the chandeliers; it was never entirely dark in this house. Lamps and wall-mounted lights were always on in some corner or other.

There was no one here. The salons and living rooms were deserted. Not a soul up in the bedrooms. Florinda's study, too, was full of silence and shadows.

Neither Zoe nor Florinda was back from Syracuse. Maybe they were already on their way to the tribunal. Or had that, too, been just a lie to lead her astray?

She checked the bathrooms, the library, even the kitchen with its open range. A draught of air made the hanging pots and pans clink. Rosa jumped, startled not so much by the sound as by herself. Her hand went to the revolver as quickly as if she knew how to use it.

Finally she thought of looking in the locked cellars. But even as she stood indecisively in the first-floor corridor, fighting down rising panic, she heard a buzzing sound behind her.

The vibrating alarm of a cell phone.

"You?"

It was only the outline of a figure, but she recognised him at once. Not until he moved into the light cast by a table lamp did she also see his eye patch, and the white ponytail hanging over his left shoulder like a bunch of cobwebs.

Salvatore Pantaleone, the boss of bosses, head of the Sicilian Mafia. He gestured to her to be patient. Instead of addressing her, he spoke to the cell phone. "Did you recognise him?... No, go ahead, do just as he says... but make a note of the number... Yes, of course, *the number!*"

He ended the call, put the cell phone away, and smiled.

"I thought you didn't use technological stuff," she said.

"The circumstances leave me no choice. At the moment everything has to move very fast."

The way she took the safety catch off the revolver must have told him how unfamiliar she was with guns.

"Rosa, Rosa, Rosa," he said softly. "You walk into this house with a weapon, but you don't keep it ready to use. You search all the rooms and corridors, but you never look in the corners properly. And you come here all by yourself, although you know what Florinda has done, and that she wants to make Zoe her heiress and dispense with you."

He went over to an armchair, an antique with gilded wooden feet and red velvet cushions, and dropped into it. Then his one eye examined her with its keen gaze.

"Florinda and Zoe aren't here," he continued. "They went to Syracuse yesterday. From there they'll be driving on to the place where the tribunal is to be held."

Ah, she thought, both of them?

"You made it easy for them," he went on. "Florinda is cunning; you should have worked that out by now. And Zoe, well, poor Zoe is putty in your aunt's hands. Florinda enticed her to Sicily with promises of wealth and luxury, and even now that she knows it all, she still hopes the money can make her happy. That's the most tragic part of it, don't you think? Florinda is obsessed, just like her mother, your grandmother. But Zoe, credulous, malleable, ever-exploited Zoe – she just chases her dream of happiness." The supercilious note gave his remarks a caustic undertone. "Florinda has promised your sister that she will succeed her. But Zoe has never understood what it means to be head of a Mafia clan *and* of an Arcadian dynasty. She's a pretty girl, she's not stupid, but she's very naive."

"What do you want from me?" asked Rosa.

"First, your confidence."

"And you think lying in wait for me in the dark and saying horrible things about my sister is the best way to get it?"

"Those horrible things, as you call them – you know yourself that they're the truth. You saw through Zoe long ago, her weaknesses, her volatility. If anyone knows that she'd never make an even halfway good clan leader, it's you. Zoe, among all the other *capi* of the families? Come off it, Rosa, you might as well throw her into a pool full of sharks and see what's left when they've finished with her."

"Does Florinda know that you're against her plans?"

"Why, of course! She's still devoted to me, but she is also full of arrogance. She refuses to admit that she's wrong. She thinks she has plenty of time to make something of Zoe – to turn your sister into something she will never be. You, on the other hand, Rosa, have exactly what it takes."

She laughed bitterly.

"You are not afraid. You've known the dark side of fate, and it didn't break your spirit, it made you grow. You are *perfect*, Rosa. There's still a lot for you to learn, but the prerequisites are all there. You're much more like your father than Zoe is, and that may be what Florinda dislikes so much. She has never forgiven him for turning his back on the clan for your mother. Maybe she's afraid you might do something similar."

Her mouth was dry, her gums as raw as sandpaper. She felt sick, exhausted. And here he was talking drivel about growth and perfection. "You're crazy."

Quick as lightning, he was out of the chair, and a few steps brought him right up to her. She was still holding the gun, but they both knew she wasn't going to fire it. At their first meeting in the forest, he had hit her, but he didn't try that this time.

He simply looked at her with his one bright, watchful eye.

"Oh, I don't mind if you call me names. Zoe never did. You have a will of your own, you're a fighter. You'll learn to show respect, and you'll learn much more as well. You'll find that I'm a good teacher."

He was burly, but no taller than Rosa, and massive as he might be, he was old and worn out. She wasn't afraid of him – so long as he stayed in human form. But Salvatore Pantaleone was also an Arcadian, and she wondered again what kind of animal slumbered inside him.

"It's been a long time," he said, "since I did anything but pull the strings from behind the scenes. I've killed men with my own hands, but that was decades ago. Later, my orders were enough by themselves to bring misfortune to others. But they've also made many people rich and influential. Ask any of the *capi*, and they'll all admit that I have led Cosa Nostra into a brilliant new age."

She tried to hit him where she hoped it would hurt. "So why do some of them secretly support the Hungry Man? Why are they waiting for him to come back to Sicily from his prison cell and take power again? Why do those men hate you so much that they'd rather follow someone who's regarded by everyone as a monster?"

He turned, moved a few steps away, and stopped in front of a painting. It was a Sicilian landscape full of sheep and bustling, cheerful peasants.

"What this picture shows was never really true," he said. "Nothing is what it seems. If you could see behind the laughter of these figures, you would recognise anxiety, fear of the coming night. And if you could look past the trees and farmhouses and church towers, you would find traces of us everywhere. The Arcadian dynasties have ruled the Mediterranean since time immemorial. They have set out from its coasts to go all over the world, gradually making realms old and new subject to them. These ludicrous peasants working in the field, with their red-cheeked wives and grubby children – they were never anything but our prey."

He turned back to Rosa, but her eyes were lingering on the painting as if it had suddenly opened a window into the past.

"But times have changed," he went on. "Back then we hunted them in packs, we ate their cattle and tore their sons and daughters apart. Today we don't rule them through fear alone; we do it through our wealth, our ingenuity, our knowledge of their weaknesses. We draw new strength from that, and anyone who denies it is a fool... but of course there are always some who don't see that. Some who mourn for the past. The Hungry Man is a living promise – a promise of a return to the old times, ancient customs and morals, unlimited killing and greed. He tried that approach in the past and failed, and over his decades in prison his hatred for human beings in general has grown even greater. He says he will give whatever they want to those who thirst for the blood of slaves, who hunger to dig claws and teeth into defenceless flesh once more. *That* is why they are preparing in secret for his return. Not because I didn't lead them well."

The revolver shook in Rosa's hand. She was clutching it

firmly, as if the gun could give her the strength she would need not to fall for his powers of persuasion. She wanted to show him that what he said wasn't getting through, that none of it meant anything at all to her.

But of course she knew better. So did he.

Pantaleone embodied the Arcadian dynasties of the present, rich and powerful in the form of Cosa Nostra and other organisations that had carved up the world between them. But the Hungry Man stood for the barbarity of the past, when other human beings had been fair game, and the Arcadians had ruled openly, wreaking havoc. An era of wild beasts.

"Do you want to be like them?" asked Pantaleone now, in a seductively gentle tone. "Do you want to be the monster, the nightmare in the night? Or would you rather go on living as before, only with a better, richer, happier life? You'll soon experience your first transformation – if it isn't behind you already."

His probing undertone tipped the scales. "I don't have to listen to this," she said. "I have nothing to do with the Hungry Man and the dynasties. If Zoe wants to stay, she's welcome. But nothing will keep *me* here."

"Not even young Carnevare?"

Had Zoe told him about Alessandro after all? With revulsion, she realised that the poison of his words was already taking effect. She distrusted her own sister.

"Alessandro has enough to do, getting to be *capo* of the Carnevares." She tried to sound indifferent, serene and cool. She wasn't sure whether she succeeded.

Pantaleone smiled, but his glance was harsh. "The Carnevares have never done anything but increase their power and wealth. That's the nature of the Mafia, you'll say, yet there's a difference. Cosa Nostra stands firmly by old values and laws; the family is our greatest good. But the Carnevares aren't like that. They sacrifice their allies, even their own flesh and blood, if it's to their advantage." He gave a short bark of laughter. "You don't believe me? You think I say so only to drive a wedge between you and that boy? Baron Carnevare let his wife be murdered – by his own adviser! In any other family that would be the greatest of crimes, and it wouldn't go unavenged. But in the Carnevare clan? The baron accepted his wife's death and said nothing. Gaia's murderer remained his closest confidant. Until Cesare finally decided it was time to be rid of the baron himself, and preferably his son in the bargain. Nothing is sacred to the Carnevares, not their own family, not Cosa Nostra."

Rosa wanted to say something to silence him, but Pantaleone quickly took another step towards her and went on. "What did Alessandro tell you? Did he say he likes you? Loves you? I'm sure that's what his father once told his mother – until one day he let her die because that was what Cesare advised. *Those* are the priorities in the house of Carnevare. So tell me, Rosa, what gives you the childish idea that it might be different, after all, with you?"

She tried to find words to contradict him, accuse him of lying, show that all this just bounced off her. Only it wasn't that simple. The baroness's death was a fact. And as for Alessandro's ambition to become *capo* himself—

"You know I'm right," said Pantaleone sharply. "Get involved with him, and you'll have his whole clan breathing down your neck. That will bring you nothing but trouble. Cesare will try to get rid of Alessandro. And if you stand in his way he'll eliminate you, too. Do you believe it's just coincidence that he's casting doubt on the concordat right at this very moment?"

All this was past history, but she wasn't sure whether Pantaleone knew it. The Carnevares had their sights set on her already, and Alessandro had indeed brought her nothing but trouble... no! She mustn't think that way. Pantaleone twisted things as it suited him. It hadn't started with Alessandro, that was the truth, but much earlier, a year ago in New York. With the death of her child.

The old man made an expansive gesture. "Ultimately, of course, it's your decision."

Her hand closed even more firmly on the handle of the gun. Her entire body tensed. Pain exploded inside her head, making any clear thought impossible for a moment.

It's your decision.

She turned and walked away.

"Where are you going?" he asked.

She did not reply.

"The tribunal will deliver its verdict at dawn," he called after her. "It's too late, Rosa. You can only decide for yourself this time – you have no influence any more!"

She hurried down the steps outside the house, left the palazzo, and strode along the path to the garages. A little later she was heading back down the drive in her father's Maserati.

At the gate, one of the guards stopped her and gestured to her to let down the window. "Here," he said, handing her a padded envelope. "Someone left this for you."

"Who?"

"Young lad. Gone again before we could ask him anything."

Rosa turned into the country road, drove the short distance to the exit for Piazza Armerina, and stopped the car on the shoulder there. Her headlights were the only ones in sight. With shaking fingers, she switched on the interior light of the car and opened the envelope. Frowning, she shook the contents out into her hand.

A cell phone. It was switched on.

The display showed a greenish infrared photo: herself and Alessandro, crossing the road outside the Villa Dallamano in the dark.

She stared at the picture for a minute.

The phone vibrated. Rosa took a deep breath and answered.

Traitors

She recognised the judge's voice at once.

Quattrini reminded Rosa of their agreement and told her that she had been shadowed ever since her return from Portugal, so of course she, Quattrini, knew that Rosa and Alessandro had broken into the Dallamanos' villa. What they were doing there, she added, didn't interest her. The one thing she really wanted was Rosa's information about Salvatore Pantaleone, which would give her the legal reason she needed to search the Alcantara property and lands. She was anxious to get her hands on the *capo dei capi*, and she was certainly not about to let Rosa pull the wool over her eyes. She was expecting that statement now. Rosa was not to move from the spot; someone would pick her up and bring her.

As soon as the connection was broken, headlights appeared in Rosa's rear window. The car must have followed her from the gate.

Tyres squealing, she took the Maserati back onto the road and accelerated quickly to over a hundred kilometres per hour. Highway 117 was well built, with broad lanes and a hard shoulder, something you couldn't take for granted in Sicily. She hoped she could keep her father's car under control even at the high speed. She was sweating within a few seconds anyway.

She had to find Alessandro and help him to rescue Iole.

The judge could wait; Pantaleone wasn't going to run away. Despite everything, Rosa felt guilty about handing him over to the forces of law and order. She was a traitor twice over: first to Cosa Nostra, then to the judge's confidence in her. But there was nothing she could do about it. She couldn't give up Alessandro. Everything the old man said might have been true about the baron – but not Alessandro.

The road was empty at this time of night; there were no rear lights to be seen ahead of her. Once something scurried across the asphalt, and she only just managed to avoid hitting it. Then she accelerated again. The legal limit here was ninety kilometres per hour, and the highway wound enough for that to make sense. Rosa was driving at 140, then 150 kilometres per hour.

The headlights in her rearview mirror kept their distance, but she had to get off this road as soon as possible. If Quattrini's people called up reinforcements, sooner or later they would cut her off ahead. But she wasn't sure how many officers the judge had at her disposal. Quattrini led a special anti-Mafia unit, probably only a handful of carefully picked men and women. If she brought in other officers, there was a danger that Cosa Nostra might be bribing some of them. Quattrini couldn't risk anyone getting a warning through to Pantaleone.

So the judge probably wouldn't mount a major search operation for Rosa. If she could shake off her pursuer, she stood a chance. All she needed was this one day. After that she would go to Quattrini of her own accord.

She cursed Alessandro for not telling her where the hunt was to take place. How was she going to find out where to drive in time to get there? And what was she going to offer Cesare in exchange for Iole's life? The Dallamano photographs and documents had been stolen by Florinda and her aides. Was there any other way to make a deal with Cesare? And what was Alessandro planning?

The steering wheel vibrated under her hands. Several times she nearly lost control on turns. Once the car went into a skid, skewing itself almost diagonally across the road, but she was able to right it quickly.

Several side roads flew past, but she stayed on the main highway. Passing one village, she had some difficulty negotiating a roundabout that she had almost failed to notice, fortunately with no other traffic on it. Insects splattered on the windshield, one leaving a mark as big as her fist. She switched the wipers on, but that made matters even worse. The yellow slime smeared itself all over the glass in a wide curve just level with Rosa's eyes.

160 kilometres per hour.

Way too fast.

Sweat was running into her eyes. She grimly clung to the wheel, and had to duck down to see under the dirty smear on the windshield. She couldn't go on like this for ever. But she was catching sight of her pursuer less and less often now.

Ahead of her, she saw rear lights. She quickly caught up with them, and without stopping to think overtook a Porsche. She saw two young men in it, staring incredulously at her.

When she moved back into the right-hand lane, she realised that she had just acquired another pursuer. Obviously the men were bent on a nocturnal race with her.

She slowed imperceptibly down. The Porsche caught up, drew beside her, and they drove on for several hundred metres side by side. She forced a smile and then accelerated again. The engine of the Porsche roared as well. The driver stayed in the left-hand lane as he tried to pass her.

Once again Rosa took her foot off the gas. The young men were yelling with glee; one of them made an obscene gesture. Then their car sped up and raced ahead into the night.

Rosa looked in the rearview mirror. Quattrini's men had disappeared behind a bend. It was now or never. At the next junction she braked sharply and turned into the side road, switched off the headlights, and stopped. A cloud of dust swirled up around the windows. Rosa stared over her shoulder in her rearview mirror. She was on a narrow woodland trail. When the dust died down, she could see a section of the main road between the trees.

With a little luck, by the time the police officers realised that the rear lights of the fast car ahead of them didn't belong to Rosa's Maserati, she would be well away from here.

She lowered the window a little way and listened for the car. Here they came.

The trees on the roadside were bathed in white light. Instinctively, Rosa ducked. The car chasing her raced past the turn, going north, its rear lights flickering several times between the trunks.

She breathed easily again only when the sound of the engine had finally died away. But she didn't dare switch her headlights on. Instead, she turned very cautiously in the darkness of the woodland track and drove back to the road at a crawl.

Lights again.

A second car was coming up along the road. It slowed down, rolled past the turn at a comfortable pace, braked, and reversed. Then it, too, turned into the woodland trail, barring her way out.

Quickly, Rosa looked around. There was a metal barrier across the track twenty metres behind her. She couldn't go any farther into the woods. She was trapped.

The headlights of the other car were switched off, but the engine kept on running. A door was opened and closed again. Someone was approaching.

The outline of a face appeared in the dark at her side window.

Rosa flung the door open with all her might. The man cried out as it hit him, and fell backward into waist-high bushes. She snatched the key out of the ignition and ran into the open air, looking neither right nor left, just making for the strange car as fast as she could. She opened the driver's door. The car was a black Mercedes. Quick as lightning, she got behind the wheel.

Hot, animal breath hit the back of her neck.

She closed her eyes. Expecting the fangs of a beast of prey to dig into her.

There was an excited whining. Then a dog's rough tongue licked her cheek.

Rosa swung her head around. "Sarcasmo!"

The dog's tail happily thumped the back seat.

Outside, the figure in the undergrowth was scrambling up, moving towards the Mercedes. Rosa only had two or three seconds to make her decision. With the press of a button, she locked the door and made sure that the passenger side was also secured.

Fundling leaned against the glass. His black hair was even more untidy than usual. His nose was bleeding.

"Let me in!" he called through the closed window.

Rosa lowered it very slightly.

"What are you doing here?" she asked. "What are you after?"

"What do you think? You."

"Did Alessandro send you?" She didn't seriously think so, and he shook his head. "Who, then? Cesare?"

"Hell, no. You nearly broke my nose."

Sarcasmo whined again and licked her ear.

"Open this door, Rosa. Come on."

"Who says I can trust you?"

"I've never hurt you, have I?"

"I'm not too popular with the Carnevares."

"Cesare doesn't know I'm here. None of them know."

"So what are you here for, then?"

"To pick you up."

She closed the window and put her foot on the gas. Just a light tap on the pedal. The Mercedes leaped forward and then stopped again. She was only two metres from the road now.

With a few steps, Fundling was beside her again. He looked nervous now, the way he had at their first meeting, when he was picking Alessandro up at the airport. He gestured to her to open the window again.

She let it down two fingers' breadth.

"Quattrini sent me," he said quietly, his lips very close to the opening. "She wanted me to fetch you because she thought you'd be more likely to trust me than her own people." The corners of his mouth twitched. "Seems like that was a lousy plan."

Her first impulse was to deny everything. Act as if she had never heard the name of Quattrini before. But then she asked, "You know her?"

"I sometimes talk to her. When she needs information. Just like you." He looked intently at her. "If you mention that to anyone, I'm dead."

Ditto, she thought. If he was telling the truth, then he was informing on the Carnevares for the judge. Until now she had assumed that he was loyal to the baron, devoted to the man who had taken him in as a baby. But Cesare wasn't the baron.

"You saw it." The words slipped out of her. "You saw Cesare kill the baron, didn't you?"

For a moment he looked surprised. Then he nodded. "I can't leave now. Cesare would think I'd given him away. He'd murder me."

"But instead you betray him but stay with him, and keep acting as his driver. Not stupid." All the same, she didn't trust him. He *was* a traitor – like her, strictly speaking – and traitors were not to be trusted.

"Will you open the door now?" he asked impatiently.

Sarcasmo was panting on the back seat.

"Did you drive them there?" she asked. "Cesare and the others?"

He nodded. "I was on my way back to the castle when the judge's people intercepted me. They sent me to you with the envelope and the cell phone."

"But the other car—"

"I was alone," he interrupted her, shaking his head. "No idea who you were speeding away from, but it wasn't anyone from her unit. At least, I don't think so. Probably just someone who happened to be driving down the road."

"Where did you take the Carnevares?"

He hesitated. "Don't go there, Rosa. It's not something you ought to interfere with."

She stared at him. "You know, don't you? What's going to happen there? To Iole?"

"They've done it often enough before. The baron was always against it, but Cesare…"

She swallowed. "Did you take Iole there?"

"No. That was one of his immediate circle. I was only driving two of his guests. One of the baron's cousins from Catania and his wife."

So there really was a whole pack of Panthera gathering to hunt the girl. Once again, she had to swallow a lump in her throat.

"Where are they?" she asked again.

"Let me in first."

She shook her head vigorously. "Where, Fundling?"

He looked down. "Gibellina. The monument."

"The *what*?"

"Don't do it. They'll kill you."

"Alessandro's there."

"He's one of them."

"No. He's different." She opened the glove compartment. There were several road maps inside.

Sarcasmo settled down on the back seat. She dared not unlock a door to let him out. Anyway, he was obviously happy enough with her at the wheel.

Fundling rattled the handle. "Please!"

All she said was, "Stand back." She gave him a moment, then hit the gas. The engine roared. The Mercedes started. Out onto the dark highway. The keys to the Maserati were lying on the passenger seat along with the cell phone.

Fundling leaped back, shouting something over the engine noise.

Sarcasmo sighed happily as he dropped off to sleep.

Rosa turned on the headlights and raced towards the expressway as fast as she could.

The Gibellina Monument

At four thirty in the morning Rosa was still at the wheel. The exit should be coming up any moment now, but she had thought that half an hour ago. After she had left the southern coastal road and turned inland again, the drive seemed to go on for ever.

Only a few more miles. She rubbed her eyes. A fog of nervous exhaustion surrounded her determination. Once she stopped the car at a rest area and burst into tears. It was a good fifteen minutes before she could drive again.

A buzzing startled her. The cell phone was vibrating, knocking against the keys to the Maserati. This wasn't the first time. So far she had ignored it, because it could only be Quattrini with more threats and accusations.

But it didn't stop. The buzzing was sending her crazy, and when it stopped briefly and then began again her nerve broke. She picked up the cell phone and pressed the answer key.

"Yes?"

"It's me." A man's voice, and one that she ought to have recognised at once. But in her present state of mind it took her a couple of seconds to place it.

"Pantaleone," she said wearily. "Where did you get this number?" The men at the gate had told him about the envelope waiting for her and had made a note of the cell phone's number. Did the old man know who it came from?

"The guards didn't recognise the boy, but it didn't take long to check him out," he said. "Next time young Carnevare has something delivered to you, he might as well just write the sender's name on the envelope."

"What do you want?" She spoke quickly so he wouldn't notice her sigh of relief.

"You need help."

"Not yours, for sure."

"Is there anyone else you can think of?"

On the back seat, Sarcasmo uttered a doggy growl in his dreams, shifted his position, and went on sleeping.

"I mean that seriously," said Pantaleone. "Where you're going, you'll need someone to stand by you."

"And you're the man?" she said derisively.

"Are you in Gibellina yet?"

It ought to have come as a shock that he knew her destination, but she was too tired even for that.

"You're playing into their hands, and you know it. Because you still hope. But hope is something many of us have lost. That's another reason why I value you so much, Rosa. You and I together can lead the Alcantaras and all of Cosa Nostra to a new dawn."

She snorted contemptuously. "The Hungry Man has you running scared, doesn't he?"

"Of course. Along with many of us."

"I told you before, I'm not interested."

"That will change. It will, believe me."

She wanted to rub her eyes again, but with one hand on the wheel and the other holding the cell phone, she couldn't. "Is that all?"

"Don't hang up. You're going to need my help. Without me, you can't rescue the girl. And young Carnevare will die."

"Alessandro knows exactly what—"

"What he's doing? No, my dear Rosa. The truth is that they picked him up some time ago. They have him locked up in Gibellina. Same as the little Dallamano girl who means so much to you."

"How do you know this?"

She could picture his self-satisfied smile. "You don't have to like me, Rosa. Or even respect me. But don't make the mistake of underestimating me. Enough talking. I'll guide you to Gibellina. Along a better route than those old road maps from your father's time."

She did prick up her ears at that. At least he didn't know she was in Fundling's Mercedes.

"What do you want from me in return?"

"Your trust. Your word that you're on my side. And that you'll listen to me without any ifs or buts."

"I could say yes and not mean it."

"If you say yes, it's a pact. The same pact I made with your aunt, and others before her. To break it would have far-reaching consequences." He paused for a moment. "Well?"

Oh fuck, she was at her wits' end. "Agreed," she said.

"Where are you now?"

"On the A29, going north."

"What's the next exit road?"

"It's for Salemi. And Gibellina Nuova."

"You don't take that one," he said firmly, going on to give her directions to the exit after next off the expressway, where she was to follow the road through an isolated chain of hills.

At first she saw signs to remote farms at the few turns off this road. Then it just went on and on, winding its way uphill around many bends. Finally the road petered out into a bumpy gravel track. Now and then along her route her headlights had shown poorly tended vineyards and olive groves, but a large part of the countryside seemed to be barren or lying fallow.

"That's close enough," said Pantaleone on the phone. "Leave the car somewhere – behind bushes or trees if you can find any. You'll have to go the rest of the way on foot."

Sarcasmo had woken up when she stopped, and was sitting upright on the back seat. His black coat stood on end at the back of his neck; he looked at her expectantly. She left all the windows slightly open and told him he would have to wait here in the car – for her or for someone else, if something happened to her. In that case, she felt sure, the Carnevares would find the Mercedes and set the dog free.

"Do you still have the revolver you were going to shoot me with?" asked the old man on the telephone. "Interesting model, by the way. With a silencer fitted. The Russian secret service likes that kind of thing."

She quietly closed the door of the car. "Yes, I have it here."

"How much ammunition?"

"No idea. How do I find out?"

He explained. In the moonlight, she felt the bulges of the cartridges in the cylinder. "Six," she said.

"And you don't know how to use it?"

"No."

"But you are American."

"Ha, ha."

"If you do as I say, and go about it cleverly, I hope you won't need it. Unless Cesare Carnevare crosses your path, in which case please be kind enough to shoot him."

"How about the concordat?"

He laughed. "Shoot him when no one's looking. But apart from that, he won't be there anyway. The tribunal ought to keep him busy all morning."

"Where's it meeting, anyway?"

"In Corleone. Only a short flight away by helicopter... Have you started walking?"

"I will as soon as you tell me where to go."

"You must follow the trail, but be careful. No one is likely to be approaching from that side, because it's a long detour and the path is so bad. All the same, keep your eyes open, and watch for headlights."

Sarcasmo didn't bark as she walked away from the car. Good dog.

Pantaleone directed Rosa along the trail for about a mile, around several bends, until an expanse of land opened up in front of her. To her right, the terrain rose higher towards the top of the mountain, to the left there were boulders, and beyond them a stony slope overgrown with bushes.

Ahead, however, there was a small plateau no larger than the marketplace of a town. It too was overgrown, but there was an asphalt path through the middle of it. On the far side, the black outline of a bizarre rock formation was visible.

Although her eyes were accustomed to the pale moonlight by now, she saw what it really was only when Pantaleone said, "You should have the ruins of Gibellina in sight any moment now."

The old man had lowered his voice. Rosa got down behind a few bushes for cover and looked at the bulky remains of walls. Her heart was pounding.

"The monument is to your right," he said.

From where she was, she couldn't see what was beyond the shrubbery. She was about to stand up and go on, when he whispered, "You must take great care now. There are bound to be guards. Take the cell phone in your left hand and the revolver in your right."

"Okay."

"Don't fire unless it's absolutely necessary. And when you can be sure of hitting your target. Six bullets aren't a lot if you want to be a match for the Carnevares and their allies."

"That's ridiculous," she whispered. "I'm not a match for *anyone*."

"Then why did you set out for Gibellina?"

She bit her lower lip and didn't reply.

"Very well, then," he said a moment later. "If you start something, you ought to see it through. But try not to kill anyone. I can make sure that the tribunal decides in favour of the Alcantaras once – a second time would be much more difficult."

"What *do* you really want me to do?" she whispered. "First you suggest I'm welcome to shoot everyone and their mother, then you don't want me killing anyone. That's not particularly helpful."

"I can't make your decisions for you. Do what you think is right. That's usually what matters to you, isn't it?" She couldn't shake off her impression that he was testing her. "Your two friends are locked up in the ruins. What you see ahead of you is only a part of what was left of old Gibellina. On the other side of the hill, down the slope, there are some more ruined houses. That's where you'll find what you're looking for."

From far away came aggressive roaring.

She had heard the same sound before, on Isola Luna. Lions and tigers. Did they roam free here, as well? The gun seemed to be heating up in her hand. Her palm was sweaty against the metal.

"What is this place?" she asked softly. "Those ruins… it's like a battlefield."

"There are two Gibellinas," he explained impatiently. "The new one near the expressway – and the old village up in the hills where you are at this moment. It was destroyed in an earthquake in 1968. Instead of being restored in the same place, Gibellina Nuova was built twelve miles farther to the west, and the survivors were resettled there. There are only ruins and rubble on the old site now. And the monument."

She got to her feet and tried to get a glimpse through the

bushes, but it was impossible. She would have to move out onto the plateau.

"I can't see a thing from here," she said.

"Don't waste your time trying. The sun will rise soon, and then you'll have much more difficulty moving about unnoticed."

"I'm going over to the ruins now."

"Brave girl."

She looked around, listened again for the distant roar of the wild beasts, and ran. Ducking low, she passed through the waist-high grass, always looking for cover behind bushes and shrubs. There was no one in sight. However, she could now see a slope rising to her right, and farther up it a farmhouse. She couldn't be sure whether that, too, was in ruins or not. From a distance it looked dilapidated but habitable. Behind it, on the nearby chain of hills, windmills stood motionless. Their white surfaces shone like gigantic bones in the moonlight.

But neither the house on the hill nor the distant windmills were what made her hold her breath as she knelt there, looking at what lay ahead of her on the slope.

The Gibellina monument was less than a hundred metres away, and at first glance she couldn't work out exactly what was before her.

But she understood at once why Cesare had chosen this place for his hunt.

The Ruins

A maze.

An immense concrete labyrinth

On an area at least the size of two football fields, the side of the mountain had been covered to a height of several metres with a layer of cement – it looked as if someone had spread a gigantic grey sheet over the ground. A network of narrow paths crisscrossed the concrete, dividing it into blocks the size of houses.

Pantaleone's breathing over the phone crackled in Rosa's ear. "You can see it now, right?"

"What's it supposed to be?"

"It's the ground plan of the old village. The paths show the former streets and alleyways, the concrete blocks between them are the buildings. An artist had the whole thing built in the eighties as a memorial to the place that used to stand here." The old man uttered a croaking laugh. "The money swallowed up by this ridiculous project could have been used to build a few decent houses for the survivors somewhere else."

"And of course Cosa Nostra wouldn't have made a red cent out of building them," she remarked sharply. "All heart, aren't you?"

"You're getting the hang of the way it works, my dear."

She hated him calling her that. However, she swallowed her reply, tore her eyes away from the cement labyrinth, and kept on moving through the grass and undergrowth, ducking low.

On the far side of the small plateau she cautiously skirted the rock formation that she had seen earlier from a distance. After a few steps she reached a ruin nestling against the boulders. There was no telling now what kind of building it had once been. The remains of the walls were sprayed with graffiti, and there were no doors left, not even window frames. Only black rectangles, with a disgusting smell of urine and carrion drifting out of them into the open air.

Farther down the slope, a big cat roared again. Cold shivers ran down Rosa's spine. A chilly wind swept across the hills, carrying the smell of burnt wood with it.

"Now what?"

"Have you reached the first building?"

"What's left of it."

"On the other side of it the slope goes down into the valley. There are a series of ruins scattered over it, far apart, and farther down are the remains of a short street. You must go there. That's the part of the village that wasn't covered over with that supposed work of art. Everything is still as it was after the earthquake."

"You know your way around this place."

"Cesare Carnevare isn't the first to have seen its uses."

She closed her eyes for a couple of seconds, took a deep breath, and moved on.

On the other side of the rocks, the bushes grew taller and closer together, and it was easier to find cover. Cautiously, she made her way through the shadows until the terrain began sloping downhill. The revolver felt as if it had been welded to her hand, with her fingers clutching the butt.

She heard voices. They came closer, then stopped. Peering over the tall grass, she saw two men walking up a steep road that had obviously once joined the upper and lower parts of the village. There were many branching cracks in the asphalt, with weeds growing through them. Ordinary cars couldn't have driven along this road; even Land Rovers would find it tough going.

The men wore black leather jackets and had headsets on. One was holding a submachine gun, the other a heavy flashlight. He had a pistol in a shoulder holster.

"What's happening?" crackled Pantaleone's voice over the cell phone.

Rosa jumped, and covered the loudspeaker with her hand.

One of the men looked around, but he walked on. The two of them were ten metres from Rosa, approaching a bend in the road. Once they had passed it, they would have their backs to her.

A little later she slipped away from the cover of the rocks. The wind ruffled her hair, blowing several blond strands into her face. She wished she had tied it back.

Below her, only a stone's throw away, stood the remains of a three-storey house. The back of it must have crumbled away in the earthquake. Rooms gaped open in the narrow wall at the side of the building, like in a dollhouse. But the front was more or less intact. There were even balconies still outside the windows of the second and third floors.

Someone was sitting there in the dark, behind its balustrade. He ought to have been able to see her, too. Was he looking in the other direction at this moment? She could vaguely make out his silhouette, but nothing else.

Alarmed, she kept very close to the facade so that he couldn't see her from above. If she was going to get past this house, she would have to pass several open doors, as well as a gaping hole where there had once been a window.

She reached the first door, then the second. Someone had painted the words DONNE and UOMINI over the doors, as if they were public toilets.

A figure came out of the third door and barred her way.

Rosa raised the revolver.

The man, in a leather jacket and jeans like the other two, held up his left hand reassuringly. He was holding a submachine gun in his right hand, with its muzzle pointing to the ground. His long black hair fell over his shoulders.

She was still wondering what to do when he shook his head and gestured to her to follow him.

"What—"

He put a finger to his lips.

"Rosa." Pantaleone spoke up again. She had almost forgotten about him.

She put the cell phone in front of her mouth like a microphone. "Not now."

"I assume you've met Remeo," said the old man. His voice sounded distorted, with a crackle in it.

"Remeo?" she repeated.

The man with the submachine gun nodded. "Quiet, now. Come with me."

Instead, she put the cell phone to her ear again. "Who is he?"

"How do you think I know what Cesare gets up to?" asked Pantaleone. "Remeo is my man in his camp. An informer, if you will. He told me they'd picked up Alessandro. And where they're keeping him and the girl. He'll take you there."

She still didn't trust Pantaleone, let alone this henchman of his, who was obviously working for both sides. But she had no choice.

Taking no more notice of her or the gun she was holding, Remeo turned and went into the house. She hesitantly followed him inside. The soles of her shoes crunched on broken glass. The narrow corridor had a back wall, but through another door she could see that there was nothing left behind it. After less than a metre the ground fell abruptly away. Old linoleum hung in rags over the edge.

But Remeo was not on his way to the back of the house. He went down a flight of stairs to a cellar. Reluctantly, she followed him through pitch-dark rooms. They finally reached the open air again on a bank below the ruined building, where tilting piles of rubble were overgrown with bushes. They were making their way through a crevice in the rubble when Remeo suddenly stopped, pointing to three houses a little farther down the slope. In the moonlight, and at this distance, they looked almost intact. Their former gardens had merged into a jungle of dense undergrowth.

"It's the middle house," her companion whispered. "The back door is open. There are several men patrolling the road outside it. And at least one in the house itself. Probably in the kitchen, or what's left of it. Your boyfriend is on the first floor, the room at the end of the hall. There's no lock, only a bolt on the outside of the door. If they catch you and shut you in there, no one can help you."

There wasn't much for her to remember, but she went through each piece of this information separately in her head.

"Where's Iole?"

"She was in the house with him, but they took her away."

"Where to?"

He shrugged.

Pantaleone's crackling voice came again. "You may have to decide between them."

If he said any more about *her decision* she'd scream. Even here.

"Thank you," she said to Remeo, and set off. After she had gone a couple of steps, she looked over her shoulder.

There was no one on the slope behind her.

The tangled jungle that the tiny garden of the house had become in recent decades offered adequate cover. Remeo had been right. The back door was unlocked, and she probably had him to thank for that, too. Very close, beyond the bushes, a generator was chugging noisily. It smelled of burnt fuel and oil.

On tiptoe, she slipped into the house and made her way along a narrow corridor. A staircase led to the floor above. The banisters had disappeared.

Light fell through an open door near the entrance. Glasses or bottles clinked inside the room. A man's voice was hoarsely singing along with an old Italian hit on a radio.

Revolver in hand, Rosa stole up the stairs. The steps under her feet seemed to be smeared with sticky resin that clung to the soles of her shoes. It felt like an eternity before she reached the top.

The singing stopped short.

Rosa scuttled around a corner at the top of the stairs. She heard loud footsteps in the kitchen, then in the corridor.

She held her breath. Listened and waited.

Nothing moved down below. Until she began to think no one was there now. But then she heard a cough, and footsteps walking back into the room. The radio was turned down, and the man did not begin his tuneless singing again.

A naked lightbulb lit the second-floor hallway. Four of the five doors were open. Only the last, at the very end, was closed. Someone had used a chunk of wood to make a bolt with a medieval look to it. It rested in fittings that had been screwed to the door itself and the wall beside the frame. Scraps of brownish wallpaper hung from the ceiling like dusty cobwebs. They blew eerily in the draught as Rosa passed under them.

As soon as she raised the cell phone to her ear, she could hear Pantaleone's voice.

"I'm in the house," she whispered. "Just outside Alessandro's door."

She distrusted her own feelings; she was torn between the confusing closeness she had felt when Alessandro, in his panther form, sat beside her at the end of the abandoned expressway, and her anger with him for leaving her behind at the palazzo like some silly little girl he'd picked up in a bar.

Soundlessly, she reached the end of the hall. The wooden bolt was heavy, and she had to put the revolver and cell phone down on the floor to lift it out of the fittings with both hands. The scraping of wood against wood sounded much too loud in the silence.

Very, very cautiously she propped the bolt against the wall. Picked up the revolver, but left the cell phone lying there. Placed one hand on the old-fashioned doorknob.

"Alessandro," she whispered as she turned it. "It's me. Rosa."

There were footsteps on the stairs behind her.

Then quiet singing…

Blood Flows

She let go of the doorknob again and swung around, arms out-stretched, holding the revolver in both hands. She aimed it down the hall as if she knew what she was doing. In fact she was trembling rather than taking aim.

A man came up the stairs. He reached the upper landing, carrying a steaming glass of hot milk. In his efforts not to spill the liquid, he still hadn't noticed her. He switched the glass from hand to hand so he wouldn't burn his fingers.

He was still four metres away from Rosa when he looked up.

The glass fell and broke on the floor. Milk splashed over the dirty linoleum.

"One squeak out of you and I fire." She hoped he didn't notice how the revolver shook in her hands.

The man came closer.

"Stay where you are!"

This time he obeyed.

"Do you have a gun on you?"

Slowly, he opened his jacket with one hand and showed her the shoulder holster.

"Pull up the zipper on your jacket." She dared not tell him to take the pistol out and drop it on the floor. She didn't know how quick he might be. "Very carefully," she said.

He was a head and a half taller than Rosa, and twice as broad. "You're the Alcantara girl."

"Zip up that jacket."

"Okay." He followed her instructions without trying any tricks. His face was not unattractive, almost humorous.

Finally he began moving again, arms raised by his sides.

"Stay where you are."

"And then what?"

Good question. The hall was too narrow for her to make him pass her and go ahead into the room. And she couldn't lock him in one of the other rooms either, because he would alert the guards outside through the window.

"You know," he said quietly, taking another step towards her, "there's only one thing for you to do. You'll have to shoot me."

She aimed the gun at his face.

"Can you do it?" he asked.

"I'll shoot you in the stomach. If you don't bleed to death, the pain will kill you." She'd once heard that in a Western.

"Then you'd better *aim* at my stomach." He dropped his left hand and patted his jacket. Her eyes instinctively followed his movement. In the same split second, she realised that she had made a mistake.

His right hand went swiftly behind his back, to bring out a long hunting knife. He must have been carrying it behind him on his belt.

Without a word, he lunged at her.

She pulled the trigger. The silencer swallowed up the sound except for a high whistling.

The man staggered as if he had been punched, stumbled back against the corridor wall. Something wet gleamed on his left shoulder as he turned to her again, his face distorted by pain.

Her hands were trembling more than ever. There was nothing she could do to stop them.

He lunged again. The knife was as long as her forearm, and its blade shone in the light of the naked bulb.

Suddenly there was someone beside her. A cool hand touched hers, gently taking the weapon from her fingers. She let go of it. The man was looking incredulously past Rosa.

"Alessandro?" she whispered.

But it wasn't Alessandro. Iole stood there instead. Unruffled, she aimed the revolver at the man – and pulled the trigger.

This time the shot knocked him off his feet. When his back and head hit the floor, Rosa saw the coin-size hole in his forehead.

"There," said Iole, pleased, as if she had finished a difficult piece of needlework.

Pantaleone's voice was shouting in agitation from the cell phone on the floor. "What's going on? Rosa? Are you all right?"

She ignored him. Iole, in front of her, had let the hand holding the revolver sink and was looking down at the dead man. She wore a white dress and smelled of soap and shampoo. Washed and dressed up to make a pretty quarry for the hunters to chase.

Rosa hugged her, and felt the butt of the gun behind her back as Iole returned the embrace. They both had tears in their eyes, but neither girl shed them.

"Have they done anything to you?" asked Rosa.

Iole shook her head.

Rosa gently took the gun from her hand. "Did your father teach you to use that?"

"My uncle," she said. "Augusto."

"Is Alessandro with you?"

"No."

Rosa looked doubtfully through the open door. No trace of him. Was it the wrong room? Maybe the wrong house?

"I'm going to get you out of here," she told Iole, although she wasn't sure who had just saved whom. She avoided looking at the dead man. Iole, however, took two slow steps towards him, put her head to one side, and examined him.

With her left hand, Rosa picked up the cell phone again, keeping the revolver in her right. "Pantaleone?"

"What the hell is going on?"

"You lied to me."

"Have you freed the girl?"

"Yes. But that wasn't what you and your friend Remeo told me." She wasn't going to say that she had expected to find Alessandro, not here in front of Iole. But the old man knew exactly what she meant. "I'm fed up with you and your tricks."

"The girl is free. That will have to do."

"This is another of your tests, right? To see if I'm made of the right stuff to lead the Alcantaras."

"You've just passed it."

"You said I'd find him here."

"Steer clear of him," he said forcefully. "The Carnevares

aren't like you and me. He'll bring you nothing but pain and grief."

"You can leave that to me." She looked at Iole, who was crouching beside the body, touching the lifeless face with her fingertip.

"You will do as I tell you now." The old man's voice was sharp. "I am your *capo*, and you will obey me."

"The hell I will. Play your little games with Florinda and Zoe if they'll go along with them."

"Forget him, Rosa. Run to the car with the girl, get out of there, both of you. You still have a chance. But it won't be long before someone notices that the girl's missing." He hesitated briefly, and then added, "Just now, when you were otherwise engaged, I was sent a message. The tribunal has made its decision."

"So early?" There was a tinge of bluish light outside the open doors. The sun would be rising in a few minutes.

"As soon as the tribunal opened, Cesare withdrew his accusation," Pantaleone said. "Your sister called a few minutes ago and told me. Cesare said that you were indeed to blame for his son's death, but you didn't pull the trigger yourself. So he got in ahead of my witnesses, avoiding a decision that would have damaged his reputation and been a bad start for a *capo* of the Carnevares. This way, however, he's shown everyone that he submits to the laws of the dynasties and would be worthy of the title of *capo*. At this moment, the tribunal should be suggesting that the Carnevares would do well to elect him their new leader."

"There's another possibility," whispered Rosa, looking at the revolver in her hand.

"Yes. There is."

"He knew I'd try to free Iole. He knew Carnevare blood would probably flow."

"Which it obviously just has," commented Pantaleone.

"And this time no one will believe I *didn't* fire the shot." She took a deep breath and turned to the girl. "Iole, do you know who that dead man is?"

"Dario Carnevare," said Iole. "Alessandro's second cousin."

Pantaleone groaned quietly. "That's the second breach of the concordat he can throw up at you. And who knows whether it will be the last, if you don't get out of there right away."

"He's been taking me for a ride."

"Possibly."

"And he knows I'm here. Now, at this moment."

"Very conceivably."

"And you knew that Cesare would lure me here."

"I only took it into consideration. I wouldn't have let you fall into his trap if there had been no way out of it. So if you hurry, you can do it. Cesare made a mistake, in spite of everything. He ought to have taken treason into account when he made his plans. Let that be a lesson to you, Rosa – double-dealing is your constant companion. But Cesare has no idea that two of his men in Gibellina are on your side. He feels confident, the fool!"

"Two men? Remeo, and who's the other?"

"You may meet him if you go to your car now, *at once!*" He was obviously tired of this discussion.

So was Rosa. "I'm getting Alessandro out of here first."

"There's no time to—"

She hung up. After a moment's hesitation, she switched the cell phone off and put it in her pocket.

"Rosa?" Iole had risen to her feet and was smoothing out her white dress. She looked rather dazed.

"We have to go." Rosa took her hand and led her away from the body, over to the stairs.

"Rosa. I know where he is." Iole smiled, but she looked strangely distracted. "I know where they took Alessandro."

❋

Ten minutes later, at the outer edge of the monument, Rosa was anxiously watching Iole move away, a patch of white in the dawn twilight. If she kept going in that direction, she couldn't fail to see the Mercedes. Rosa had described the place where she had left the car and made the girl promise to hide near it and wait for her. If Rosa wasn't back by full daylight, she said, Iole must set out on foot. Two hours' walk down the road would take her to the nearest village.

At the moment Rosa couldn't do anything else for her. The northern route seemed to be reasonably safe. The Carnevares, and others who had come to Gibellina for the election and the hunt that would follow it, had left their cars in the valley south of the ruined village. In the dim light of early morning,

Rosa had seen them some way farther down the slope. She thought, and hoped, that Iole could get away unnoticed on the inhospitable and winding road to the north.

Several men were preparing for the hunt in the concrete alleys of the monument, setting up floodlights and generators. Rosa crouched in the tall bushes, assessing the best way to avoid Cesare's henchmen.

Time was short. The sun was coming up over the hills in the east, turning the sky a fiery red. Morning mists rose from the surrounding valleys, dispersing among the untended vineyards. Rosa set out on a wide detour around the concrete labyrinth on its western side. Ducking low, she ran up the slope, taking what shelter she could find in the bushes and the rubble. No one had yet realised that Iole had disappeared. It was possible that Remeo was covering up for her down there.

Above her was the lonely rough-hewn stone farmhouse that she had seen when she'd first arrived. It stood on the slope above the monument, apparently unoccupied.

So far she had seen only a single patrol, and avoided it easily enough. All the other men were busy putting up floodlights, laying cables, and preparing a large festive table in the shelter of the mighty rocks at the edge of the monument, out of the wind. Crates of wine were carried, clinking, up a path that ordinary cars couldn't manage; wooden benches and folding chairs were set up. A huge barbecue with a spit big enough to hold a whole calf was being hauled up the hill by four men. Rosa had a horrible idea of *what* the long spit was intended for.

Was this the way the Arcadian dynasties had helped the savage lusts of antiquity to survive into the present day? What barbarity would there be if the Hungry Man regained control of the dynasties again, reviving King Lycaon's cult of cannibalism?

As she climbed the last part of the way to the house, she wondered again about Cesare's motives. It seemed strange that he wasn't mounting a search for her. Unless, it suddenly occurred to her, he had indeed given orders for one, but they had never arrived at the Gibellina monument. If so, Pantaleone's second informer must hold high rank within the Carnevare clan – high enough to countermand Cesare's message.

Up above the monument, Rosa crossed a narrow path – asphalted, but the surface was breaking up – and then she reached the outer wall of the old farmhouse. Keeping low, she was moving into its shadow when she heard a noise far away. It was the rhythmic hum of an engine, rapidly getting louder.

Cautiously, she peered around the corner of the wall. The dismal concrete expanse of the monument stretched out below her.

In the sky to the east, gold in the rising sun, a helicopter was arriving.

The Informer

The helicopter landed on the open space at the edge of the concrete labyrinth. The men busy with preparations for the celebration stopped work when the wind of the rotor blades and swirling dust whipped across the slope.

Rosa was about two hundred metres uphill. No one could see her from below. Her heart was hammering so hard that she could sense the pulsing at her throat.

The side door of the helicopter opened and Cesare Carnevare climbed out, accompanied by three bodyguards, all of them in black suits. One of the men who had been working on the monument hurried towards Cesare.

Rosa withdrew her head and leaned against the wall for a moment. Even if Cesare's orders to his men in Gibellina to look for her had never reached them, it wouldn't be long before someone went in search of Iole and Alessandro.

She hid behind an abandoned stable a little way up the slope and found that she could peer cautiously around its corner and see the front of the dilapidated farmhouse. New windows had been set into the facade.

Two Land Rovers were parked outside the entrance. There were no guards in sight, but she couldn't be quite sure. So she ran first into the cover of one vehicle, then over to the other. There were ten metres now between her and the farmhouse door.

She was betting everything on a single card. She ducked low and ran across the open space of the farmyard. A light shone behind one of the dirty windows. Crouching down, she heard men's voices inside the house, talking in low voices. Two at least.

There were still four bullets in her revolver. She wasn't sure what her best course of action would be. All she knew was that Alessandro was being held in this building, and she had to do something.

A cell phone rang inside the house. The men stopped talking. A brief silence, and then one of them said, on the other side of the glass, "No, all in order here. No problems. But Gino will take a look around outside."

"Why me?" protested his companion, but the next moment came the scraping sound of chair legs being pushed back.

Rosa raced away, retreating behind one of the Land Rovers. In a panic, she looked around for a better place to hide, and at the last second rolled under the vehicle. She lay on her stomach in the dust, the gun in both hands, looking towards the house.

The front door opened; faint light fell out into the farmyard. A man came out with a submachine gun in one hand and a torch in the other.

Rosa didn't move. She held her breath.

Slowly, the man crossed the yard. His shoes disappeared behind one of the high tyres. She couldn't see him now, although he was less than two metres away.

"Anything unusual?" asked a voice as the second man appeared in the doorway.

"Not a soul in sight."

"Go and look all around the house."

"What are they so scared of all of a sudden? Cops?"

The man in the doorway shrugged his shoulders. "We're to keep our eyes peeled, that's what they said. Signore Carnevare is coming up. He wants to speak to the boy."

Gino, the man standing between the Land Rovers, groaned. "Okay, I'll look around. Leave some of those *cannoli* for me."

No sooner had he disappeared around the corner of the house than a third voice called, from the trail leading up to the house, "All clear with you?"

Rosa couldn't believe her ears.

The man in the entrance shone the light of a lamp on the new arrival. "Does anyone say anything different? Why do they all seem to think we're not up to the job?" Morosely, he stepped out of the door. "So what do you want?"

"Signore Carnevare sent me. I'm to take Alessandro to him down by the chopper."

"Just now they said he was coming up here to us."

"Then he's changed his mind." Footsteps crunched on dust and gravel. Turning her head, Rosa saw trainers and jeans moving over the yard outside the house from the path below.

She knew that voice.

"Are you alone?" asked Fundling.

"Gino's just checking the back of the building. Wait there while I call them down below so that they can—"

"No need."

Two shots hissed through a silencer. The man in the doorway collapsed without a sound.

Rosa still didn't move.

Fundling was faster. She could see him now, bending over the lifeless man and hauling him into the house. After a last glance into the dawn twilight, checking the surroundings, he closed the door from the inside.

Maybe he had hot-wired the Maserati. Or someone had picked him up and brought him here. The judge's people? But wouldn't they have intervened long before?

Rosa glanced at the corner of the house. Gino wasn't in sight yet. She quickly rolled out from under the Land Rover, ran on tiptoe to the window, and peered in. No one there.

She switched the gun to her left hand so that she could wipe her sweating palm on her jeans. Then she took the butt in her right again, stole over to the door, breathing deeply – and opened it.

She aimed the revolver into the house.

Fundling was standing in front of her, with the muzzle of his own firearm pointing her way.

"Rosa!" Relieved, he lowered the pistol.

She kept her gun at the ready and stepped inside the door, kicking it closed behind her with her foot.

"Where's Alessandro?"

Legs apart, Fundling was standing over the dead man's feet. "You don't have to wave a gun at me."

"What are you doing here?"

He shrugged. "You left me the Maserati."

"Did Quattrini send you?"

"She's looking for you."

Rosa pointed at the body of the dead man. "What was that for?"

"We have to hurry. Before Gino comes back." He put the pistol in his waistband and started dragging the body away from the door. They were in a narrow hallway. To the left was the lighted room where the guards had been sitting. The door on the right was closed. Fundling manoeuvred the corpse through the third door, at the end of the tiny hall.

Rosa never took her eyes off him. The gun in her hands wasn't shaking nearly as badly now. She was still confused, but she was regaining control over herself. She waited.

Fundling came back into the hall, closing the door behind him. He had the pistol in his hand again now. Rosa kept aiming at his chest.

"Now to look for Alessandro," he said.

"You just shot that man."

"Well, what exactly were *you* planning to do?" He nodded at her gun.

She heard footsteps outside in the front courtyard.

Rosa swore. She was still standing with her back to the front door. Time to get out of there, fast. She quickly made her way into the room on the left, just in time to see Fundling aiming his pistol at the entrance to the house.

Gino opened the door. "Nothing there. No idea what they—"

Fundling fired twice. Through the narrow gap, Rosa couldn't

see either of them. But she heard the heavy thud of a body falling. Fundling hurried to the door. A moment later he was dragging the second dead man to the end of the corridor.

The room where Rosa was standing smelled of sweet pastries and coffee. Two cardboard cups stood on a table, with a thermos jug and a plastic plate of *cannoli*.

Outside the room, the door at the end of the corridor closed, and then Fundling shut the front door as well. Seeing a trace of blood on the floor, he cursed under his breath.

"Once again," said Rosa, "what are you doing here?"

"Keeping an eye on you."

"Keeping an eye on—" She was lost for words. "Quattrini knows I'm here, and she sends you? What exactly *are* you, her fucking intern?"

"She has no idea what's going on here."

Rosa stared at him. Suddenly she remembered what she had been thinking earlier. "It's *you*? Pantaleone's second man in Cesare's camp?"

His nod was surprisingly frank, although he avoided her eyes with a touch of shame the next moment. "It's complicated."

She'd been wrong. The second informer did not hold high rank in the Carnevare outfit; his was about as low as you could go – he only ran errands for them. That was how he had been able to intercept Cesare's message to the others.

She lowered her weapon a little way. "You're informing on the Carnevares to the police *and* to Pantaleone?"

"I'd help any enemy of Cesare's, never mind who else they are and what they want."

"Because he—"

"For the same reason as Alessandro," he interrupted her, "only by other means. He wants to kill Cesare but protect the clan. I couldn't care less about the clan. Cesare murdered Gaia and the baron. I owe more than my life to them. I won't allow Cesare to become one of the most powerful *capi* in Sicily through murdering them."

"Pantaleone told you to help me?"

He nodded. "But I was already well on my way here by then. This has nothing to do with either Pantaleone or the judge. I'll explain it all to you later, if you like, but right now we don't have time."

"Cesare's coming up here," she managed to say.

"Yes. We have two or three minutes at the most."

Hesitantly, she lowered the revolver as Fundling pointed behind her. "The cellar door."

She looked over her shoulder, but still didn't dare turn her back to him. This room must have once been a kitchen; a cast-iron stove stood against the rear wall. There was a narrow door beside it.

"Is he in there?" she asked huskily.

Fundling nodded again.

"Why doesn't he say anything? He must be able to hear us."

"They'll have bound and gagged him. And probably chained him up. Because of the transformation."

She hurried over to the door. The key was jammed.

"Rosa," said Fundling gently, "wait."

"We don't have time. You said so yourself."

"Do you know *what* you're planning to set free?"

"Fundling, I'm one of them. I'm not afraid of him."

He was about to say something in reply, but at that moment there was a crunching of tyres on gravel as a vehicle drove up outside. The headlights passed the two parked Land Rovers and shone through the window. Bright white light filled the room.

Fundling took a step forward, grabbed hold of Rosa, and tore the cellar door open. She stumbled into the dark. A narrow flight of well-worn stairs led down without any rail. She leaned the palm of her hand against a bare stone wall.

Fundling let go of her. Suddenly she was alone on the steps, with nothing but darkness below her.

She looked back over her shoulder.

Fundling slipped smoothly back into the kitchen. Their glances briefly met. Then he closed the cellar door from the outside. She heard the key in the lock.

She was trapped there in the blackness.

In the Dark

Cursing, she stumbled up the three or four steps to the top of the cellar stairs again and felt her way along the wall. When she reached the door, she hammered on the wood with the butt of her revolver. "Damn it, Fundling, open up!"

Car doors slammed outside the house. An engine was turned off. She heard muted voices in the distance.

She was gasping frantically. She breathed in the damp, musty air of the cellar. If she called and knocked again, it would draw the attention of Cesare and his men to her even sooner.

She slowly turned around. Below her everything was dark, no light at all. As if she had been dipped into a cask of black ink.

"Alessandro?" she whispered.

Something was moving down there. She heard rattling. The clink of chains.

"Alessandro, is that you?"

Outside, the voices were all talking at the same time, until one rose above the others. Cesare. She couldn't make out what he was saying.

Cautiously, she felt around for the top step with her foot and began the downward climb. Her fingers were touching the cold stone of the wall again. There was nothing to give her any idea of how large the cellar was.

After ten steps she reached the bottom of the stairs. The wall went straight on ahead to her right. Rosa groped her way hesitantly along it.

"Where are you?"

The rattling grew louder. Even noises were swallowed up by the blackness. It was cold in the ancient stone cellar, but part of the chill came from herself. A shudder raced through her legs, took over her upper body. She had to stop for a moment to calm down.

"Where are you?"

There was a growl, and then vigorous rattling of the chains again. Farther ahead or to her left? She was having difficulty locating the sound.

"I can't see anything," she whispered. "I can't find you unless I hear you."

She followed the course of the wall. The rattling was in front of her now. She sensed the presence of someone very close.

Slowly, she put out a hand. It was unnerving to move away from the wall and the sense of direction it gave her.

Her fingers met a void.

After a moment's hesitation, she crouched down.

She felt fur. Alarmed, she withdrew her hand. But the next moment she reached out again, and yes, there it still was. Warm, smooth fur over a supple, breathing body.

The growl turned to a gentle purring, curiously muted, which finally told her that he had been gagged. Maybe with the kind of muzzle dogs wear. He moved again, and once more links in the chain scraped over stone.

"Can't you change back?" she asked quietly.

His anger with Cesare, maybe with himself as well, must be holding him in his animal form. His feelings were out of control, just as they had been a few days ago when he sat beside her in panther form, helpless to do anything about it, unable to turn back into human shape until she had left him alone. She had to calm him down. Get rid of the gag. Get his chains off.

There was a crashing sound on the floor above. Something had been pushed over, or smashed. A shot made her jump. No silencer, so it hadn't been fired by Fundling.

Although she was trembling, she passed her hand gently over Alessandro's fur. It was soft and silky. She could feel the arch of his backbone. He was lying on his side with his back to her. The chains were too short for him to stand up. The angrier he was, the harder it must be for him to change back. Older Arcadians might be able to control their transformations, but Alessandro was a victim of his emotions.

Her fingers wandered along his back and up to his neck. If he had been lying there in human form, she would have felt more timid about touching him like that.

He kept his heavy panther head perfectly still as her fingertips rubbed between his ears and hesitantly stroked his skull, then his cat-like face. He closed his eyes when her fingers passed over them. Then she touched a strap. It was indeed part of some kind of muzzle. She quickly undid the buckles and took the leather thing off his face.

He let out a sharp snarl. When she flinched back, he calmed down again. He had never said how often in the past he had changed to his panther shape, but she now guessed it couldn't have been very often. Up above, she heard two more shots. Who was firing at whom? Had Fundling entrenched himself in the house? All that seemed very far away, as if it had nothing to do with her. An unnatural calm took hold of her. At the same time, the cold sensation moved on to her fingertips.

"Just lie there, okay?" she whispered.

He purred like a domestic cat.

Her hands moved down his muscular forelegs until they met iron rings above the paws. The chains holding him were no broader than her little finger. Then she felt for hind legs, and to do that she had to lean far over him. Her upper body touched his fur. A strange tingling ran over her skin. She tried to ignore it, let her fingers move down his legs, and found two iron rings there, too.

"Did they tranquilise you to get these things on you?"

He rubbed his head on her knee, which she took to mean yes.

Upstairs, glass broke. Someone started shouting, but farther away, probably outside.

"I still have four bullets in my revolver," she said. "I can try to shoot the chains apart."

His head rubbed against her leg again.

"I'll have to put the muzzle of the gun on a link in each of the chains. Can you stretch them tauter?"

A decided snarl of assent.

She picked up the revolver, as several more shots rang out in the house overhead.

In the dark, relying only on her sense of touch, she made her way around him. "First the left foreleg." He straightened it until the chain between the iron ring around his paw and the wall fastening was taut. She felt the tips of his retracted claws, counted four links down in the chain – she hoped that was enough not to injure him. She put the muzzle of the revolver on the metal there, took a deep breath, and concentrated.

"Ready?"

He growled.

"Here goes, then." She pulled the trigger. The recoil was violent. A whistling explosion showed that the projectile had hit something and was now ricocheting through the darkness.

"Are you all right?" she was quick to ask.

He scraped his leg on the floor, and she realised that it was free. Her idea worked. If none of the ricochets caught her, she could get the chains off.

Someone shouted up on the first floor, someone else replied. A submachine gun chattered. More broken glass.

"We have to move faster," she managed to say.

Soon his second foreleg was free, then the first hind leg. He tried to stand up, but she quickly laid her hand on his side, to tell him he must be patient. Only one chain now. And her last bullet.

The shot blew the links apart. This time she thought she felt the sharp blast of the ricochet close to her temples.

Alessandro leaped up, staggered, and collapsed again,

almost buried her under him. At the last moment he swerved, scraped the cellar floor with his paws, and found his footing. He seemed to be standing upright now. His soft panther muzzle pressed against her throat, his hot breath sent a shiver through her. She had goosebumps.

He purred quietly and then withdrew.

All was suddenly quiet on the first floor above them. No more pistol shots, no further salvos of gunfire.

There was a groan beside her. His transformation was beginning. Soon, shaking fingers felt for her. "Thank you," said a hoarse voice that was not yet entirely his own. His fingers were much warmer than hers.

And suddenly she felt his lips on hers, his hand gently placed on the back of her head. He was naked, she knew that without seeing him, and something was happening to her. What she had taken for goosebumps was really something else. Scales rustled now whenever she moved. The tip of her tongue touched his, and divided.

A grinding sound came from the cellar door. Someone was turning the key in the lock.

Rosa flinched, whether because of the noise, or because of what she might be changing into, she wasn't sure.

"I'll see what that is," said Alessandro. Now it was undoubtedly his voice, although it still didn't sound quite right. His metamorphosis wasn't complete yet. And what was she herself? A girl showing the first signs of turning into a snake? The cold inside her threatened to overwhelm her, spreading to every part of her body.

When he moved away from her, her tongue changed back. Her eyes widened painfully and took on human form again. The rough scales on the backs of her hands smoothed out, growing together and merging into skin.

"Alessandro?"

"I'm on the stairs."

Swaying, she moved as if she had to get used to her legs. Her hand felt the cellar wall, her feet found the steps. She followed him up and noticed with relief that he was waiting for her.

They went up to the closed door together. All was quiet on the other side.

"Ready?" he whispered to her.

"Not in the least."

She heard him laugh quietly, and pictured his dimples when he smiled, the sparkle in his green eyes.

"There's something else I have to tell you," he whispered.

At that moment the cellar door was flung open.

Panthera

Rosa blinked at the brightness. Morning sunlight was falling through the window into the former farmhouse kitchen. There were bullet holes in the walls, and motionless bodies lay on the floor.

"Come out," said the long-haired man who had opened the door. He was holding an automatic pistol in one hand.

"Remeo?"

He impatiently beckoned her out of the cellar. "Hurry up. Most of them are dead, but I don't know about anyone down in the valley. Some of them may have stayed behind there."

Rosa stopped in the doorway and turned around. She reached out a hand to Alessandro. He had no clothes on, but nor was he naked. Black panther fur covered parts of his body, although it was visibly thinning out. The iron rings with the remaining links of chain lay around his wrists and ankles.

His emerald eyes moved away from her to linger on Remeo and the gun in his hand. "What happened?"

"He works for Salvatore Pantaleone." Rosa stepped back and impatiently took Alessandro's hand. "He's on our side. Let's get out of here."

Alessandro didn't move. His voice was fully human again, but there was an odd note in it. "He saved *you*, Rosa. He has other plans for me. Isn't that right, Remeo?"

She whirled around and stared at the man with the gun.

Remeo shrugged his shoulders.

Her cheek muscles tensed. "What's that supposed to mean?"

"Get out of the way," Remeo told her. "No harm will come to you."

Instinctively, she moved in front of Alessandro. "Pantaleone's given you orders to kill him?"

"Of course he has," said Alessandro, behind her. "This is his best opportunity to eliminate the Carnevares. It'll look as if it happened during the shoot-out. No one will think of this guy turning on his own people, still less would anyone suspect Pantaleone. They'll pin the blame on Cesare." He tried to put Rosa gently aside, but she didn't budge from the spot. She was standing in the middle of the doorway, with her back to Alessandro and the cellar stairs.

Remeo didn't move a muscle. He looked at her as if she were some package that he had to deliver before he would be paid.

She stared at him with all the determination she could summon up. "Pantaleone wants me to lead the Alcantaras for him. He won't dare kill anyone who's under my protection." It was a bluff, but she had to gain time somehow.

"He's the boss of bosses," Remeo contradicted her, "and you're only a child. You'll forgive him. Now, get out of the way."

She lunged forward and struck him in the face. It was not a move that could seriously stop him, but it took him by surprise. Cursing, he dealt her a blow that swept her aside, and raised his pistol.

Rosa collided with an overturned table. Beyond it, legs were sticking out, the lower half of a lifeless body. A pistol with a silencer lay beside it.

Fundling's gun.

Remeo fired at the cellar doorway. Alessandro was faster. The leap with which he avoided the bullet carried him out into the room. Even in midair he was changing into a black shadow, and he landed on all fours.

Remeo swung his firearm around and shot for the second time. The bullet grazed Alessandro and made him stumble. His leap just missed Remeo.

"Remeo!"

Rosa was holding Fundling's pistol. She took aim.

For a moment Remeo looked at her, frowning. But then he pointed his gun at Alessandro again.

Rosa pulled the trigger.

The pistol clicked. The magazine was empty.

She cried out furiously, braced herself upright where she had landed on the floor, and flung the useless weapon at Remeo. He ducked without taking his eyes off the panther. Alessandro was bleeding from a wound in the neck. The first shot had grazed him; the next would hit home.

The panther leaped off the floor. Rosa saw the huge cat as if in slow motion, carried through the air about a metre along the wall before springing off it and towards Remeo, who swung his gun around again. Alessandro was racing at him, panther jaws wide open.

Before Remeo could fire, he was knocked backward by the weight of the impact. Alessandro landed on him and dug his panther fangs, with a crunching sound, into the man's face. Remeo's features disappeared between his assailant's jaws.

Rosa crawled over to the lifeless Fundling. His clothes were drenched in blood. There was a wound on his forehead.

Remeo's screams died away behind her. Alessandro let out a wild panther howl, triumphant and desperate at once.

She didn't want to see what he had done to Remeo. Instead, she felt frantically for Fundling's wrist, tried to find a pulse, and failed.

But yes – there *was* a pulse! It beat very faintly.

Fundling must have barricaded himself into the house to keep Cesare away. He could have had the same orders as Remeo from Pantaleone. Or perhaps he had done it all for her. Finally, however, Cesare's men had stormed the place. They hadn't been expecting another traitor to come up behind them. Remeo had probably been able to pick them off one by one at his leisure. One lay dead at the entrance to the room, another out in the corridor.

"Fundling's still alive!" she called to Alessandro. "We have to help him."

But the panther didn't seem to hear her. He let out another roar, turned away from Remeo's body – and leaped in Rosa's direction.

She ducked. Alessandro, passing over her, collided with something else – something as large and powerful as himself. The force of the collision carried both creatures to the floor, only just missing Rosa and Fundling. Rosa staggered back, and realised, at that moment, *who* Alessandro had attacked.

A lion with a shaggy mane was digging his claws into the panther's coat. The big cats were biting each other, rolling over and over, snarling and roaring. They crashed against the wall, crushing a chair under their weight, yet they would not let go.

Rosa took Fundling under the armpits and dragged him to the door. One of the two dead bodies was barring their way; she would have to move it aside first. In the room, the panther and the lion were fighting savagely, striking out with their claws, each trying to tear the other's throat to shreds.

Rosa tugged more and more desperately at the corpse in the doorway. The man was too heavy. And the other dead man still lay in the hall.

Her eyes fell on a submachine gun. But if she used that, she might hit Alessandro and not the lion.

At last she managed to haul Fundling out of the room and into the corridor. She found another pistol there. She picked it up and staggered back to the doorway.

The two big cats were still locked in furious battle in the ruins of the room. The lion's left eye was closed, a trail of blood passing over it. Rosa tried to take aim with the pistol, but they were both moving too fast. Even at such close quarters, she risked hitting Alessandro.

Furious, she stuck the gun in her waistband and turned back to the dead man at the front door of the house. With an effort, she pushed the body far enough aside to allow her to pull Fundling past him and into the open air.

The morning sun was still low in the sky, casting long shadows over the farmyard. Several bodies lay dead in the dust.

One of them had been flung over the hood of one of the Land Rovers by the shot that killed him. A black Jeep, its doors open, stood beside the two other vehicles. The car radio was quietly playing a song that seemed familiar to her. 'My Death'. Or maybe something Italian.

As soon as she had hauled Fundling's legs out of the doorway, the kitchen window exploded. Lion and panther fell out into the farmyard in a shower of broken glass and splintered wood. Cesare landed on all fours, Alessandro on his side. The lion looked up, fixing his gaze on Rosa.

She fired the pistol.

The bullet struck Cesare's flank and threw him aside. He staggered, turned his mighty head around, roaring, and looked at Rosa with sheer hatred.

Wounded as he was, he was still heading towards her, about to pounce.

Alessandro intercepted him as he sprang, colliding with him sideways and bringing him to the ground. Once again they landed in the dust, a fighting tangle of limbs. The panther's paw robbed Cesare of his remaining eye. His terrible roars made the farmyard echo. His back legs collapsed under him, and then he sat there striking out helplessly with one paw, while the panther prowled watchfully around him.

In the end it was quick.

Alessandro pounced, sank his teeth into the lion's neck, and tore his throat out. Cesare's head fell heavily to the dust, the mane sticky with his own blood.

Silence fell over the farmyard as the corpse was transformed.

The shape of the gigantic lion changed back into the body of a man. Rosa looked away as the lion's coat receded from the wounds and exposed human flesh.

Breathing heavily, Alessandro crouched over his adversary and waited until it was over. Then he threw back his head and let out a roar of triumph. Rosa shuddered.

She wanted to go to him, but something held her back. Fundling's ribcage was rising and falling so slowly that she could hardly see its movement. He urgently needed a doctor, and she wasn't going to give him up, not after all he had done for her, whatever his motives.

Music was still coming through the open door of the Jeep, a nostalgic, sentimental song, as if the final credits were about to roll over this scene strewn with dead bodies.

The panther lowered his head. He looked down at the dead man, and Rosa wondered whether, at this moment, Alessandro felt satisfaction because his mother was avenged.

She dragged Fundling over to the Jeep, and with the last of her strength heaved him into the back seat.

The panther turned his head and looked at her, sad-eyed.

She waited, giving him the opportunity to come over to her.

He stayed where he was.

The pain in her breast was worse than any of her bruises and abrasions, and it hurt more with every heartbeat. "Go to your people," she said tonelessly. "You've done it. You're their new *capo* now."

The key was in the ignition. When she turned it, the music stopped and then immediately started again.

The engine faltered and jolted as she got the hang of the manual gearshift. In the rearview mirror she saw Alessandro at the beginning of his transformation back into human form – and maybe the end of what had been between them. Fundling's condition gave her no time to find out.

Farther downhill, on the gravel track up the slope, she found Iole and Sarcasmo. The girl had let the dog out of the car, and now he was asleep beside her in the bushes, his head lying peacefully on her lap.

In silence, they drove north.

Zoe's Message

Rosa and Iole sat side by side on plastic chairs outside the entrance to the operating room. The young man at the hospital reception had promised to look after Sarcasmo.

A uniformed security guard stood a few metres away, keeping an eye on them both. The loudspeaker system was calling for a doctor to go straight to surgery.

Iole was wearing a red bathrobe over her white dress; one of the nurses had given it to her. Someone must have left it behind at the hospital. It was several sizes too big for Iole, who had rolled up the sleeves and wound the belt three times around her slender waist so she wouldn't trip over the ends of it.

"I don't know anyone who drives as badly as you," she said without looking at Rosa.

"My first time using a stick shift."

A doctor hurried past them and through the connecting door to surgery. A notice on it said hospital personnel only. For a moment, looking through the crack in the doorway, Rosa saw men and women in green coats hurrying about between the operating rooms.

"Do you think he'll pull through?" Iole asked.

"I don't know."

"Why isn't he dead, with a bullet lodged in his skull?"

"I'm not a doctor."

Iole turned her head to look at her. "What *are* you? I mean, what do you do?"

"Not so many months ago I was still at school."

"Then what?"

"Something happened, and I stopped going."

"I'd have liked to go to school," said Iole, lost in thought. "But now I'm stupider than everyone else because I missed out on six years."

"You're not stupid."

"I don't know anything at all. Only stuff off television. The name of the girl assistant in the blue dress, why the anchorman on the breakfast TV show doesn't like to travel by subway, that kind of thing."

"You're free now. You can catch up on it all."

Iole thought that over. "I'll probably just stay home watching TV. I know how to do that."

"We'll find something else for you to do, don't worry."

"I can't go to school. I'm fifteen. I'm not going back to fourth grade." She smiled, but her eyes were serious. "Everyone would think I'd had to repeat a year six times running."

Rosa put an arm around her shoulders and drew her close. "Everyone would want to hear you tell exciting stories. What it's like to be kidnapped by the Mafia."

"Not exciting, for a start."

"No." Rosa sighed.

"What happened? I mean, to keep you out of school."

"I was pregnant."

"In love?"

"No, only pregnant."

"Oh." For a moment Iole seemed to be wondering whether it would be all right to ask more questions. "But then where's your baby? At home?"

Rosa shook her head.

"Did it die?"

"I'm not sure if it was ever really alive."

"It hasn't missed much not watching TV, anyway."

Rosa gave her a smile. Iole shyly returned it.

A quiet signal sounded. "'Scuse me," said Rosa, taking the cell phone out of her jeans pocket. After their arrival at the hospital she had called the judge. Quattrini and her team were already on their way from Catania to Palermo, right across the island. It would take her ninety minutes by helicopter. Quattrini had said two hours at the most.

At the moment Rosa was not interested in the possible consequences of her call. All she knew for certain was that she was going to hand Pantaleone over to justice for his orders to kill Alessandro, and she had said so to Quattrini on the phone. "I'm standing by our agreement. We'll talk when you get here. But keep the police off our backs until then. Can you do that?"

Yes, she could, Quattrini had assured her. On the condition that Rosa and Iole didn't move from the hospital.

"Okay," Rosa had said.

"Can I count on you this time?"

"Sure."

"I'd like you to swear it."

"I could be keeping my fingers crossed and you'd never even notice."

"Swear on your aunt's life."

"What?"

"You heard me. On the life of Florinda Alcantara."

After a moment's hesitation, she had replied, "I swear it. If I'm lying, may Florinda burn in hell… not that I can promise you they'd want her there."

Now, an hour later, she was staring blankly at the cell phone.

Iole realised that something was wrong. "What's the matter?"

Rosa did not reply. Her fingertip was hovering over the keypad, but she still hesitated.

"Rosa?"

"A text message," she said. "From my sister. From Zoe."

"What does it say?"

"She probably just wants to tear me a new one."

"But you haven't even read it yet."

Rosa got to her feet. "Wait here, okay?"

Iole pointed to the security guard. "He's not going to let us leave. When you bring someone to the hospital with a bullet in his head, they don't let you go home just like that."

"I'll only be a minute, okay?" Rosa left her on the plastic chair and strode down the white corridor. The security man in his dark blue uniform moved to intercept her, but Rosa pointed to the nearby door of the ladies' room, and he nodded.

She shut herself into one of the cubicles. The message was

from Zoe's number, no doubt about that. Reluctantly, she read the text.

we need help, it said, but she had to read it three times before she could take it in. *were captured went in car not sure where deep ravine.* And finally: *not too good but alone no guard ask alessandro he may know where come help us.*

As if dazed, she stared at the characters. The message looked like any other: black lettering on a white background.

Had Cesare sent his men to intercept Zoe and Florinda on their way back from the tribunal? He would have to eliminate them to cover up for a breach of the concordat. And everyone who had known their whereabouts was very probably dead.

She didn't need Alessandro's help to identify the place. The end of the unfinished expressway. Cesare must have planned for them to disappear inside one of the ancient Siculian cave tombs on the rock face of the canyon. If they were held captive in there, it would be next to impossible to find them. But if they were still out in the open, it wasn't too late.

She couldn't wait for Quattrini. Couldn't just sit there doing nothing.

Taking care not to let anything show, she went past the security guard and back to her chair, where she talked quietly to Iole.

Soon after that, the girl suddenly threw a fit of hysterics. Screaming, Iole flung open the door to surgery and raced along the corridor, calling Fundling's name again and again.

"Hey!" shouted the security man. Cursing, he gave chase.

Rosa waited two or three seconds, then jumped up and

hurried in the other direction, walking faster and faster until she was almost running.

Two minutes later she drove the black Jeep out of the parking lot, turned onto the A20 going west, and raced at top speed towards the end of the world.

The Secret

She had nearly reached her journey's end when another text message came in.

florinda dying come quick.

Rosa tried to call Zoe back, but only got her voicemail.

When she had passed the barricades and was turning onto the asphalt, the next message reached her.

gagged only fingers free idiots forgot to take my cell phone

Rosa tapped in an answer:

can you read this?

yes

sure there's no one with you?

After a few nerve-racking moments of waiting:

yes

She briefly contemplated asking Quattrini for help after all. But the judge was likely to be unforgiving, now that Rosa had made herself scarce yet again.

Suppose she tried Alessandro? As soon as the idea of him came to her, her mind was in turmoil, and she couldn't think straight. But there was no use hesitating now.

what's wrong with Florinda? she texted Zoe back.

injured came the answer, after an endless wait. *bleeding to death*

Rosa's arms felt too heavy to hold the wheel. Even driving straight ahead cost her an effort.

It was midday now. Dense grey clouds were moving north, rolling over and over in the sky like smoke from a gigantic fire. As if all Africa was in flames on the other side of the Mediterranean. Storms were raging in the upper strata of the atmosphere, and strong gusts of wind buffeted the Jeep.

with you soon, she typed, to reassure Zoe and herself. Only a couple of miles now. On her visits to the unfinished expressway with Alessandro, it had never seemed so long. Today it went on and on to the horizon.

zoe?

hurry

Quattrini would have tried to stop her, so she called emergency services and asked them to send an ambulance. Asked how many injured people there were, she had to answer evasively. "Probably two. One seriously injured." They wanted to know her name; she declined to give it. Was she sure, they asked, that this wasn't some stupid hoax call? "No, goddamnit, it's not!" Then she must give her name. "Lilia Dionisi," she said.

When she broke the connection, she had a devastating feeling that she would wait in vain for help to arrive. She stared grimly ahead over the steering wheel, but she still couldn't bring herself to call the judge. Not yet.

A text message from Zoe arrived. *can hear you*

And next moment, *and see you*

Rosa slowed down as the horizon sank lower and lower, and the mountains on the other side of the ravine came into sight. The place where the road stopped short loomed ahead.

A dark line at the edge of the abyss.

Someone was lying on the asphalt about a metre from the drop.

She trod on the gas once more. Everything was muted: her perception, her feelings.

As she came closer, she could make out details. A woman's slender body in a black skirt suit, torn pantyhose, no shoes.

She was lying on her side, facing the abyss, with her back to Rosa. Her long blond hair fanned out over the ground. The cold winds from down below blew single strands in the air, making them dance around her head like golden snakes.

Florinda, thought Rosa. But where was Zoe?

As she braked she looked around. Builders' rubble was piled on both sides of the road, and the remains of structures to consolidate the former bridge. The debris formed an irregular rampart, metres high in some places, broken down in others. Walls of rock rose high beyond it, the edges of the track that had been blasted into the mountains to build the expressway.

She stopped the Jeep only a few metres from the edge. Florinda lay a metre from the driver's door, motionless. Rosa couldn't see whether she was breathing.

Before she got out, acting on a sudden impulse, she opened the glove compartment. She was driving a Mafia vehicle, so there should really be—

No. Chewing gum. Tissues. But no gun.

Now she did tap in Quattrini's number after all, placed her thumb on enter, but didn't press the key. She kept the cell phone clutched in her fist as she got out and went over to her aunt.

"Florinda?"

Even as she said the name she realised her mistake. The clothes were Florinda's, yes, but it wasn't her wearing them.

"Zoe!"

She fell to her knees with a cry. The cool winds coming up from the depths below tugged at her hair. She began to feel terribly cold.

She let the cell phone drop and rolled Zoe over on her back. Blond strands spread over her sister's face. Her eyes were closed. A rivulet of blood at the corner of her mouth had dried and cracked; red flakes of it were falling over her white throat.

Her hands trembling, Rosa tried to feel Zoe's pulse. She couldn't find it.

She threw her head back and let out a wail of agony. It echoed through the ravine like a chorus of ghosts replying from the ancient cave tombs in the rocks.

Her fingers were shaking too much to search for the pulse again. Frantically, she tried once more. At Zoe's throat. Her left wrist. Then her right wrist. Her sister's skin was cold and white.

Deep in her mind, doubts stirred, although pain and despair almost numbed them. There was no cell phone here. *Zoe couldn't have sent any text messages.*

"Good afternoon, Rosa."

She was taken by surprise, yet not truly shocked.

Salvatore Pantaleone stepped out from the stones and rubble beside the expressway. The old man's white ponytail was tossed over one shoulder. His eye patch was like a black hole in his face, attracting far more attention than a good eye. This was the first time that Rosa had seen him by daylight, and he looked to her greyer, bowed down with worries, exhausted.

He had Zoe's cell phone in his right hand.

"I've learned more about using this thing," he said, looking at the little device as if he surprised himself, and after a moment he shrugged his shoulders. He swung his arm back, and then flung the phone with considerable force down into the abyss.

"It was you."

"We had to meet somewhere you wouldn't set your new friend the judge on me."

She had pushed one hand under Zoe's head and was still keeping it off the asphalt. Now she laid it gently down on the road surface, stroked her sister's cheek with her left hand, and struggled with her grief.

But her body refused to obey her. It was as if it had been separated from her mind. She had to force herself to turn her attention back to him.

"Did you kill Zoe?"

"I did it for you. I regret it, but it was necessary."

Rosa tasted vomit rising in her throat, and swallowed it down. "Where's Florinda?"

"Not here."

"Is she dead, too?"

"You are the new head of the Alcantara clan now. Just as I said you would be. We'll work together as a team, you and I. It may take a little while for us to get accustomed to each other, but—"

Every word, every breath was a struggle. "You know that I've informed on you to the judge. And you still want me to help you?"

He nodded. "But first I will help you. You'll be needing it. You're only seventeen. Florinda's advisers and business managers will soon be clustering around you like flies, trying to take advantage of you for their own purposes. There may be one or two of them who can be trusted, but the rest are a pack of bloodhounds without a shred of conscience."

"You fixed the whole thing. All of it."

The old man came closer, shaking his head. "Much of what Cesare Carnevare did has turned out to be useful in retrospect. But that had nothing to do with me. I merely took my chance when it presented itself. The fact that Remeo was there and could do what he did... well, sometimes you also need a little luck."

"Zoe and Florinda... were they at that tribunal at all? Or were they already... elsewhere when we met at the palazzo?"

"A body dead for several hours doesn't feel like that, my child. Of course they were there." He nodded towards the lifeless Zoe. "I liked your sister. For a long time I thought she might be the one to... but she doesn't have your edge, your tough mind, your determination. And then there was that business with the other girl. Unfortunate."

She had to force herself to go on asking questions as she looked for a way of killing him. Here and now. Even without a weapon. Slowly, she straightened up until they were facing each other over Zoe's body.

"And Florinda? What was it about her that didn't suit you any longer?"

"Her bitterness. Her uncontrollable rages. The way she assessed many deals – well, let's say emotionally, thus wrecking them. Your father ought to have led the Alcantaras, but he insisted on leaving Sicily with your mother. Florinda was never fit for the position."

"Nor am I, any more than Florinda. And I don't want it, either." She could hardly open her lips. Her tongue felt cold and hard, as if frozen.

He wagged his raised forefinger at her. "You just don't yet know that you do want it. Or maybe you don't want to admit it to yourself." He took a step closer, and was now right in front of Zoe's body, not two metres away from Rosa. "You and I have what it takes to stand up to the Hungry Man."

"Me!" she exclaimed scornfully. "Oh, sure!"

"You and I," he repeated. "You as my right hand. Because deep down you have moral standards that Florinda lacked. The reborn Lycaon can't be fought with cruelty and brutality; he and his supporters have more than enough of that themselves. But conviction, and a kind of sense of justice that has nothing to do with the fatuous ideals of your friend the judge... those are valuable weapons to use against him."

"Nonsense," she whispered, and let the wind carry the word over to him. She looked down at Zoe again, and welcomed the cold spreading through her body. By now she had no sensation at all in her arms and legs. That felt good.

"TABULA," she said quietly. "Maybe they have the right idea."

He smiled. "I'll teach you things about them, too. And about the gaps in the crowd. There are answers to such questions, did you know that? The answers to everything lie deep down in the sea."

Have you ever wondered who's in the gaps in the crowd? That was what Fundling had asked her, in the car on the way to the harbour where the yacht was moored.

A voice whispered, "Rosa?"

Zoe's pale hand moved up Rosa's calf. Her voice was so faint that the sound of the wind almost drowned it out. But it *was* her voice, too weak to give Rosa much hope, yet all the same—

"Poor, persistent little thing," said Pantaleone, drawing a pistol.

"No!" Rosa leaped across her sister, charging at him. Even as she jumped, the cold overpowered her. Finally became one with her.

Ice crystals ran through her blood vessels. Frost covered her eyes and then faded away again. After that, she was someone else.

Pantaleone smiled.

Only very briefly. Almost proudly.

His eyes widened. Turned dark. The pistol fell to the ground. He was also changing.

Then she was on him.

Two Animals

If there had been anyone else in this place at the end of the world, close to the precipitous drop of the deep ravine with the cave tombs on the far side of it, he would have been presented with an astonishing sight.

Two animals lying motionless on dusty asphalt. They are not far from a jagged, broken edge where the road once led to a bridge. Today it ends in nothing, in a fall into a canyon of fissured rock.

One of the creatures is a snake almost three metres long, with a body as thick as a human thigh. Her scaly skin is the colour of amber, patterned with brown and yellow and deep, dark red. Her head lies on one side, her eyes are wide open – the slits of the pupils are a glacial blue, unusual for a reptile. She has two fangs, long, curved, sharp as daggers, and a forked tongue.

The snake's body winds in a spiral around the other animal, a mighty wild boar with a grey coat and only one eye. He lost the other long ago, and the eye socket gapes open like a knothole in the branch of a tree. He lies lifeless on the asphalt, legs slack, mouth with its huge tusks open. His tongue lolls out, not delicate like the snake's, but coarse and grey. His body is covered with old scars. Death has only just taken him, and the flies don't yet dare to settle on the corpse. Several of his ribs broke when the snake wrapped herself more and more tightly around him, crushing the life out of his lungs. It took him a long time to die, but now it is over at last.

And while three eyes stare at the stormy sky, a transformation suddenly begins. The shape of the boar distorts in the huge snake's embrace. At the same time his coat disappears under his skin. His muzzle flattens, turning inward, and is smoothed out; his forelegs become arms. One of his broken ribs pierces his wrinkled chest, because human skin will not stretch enough to cover the splintered bone. His tongue retreats between split lips, the yellow tusks disappear. Soon no more of the boar can be seen.

And now the snake's own metamorphosis begins. Her body grows shorter, thickens in some places, becomes more slender in others. The eyes change shape, their glacially bright blue intensifies. The ends of the forked tongue merge, and the fangs disappear. Finally the scaly skin on the snake's head divides into strings that swiftly split again, first into strands, then into separate hairs. Soon a wild mane of blond hair surrounds the head of the girl who, only moments ago, was a snake. There is nothing left of the reptile except a few dry scales on the asphalt.

Rosa wakes and blinks at the daylight. Naked and weak, she crawls away from Pantaleone's body, finds the cell phone, presses a key with shaking fingers.

"Quattrini," she whispers, without raising the phone to her mouth. "You can have the old man now."

＊

Zoe's life ebbed out of her in a single long breath. Rosa had been kneeling on the ground, cradling her sister's head and shoulders in her lap, gently stroking her long hair. Zoe's eyes sought hers, but she could see that they were barely able to take in any of her surroundings.

"Was it us?" Zoe managed to gasp.

"Don't talk now. Help will soon be coming."

"Was it... us?"

Rosa saw one of her own tears drop, as if in slow motion, on Zoe's cheek. "I don't know what you mean."

"Were we... the traitors?"

"I went to a judge. I broke the law of silence."

"Not that." Zoe's lips quivered. "TABULA," she whispered.

Rosa's memory lay hidden behind a wall of pain and grief, yet something stirred slightly in her mind. One of the families had given the Arcadian dynasties away to TABULA – the Alcantaras, Cesare had said.

"It could have been anyone, maybe even the Carnevares themselves." She listened to her own words; it kept her from losing her mind then and there.

Zoe coughed up blood. "You must... must find out."

"Why?"

"Because..." She broke off, her breath coming noisily as she relaxed her face muscles. "Because of Dad," she whispered.

Rosa shook her head. "Listen, now you must—"

"Because of *Dad*, Rosa. Because of him and TABULA."

Then Zoe smiled, and died.

A Message

Life-support machines hummed around Fundling's bed. His head was bandaged, and propped on white pillows to keep it from tipping over sideways. Someone had shaved his black hair off. His eyelids were closed, but the eyes under them moved feverishly.

Iole had put a photograph of Sarcasmo on the bedside table. The dog seemed to be laughing; his eyes shone. She and the black mongrel were crazy about each other. Ever since moving into the Palazzo Alcantara, Iole had shared her room with the dog, and never left the house without him.

This afternoon, five days after Zoe's death, Rosa was the only visitor in Fundling's room. Wearing a black coat from her sister's wardrobe, she sat beside him. Out in the hospital grounds, a stormy wind shook the tall oak trees. Fundling's condition had stabilised, but no one could say whether he would ever come out of his coma.

"You know, don't you?" She was looking not at him, but at the garden outside the window. "You knew more than most people all along. About TABULA, and about those… gaps in the crowd. About the Hungry Man. And the laws of Arcadia."

She got to her feet and leaned over him, very close to his face.

"Where do you really come from? And what were you doing as a baby, alone in the hotel that the Carnevares burned down?" With her fingertip, she touched her lips and then his forehead. "One of these days you'll tell me the truth. One of these days you'll tell me everything."

✳

Outside in the hallway, she met the judge.

Quattrini had seen to it that no legal proceedings were taken against Rosa. The death of Pantaleone had been a setback for her. She had hoped that, once arrested, he would provide information about the extensive network of Cosa Nostra's business deals, and perhaps details of the bloodbath at the Gibellina monument as well. Much of that would now remain unexplained.

The greatest mystery, however, was Pantaleone's death itself. Rosa claimed to have pushed him over the edge of the precipice in self-defence after he murdered her sister. But no one could explain what had caused a spiral of hematomas all around his body as he fell.

"How is he?"

"No change," said Rosa. The judge seemed even smaller than on their earlier meetings. She had to look up at Rosa, but that didn't appear to bother her.

"I was told I'd find you here. I'm afraid I have bad news."

Rosa looked down at the floor briefly, and then met the judge's penetrating gaze. "You've found Florinda, I assume."

"You don't seem particularly surprised."

Pantaleone had called her the new head of the Alcantara

clan, and he certainly had his reasons. "I broke the oath," she said. "It was bound to happen."

For a moment the judge seemed genuinely distressed. "I'm sorry. About your aunt, and that stupid oath."

"Don't apologise if you don't mean it. You guessed what would happen."

Quattrini looked over her shoulder. Stefania Moranelli and Antonio Festa, her two bodyguards, were standing in reception at the end of the hall, staring at them. "There were indications of conflict between the families," she said, turning back to Rosa. "I didn't have to be a prophet to foresee that blood would flow. But what I am still not clear about is your own part in all this. And the boy's."

"Fundling?"

The judge shook her head. "You know who I'm talking about: Alessandro Carnevare."

"Ask him yourself. I haven't seen him for days." She added, more coolly, "I imagine he has a lot to do."

Quattrini nodded, as if confirming something that she had known for a long time. "I *will* ask him, don't worry."

"Where did you find Florinda? And what had happened to her?"

"She was shot. Not with the same gun as your sister, and probably some hours earlier. Her body was washed up on the shore of Panarea."

"Panarea?" asked Rosa, only for something to say. Her voice sounded husky.

"Panarea is one of the Lipari Islands, north of Sicily.

Did your aunt perhaps set out on a sea voyage a few days ago?"

"Not as far as I know."

Pantaleone must have given orders for Zoe and Florinda to be brought to him from Corleone. Maybe Florinda resisted, and so she was shot and her body thrown out of a helicopter somewhere over the sea.

"I'd like to have them both laid to rest in our family vault as soon as possible," said Rosa.

"Of course."

"And Iole can stay with me for the time being?"

"If that's what she wants. We haven't been able to find any living relations. Whoever eliminated the Dallamano family six years ago made a thorough job of it."

"You're forgetting Augusto."

"He's not alive any longer. Not officially."

Rosa nodded. "Goodbye, Signora Quattrini."

She walked past the judge and down the corridor. Quattrini did not follow her, but she could feel the woman's eyes on her back.

"Rosa?"

She looked over her shoulder.

"My congratulations."

"On my aunt's death?"

"On your inheritance," said Quattrini. "You are the head of the Alcantara clan now. I only hope you stay alive long enough to enjoy it."

Rosa turned again and left.

She didn't burst into tears until she reached her car.

A Farewell

A column of black limousines was winding its way up to the Alcantara property.

Rosa stood at the entrance to the funeral chapel with Iole, watching the *capi* of the other clans arriving. She wondered how many of them were Arcadians behind their masks as prosperous businessmen.

Not only were the bosses and their families attending the funeral, so were the business managers of the Alcantara companies in Palermo, Milan, and Rome, together with several of those advisers against whom Pantaleone had warned her. She knew that later she would be expected to accept their condolences. But she wasn't here to live up to expectations.

The mourners formed two long lines outside the chapel. Rosa had been inside it only once before, when Zoe took her to see their father's grave. This morning she had looked at it again. Just the name DAVIDE ALCANTARA carved into the stone slab, no date of birth, no date of death.

The sweet smell of lavender and furze flowers hung in the air, mingling with the fragrance of countless floral arrangements. Most of those had been delivered first thing in the morning. The undertaker's staff had used them to decorate the vault and the porch.

One of the last limousines to draw up outside the palazzo came to a halt, and Alessandro got out.

He was wearing a well-cut black suit, and sunglasses. His hair was shorter. He somehow looked more grown-up.

Unlike the *capi* of the other clans, Alessandro had come alone. No bodyguards accompanied him from the front courtyard to the chapel. He did not exchange greetings with anyone but joined the far end of the long line of mourners, took off his sunglasses, and looked in Rosa's direction. From this distance she couldn't read his expression.

When their eyes met, she realised that she had thought she was armed against him, assuming that grief for Zoe would preoccupy her so much that his presence would make no difference. But now that they were meeting again for the first time since the events at the Gibellina monument, the sight of him was like an electric shock.

Iole touched her hand and gave her an affectionate smile. In the last few days, she had undergone a remarkable change. She seemed more mature, less childishly confused than at their first meeting on Isola Luna, and she attracted curious glances from many of the mourners.

Rosa had tied back her mane of witchy blond hair in a ponytail and had had some of the clothes from Zoe's wardrobe altered for her by women from the village. The black skirt suit she had chosen to wear today gave her a businesslike appearance, and she looked to herself like a stranger in the mirror. She was already missing her metal-studded boots.

Three days ago she had called her mother in New York to break the news of Zoe's death. Gemma had not disappointed her. After expressing genuine shock, and then indulging in an outburst of grief, she had rejected Rosa's offer to send her air tickets for a flight to Sicily. Not even her daughter's funeral could induce her ever to set foot on the island again. Rosa didn't try to change her mind. She promised to call again when it was all over, but silently decided that this was goodbye once and for all. If her mother didn't try to get in touch, then she wouldn't either.

The funeral itself seemed like some bizarre kind of theatrical show, a play in which someone had made her go onstage to take the leading role. She was glad when it was finally over. She still didn't know how she was going to come to terms with Zoe's death. The sadness of the past few days, now this ritual, which meant nothing to her – that couldn't be all. But whatever she was waiting for didn't happen. It was as if all her reserves of tears had been exhausted over the last year.

Outside the chapel, men and women were waiting to commiserate with Rosa. She left without so much as glancing at any of them. These people had hated Florinda and Zoe. Refusing to accept the condolences that they were honour bound to offer was like a slap in the face for the *capi*. She knew that. She didn't care.

Holding herself very erect, she walked past the rows of guests and finally stopped in front of the one who was still standing at the end of the line, looking at her.

"Come on," she said, "let's go for a walk."

The sun was shining through the gnarled branches as they entered the shade of the olive groves. It cast dappled light over their bodies, surrounded them like glowing tendrils, then let go of them again at the next step they took.

"I've been to see Fundling in the hospital a couple of times," he said. "I'd hoped you would be there as well."

"You could have just called."

"Yes, maybe."

"So now you're what you always wanted to be," she said without looking at him. "The *capo* of the Carnevares. Does it feel the way you imagined it would?"

He sighed slightly. "The account my mother left has convinced the clan members that Cesare was going behind their backs. But that doesn't mean they're all convinced by *me*." He glanced sideways at her. "How about you?"

"I feel as if I inherited all this like an old car that no one wants to buy. Now I'm stuck with the picturesque old heap of rust and I can't get rid of it."

"There ought to be plenty of people taking an interest."

"You?" When she realised how he might take that, she left him no time to reply. "I'm going to try to change a few things. Lose a couple of branches of the business." A smile flickered around the corners of her mouth. "Build more wind turbines."

They were far enough from the house now to hear the mourners' voices only as vague background noise. Alessandro stopped, took her hand, and gently pulled her around to face him. The sunlight breaking through the branches of the olive trees lit emerald flames in his green eyes.

"Are we enemies now?" she asked. "Like our families?"

"My immediate family is dead. I only have" – he shrugged his shoulders – "I only have employees. You at least have Iole.

Looks like you're going to be the big sister now."

Her fingers intertwined with his as if of their own accord. "You didn't answer my question. Do we have to be enemies now?"

"Well, the concordat will see to it that we don't actually harm each other."

Frowning, she looked at him, and then saw that his dimples had almost imperceptibly deepened with laughter. "Idiot."

"That's what I told myself, too, after that whole thing in Gibellina." A shadow appeared in his eyes. "I ought to have driven to the hospital with you. Instead I—"

"You made sure that your clan didn't fall apart," she reminded him, and meant it. "I managed the aftermath on my own, no problem."

"You ought to have left the island," he said quietly. "I'd hoped you would be sensible and leave all this behind. I didn't want to stop you – and then blame myself if anything happened to you."

"So why haven't *you* given it all up? Don't tell me it's any less dangerous for you to take over from your father."

"I was born into this world. It's what I know. But you're different. All those advisers, and your firms' business managers, any moment now they'll be crowding around you, each trying to grab the biggest slice of the cake for himself."

"We'll see about that."

His eyes rested on hers. "Considering how many people would sooner shoot me in the back today than tomorrow,

I ought to be thinking about Carnevare business – instead I think about you day and night."

She was shocked to hear him speak with such honesty, although it was exactly what she had so often wondered. They looked at each other in silence. Then he leaned forward and kissed her.

She responded to the touch of his lips hesitantly at first, then with a fervour that surprised her. It felt different from their first tentative kisses, as if they suddenly knew exactly what they were letting themselves in for.

After a moment she whispered, "No one can know about this. Our own people would murder us."

His smile showed determination. As if it were a challenge that he would happily accept. "When everything has calmed down, and—"

"Nothing's going to calm down. The Hungry Man will be coming back to Sicily. And that's not all."

"You're talking about that statue?"

"You want to know too, don't you? What it means?"

He nodded.

"There have to be more of them down there. Pantaleone said the answers lie at the bottom of the sea. And it's not just about Lamias and Panthera – there has to be more behind it. The dynasties, TABULA… Those gaps in the crowd. Fundling and Pantaleone both talked about them, and—"

He cut her short with a long kiss. "This is about us," he said. "Just us."

Sunlight wandered over the ground, golden and decorative,

weaving the shadows of the branches together. She held him close, kissing his throat, his cheeks, and then his lips again.

"I know it is," she said, sounding neither affectionate nor cool, just stating the fact because it was true. "But we shouldn't see each other for a while. Give the others time to start racking their brains over something else."

"How long?"

"A month. Counting from Gibellina." She smiled. "It'll feel better once the first week is over."

"And the other three will pass quickly." He didn't look as if he meant it.

"Oh no," she said seriously. "Three weeks will be a long time."

She kissed him one last time.

Then they set off on their way back, up the slope and past the double line of olive trees that met above the path.

Epilogue

The ship's bows cut through the blue waves of the Strait of Messina. The sky was clear and radiant; seagulls flew from the shores of Sicily in the west to the sandy bays of Calabria in the east. Open sea lay between them.

Wearing a black neoprene diving suit, Rosa sat by the rail in a deckchair, looking out over the water. It was smooth and calm, with only a light breeze blowing, warm for this late in the year. Here on the surface there was nothing to indicate that the sea floor was furrowed like a battlefield, crisscrossed by deep clefts and underwater canyons.

She had seen charts and diagrams, not least in the stolen Dallamano papers, which she had found in Pantaleone's house in the forest. Florinda must have handed them over to him after the raid on the Dallamano estate in Syracuse. They clearly showed how severely the frequent underwater earthquakes had disrupted this part of the Mediterranean sea floor.

"Nearly there," the captain called down to her from the bridge. She took a deep breath, raised a hand to him in acknowledgement, and jumped up. This was only a small vessel with a six-man crew. She had not wanted to attract attention by ostentatiously equipping herself for a treasure hunt.

She wanted to do the first dive on her own. She had been training for the last three weeks with a personal diving instructor, first in the Lago di Ogliastro, not far from the

Palazzo Alcantara, then in the sea off the south coast. That would have to be enough for what she had planned for today. Not an expedition, certainly not an attempt to bring anything up. Only a look at what the Dallamanos had found down there.

The diving lessons had been not just preparation, but also a welcome distraction from the visits of the presidents and business managers of the Alcantara companies, who came to take a suspicious look at the *piccola ragazza*, and on whom her fortunes would now depend. She had made an appointment with the diving instructor for as early as possible every morning.

Her equipment was lying on deck, not far from a gap in the rail. She checked the instructions on the oxygen cylinders again. One of the crew came over and was helping her to get the cylinders over her shoulders when the captain suddenly called, "We have a visitor. Another craft to port. She's making straight for us."

She wasn't about to waste time getting the heavy oxygen cylinders and her flippers off again. Impatiently, she waddled over to the opposite rail in them. Suddenly the sun seemed even warmer.

"I know that ship," she said.

The sailor beside her shouted up to the captain, "She says she knows the ship."

"She's the *Gaia*."

"She's the *Gaia*," the man shouted.

Rosa gave him a look that silenced him.

The snow-white Carnevare yacht came racing up on a crest of foaming sea spray. The engines of both vessels cut out when they were ten metres apart. Both of them were at the precise spot of the coordinates Ruggero Dallamano had marked on his charts. The statue of the Panthera and the Lamia ought to be standing on the sea floor forty metres below them.

There was no one in sight on the deck of the *Gaia*, and her mirrored windows allowed no view of anyone inside the cabin.

Then, unexpectedly, the sound of trumpet fanfares came over the yacht's loudspeakers. Rosa recognised the introductory accompaniment at once. The next moment a song was ringing out over the water, clear as glass. A song she knew very well. 'My Death'.

Soon the volume was turned down and Alessandro appeared on the lower deck of the yacht in a dark blue diving suit, with oxygen cylinders on his back, his diving mask pushed up on his forehead. He held something that glittered metallically in one hand.

"He has a gun!" shouted the man beside Rosa.

"No," she placidly contradicted him, "that's not a gun."

Alessandro grinned, and with his forefinger he traced a figure 3 in the air. The others onboard must have thought he'd lost his mind, but Rosa smiled.

She stepped clumsily over to the deck chair. Her iPod was lying beside it. She took the cable out of the earphones and went back to the rail with it. Sunlight shone on the silvery case. As it did on the device in Alessandro's hand.

" 'My Death' was my mother's favourite song," he called.

"She used to listen to just that one song. After her death I played it over and over again myself. But then, on that plane – I thought it was time to put an end to it. Or at least try to." He shrugged his shoulders. "Didn't work too well."

"You switched them. While I was asleep."

"You knew?"

"I've known for quite a while. When I was in your mother's villa that first time… the song felt like a part of it." Like Gaia's ghost.

He raised the player in his hand and let the sun sparkle on it. "This is yours. I thought I'd bring it back to you. Maybe you can use it."

"Underwater?"

"Who knows?"

She weighed up the flat device in her own hand and swung back her arm.

Two silver arcs cut through the air above the sea. The crew exchanged baffled glances.

The iPods collided in midair at the highest point of their trajectory and fell into the sea.

Alessandro sighed. Rosa laughed. They looked at each other, grinning.

"Let's go after them!" she called over to him.

And they both dived into the deep blue sea at the same time.

Coming in 2013...

ARCADIA
BURNS

KAI MEYER

Intense, dangerous and seductive, Arcadia Burns is the second title in this gripping new trilogy.

Following the shattering events in Sicily, Rosa is now head of the Alcantara clan. Scared and scarred, she flees to New York to consider her future. There she encounters the American branch of the Carnevare Mafia family, also Panthera Arcadians. Forcibly injected with a serum that temporarily prevents the metamorphosis, Rosa is pursued by the Panthera in a deadly chase. Narrowly escaping with her life, Rosa returns to Sicily and to Alessandro.

Hunted by their enemies and manipulated by their allies, Rosa and Alessandro encounter corruption, intrigue and mortal danger at every turn. Will it force them together or drive them apart?

ISBN 978-1-84877-640-1

 facebook.com/templarfiction   @templarbooks